THE RAID AT
LAKE MINNEWASKA

THE RAID AT LAKE MINNEWASKA

Book I:
A Minnesota Lake Series Novel

J. L. LARSON

Library of Congress Control Number: 2022900967

HARDBACK: 978-1-957575-09-4
PAPERBACK: 978-1-957575-08-7
EBOOK: 978-1-957575-10-0

Ordering Information:

For orders and inquiries, please contact:
1-888-404-1388
www.goldtouchpress.com
book.orders@goldtouchpress.com

Printed in the United States of America

Dedication:

To Charlotte...my most loyal reader

...and Mother

ALSO BY J. L. LARSON

The Disappearance of Henry Hanson

The Choices of Adam Bailey

The Accident at Sanborn Corners....and Other Minnesota Short Stories

The Assumption

The British-made engine purred as the old air machine doggedly continued its flight into the uneasy skies of central Minnesota on that Friday, June 5, 1931. It was almost fourteen years since that biplane had made its last reconnaissance flight over the English Channel. Since then, after a small respite, it had surprisingly continued to be quite airworthy and active. Known as the Sopwith Camel, it had risen from post-war salvage to become a privately-owned craft. Some said this re-conditioned biplane never looked better; others said before its initial flight, how could it look worse.

It was late that afternoon that the owner of the aged biplane, James Lawton, was heading towards Lake Ida near Alexandria, Minnesota from the Twin Cities. It was to be a weekend spent with some college and business friends playing some golf and mostly having two days of good times. Flying over Kimball, Minnesota and heading on towards Paynesville, Lawton never got over the shear beauty of the peaceful countryside. It was like a painting with the spread of lakes and marshes as far as the eye could see. Glancing at his watch, he was satisfied with his progress despite a growing head wind. Unfortunately, there was a problem developing ahead that was hard to ignore. He'd been hoping to beat a distant thunderstorm but it was becoming evident he wasn't going to win. The shear size of the darkening hue had dulled his awareness of the growing cloud system. With each passing mile, it became more defined and quite apparent more than a minor rain shower.

The system created a blackening tinge from the Willmar area on his left to as far as the eye could see northward on his right. So far there was no lightning in the immediate distance, but there was no denying the huge low-pressure weather formation could be packed with punch. He swore under his breath. Making it to Lake Ida didn't look promising. One thing for certain, he'd learned not to test his courage against Mother Nature. If all hell was going to break loose, he intended to be on the ground under some shelter.

Seeing a slight opening in the large weather system to the west, he maintained a slight hope. As he flew past Paynesville, he re-directed his course slightly north towards Sauk Centre hoping to slip between the approaching storm cells. Within minutes, though, even that maneuver showed little chance of success. The sky to the northwest had turned darker and the headwind had become more pronounced.

Nonetheless, that small sliver of lighter sky on a more westerly course kept his hopes alive. Lawton was determined. He had to give it a try. Again he changed his heading. If it worked, it would be something he could brag about to his friends...that he snuck his air machine between the two major thunderstorms just before they joined.

Peering over the side of the fuselage, Lawton had a sense where he was. Locating State Hwy. #28 below, he knew he was above the roadway from Sauk Centre to Glenwood. With Lake Amelia near Villard straight ahead, he anticipated flying around the south edge of the lake where he could better evaluate his chances for completing his flight. The main challenge he faced was how fast the storm to the southwest was approaching the more northern storm as it moved eastward.

His defying the odds ended less than a minute later. It was then he saw the first flash of lightning. It was in the direction of his destination. It was no doubt pouring rain in Alexandria. Just like that he was no longer interested in being in the air. There would be no flying around or between anything. He didn't compete with lightning whether on the golf course or in the air. An open air cockpit and a thunderstorm were not a good mix.

Then another flash appeared straight ahead much nearer than he expected. No more delays. It was time to find a reasonable landing area and get his machine safely on the ground. He felt no panic or great discomfort. This experience was not new. He'd lost count how often he'd had to land someplace quickly whether for mechanical failure or inclement weather.

Descending to a more visible altitude less than a thousand feet above the ground, he examined the curving State Hwy. #28 right below him. He was aware the town of Glenwood was straight ahead, but he wasn't familiar with the location of the town's airfield. He remembered one of his flying buddies talked about the Glenwood airfield being located on the bluffs above Lake Minnewaska. He wasn't excited about going in search of this landing strip with the conditions deteriorating by the minute.

Then a brilliant display of lightning on the north side of Lake Amelia to his right again caught him off guard. It was extremely close. The storm was moving much faster than he'd estimated. Now less than five hundred feet above the ground, his head was hanging out over the edge of the fuselage scanning the area for any dry, flat patch of ground. He swore a blue streak having put himself in this dire situation... something he'd promised himself repeatedly to never do again. Now because of his impatience in getting to Alexandria, he'd inadvertently put himself in danger. Moreover, his concern wasn't just about his personal well-being, but he wasn't in the mood to have to pay Sam, his mechanic, for major repairs on his old relic.

Another flash of lightning and he brought his biplane down less than two hundred feet over State Hwy. #28. The atmosphere ahead to the west had become as dark as the sky to the north. Lawton strained to see any dependable landing field. Another streak of lightning straight ahead with an accompanying clamorous echo of thunder made that search no longer a consideration. The storm was coming at him just too aggressively. The wind had increased and his flight had become choppy. He'd definitely misinterpreted this entire weather system. It was time to set the biplane on the ground even if he had to land on State Hwy. #28.

Descending to less than forty feet above the roadway, some droplets of rain began pelting his face and small windshield. Countless times in his flying career, he had chosen caution over valor when bad weather was in front of him. His mind clicked back to the times he'd landed on anything that resembled solid ground. If no flat land then roadways were preferred for emergency landings... especially in the marshy terrain of rural central Minnesota. The concern pilots always had to face was whether the unfamiliar ground was actually firm.

State Hwy. #28 had become his only alternative. With a roadway landing his eyes scanned nervously for some kind of cover once on the ground, even if it was just a grove of trees. That initiated another flash, but this one was in his mind. Cars logically tended to have the priority over airplanes on the highways. By far he'd had more close calls with automobiles or horse-drawn wagons when making emergency landings on roads than difficulties with his biplane while in the air. He'd often contemplated if his air machine landed on a lonely country road and slammed into a car at an intersection, would the accident and his ensuing death be classified as just another traffic fatality?

Approaching Glenwood, he made a quick glance backward toward the beautiful, spring fed Lake Amelia. The sky was so black he couldn't make out that lake's nearest shoreline. He was officially in the middle of a major storm center and he was not yet on the ground. The hilly, curving road made it difficult to put down. Ahead he was aware of the massive Lake Minnewaska. He'd seen it in the distance in previous trips to Alexandria. Now he was just a few short miles from the lake, yet it remained unseen. That brought on another concern. There were bluffs above the lake. If he suddenly reached those bluffs, there would be no more flat terrain or roadway for him to land. There would only be a steep descent into the community. Landing downhill onto a tree-lined street entering Glenwood...he didn't like his chances of his plane or himself surviving that type of emergency landing. For the first time he accepted his hazardous situation had transformed into a deathly one. He had to land immediately on the road above the bluffs whether the roadway was straight or not.

He readied his biplane and himself for a gusty...and gutsy... landing on the state highway now right below his wheels. He strained to look ahead praying there was no on-coming traffic. He again felt extreme anger having put himself into a baleful situation despite self promises never to do so again.

A bolt of lightning hit the ground dead ahead momentarily giving him the picture of how close he was to the very crest of the hill overlooking Lake Minnewaska and the town. He lowered his biplane one last time awaiting the feel of his wheels touching down on the cement covered highway.

Then two things happened concurrently. A gust of wind and heavy rain hit Lawton's air machine head on causing his plane to lurch upward...and simultaneously a vehicle appeared out of nowhere coming right at him. There would be no reason to believe the driver would ever contemplate a flying machine could be bearing down on him. It was one of those random situations pilots and a driver in a car could have no control over...and it was about to take place in seconds.

Then, as if divinely guided, the vehicle veered into a farmyard driveway just before the biplane's wheels made contact with the highway...as if the two of them had rehearsed that moment several previous times.

The biplane blazed by the driveway with the left wings barely missing the back of the farmer's automobile. Lawton wondered if the driver had even seen him.

Once on the pavement, his air machine slowed abruptly against the gale wind. He barely sensed the heavy rain pelting him in the face given the sweat pouring down from his brow. He let out a roar of exhilaration and relief for surviving the landing. Looking back toward the farmhouse, he watched an old Plymouth sedan gamely drive up the long, potted driveway seemingly oblivious to the potential death despising incident the car had just avoided.

Quickly Lawton gathered his wits. Another vehicle could be coming down the road with little time to stop. More worrisome, the wind threatened to tip the plane if he didn't turn it around, head back up the roadway with the wind at his back, and drive off onto that same driveway where the vehicle had turned.

The entire sky then burst forth with an electrical storm that seemingly had no boundaries. Lawton felt like a target on that open road vulnerable to the next series of lightning bolts. The biplane had to be put under some cover or he'd face losing the small craft. Revving up his engine, he hurriedly turned toward that pathway. Something or somebody on that farm would have to give him safe refuge and a windbreak for his beloved plane.

As he coaxed his biplane along the potted driveway, he doubted the family living at the farm would hear the roar of his engine through the din of the torrential wind and rain. Arriving at the farmyard, he guided his machine over toward the leeward side of the barn. Crawling out of the cockpit, he hastily unraveled some canvas from within the fuselage. Before he threw it over the cockpit opening, he unstrapped his saturated golf bag and clubs behind his seat and slung them over his shoulders. His suitcase remained in the biplane. Even in the worst of conditions, there were priorities.

After blocking his wheels, Lawton slogged through the wind, rain and lightning to the farmer's front door and loudly knocked. A slightly wet, but tall, slender, pleasant-looking fellow answered the door. The man had literally just run into his house from his old truck and had obviously not been aware of any other arrival...unique or otherwise...to his farm. The farmer just stared in astonishment for a couple seconds at the pitiful vision in front of him.

Standing there looking like a drenched dog, his goggles half askew over his face, and his golf clubs slung over his shoulders, Lawton was tempted to jokingly ask the farmer where the #7 tee box was located. Seeing the surprised look on the man's face, though, Lawton decided not to waste any attempt at subtle humor.

Instead it was Lawton who was caught off guard by the farmer's first comment. "You lost," he innocently shouted above the clamor of the storm, "or are you here for the golf tournament?"

Momentarily speechless, Lawton wondered how a farmer living in the middle of nowhere outside of Glenwood, Minnesota might know or even care about golf much less a golf tournament. Certainly, at the very least, it was a very strange greeting. Without responding, Lawton barged his way through the front entry to escape the downpour.

Shouting above another burst of thunder as he put down his golf clubs in the entry way of the small home, Lawton retorted "My friend, I hope you don't mind if I leave my vehicle out by your barn?"

The farmer, a man named John Bailey, looked back outside toward his parking area and then to his barely visible barn. His squint followed by a look of utter amazement was priceless. He had expected to see an automobile. Instead Bailey saw what must have looked like something from another planet. His jaw dropped noticeably. Without blinking he looked at Lawton in his soaked flying suit and then back towards the biplane.

"I'll be damned" was all he could say as he invited the pilot into his humble but dry little farmhouse." As he closed the front door, he said it again.

Coincidences so often contribute to new paths in people's lives. It was pure happenstance when James 'Jamie' Lawton was forced to land his storm threatened biplane that Friday evening on Hwy. #28 one mile east of Glenwood and then sought safety at the John Bailey farm. That landing would be the first step of a strange set of occurrences in which he...and Bailey...and three other individuals would come together quite by accident during that weekend. Their lives would be literally uprooted and changed forever just because of that emergency landing.

What was odd from the very start was how these five individuals even came together at all. Three of them happened to be in town only temporarily...two on a lark and one on what can be described as 'a work assignment'. The other two individuals, John Bailey and his son, Adam, were local area residents who lived on that farm on the bluffs above Glenwood overlooking the picturesque Lake Minnewaska.

The two people 'on a lark' had no intention of being anywhere near Glenwood that weekend had it not been for Lawton's desperate landing. Lawton and his friend, Charlie Davis, were attorneys by trade and close friends since their first days of law school at the University of Minnesota. Since squeaking by the state bar exam seven years before, they had maintained their friendship despite living one hundred fifty miles from each other. Lawton was a business attorney and partner in a four-man law firm in downtown Minneapolis. Davis was a sole-practitioner in his home town of Alexandria, Minnesota, up State Hwy. #29 thirty miles north of Glenwood.

The two locals, the father and son...John and Adam Bailey... had lived on that barely productive farm since the son's birth. The best thing that could be said about the decrepit Bailey property was the location of the farmhouse. The view from the porch overlooking the sprawling lake was impressive. The older Bailey, a widower, was facing not only the stress of keeping his farm solvent and food on the table, he was also dealing with his own wrenching emotion regarding his son. Eighteen-year old Adam was leaving that fall for his freshman year at the University of Minnesota. The older Bailey's feelings were paradoxical. A part of him would have preferred his son remain home as was the custom of most 'eldest' sons in a farm family. But, Bailey didn't want that option to be his only son's primary choice. And, he definitely didn't want Adam to feel obligated or be saddled with the responsibility of the family farm. To Bailey, that college education would open his son's eyes to more of the world and give him some depth to better deal with the challenges in the future. If Adam never returned to the tough, thankless farm life that had possessed the Bailey heritage for three generations in the U.S...and most assuredly many previous generations in the old country...John Bailey knew he'd be a very contented man.

As for the fifth member of this accidental group, Lindy MacPherson, she was definitely not in Glenwood on a lark. She had an assigned task. Everyone in town thought the twenty-eight year old was an independent writer who worked for a travel magazine. She had explained her purpose to the folks in the Lake Minnewaska area as being asked to compose a promotional article emphasizing some of the lakeside resorts still open for vacationers despite the Depression years in full swing. Her arrival a week prior to Memorial Day weekend made sense as it was just days away from a ten-day town festival welcoming tourists and sportsmen to the official opening days of the summer season at Lake Minnewaska.

In fact, her stated intention was anything but her true mission. Miss McPherson was actually an attorney, like James Lawton and Charlie Davis. Her tale of being a travel magazine writer was only a cover. As a relatively new addition to the Minneapolis branch of the U.S. Attorney's office, her real job was to explore a rumor about illegal gambling allegedly taking place at a resort located in the vicinity of Lake Minnewaska.

Her investigation was supposed to be a simple task with the sole purpose of giving her some investigative experience. The undertaking was intended to be neither lengthy nor precarious. Her orders were strict. If she were to find any evidence relating to the matter of illegal gambling, she would promptly return to the Twin Cities office, inform the state patrol or an agent of the Bureau of Investigation, and let them provide any further examination of the potential for arrest warrants.

Fortunately...or unfortunately...Miss MacPherson did not have an exemplary record of following 'strict orders'. This was especially the case as she made more discoveries during her two weeks in Glenwood. It didn't take long for her to realize her simple assignment had more teeth than originally assumed. She knew she could call in the state police at any time, but different things kept popping up indicating she was on top of a powder keg of illegal activity. By calling in the authorities too soon to make some obvious and notable arrests, she might blow the chance to end something much, much larger than a small gambling operation.

Originally scheduled to be in Glenwood less than a week, she felt compelled to invest more time into her investigation. With her cover working out so well, she stayed in Glenwood throughout the ten-day festival. This would be the second major coincidence that would eventually bring these five individuals together.

And, in the short time they were together, the actions of these five individuals would have a major impact not only their own lives, but the futures of the people in town as well as the inimitable guests at Chippewa Lodge on the east edge of Lake Minnewaska.

❧ CHAPTER ❧

2

James Lawton... 'Jamie' to his friends... was a thirty-one year old Minneapolis attorney, confirmed bachelor, golfer, and private aviator. Lawton had been an attorney in downtown Minneapolis since finishing law school in 1924. On that June day when he flew into the oncoming storm, he was thirty-one years old having been one of the first human beings born in the twentieth century in Minnesota. He was a quarter of inch north of six feet tall, but looked taller because of his slender build. Called 'Jamie' since childhood, he joked that his close friends called him a host of other less flattering names.

With the slender Scandinavian look including the wavy blond hair and easy going manner, he played the innocent role, sometimes legitimately, only because it was had often proved successful in winning attention from various ladies. His hair tended to be too long relative to the style of the day. It was not that he couldn't afford a haircut; it was just that a trim was a lower priority.

He was distinctive for those times. During the week he was a dedicated, highly responsible lawyer committed to his profession and his client's concerns. On the weekends...especially the summer weekends... he was anything but the steadfast barrister. During those warmer months in Minnesota, weekends found him some place out of the city with his college and law school friends enjoying the amenities of someone's lake home...and preferably playing in some kind of golf competition. His friends kidded him constantly about his weekend adolescence.

And nothing typified his devil-may-care approach to life than his predilection with flying. For years his friends watched him land and take off in his worn-out biplane he'd purchased prior to his first year in college. Somewhat amazingly, he was still flying that same contraption in that spring of 1931 as if it had just come off the Hughes Aircraft production line. Everyone calculated he'd gotten more than his original investment out of that machine, especially since they swore he was still using the same war-time engine! Having seen the biplane in its post-war deplorable condition, those friends refused to fly with him. They referred to him by various feline names believing he used up one of his nine lives every time he took the biplane airborne. As far as Lawton was concerned, there were a lot of cats still living...and he was one of them. He considered his craft a very reliable flying machine.

By 1931 he had owned the very old and very dependable biplane for over a third of his life. His particular Sopwith Camel had quite a history. It had been built and assigned to fly search and discover missions back and forth across the English Channel during what people referred to then as the 'Big War'. In other words, it was an original 'spy' plane. Unfortunately, it was slightly damaged during a World War I reconnaissance flight when it got too close to the German borders in 1917 and got shot up. When the war ended, it was brought back to Wold Chamberlain Air Field in Minneapolis for repair and public viewing. Its reputation should have earned it plenty of historical importance at war's end. Unfortunately, there must have been other flying machines that took the bulk of the post-war glamour. The idea of it becoming a museum artifact never caught on.

It was about to be junked when Lawton heard of the biplane's pending last rites. Having just completed flying lessons, the young man put his savings together plus $60 borrowed from his father and bought the plane a month before he began his undergraduate studies. He personally brought the biplane back to life that fall with help from a mechanic friend. He even took it airborne twice that autumn before the weather forced the plane back in the hanger until the spring. That air machine and Lawton had been close ever since.

For a lad living in the St. Paul area, his purchase was considered rather odd. But, he had an impulse and he played on that inspiration. Through college he barnstormed in his plane to county fairs and town festivals in all parts of Minnesota, some parts of western Wisconsin and a few times into the Dakotas. It was easy money to offer ten to fifteen minute flights to patrons at these county fairs for $3 to $5 a head. His summertime exploits earned him enough extra cash to keep his flying machine maintained and airborne with enough profit left over for some spending money and college tuition.

And there were perks! As a rather romantic figure roaming the Midwestern skies, he enjoyed additional pleasures. There were introductions to various local ladies. He enjoyed many free dinners and even some invitations to play golf when folks saw his golf clubs stored in the back fuselage of his biplane. As for the experiences with the many ladies he met, those were dividends he'd never figured on but certainly appreciated.

There were other parts to his life, but none as exciting as his habit of flying. His social life was active at times. Mostly it was seasonal... warmer in the colder months and practically non-existent in the summer months when he traveled most every weekend. When the cooler latter months of autumn arrived and he remained in the Twin Cities, he dated an assortment of lady friends. He was considered a gentleman but certainly not innocent. Most of all, the reputation he carried amongst the female crowd was that he was simply not serious about any long-term relationship. He rarely dated a woman more than a few times.

The reason for his sporadic dating practices went beyond just the vagaries of the weather. He had become aware that as his law practice developed, his attraction was too often focused on his professional position and probable wealth. He saw too often his dates with flashing eyes introducing him to their friends as that 'lawyer I was telling you about'. He felt like a commodity. The thought became distasteful enough that his interest in settling down became even more firm.

The real corker, as he often laughed and told his close friends, if only some of these females had any idea of his true net worth. They most assuredly would have been shocked how slight his apparent prosperity actually was. He wasn't as impoverished as so many folks were during those difficult times after Wall Street crashed. He simply appeared better off than he actually was.

He did own a home outright along the shoreline of Lake Johanna in St. Paul. It had been his parent's house and his boyhood home. That advantage saved him some money. However, with expenses from the biplane, his travel whims during the warm months in Minnesota, and his social and country club expenses throughout the year, his savings were negligible.

His life style really had not been altered since law school. Flying his biplane almost every summer weekend was a habit he simply didn't want to break. Rightly or wrongly, his attitude in the warm Minnesota months was what had to be done on Friday could be completed on Monday. It was a popular mentality by many businessmen in that state...at least from May through early September. Funny how those Fridays in the winter didn't have the same social priority as those Fridays in the summer.

September meant that golf outings and tournaments ended as well. It didn't take much to convince him to discontinue his flights when the air became frosty. That was when he reciprocated by inviting friends down to the Twin Cities for a Minnesota Gopher home football game. His house along Lake Johanna provided a more than adequate place for his friends to stay. While he and his cronies hunted and fished in the late fall, as it got even colder, speakeasies, cards, and parties replaced the outdoor entertainment.

The money he'd made as a fly boy had been good during the early 1920s. At times he had been tempted to make that avocation into some kind of career. But, luckily a very good friend of his late father eventually convinced him to come down to earth long enough to earn his law degree. During those cold days of the fall, winter, and spring, he was especially satisfied he'd followed the advice.

As he hit that magic age of thirty, he didn't slow down his business and social schedule. He did contemplate, though, how he'd become a bit more conservative...but only relative to his wilder younger years. He just did not take as many unnecessary chances. Too many of those barnstorming buddies he'd laughed heartily with in his early 20's were now flying with their own wings way, way up high after only one mistake. That's all it took, one mistake in the air, and a pilot could earn his own personal wings.

Lawton often chuckled whenever he thought himself as becoming conservative. His friends would never use that word ever to describe him. How many people would be flying repeatedly to some small town golf affair in an open cockpit biplane with an engine that needed to be overhauled? While he was not a dare-devil, he guessed he was hardly old-fashioned. For certain, his age had helped him gain enough experience to become more cautious and not be embarrassed about it.

That was the life of Jamie Lawton during the latter years of the 1920s...and how it continued into the tamer 1930s. At times his friends' kidding remarks about his seemingly frivolous life style would cause him to pause. When he'd see a couple strolling down the streets of Minneapolis hand-in-hand he did wonder if his peripatetic social life would ever change. When he turned thirty shortly after the stock market disaster, he even seriously considered changing his light-hearted habits. He went so far as to allow a longer term friendship develop with a girl he'd known since undergraduate school. He wanted to experience whether a worthwhile relationship might turn into a more preferred life style given his 'advancing' age.

She had a lot of qualities. Bernice Donaldson was a capable businesswoman in her father's small business in downtown St. Paul.

It was just a question of time before she'd eventually take over the family-owned department store. More importantly she was attractive, energetic and intelligent. As a bonus, she even liked to fly with him. He kept asking himself what wasn't right about her.

They had been going together since the fall of 1929 for seven months when the warm days of April arrived. That good-looking female and Lawton had a falling out following his first solo flight of the spring to St. Cloud to play some weekend golf with friends. She couldn't believe he preferred golf to her. It wasn't necessarily the case, but he could understand her perception. It only proved he wasn't ready for the extraordinary and unwanted change in his summer plans if he had to feel guilty every time he flew off to see his friends without her.

It was an issue without an immediate answer...and certainly something he didn't want to have to negotiate. He was relieved when the two of them eventually went their separate ways.

He did meet one other girl a month later at his country club, Midland Hills, in St. Paul. Unfortunately, he was blinded by her competitiveness, her crass humor and her ability to play golf. Those factors ended up being her most favorable attributes...that along with her employment schedule requiring her to work most weekends. For a couple days Lawton sensed he may have found the perfect relationship. However, there was another pertinent factor...or two...causing that courtship to end. It wasn't so much her swearing like a construction worker after one drink as it was how she reminded him of one as well. Looks weren't everything, but he knew they wouldn't be spending all their time on the golf course.

Those two experiences convinced him there was no magic about turning thirty requiring him to get married. It helped that many of his friends were still single and enjoyed various lady friends as well. In the end, until a better plan was discovered, he became even more content to glow in the pattern of his single life.

As for his law career, his partnership with a couple of other lawyers in downtown Minneapolis was still in the growth and development stages. That was another way of saying the partnership was viable and compatible, but financially burdened. The firm was paying its bills on time and salaries were being met, but the financial crisis around the state and the nation certainly had an affect on the firm's receivables since their own business clients were stressed as well. It made those summer Friday afternoons easier to split from the office. Still, if a Friday night meeting was important to gain or hold a client, there was no question that would take priority. Leaving Saturday morning very early didn't interrupt his weekend plans that badly.

His practice had taken on a slightly different emphasis since the end of 1929. Survival was the mode of so many of his corporate clients. Only a few years before, it had been acquisition and revenue building. Now, so much of his work had to do with bankruptcy law, some real estate law, and lately even tax law and criminal law. In fact in the recent year his firm's revenue had not been consistent with him and his partners' timesheets. Delayed client payment had become the norm. It was just a pattern of the times.

Despite the tough times, he was quite proud of his firm's growing reputation. In the five years his partners and he had been together, they'd gained a strong image since placing their shingle on the outside of the Grain Exchange Building in downtown Minneapolis. The middle 1920s was a great time to begin a law practice. There were plenty of new ideas and investment money to start new businesses. He and his partners had been so busy garnering clients they barely had time to do the legal work.

By 1929, the Minnesota Law Journal had named his firm the top new law firm in Minnesota. It was a special honor. He remembered how he and his partners joked how glad they were the judging wasn't based on their financial records. They had spent plenty on publicizing their firm's name within the bylaws of the Minnesota Bar Association. As a result of their expenditures to gain clients, they figured they had the lowest capital base of any multi-person firm in Minnesota at the time of their award. It seemed their expenses were eating revenues about as fast as the clients paid their invoices. Luckily he and his partners had accepted the circumstances and expenses as necessary cost of growing a law firm and increasing their client base. They had agreed upon taking a limited salary plus a year-end bonus based on remaining revenue after expenses. It offered a reasonable income for each of them for the times. However, in the two years since the stock market crashed, while the salary base was maintained, the year-end bonuses couldn't buy a new set of golf clubs. Ever faithful, though, they all believed 1931 would be better than the previous year. They'd said the same thing in 1930.

In January, 1931, Lawton's law firm moved to one of the higher floors at the Foshay Tower, a building that had recently become the tallest skyscraper in downtown Minneapolis. The four partners had thought it important they re-locate to a classier location. Their former offices in the Grain Exchange Building just didn't reflect the image they wanted.

Lawton had hoped for a simple flight that Friday afternoon. All morning he'd sat at his twenty-first floor office desk with his mind wandering. He was finding it hard to concentrate on the legal documents in front of him. His feet were up on the back credenza as he stared out his office window toward Lake of the Isles, a beautiful lake area southwest of the main downtown portion of the city. It was already a surprisingly muggy day. That day's *Minneapolis Star* hinted there might be an evening rainstorm heading toward the Twin Cities. He didn't pay much mind to weather forecasts. To him having the weather report say it might rain was similar to reporting that the stock market was certain to recover from the 1929 debacle....eventually! 'Thanks for the worthless bulletin' was his only thought. As a pilot, he was used to making weather decisions for himself. Unfortunately, that day he was having premonitions from the high humidity that bad weather was probable. As a result, he planned on leaving the office earlier that afternoon.

He didn't give the weather much thought again until after lunch. A couple calls from worried clients had brought back his concentration. By then it was eighty-two degrees with some increasing cumulous clouds and a distracting haze to the far southwest of the city.

Leaving the office after a quick 2:00 meeting, he popped his vintage 1925 Julian Sports Coupe in gear and pealed out Hennepin Avenue toward Flying Cloud Airfield, southwest of Minneapolis. Upon arrival, just like every other weekend when he was about to fly, his sturdy biplane was already out of the hanger waiting for him. Sam, the local manager/mechanic was sitting by the tin-roofed garage smoking a cigarette and enjoying an illegal beer. He was staring at Lawton's old relic with some disapproval as was his habit most weekends when Lawton arrived at the airfield.

Lawton had gotten to know Sam over the previous decade, but not as closely as would normally be the case. The last name was some kind of Czechoslovakian derivation, difficult enough that few people would try to pronounce it. Mostly, Sam was just 'Sam', a cantankerous, but thoughtful forty year old man with permanently oil stained clothing and completely unmotivated to do much else with his life but manage the flying field. Still, he was a skilled airplane mechanic and serviced the planes at the airfield like they were his own offspring.

Lawton knew part of the fellow's story. Previous to Sam's taking the job at Flying Cloud, he worked on warplanes in France and England during the 'Big War'. The scuttlebutt was that Sam saw too many of his fly buddies go down during the war...and it had affected him. He came back to his home in Hudson, Wisconsin and just sat around for about a year before he suddenly showed up at the airfield in Hudson announcing his intentions to work there. Before the airfield owner and manager told him to get lost, he had the sense to inquire about Sam's mechanical skills and flying machine background. Sam was offered a job not two minutes later. He eventually took the airfield manager position at Flying Cloud Airfield because the job included a small apartment above one of the garages. It came free of charge with the deal he was offered.

Sam could have had the same position at the big field at Wold Chamberlain, but said he preferred a smaller airfield. He claimed he didn't want the responsibility and didn't particularly need a lot of money. The owner of the Flying Cloud Airfield was happy to oblige. It took a few years before Sam began to reconsider what he'd said. Lawton helped him out by speaking to the owner of the airfield and forcing a nice raise. Sam never forgot that act of kindness.

Of course, even before that small favor, Sam had taken a liking to Lawton. Sam had been at Flying Cloud Airfield about a year when Lawton began storing his biplane there during college. He said Lawton reminded him of a certain pilot he knew back in France. He always talked of that pilot in the past tense.

Sam began servicing the old war plane when Lawton began his days as a barnstormer beginning in the summer of 1920. Lawton not only did air shows at county fairs, but developed a small letter delivery and package transport business. The size of his biplane was about the only limitation for him to have grown the business more profitably. But, no matter where he was, those fifteen-minute rides in his biplane for $3-$5 were quite popular. His only exception was charging as little as $2 if the girl was pretty...$1 if the girl was pretty and she offered to cook him a meal.

When Lawton eventually gave up his barnstorming career to become a lawyer, Sam found it difficult to comprehend. Sam couldn't understand why anyone would give up flying for any reason. Lawton patiently explained that making a reasonable income as a lawyer afforded him the opportunity to continue flying...and eating...and playing golf. Years later after the stock market crash, Lawton at times wondered which of the two of them actual cleared a better profit... especially after life style expenses.

That Friday afternoon Sam greeted the arrival of the Julian Sports Coupe with his easy going wave. He pointed to the smaller garage for Lawton to park the vehicle for the weekend. Then he got busy making some final checks on the biplane as Lawton made his own preparations and changed into his flying suit.

Within minutes the suitcase and golf clubs were secured in the back of the fuselage. Lawton was excited about trying his new Gene Sarazen sand wedge against his golfing friends the next day at the Alexandria municipal golf club. He knew they'd be jealous of his acquisition.

Both men gazed wistfully at the sky. The clouds looked full to the southwest, but not particularly dangerous as long as Lawton took a heading around the north edge of the cloud bank. Besides, potential bad weather was just part of the adventure of flying.

Sam was wiping off the engine as Lawton made his final personal checks on the plane's condition. The mechanic was always worried about his young client's safety, while Lawton seemed more concerned about the security of his golf clubs.

Sam yelled out, "Jamie, you've got to watch that oil leak. I don't want to hear you had to glide your plane in for a landing because of a dead engine."

Lawton nodded as he did every time Sam made the same statement. For the thirtieth time Sam suggested a new engine. For the thirtieth time Lawton responded, "Thanks Sam, I'll think about it." They both shook their heads and smiled at their repeated performances.

Getting into the cockpit Lawton checked his instruments and then his flaps. Sam stood by the propeller ready to assist in starting and revving up the engine. When the engine finally turned over, the relative solitude gave way to the deafening noise of a reasonably healthy engine.

Lawton waved his thanks for the assistance and then remembered something. He pulled an envelope out of his jacket and held it out for Sam to grab. It contained the monthly maintenance and hanger fee expense...plus a little extra. The extra wasn't mandatory, but it was something he always did. Sam held Jamie's life in his mechanically sound mind and capable hands. Lawton wanted this man to maintain his concentration on keeping the old spy plane in the sky.

Uncaringly, Sam shoved the envelope into his shirt pocket as both of them listened to the revved up engine and its mechanical reliability. For good luck, they shook hands again before takeoff. Lawton placed his goggles over his eyes, checked his gauges and flaps once again, and moved away from the hanger. He frankly thought his biplane's engine sounded better than ever. His friends thought it was just wishful thinking.

With the engine purring strongly, he was ready for take off. Lawton gave a final wave to Sam and proceeded toward the grass runway.

The takeoff against a westerly breeze was exhilarating as always. Flying low along the bluffs above the Minnesota River valley with the river town of Shakopee on his left, he looked below and saw State Hwy. #5 crawling up the side of the hill overlooking the valley. Another glance towards Shakopee and there was the ball field just north of the center of town. The Minnesota River gently flowed too close along the left field fence.

When he reached one thousand feet, he changed his heading northwestward in the direction of Alexandria, some one hundred fifty miles from the Twin Cities. Glancing westward along Hwy. #12 toward Willmar, he noticed the faint hint of a darker cloud mass, but paid it little thought since his intention was to go north of that cloud bank anyway. He'd been flying around the Midwest for many years. His experience told him he'd have a good chance of missing the storm system...unless there was another unknown thunderstorm mass coming at him from the Alexandria area.

Even then he wasn't worried. He knew the towns where there were airfields...or flat spots on the roadways near other communities. He'd traveled through some horrible conditions in the past and landed in some pretty rough terrain. In his early pilot days he bragged and immaturely scoffed with other barnstorm pilots about their close calls. Then his group was composed of other young and brave men who distained fear. After all, the new wave of fighter and reconnaissance pilots from the 'Big War' had to face tougher pressure than mere inclement weather.

As he leveled off at three thousand feet, he looked down upon some small towns where he'd given rides at county fairs during his college summers. Even during law school at the University of Minnesota, he had continued this avocation. While the rides at county fairs and the air shows had been profitable for him, his package delivery business had the real potential. But, he'd never followed that opportunity. As it turned out, the contacts from that small business nonetheless provided him some very important connections that helped launch his law practice in the Twin Cities.

Increasing his altitude to five thousand feet while passing west of beautiful Lake Minnetonka, he kept his left wing parallel to State Hwy. #55 just below. Gazing down at the huge lake with the many beautiful shoreline homes, he thought about his clients living in some of those exclusive homes. A couple of them were depending on his law practice to advise how to keep their business or family fortunes afloat. Given the full-fledged depression of the nation's economy, too many of his business clients were just hanging on.

An hour into the flight, Lawton still believed he could make Alexandria before meeting any real inclement weather even if he had to go further north than normal. There was a darker hue to the western sky, but he was moving along nicely despite a noticeable head wind. His routing along State Hwy. #55 northwestward out of the Twin Cities had become a very comfortable passage. He was familiar with the topography by air as well as having driven the roadway. Landmarks like the hills around Kimball and the lakes around Paynesville, St. Cloud, and Alexandria were quite recognizable from the sky. Once he flew over the main street of Alexandria there was always a very dependable landing area along Lake Ida awaiting his arrival. It was a wide strip of grass cut near a large barn. He could land and drive his unfailing biplane right into that oversized barn doorway thereby protecting his air machine from any elements.

That clean-cut grass landing area was the work of none other than his law school buddy, Charlie Davis. Davis owned the landing strip plus an impressive amount of acreage on the shoreline of Lake Ida next to the private little airfield. He had become something of a land baron... or so Lawton kidded him. Davis' small town law practice emphasized real estate law, but handled other general law needs as well. His friend had indeed built a very successful law practice in just a few short years.

Davis was akin to making some notable land investments. As the resort atmosphere of the Alexandria area grew in popularity in the 1920s to lake loving Minnesotans, Davis recognized the profit potential for lakeside property. By the end of that decade, his lake property investments had become the talk of central Minnesota. In a few short years, Davis had amassed a veritable real estate fortune for someone of his moderate age. With the stock market crash, his wealth remained mostly in land. With real estate as his leverage, he came through 1929 in much better shape than if he'd invested in securities. While the real estate value may have dropped, at least he had something to show for his investment dollar.

Business acumen aside, Charlie Davis looked anything but a well-to-do land mogul. There was always a certain unkempt look to this man. His normal appearance was extremely casual...as if he'd just finished mowing that air strip by his house and barn...or just completed eighteen holes of golf at the Alexandria Municipal Golf Course in 90-degree heat. Lawton always marveled at how little time and success had changed his good friend.

Davis had always defined informality. He was as untailored as he was that first time Lawton had seen the tall, slightly overweight classmate charge up the steps of Fraser Hall at the University of Minnesota for his first law class. Lawton recalled that morning how Davis had arrived literally with suitcase in hand, a pencil, and a notebook. He'd taken a bus from Alexandria the night before and didn't have a place to clean up and unpack much less sleep. When asked, he vaguely described sleeping someplace on campus. His voice had then tailed off as if completely oblivious to any worry about his immediate future. Lawton couldn't help but take pity on this laid-back country bumpkin and invited the big man over to his folk's place for the evening...or at least until Davis could get himself settled. That night Davis slept in a bedroom out in the Lawton boathouse next to Lake Johanna. Three years later Davis got his law degree and moved out of that same boathouse bedroom back to Alexandria.

Davis did at some point offer to pay rent for use of the boathouse room, but that was two weeks after arriving. By then he'd gotten so close to the Lawton family any discussion of his moving elsewhere simply dissolved....as did any talk of rent.

In those three years, Charlie Davis and Jamie Lawton built a strong bond. There was a definite loyalty between the two of them...with the only exception being when the female gender came into view. Conflicts occurred if the two of them happened to have their eyes on the same girl. Like any friendship they learned how to deal with that inconvenience. They cleared the matter of 'first attempt' with any game of chance to their liking. At first, they shook dice or cut cards, but that proved unsatisfactory to their basic competitive needs. What became more popular was playing eighteen holes of golf for the right between the two of them to initiate contact when next they both were focusing on the same winsome lass.

Golf turned out to be as prevalent in their lives as going to class. Had there been classes in the summer, neither would have graduated. They played a lot of golf together competing in tournaments around the Twin Cities. Mostly, though, the two of them made constant use of the Lawton family membership at Midland Hills Country Club.

It was within weeks after starting law school that Lawton moved his clothes and personal items from the main house out to the other room in the boathouse. He found it easier not to have to explain his whereabouts to his curious folks after a fourth night in a row of arriving home after 3:00 AM.

Somehow the two of them did make it through law school and passed the bar exam in 1924. Needless to say, neither one of them was offered positions at the top law firms in Minneapolis or St. Paul.

It didn't matter. Davis already had his plan to continue his father's local practice back home. Lawton's aim was to remain in the Twin Cities. With three other classmates, they had a shingle out within two month of graduation.

Though the two friends went their separate ways after graduation, it was probably a good thing. They might not have survived given the life style they'd created during law school. Nonetheless, they maintained their strong friendship which included a group of twelve other law school and undergraduate friends.

Despite there being one hundred and fifty miles between their two offices, they often talked about setting up joint offices in Minneapolis and Alexandria. The logic was since Davis was in Minneapolis so often in the winter and Lawton was up at the lake near Alexandria so often in the summer, why not?

Still, the idea just never took root. With Lawton's growing client base in the Twin Cities and Davis' uniquely effective practice in the Minnesota lake region, it was financially sound not to upset each other's business progress. Lawton would of course kid Davis that the only reason his friend wanted Lawton's name on the shingle outside his Alexandria law office was so Charlie had some added class to his practice. Davis countered by claiming that Lawton's practice was too traditional…that it couldn't tolerate law billings getting paid with land as was Charlie's preferred payment as a sole practitioner.

During the first two years of their respective practices, Lawton did tease Davis about his constantly changing living arrangements in the Alexandria area…and that he was more a real estate tycoon than a lawyer. A move seemed to occur about every three months for Davis. To Lawton it seemed his friend was buying, trading, and selling real estate daily.

Davis never disagreed. His standard response was repeated often. He'd say, "Jamie boy, lake property is money in the bank." He proved that maxim to Lawton and others many times over, especially after 1929.

It was in 1928 that Davis moved again, but this time into a more permanent lake home. This acquisition was a substantial payment for a number of on-going legal fees. It was a beautiful home overlooking Lake Ida. A large barn, twenty acres along the lake, a boathouse, and a dock with sailboat were included in the transaction.

Before Lawton saw the property Davis was promoting the room in the boathouse as Lawton's sleeping quarters any time he was in the area. He said it would be reimbursement for those three years Davis stayed in the Lawton boathouse.

The act of generosity ended there. The Lawton boathouse had been finished and had its own heating system. When Lawton finally made it up to Lake Ida that spring, Davis' boathouse was somewhat less inspiring. Lawton compared it to a preserved 1820 hut on the bluff by Ft. Snelling along the Mississippi River. The upstairs room in the boathouse was actually a storehouse for firewood. Davis played hurt when Lawton chose an alternative more comfortable room in the ample main house. As it worked out, this large home became the main meeting place for Davis' and Lawton's college group on those many summer weekends.

As for Lawton, Alexandria and Lake Ida became a convenient escape from the city life. It was comforting for him to know he always had a place to park his biplane and his body in the lake country of central Minnesota. Of course, the reciprocity continued at Lake Johanna for Davis when Lawton acquired the deed to the house when his father passed in 1927. Lawton's mother remained at the house except during the winter months when she lived in a development called Palm Beach in Florida. Her presence during the late spring, summer and early fall at least brought some orderliness to the bachelor quarters.

Flying, though, was somewhat of a stumbling block between the pair. Davis would eventually get over his discomfit with heights. Nonetheless he was scared silly of flying in Lawton's old spy plane. He claimed it was sacrilegious to be flying such a long dead museum piece. Irregardless, he kept the airfield by Lake Ida manicured for his friend's landings. While he claimed he wanted a safe place for Lawton to land, there was an additional reason for the effort. Davis also enticed Twin City businesspeople to utilize the popular new form of transportation and land by his homestead in Alexandria to consider purchasing some of his choice lake properties. That landing strip was well marked and many prospects stayed right at the Davis lake home adjacent to the landing field. Charlie Davis was no dummy in business matters.

As Lawton continued his flight toward Lake Ida late that Friday afternoon, he'd become entranced with that sliver of light between the two weather systems. That wasn't his first miscalculation on that flight, but it would turn out to be his most egregious one. While he couldn't have known the size and speed of the approaching cloud masses, his impatience in trying to beat the storm systems to Alexandria had truly clouded his judgment. On more level-headed days, he would have landed back at Sauk Centre or even Paynesville and wait out the squall.

How different his future would have been had he landed in one of those two municipalities...as would have been the lives of Lindy MacPherson, Charlie Davis and John and Adam Bailey...and countless people in town and those gruff, fun-loving guests out at Chippewa Lodge.

CHAPTER
3

James Lawton's emergency landing east of town that Friday night and the investigative efforts by Lindy MacPherson around Lake Minnewaska were certainly a critical part to the eventual turmoil that occurred that June weekend in 1931. However, both actions would have had little correlation if it hadn't been for one other key factor. It had to do with the town of Glenwood. There had been things going on in that community for quite a few years…things long accepted… that caught the attention of both visitors in entirely different ways.

It should first be explained that this rural lakeside village seemed always to have a more refreshing, even more invigorating environment than most other small lake towns. It wasn't markedly so, just the feeling was noticeable. It had nothing to do with the people being smarter or friendlier…or more religious or more playful than other communities. There wasn't one particular large employer providing more jobs to the local citizens. There wasn't even a prominent state politician or athlete living anywhere near the community. The difference had always been topographic…and too often it took visitors to remind Glenwood citizens about the town's amazingly beautiful landscape. The view was truly grand. On the north and east sides of the town bordered a high bluff offering a vast view of the surprisingly large and picturesque Lake Minnewaska. It was a perfect picture for a postcard. Anyone looking at the lake from those bluffs couldn't help but be impassioned by the beauty and somewhat envious that their town didn't have such a site. It resulted in Glenwood and surrounding resorts benefiting from a tourism trade that brought extra revenue into the community.

Without that tourism trade, Glenwood would have been just another rural Minnesota farm community trying to survive the harrowing difficulties of a bad agricultural economy. And, during the era of the early

1920s, the dismal, uncompromising agricultural economy was putting even the better-than-average little town of Glenwood on its knees.

As that decade progressed, Glenwood had been lucky enough to still enjoy some tourism trade, but the resorts around Lake Minnewaska began to close in direct relation to the decreasing number of people who could afford lake resort vacations. The tough times just wouldn't cease.

Yet, it was still the rousing 1920s. Citizens in Glenwood and other the rural towns were well aware of the exciting image of the 'Roaring 20s'. It was just that financial circumstances in rural America generally prevented them from taking part in that wild imagery. There were speakeasies in the rural areas to be sure. The illegal hooch offered at back alley dives gave the country folk some opportunity and taste for what the better life might be like...or at least gave them a chance to momentarily forget their woes.

Up until the 'Crash', it was the city folk who were grudgingly credited with helping keep lake resorts barely solvent. One might assume the rural lake towns would have been thankful for any outside business. That wasn't necessarily the case. Country folk were disgruntled as they believed city inhabitants just didn't have it as tough. Their assumption, which could have been more truth than fiction, was that city folk had more money. Only the city folk could afford fancy cars. Only the city folk could live lavishly and spend freely. Only the city folk had the money to make a killing in the stock market if they chose to invest their money. With this exaggerated perception, it followed that only the city folk were frolicking in the Roaring 20's and had the means to do things like vacation at a lake resort.

With the implosion of Wall Street, many of these seemingly advantaged 'city folk' suddenly and severely felt the wave of the hard times...sometimes overnight. Jobs vanished. Homes were lost. Feeding families became desperately difficult in the city. The tables weren't exactly turned, but the city folk had become part of the hopeless times.

In turn, city folk came to perceive that the farmer at least had some land and could survive self-sufficiently. Further, the farm house might be small with a leaky roof, but it did provide some shelter and privacy. It beat the miserable alternative. Of course, as time went on, even the rural folk were losing their land and farm homes, so overstressed perceptions no longer lingered. By the 1930s few people no matter where they lived had anything that offered much encouragement.

With bleakness having become the way of life in rural America, people longed for anything that might bring some sense to such difficult, dire days. Heroes were sought who could give some hope or bring some vicarious excitement to the dull existence around the country. Sports figures enjoyed prominence like never before. Movie stars caught the eyes and ears of the desperate populace. Even mob activity reported daily in newspapers provided a kind of macabre romantic vision. To many depressed souls, thievery was an example of people beating a capitalistic system that had somehow become flawed. Criminal and mob activity showed that America was still the land of opportunity, even if it was on the wrong side of the law.

In 1927 a brave Minnesotan from Little Falls gambled with his life and flew solo across the Atlantic Ocean. Maybe with the conditions of the time, gambling with one's life, like Charles Lindbergh did, simply fit into the character of the country. In some ways it epitomized the ultimate despair. One's life may well have seemed like the only collateral to back up a wager, dare, or risk. What added to the gloom in rural America was the obscure leadership of the Calvin Coolidge administration. Unfortunately, it then got worse when Herbert Hoover took over as President in 1929.

As far as Glenwood, Minnesota was concerned, the town still hung on to its beautiful view from the bluffs above Lake Minnewaska like it was the gates of heaven. But, as the farm economy continued to skid during the latter half of the 1920s, tourism followed suit. Many Minnesota lake resorts were forced to close. Lake Minnewaska saw three-quarters of their resorts lock their doors by 1926. Those lake resorts still able to survive in the closing years of the decade seemed to be living on barely enough oxygen to exist. When Wall Street went bust, even those vapors seemed to disappear. During those years the incessant wave of negativity was like the constant, bitter northwest wind of winter so prevalent during the long cold months in the Midwest.

And then like a hiccup in the downward trend, something happened in the spring of 1926. It took place no where else in Pope County or in that central Minnesota lake region. It happened only in Glenwood.

The change was gradual and became more perceptible during the remainder of that year...and then continued more noticeably in the following years. It was hard to define; many didn't want to try. In a nutshell, things got better. More and more businesses in town were not just surviving; some showed a surprising profit; a couple even began flourishing. There were more jobs. More families seemed not as desperate. There evolved a kind of energy, even vibrancy, to the community. People weren't trudging down the street with stooped shoulders and a hopeless outlook. There were more smiles amongst the townsfolk. Citizens seemed more interested in taking better care of their property. Attendance was up at churches. Even those churches were better maintained. Repairs were done when needed since the offertory plate was providing slightly more revenue since 1926. More important than money was the willingness for local citizens to help one another in times of need. It was as if a new sense of pride and caring about one's neighbor permeated each flock at each congregation.

Naturally, there were exceptions. Predictably, the Church of the Nazarene had looked as down-trodden as the day the construction had been completed. It continued to look as austere and uninviting as ever. Also, people still got drunk on Saturday night. There were still disagreements over national and state politics anytime two or more people gathered. And, there was no change in hearing various citizens complain about the country going to hell. While that complaint had some truth to it, Glenwood at that time certainly was not an example of that allegation.

To the locals, they didn't really acknowledge their good fortune. To them their new found spirit was normal...what life was supposed to be. When the subject came up in reference to the town's alleged advantageous conditions, credit tended to be given to hard work finally paying off, strong town leadership, and naturally, the benefit of having Lake Minnewaska and its natural beauty. The point local citizens tried to make was that with these 'inarguable' factors, why wouldn't life be just a bit better in Glenwood?

The town spirit also showed in a number of community projects. The biggest task initiated in the late 1920s was the refurbishing of what locals called 'City Park'. It included the completion of the band gazebo, the horseshoe pit, a tennis court, a softball diamond, and the beautification of the lake shore. There were other things not as noticeable, but completed nonetheless. The local school got a new roof and an improved heating system. Also, the courthouse tower was repaired along with upgrading the jailhouse.

All in all, the improvements in the town prompted by the enhanced attitude of the populace... and the willingness to put in the time, effort, and money to pay for the enhancements...were truly significant given the times. And, this aura did not go unnoticed by visitors. They saw no boarded up windows on store fronts in Glenwood. They observed people in town busier... friendlier...even, if one might say, happier. At times, these visitors voiced their observations as if trying to find out the real reasons why their own community wasn't thriving as well. While the compliments were certainly appreciated, most Glenwood citizens just looked blankly back at the questioner. Sometimes, that look was even smug. The despair shared by other rural towns around the country just seemed to have skipped over Glenwood. Most visitors left Glenwood, Minnesota wishing their town worked half as effectively.

Though the true difference was never admitted, there was most definitely a cause of the good luck...and in no way was it related to just harder work or to a more attractive geographic location. To the good fortune of the community, the explanation was understood, if vaguely, by the real town leaders. People like Mayor Charlie B. Good, Big Bud Bunsen, owner of Big Bud's General Store, Pastor O. E. Olson of the First Presbyterian Church, Wilbur 'Nosey' Newberg, the local newspaper editor, and a fellow named Henry Hanson, the local manager of the Feed & Grain Mill. They were well aware of which side their bread was buttered. They rarely discussed the subject...as if conversing about the good luck might somehow end the town's wonderful advantage. Like all locals, they just wanted the good fortune to last forever if that was possible. And, as town leaders, they weren't going to let anything...if possible...to upset the apple cart.

The reason for this unforeseen and unexpected change in Glenwood would take root in that spring of 1926. It was late April when the seed of change was planted, and actually, it didn't originate directly in the town. That was another reason the change wasn't so readily noticed. It was actually sewn at that aforementioned secluded little resort near the town. Chippewa Lodge was one of those lake properties barely holding on and far enough from town that locals hardly paid it much heed.

That month the chill seemed to hang in the air even though the sun was shining and the ice coating had disappeared weeks before. People in the area were generally content they'd survived another cold, heartless winter. Therefore, the cooler spring didn't matter. While there were no expectations for a better year, the sparkling Lake Minnewaska still worked its magic even though the water was still numbingly chilly. Under the warmer sunlight there was a natural springtime sensation for lakeside dwellers as the winter melted away. Unfortunately, the 'times' had made that emotion more temporary. Any positive feelings of spring historically would dissipate by June. The hot, dry summer eventually would beat down on the populace along with the dreadful economic news. The frets of local area farmers carping about either poor crop prices or lack of rain would echo around the community.

But, that summer of 1926, the downward spin just didn't happen. By the fall, most townspeople saw hints of things looking better in their town. Business owners were already aware. They knew the catalyst. They just didn't understand the why. It had become more and more evident that the isolated resort called Chippewa Lodge was unexplainably enjoying more occupancy. Not only that, but the resort 'guests' were extending their stays and coming into town for needed goods and services.

As nice as it was, locals thought this extra business would slow down when the summer ended. They were pleasantly surprised when they were wrong. High occupancy continued at the resort. Patrons just kept flowing into Glenwood to get their supplies. Local business owners didn't comment much amongst themselves about their improved profits. They only continued their silent prayers hoping the added revenue would continue before the real cold hit the area in November.

As for the 'Lodge', as locals referred to the resort, it had always seemed to have the potential to be one of the better vacation locations in the area, including those lake resorts around the Alexandria area to the north. But, as luck would have it, its legacy had been better known for its record of repeated foreclosures.

Yet, it would be clear to most locals that Chippewa Lodge had to have some notable qualities to have survived at all through the 1920s. Certainly the bucolic setting invited comfort and privacy. A pine-walled, slightly musty smelling restaurant and social center opened early and closed late to feed the needs and pleasures of the patrons. The docks within walking distance across the entry road to the Lodge offered boats for fishing and sailing. The swimming area was clean and had a sandy beach area for games and sunbathing. And, given its countrified setting, fishing and hunting was convenient. Still, as nice as those amenities might be, quite frankly other lake resorts still open in 1926 could boast the same features.

There had to be at least something more distinctive at this resort for it to remain open...or for that matter, to have enticed a number of new owners to have tried to make a go of their investment in the Lodge.

And, there was. On the property was a picturesque, competitive and hilly nine-hole golf course that answered a growing interest in the sport. Golf had taken on more popularity with the exposure of nationally renowned golfers like Bobby Jones, Gene Sarazen, Walter Hagen, and even the on-going legend of Francis Ouimet, the young amateur 1913 U.S. Open winner. Chippewa Lodge was able to offer this particular 'sport of royalty' to its guests.

Going back to the original owner and developer, Charlie Gordon had built the resort golf course in the early 1900s with help from his cronies in Glenwood and nearby Villard. Unfortunately, Gordon owned the land and the resort for only a few years before it was forced to close. Successive owners had no better luck.

In fact, Chippewa Lodge should have been more successful prior to 1925, but nothing seemed to work. The resort might have been too rustic...too isolated from the Twin Cities...and maybe even too far from Glenwood. Additionally, the years had not been kind. Misfortunes interrupted the previous owners' hopes for profitability...World War I being the big one. During the war, vacations seemed frivolous and disrespectful with American doughboys fighting and dying on the Franco-German border and in the fields of Belgium.

By rights, the 'Lodge' should never have even opened when Mr. Darrell O'Donnell bought the fledgling business in the summer of 1925. A golf course superintendent in St. Paul, he'd been left some money from a deceased uncle. He was looking to leave the big city and invest in a business. The Lake Minnewaska property's price... including the golf course...coupled with the quaint, quiet location were just too intoxicating for him. He bought it for a song and still had money left over to make some badly needed improvements. Mr. O'Donnell became the owner and manager...and everything else at Chippewa Lodge... including the maintenance man, the restaurant coordinator, the front desk clerk, the clubhouse golf pro, and the head greenskeeper. He did whatever he could to save operating costs. It was shear determination and stubbornness that kept the place open through the rest of that remaining summer and fall.

O'Donnell did have some limited paid staff. Thanks to access to some illegal booze, the restaurant almost broke even over that first summer. The golf course was kept groomed by a number of local townsmen who traded maintenance work for free play. O'Donnell, though, knew he'd have to face not opening the Lodge or the golf course after the very hard winter of 1925-26. The response to his advertising and promotion was poor to go along with the general drop in occupancy rates at lake resorts all around Minnesota.

Opening the gates of the resort in the spring of 1926 seemed unpromising. Just the cost to get the golf course into playing condition that April was financially crippling. He knew his occupancy rates would have to miraculously pick up for him to last into the real warm months of summer. That probability looked as likely as a major convention being staged on his property.

Despite grave doubts Darrell O'Donnell did convince himself to keep trying. He opened the resort on the fifteenth of April, 1926, after the ice on the lake had melted and that previously mentioned 'spirit of spring' mentality offered him renewed if illusory hope. He decided he was going to keep the grounds open and his cabins cleaned until the first night he had no guests and his future reservation ledger was blank. Even then, he figured to keep the golf course open until the first frost of fall.

Still, with the golf course operational by the last week of April, things continued to look bleak. That month there was a 90% vacancy rate on his cabins. If it wasn't for his illegal booze shipment from Canada, his restaurant would never have remained open. Bookings for May didn't look much better than April. Holding out until June when some of the summer business might give his resort a needed boost was his last hope.

And just when the world looked the dimmest...when day threatened no light...when running a business seemed the height of idiocy and carried no whim of success, 'chance' blossomed like the new tulips in spring.

In early May, 1926, the Chippewa Lodge resort and soon the town of Glenwood would have a most unanticipated miracle literally drop at their feet. It was so unexpected...so incompatible with the unrewarding, seemingly futile atmosphere during that time period.

The phenomenon wasn't even recognized right away by the small staff at the Lodge, but Darrell O'Donnell spotted the opportunity the very minute it arrived. Like a starving tiger stumbling upon a limping wildebeest, he read the potential when a group of rather boisterous, out-of-state visitors arrived unannounced wanting to rent four cabins for three nights. They primarily expressed interest in testing the golf course, but became impressed by the quality of the restaurant...and the artery of illegal 'booze' O'Donnell was able to guarantee. These men were obviously city slickers in the way they dressed and their mannerisms. O'Donnell's heart had leaped when he saw that late-model Packard driving into the resort. The men exiting the vehicle were smoking large stogies. He almost fainted when the cabin rentals were paid ahead of time.

One of the men, a huge man with cigar stains on his shirt and tie talked with a voice so gravelly it seemed impossible to imitate. He mentioned casually to O'Donnell after the first night's stay that his group was looking for a 'getaway'...then quickly corrected his wording to describe that he meant a place guaranteeing quiet and seclusion. O'Donnell literally gulped with anticipation and didn't hesitate substantiating how the Chippewa Lodge resort was the answer to the man's needs. The big city fellow just nodded, not agreeing or disagreeing.

During those couple days, this group of raucous men played a lot of golf and kept endlessly late hours at the resort restaurant. They couldn't stop talking about the pipeline of illegal booze. O'Donnell made it sound harder to get the booze than it really was. With false modesty he responded, "Yes sir, it's easy to get beer and alcohol shipped in from Canada...if a person knows the right people."

The cigar chomping guest appreciated the comment. He replied, "O'Donnell, my guys don't care about your source. They just care that it's there when they reach for it."

While O'Donnell desperately wanted the continued business, he took note of the odd behaviors amongst these big city chaps. Though smartly attired, their behavior and speech were consistently loud and crass... not exactly the family clientele he had been pursuing. Of course, that particular market...the families...were not beating down his office door to rent cabins. He had no problem with bad behavior and crassness as long as money accompanied the conduct.

And, money spoke unmistakably during the city slickers' stay at Chippewa Lodge. O'Donnell didn't care who rented the cabins as long as they were occupied. He was ready to make a deal with the devil as long as it meant revenue for his struggling resort. Little did he realize he was closer to that reality than he ever could have guessed.

The third day of their stay, a few of the men went fishing off the resort's docks across the roadway while the large man with the stogie in his mouth, a Mr. Loni D'Annelli, took time to talk with the resort manager. The conversation centered on the possibility of D'Annelli and his friends renting some cabins for an extended period of time.

O'Donnell couldn't believe what he was hearing. The man gave every impression that he and his group could afford much better quarters, but D'Annelli admitted his people were quite taken with the secluded resort, the accompanying golf course, and the continuous flow of Canadian booze. D'Annelli suggested he might want as many as five cabins right away... eight for the following month...and for each night! The gargantuan city slicker looked the giddy owner of the resort right in the eye and added, "Yeh, O'Donnell, if things work out, we might need double that number of cabins by July...and for the rest of the year."

O'Donnell feared he might need a paper bag to balance his breathing and keep from passing out. The light-headed resort manager didn't know what was meant by 'things working out', but he was going to make certain things would indeed work out. All he recognized was that out-of-state money was as good as any other cash. His only wish from that moment onward was to appease his new 'guests'.

A deal was struck that afternoon. An important part of the agreement for D'Annelli was that O'Donnell and his staff paid no heed as to who would be staying in the rented cabins. As D'Annelli explained in his inimitable gruff manner, "O'Donnell, we'll do business as long as you and your staff keep your traps shut, the cabins clean, the booze flowing, and the golf course playable."

O'Donnell agreed to those additional terms with an eager nod and a bladder he thought was going to burst. Suddenly because of this early season cash inflow, he could commit to keeping his little resort open and solvent through the summer and very likely to the end of the year as well.

He could not believe he was receiving such glad tidings. He thought only the Presbyterians could be so hallowed. Since he was Lutheran, he was damn well certain he'd never mention his good fortune to any of his fellow church members. They'd find something evil in his business saving transaction. And to his staff, he expressed in no uncertain terms the conditions of their employment. What they saw or heard at the resort from these out-of-town 'guests' would remain at the resort or the workers would be responsible for him having to close the resort and for themselves out of a job.

O'Donnell didn't know it, but he'd just made a deal of Faustian proportions. Mr. Loni D'Annelli had introduced himself as a union boss from the 'Windy City'. To O'Donnell that meant a man with connections...and might even refer his union members to vacation at a certain lake resort in Minnesota. However, D'Annelli had not given the resort owner the complete and more telling portrayal of his background. The man from Chicago was a mob kingpin who had ideas far beyond just renting some cabins for his 'friends and colleagues'. D'Annelli had an assortment of business interests...some still in the idea phase. His location in Chicago had been preventing him from acting on those ideas. He'd been trying to find a more ideal location away from the keen eyes of the law and the hairy noses of the press. When he arrived at Chippewa Lodge he sensed he'd just found the perfect secluded setting.

Had Darrell O'Donnell been made aware of D'Annelli's underworld background, it doubtfully would have been a deal breaker. He was in a desperate situation. O'Donnell simply thought his sporadic church attendance and his attempts at reducing the use of God's name in vain had finally paid off.

Within weeks of striking the deal, more and more rather questionable characters registered as 'guests' at the Lodge...and not just for a few days. Some appeared they were setting up quarters in their cabins for an extended period of time. O'Donnell was seeing men register from unlikely places like Milwaukee, Detroit, Omaha, and even New York...as well as Minneapolis and Chicago. Their names were not of Scandinavian, English or German ancestry. They were more of Italian heritage. And when these men rarely responded to the names logged onto to the register, that didn't matter to him either. The cabins were paid for in advance...that was the part that did matter!

As a result of his sudden and on-going revenue increase, there was another byproduct he never fathomed as his occupancy rate increased. There was an ancillary business boost beyond the gates of his lake resort. Owners of local Glenwood businesses began to profit from the services and supplies needed by this unruly but moneyed group of 'guests' and from O'Donnell as well. He began receiving shy but friendly greetings from local folk whenever he happened to be in town. It made him feel kind of important. For the son of a barber from Park Rapids, Minnesota, the massage to his ego was quite gratifying.

That the serene, lazy town and the secluded little resort were chosen as a preferred 'vacation' spot by an underworld figure from Chicago exceeded all odds. As D'Annelli had taken note of the solitude and isolation the resort offered, he was further satisfied how both the resort staff and even the citizens in town were patient with his noisy and disruptive colleagues. It became quite evident to him as the weeks and months progressed how grateful the folks in Glenwood were for the additional business the 'guests' of Chippewa Lodge required. Townsfolk blind and deaf to any misgivings caused by the animated and unruly clientele. As time went on, D'Annelli was forced to reason with the men living in the cabins. He stressed the importance of them sticking by the normal rules of conduct when in town. As he told them, "You mugs need to understand our little private resort will work just fine as long as all of us remain welcome in Glenwood."

Throughout the remainder of 1926 and into the spring of 1927, various groups of men stayed at Chippewa Lodge each season of the year...even during the harshness of winter. Guests stayed for months... some for the entire year. At other times, a cabin might be rented but used only sporadically during a thirty-day rental. But, since it was always pre-paid, it was available to whomever D'Annelli invited to use that cabin.

Often times O'Donnell would notice 'guests' who hadn't even registered as they walked back and forth from the cabins to the restaurant or lake...or when they teed off at the resort golf course... or as they loaded up on booze and food while they played cards in the backroom of the restaurant. More than once he wondered if he'd lost complete control of his own resort. Then he'd look at his ledger, smile and remind himself that 'control' wasn't as important as revenue.

As for these 'guests', they were a hardy lot. The restaurant's back room became a perpetual card room. Besides the card games, the 'guests' bet on anything from golf to the boat races to fishing contests to road races on the back roads of Pope County. They also drank like they had two livers and ate as if each meal was their last one. Just as important, their "nieces" visited them....and often!

During the warmer months that first summer, there were ten rented cabins mostly filled each night. A year later there were more than double that number occupied at all times. Golf was like a religion to these 'guests'. It was played seemingly every minute there was daylight and no rain. Sometimes even darkness and rain weren't a deterrent.

Fancy cars drove in and out of the resort through the seasons. Occasionally O'Donnell would be cautiously asked by local citizens what he'd done to pick up his business so dramatically. O'Donnell, the picture of phoniness, would simply crow, "word of mouth"...implying that once a person stayed at his resort, they were sold on its comforts and were recommending the place to friends. It was a nice catch phrase and as pompous as it was untrue.

As for local businesses, they didn't care if he was being pretentious. They just loved the additional trade...especially places like Big Bud Bunsen's General Store, the Glenwood Café, crusty druggist Warner Kemp and his Apothecary Shop, the town's dentist, Cal 'Cavity' Carlson, the tailor, 'Thread' Nelson, 'Engine' Joe Goodbody, the local auto mechanic, and of course, Curly Gaston, the barber. All of them showed improved business paralleling the increased occupancy rate at Chippewa Lodge.

Big Bud Bunsen's store was the real beneficiary. With Prohibition being the law of the land, Big Bud trucked in enough Canadian beer and booze from Winnipeg, Manitoba to keep the boys out at the Lodge well satisfied. But, the astute businessman didn't stop there. His local friends in town benefited as well. He had a sizable private storage room off the back of his store he parlayed into a place all ages of male could engage in acts of sin like drinking and card playing. On Friday and Saturday nights, Big Bud's 'backroom' was one of the busiest speakeasies in the area...including the better known lake area hangouts thirty minutes north around Alexandria.

Through all this time, the local law enforcement officers remained curiously uninterested and unaware. It was as if they wanted to remain distant from the 'guests' at Chippewa Lodge. Yet, this behavior by the local and county police force had not just happened. Loni D'Annelli had not arrived at his station in life by luck or being dim-witted. He'dd taken time to introduce himself and win over the local leaders of the town including the leading two law enforcement officers, the Pope County Sheriff Clarence Petracek and the town's Chief of Police, Rich Brey. Furthermore, D'Annelli charmed to the town's citizens by donating money for the resurrection of City Park. Civic and church organizations enjoyed his financial support as well. Not only did church offertory plates have a bit more money than normal each month, but any food or clothing drives...or bake sales... the 'guests' out at the Lodge were behind them.

However, the biggest act of benevolence from 'Mr. D'Annelli', as he was known in town, was his invitation to the church and civic organizations to help out with his first annual charity golf event he scheduled in June, 1927. He explained to the town council his idea of inviting celebrities and prominent businessmen to play in a two-day event to be held out at the Lodge golf course. He told them his need for support from various organizations in town to help with spectator transportation to and from town, parking out at the resort, ticket sales, and of course food stands...plenty of food stands. D'Annelli then generously offered that any profits from all this support by the civic or church groups should go right into their coffers.

The town council was bowled over by both the idea and the extreme bigheartedness. What they didn't know was this charity event was all part of a master plan. D'Annelli's efforts were done specifically to continue winning the hearts and minds of the local populace thereby further ensuring privacy and confidentiality. He wanted the townspeople so immersed in the benefits they were receiving from him and his 'guests' that any nosiness or inquisitiveness would be assuaged. His gamble was that if any citizen got wind of some unfavorable gossip pertaining to the 'guests' or activities out at the Lodge, they would tend to look the other way. It turned out to be one of his safest bets.

By the end of that second summer in 1927 following his first annual charity golf invitational tournament, even D'Annelli was amazed how well his choice of Chippewa Lodge was working out. He expanded his business plan to include even more of his ventures to be based out at the isolated resort. The kind of privacy he had at the resort was not possible back in Chicago or even Milwaukee where cops and reporters seemed to be around every corner.

If the townsfolk in Glenwood had only known what was going on at the Lodge property by the end of 1927, most of them would have been uncomfortable. But, D'Annelli's belief held true that generosity and friendliness, even if factitious, would always be his strength in maintaining loyalty from the citizenry. From that summer of 1927 to that astonishing June weekend in 1931, Loni D'Annelli had the Lodge and the town of Glenwood in the palm of his hand.

Many years later townsfolk still living in the community couldn't agree on why or when the town of Glenwood seemed to get 'blessed' back during that era of the 1920s. Some admitted it was that spring of 1926 when those 'big city' fellows began arriving in the area. Still others gave credit to the ten-day town festival, an unabashed, almost immodest display of the town's good fortune that began in June, 1928.

Still others believed the town was just fortunate to have a couple energetic and uniquely effective leaders who guided the town so effectively in the late 1920s.

The person they were primarily referring to was surprisingly not Mr. Loni D'Annelli from Chicago. He might have supplied generous amounts of money, but it took some town leaders to help the community take advantage of the circumstances. While there was more than one of these type of leaders living in the community at the time, one particular fellow seemed to stand out far above the others. He was a respected and admired person throughout the time he lived in Glenwood. He maintained that stature for an entire generation even after he left the community. His name was Henry Hanson and he'd been part of the town for almost the entire decade of the 1920s right through that extraordinary June weekend in 1931.

He wasn't an impressive looking man if seeing him amble down the street to or from his work as General Manager at the Feed & Grain Mill. But, he could be recognized from blocks away for his long even strides in a body that was too tall and too thin. He wasn't really outgoing, but he was friendly. He had a way of making people feel good no matter their age just in the way he greeted them. And, his loyalty to the town of Glenwood was unquestioned. He praised people who kept up their properties; he stressed the need for investing in the school; he commended many churches for messages underlining neighbors helping neighbors. He took on civic responsibilities even though he disliked town meetings. He became the financial manager at the First Presbyterian Church even though his attendance at church was spotty.

When he talked people listened, especially after one of his many vacations he took during the year. He was a traveler at heart. Hanson liked history and exploring new places. Down at his Mill office, he had subscriptions to magazines covering various historical and travel locations around the world...especially in Western Europe where he'd been stationed during the 'Big War'. And, when he returned from one of his vacations, townsfolk would stream into his Mill office welcoming him back and hearing his stories of New York City, Washington D.C., Chicago, Boston, Philadelphia, and various Civil War battlefield sites he'd visited.

When his leadership was called upon, he had a knack for helping, especially the town council members, understand both sides of an argument or issue. He rarely expressed strong opinions himself...or so it seemed. And, regarding any community improvement, he did everything he could to get people involved... including getting his own hands dirty as well. For his sincere efforts and absolute trustworthiness he earned a moniker. He was referred to as 'Honest Henry' as far back as anyone could remember...and a description that stayed with him long after he'd left the town.

It was in the spring of 1928 when the two-year quiet relationship between the townspeople and the 'guests' out at Chippewa Lodge was put to the real test. Whether it was Henry Hanson or Loni D'Annelli getting the credit, it took both men from both their perspectives to persuade the town council into establishing a multi-day town festival to be run in conjunction with D'Annelli's second annual charity golf tournament. With the positive results of the previous year's charity event, it gave D'Annelli added credence in selling the bigger idea. However, it was Henry Hanson who saw how the community could truly profit even more from such a venture. He even favored the eventual decision to make it a ten-day town celebration to help usher in the summer tourism season at Lake Minnewaska. In addition, he took on the thankless job as festival chairman and remained in that capacity right up to and including the gala event in June, 1931. With his guidance, each year that town celebration got bigger and better.

What was further interesting was how these two men got along so well. Opposites in so many ways, the gruff, over-confident D'Annelli and the rock solid, quiet Hanson appeared to complement each other in setting up this huge town celebration. Their confidence helped the entire community of Glenwood exude the energy and enthusiasm required to take on such a grandiose event...especially in such troubled economic times. With the aura of D'Annelli and Hanson, the advantages of topography, the right people as members of the town council, and the willing volunteer church and civic organizations, the chemistry was there to further solidify that special relationship between the peculiar 'guests' out at the Lodge and the willing, but oblivious, citizens in town.

What most people didn't realize once the ten-day festival measure was passed by the town council in January, 1928, D'Annelli more or less disappeared from any public leadership role. He'd accomplished what he'd wanted in getting the town and its citizens to feel even more obliged to his benevolence. That was when Henry Hanson and the other key town leaders blindly took charge of the entire ten-day celebration...just like D'Annelli had hoped.

And what a ten-day festival it was. With Memorial Day weekend kicking off the festival, the following weekdays were filled with planned sporting contests including nightly horseshoes, kitten ball tournaments, boat races, fishing competitions, and countless activities for the kids. For the more sedate citizens, the games at booths in City

Park and prizes for the best farm products and baked goods satisfied those other competitive urges. The grand party ended the next weekend with a beauty contest, a band concert at the City Park gazebo, and a large street dance on Saturday night. On the final weekend of the festival, there was the charity golf tournament and of course the 'finals' for all other sporting events.

The guidance and management to sustain such a festive week didn't rely just on Henry Hanson. Besides the trusted, civic-minded Henry Hanson as chairman, there was the ever promotion minded... especially for himself...the honorable mayor, Charlie B. Good... the energetic and vibrant minister of the First Presbyterian Church, Pastor O.E. Olson... and that very willing town businessman, Big Bud Bunsen who seemed able to find anything for anyone as any capitalist ever born. Still it was the townsfolk who volunteered and teamed up that made Glenwood's community festival one of the best supported events outside of the Twin Cities. And, this effort might not have been so freely and generously given if the carnival atmosphere didn't bring in the impressive financial gain the way it did to the churches, the civic organizations, and the local businesses.

So, those were the circumstances in Glenwood...and the atmosphere out at Chippewa Lodge up to that Friday, June 5th, 1931. The months had turned into years of seeing surly looking and deviously acting strangers staying at the Lodge and frequenting the town. The seasons of continued business profiting and surviving in Glenwood had unmistakably coincided with that loud and brash bunch at the resort. As long as the townsfolk didn't question who the Lodge 'guests' were and those same 'guests' didn't create too much trouble in the community, the peaceful coexistence remained strong.

By that final weekend the locals were looking forward to a big finish of their best ever celebration. Friday, June 5, was a particularly busy day in town getting ready for the finals of the various competitions, the big dance on Saturday night, and the rich charity golf tournament both Saturday and Sunday. There was already a record crowd attendance according to the excitable Mayor Good. Even local newspaper editor, Wilbur 'Nosey' Newberg, normally with a more balanced perspective to the news, agreed. It was also the largest group of 'guests' ever assembled at the Lodge through invitation from Loni D'Annelli. The upcoming charity golf tournament commencing Saturday morning promised to have an even bigger spectator turnout judging by the pre-purchased tickets.

CHAPTER
4

Sitting at the Bailey farm that Friday night, the storm was still fierce two hours later. James Lawton was having a cup of coffee on a bland-looking, worn, and scratchy couch in the farmer's living room. The house was actually quite comfortable inside...quite the opposite of what it looked like from the outside. Bailey turned out to be a very big-hearted man and generous host providing Lawton with some dry clothing. Considering where he could be at that moment, Lawton pronounced himself quite lucky in the safe confines of that old house.

Initially Bailey was quiet as he listened to Lawton's travails about failing to outguess the direction of the storm and facing the reality he'd have to land on the highway. Bailey had no idea his truck and Lawton's biplane had come perilously close to colliding just before Bailey had turned onto his driveway. As he became more at ease with Lawton, the farmer became more talkative. Bailey kept inquiring about both the biplane as well as what his guest did for a living in the Twin Cities. For Lawton, his travels around the Midwest had taught him many things. One was not to necessarily divulge his legal occupation unless necessary. Informing rural folks he was a lawyer often made them uncomfortable.

That was how he judged John Bailey upon entering the house. If asked he figured to stick with his other more exciting former part-time occupation, that of an aviator. That side of his life never seemed to disappoint the folks he met. It led to more relaxed conversation.

As they talked, Lawton's eyes gazed around the home. The interior was very austere. It occurred to him there was no female to add a softness or any decorating appeal to the inside. There was also something in Bailey's conversation...a seriousness...a difficulty finding humor...that made Lawton careful with his own questions. He chose not to ask his host about his family, especially since the farmer didn't seem concerned as to where his family members were during the torrential rain.

Soon Bailey's questions changed to a much different and more surprising direction. "So, Mr. Lawton, have you played in the local tournament in prior years or is this your first time?"

Lawton wrinkled his brow having no idea what the man was referring. "What local tournament? I'm playing golf tomorrow but in Alexandria with some friends. Why do you ask?"

Bailey now looked puzzled. "I don't know about any tournament up in Alexandria, but the one at Chippewa Lodge starting tomorrow morning is one of the best charity tournaments in this part of the state and to my understanding one of the most unbelievable money tournaments played at any golf course."

They were talking on different frequencies. Befuddled, Lawton queried, "You mean there's some kind of professional tournament being played in the area this weekend?"

Also confused, Bailey shook his head and chuckled, "Well, Mr. Lawton, you really did just drop from the sky. I guess there'd be no way you'd know about this small charity golf tournament unless you received an invitation or lived out in these parts. I'm talking about a high stakes gambling tournament having been played every first weekend in June locally for the past couple years. Not a lot of people know the players competing in the event. They're mostly professional businessmen from out of town who obviously have a lot of money. What you wouldn't believe is the amount of cash that exchanges hands at the end of this so-called charity golf contest. And, from what I hear, these players are anything but professional golfers. I guess a lot of the locals wonder what type of actual work these competitors do considering the way they throw their money around."

Lawton wasn't following everything the farmer was saying. Unmindful, Bailey just kept talking, as if enjoying the chance to share an interesting story. "When I saw you with your golf clubs at my front door, I just took for granted you were one of those "high rollers" arriving in time to tee it up tomorrow morning."

Just the way Bailey rolled his eyes as he used the term 'high roller' grabbed Lawton's attention. In fact, Lawton's tentacles would rise even higher in the next hour as he heard more about this strangely unknown tournament, since he happened to be a scratch handicap golfer. Like any skilled player, when an opportunity like a golf match with a lot of money riding on the outcome, any competitive golfer would be interested. Lawton was no exception. He could vividly see the image of human pigeons wearing the latest style of golf knickers and very willing to risk an abundant number of greenbacks in a sporting atmosphere.

As Bailey described some of the players as not being as skilled, the smell of opportunity became even more redolent. He had seen many of this type of golfer. Most talked better than they played. They would swear at errant drives and missed putts as if they had the same skill level as Bobby Jones or Walter Hagen.

Lawton wanted to hear as much as Bailey was willing to say about this tournament without appearing too greedy or too eager. When Bailey sounded as if he was done, Lawton trying to stay calm inquired, "So, John, how does one enter such a competition?"

Bailey remained quiet while eyeing his guest. The farmer got up to refresh his coffee cup not saying a word. In those seconds Lawton thought about his state-wide travels and how was it not possible he'd not heard of this golf event. He'd been distantly aware of Glenwood's annual June festival but hadn't thought that community event had anything to do with golf.

The rain continued to pour as Bailey returned to his living room chair. Where the farmer had been reticent at the beginning of their conversation, he was now quite relaxed with Lawton. He broadened his story to explain how the charity golf tournament was the last big event of the town's ten-day opening of summer celebration. He spoke incredulously about the ever increasing number of spectators who came to watch the golf event.

A distant rumble of thunder echoed across the farm land as Bailey lazily added, "Yeh...and this ten-day town festival has been quite a ride for Glenwood. Locals really support the celebration and the golf event. It's worth a lot of money to the town. Even my own son has profited. He caddies in this tournament and makes enough money that we could probably survive comfortably for a couple of months if the crops didn't mature for fall harvest or the farm animals all died.... God forbid, of course."

Lawton thought of what he normally paid a caddy and was unimpressed. He immediately decided Bailey must really be struggling on his farm if he could live on what a caddy was paid.

Without offering names, Bailey described some of the unique players participating in the tournament. "They come as far away as Chicago, Milwaukee, Omaha, and even St. Louis. These guests arrive sometimes a week before the charity golf event and play golf every day at the Chippewa Lodge golf course in preparation for the tournament.

Some attend the events at the festival during the week, but mostly they don't leave the resort."

Bailey then looked over at Lawton's golf clubs drying by the front door. "I'd have to say by the looks of those golf clubs, you like the game. Tell me, have you participated as a player or a buyer in something called a 'Calcutta' during any golf tournaments where you've probably played?"

Lawton nodded surprised that a non-golfer like John Bailey knew of this term. What he was talking about was something commonly done at private country clubs before the occasional weekend club tournament. Players would be sold like horses to encourage outside betting among non-players. Payouts were then given to the winning buyers based on the results of the competitors....typically the top three places made the money for the bettors. Since the Calcutta was accomplished within the confines of a one-time tournament, the illegality of gambling could conveniently be overlooked by local law enforcement. Still, the gaming was done very secretively so as not to stir up any police action or legal trouble. The actual auction of the players transpired usually in the clubhouse bar or away from the club at a private location. Even in the recent tough times of the 1930s, Lawton was often surprised by the amount of money being wagered in some of the tournaments he'd participated.

Bailey continued, "Well, if you're familiar with this type of gambling action, the calcutta at this Chippewa Lodge charity event doesn't just casually happen. A couple staff people I know out at the Lodge have witnessed the true magnitude of the wagers. It's an incredible amount of money in the Calcutta "pot" for this tournament. People can lay down bets on various individual player scores or bet on a particular team. There are even a couple betting booths outside the resort to give even outsiders a chance to place their wagers."

Until that statement, Bailey's explanation was understandable. Where Lawton participated in this type of gambling over his amateur golf career, it was all done very prudently. But, hearing about the outsider betting booths...that went too far. To Lawton that effort would make the entire gambling affair way too public and probably crossed the line of being way too 'illegal'.

Then Bailey shook his head disapprovingly. "I've been watching this whole cotton pickin' little game go on for a couple years. It's a strange situation. So many churches and civic organizations in town benefit from this golf event. The town leaders are thrilled. Hell, the Presbyterians are in charge of the betting booths...one down in City Park and another outside the gates at the resort. Those Presbyterian

Men's Clubbers who work at the booth call the Calcutta a horse race. They don't know the first thing about golf; they just take in the bets."

Then he paused wrinkling his forehead. "You know, at times I think those fellows have to be taking bets on other types of action than our little old charity golf tournament. But, they don't say a word. The workers are bound by secrecy. They act like the world will end if they say anything about their volunteer work at either of the betting booths. I don't get how the whole thing is legal, but it must be. Our law enforcement people aren't too concerned. But, I got to tell you, there are more players...more guests...more fancy cars...and from what the rumors are, more money in the Calcutta each year. It certainly has good for the community. I know some people are holding their breath praying the whole damn thing won't blow up in their faces."

Lawton wasn't quite certain how to react to Bailey's story. He didn't have to be a lawyer to sense some laws were being stretched beyond their intent. There was an uncomfortable silence in the living room as both men got up to stretch. They moved out onto the porch to observe the dying storm. Occasional lightning still lit up the skies to the east as the worst of the storm had passed. It was turning into a breezy and refreshing evening that so often followed a Minnesota thunderstorm.

Bailey then lit a cigarette and commented, "Even our honorable mayor, Charlie B. Good has magnified this annual celebration to bring in more visitors and tourists. Yeh, old Charlie B. was elected in 1928 with the slogan, 'Things will be good with Charlie B. Good'. And, that pretty much has been the case, not that the mayor can take full credit."

The farmer blew some smoke into the air and sighed, "Someday, and I don't think it's too far off, we'll find out what really is going on at the Lodge. My neighbors in town are so very careful not to say anything negative about the resort or the 'guests' out there. It's like no one wants to be accused of upsetting the apple cart. Golf tournament admission tickets are sold by the Methodists. The Lutherans and the Baptists handle the parking. Every church has a concession stand. For two bits a head, the Church of Christ folks will give carriage rides to curious golf enthusiasts who want to ride along the lake on the way out to the Lodge golf course.

And the Presbyterians....they really lucked out. Like I told you, their take at the Calcutta betting booths apparently is incredible. A friend of mine, a manager down at the Feed & Grain Mill is in charge. His name is Henry Hanson. Henry trains a select group of church club members how to take the bets while he handles the money and compiles the results and pay-offs. He won't tell me the figure that the

Men's Club earns; he just whistles when the topic comes up. Hell, all these churches make more money during festival week than a century's worth of bake sales."

Bailey began to chuckle at his own joke. "And you should see some of these 'professional businessmen' playing in the charity golf tournament. I swear a few of these fellows have a very familiar look... like their pictures have been in the newspapers...and not for heroism. But, they keep a low profile and rarely go into town. Sometimes you see them eating down at the café, but not often. You can tell they're from the big city because they wear suits instead of farm clothes. Not often, but periodically, some townspeople comment about 'so and so' visiting right here in Glenwood. The local folk have become mesmerized with the celebrity aspect of a couple of these players whose backgrounds have not been stellar.

Most visitors who come to our community for the golf event don't really know or care who the players are. They just get caught up in the competition when they hear about the high stakes."

Showing a big smile, Bailey chortled, "And, something that really makes this tournament one of a kind is some of the antics that go on among the players. It's a golf competition the likes of which you've never seen. I'm not a golfer, but I know enough about the game to realize some of the actions...well...it isn't exactly good sportsmanship."

Lawton thought that an odd comment. He'd played in a lot of tournaments and seen a lot of strange things on the golf course. He interrupted, "John, that's quite a statement. What do you mean?"

John's grin remained on his face. "When my son, Adam, gets back home tonight, I'll let him fill you in on what goes on during the actual competition. He's a golfer. I think only then will you get some true idea."

Lawton found John Bailey to be a surprisingly bright and genuine fellow. He didn't know why he was so surprised. He just didn't expect a lonely farmer to have such well stated thoughts. He sensed Bailey was likely a highly respected man in his community.

Some lights suddenly flashed on the barn. Both men jumped as if lightning had struck nearby. They relaxed again when they saw headlights of a truck rumbling up the driveway toward the farmhouse. Bailey immediately excused himself and went into his house as if he'd gone through this routine before. He began busying himself with preparing something to eat. He yelled out to Lawton on the porch, "If you're hungry, I'll make extra."

Lawton shook his head and yelled back, "Sure, I'd appreciate something to eat. Thanks very much." Bailey was thoughtful if not prompt with his invitation for dinner.

Seconds later a young man burst out of a rusty old Plymouth truck and bolted toward the front door jumping over mud puddles onto the steps before rushing through the front screen door. He rushed past Lawton without seeing him on the rocker at the far end of the porch. The lad was like a cannon shell compared to the quiet nature of his father. He was lanky like his father, but appeared taller because of his thinness. He guessed the kid to be in his later teen years.

Adam Bailey began chattering to his father before the screen door slammed shut. He was excited and laughing uproariously despite his clothes being saturated to the skin. Lawton heard him breathlessly explain to his father about the group he'd caddied in earlier that afternoon before the downpour. He referred to the man he caddied for as 'Loni'.

Gasping, he said to his father, "Dad, it was just a pre-tournament practice round, and he gave me $50 for my caddying efforts. He said it was also part high school graduation gift."

The usual caddy fee was 50 cents for nine holes or $1.00 for 18 holes. Lawton noted the extra $49 was truly a nice graduation gift.

The young man then launched into a story about his profitable afternoon. "Dad, a bunch of the fellows started kidding Loni about wanting to bid for my caddy services. These guys said they wanted me caddying exclusively in their group both Saturday and Sunday because of my knowledge of the course and reading the breaks in the putting greens. But, Loni put the clamps on the bidding. He simply said, 'Forget it boys. Adam's my caddy and that's the way it is.' I tell you, there were no more words said about it.

After caddying eighteen holes, I cleaned the interiors of some of the cars until it started raining. I also drove into town to get more supplies and food for the restaurant and a case of booze for Loni's cabin. I saw Big Bud. He says to tell you 'hi'. Anyway, I got $20 in tip money for all that work. If this week were a month long, I'd have to contemplate retirement."

Both father and son burst into uncontained laughter over the son's good fortune. Lawton couldn't help but chuckle as well as he got up from the rocker on the porch and stood by the screen door. He observed what had likely become a father and son ritual. Having warmed the food and placing a plate of beans, meat and some carrots in front of his son, the father watched Adam dig in like he hadn't eaten in days. As the young man inhaled the food, John smiled at his entertaining son and patted his shoulder. It was a warm scene. The father was obviously very proud of his son.

It again crossed Lawton's mind as to where Bailey's wife might be… and if there were other family members. Something was missing in this home despite the wonderful picture of a strong father/son relationship.

Lawton remained outside the door as Adam relayed another story. He marveled at the young man's unbridled enthusiasm. It brought back his own memory of having the same kind of personality. In the present day Lawton still laughed and enjoyed life, but he'd long since lost that certain innocence reflected so much in young Adam's behavior.

Standing there and listening to Adam relate more stories about the golfers that day, Lawton found himself wishing he'd known about this golf tournament in years past. There may be some colorful characters making up the roster of competitors, but he was no choirboy himself. He'd beaten a man in the first round of the State Amateur Tournament three years before who was now behind bars for murdering his wife. His friend, Charlie Davis, joked that the loss probably put the man over the edge. It was the final straw. The man had lost patience and strangled his poor spouse. Davis then rationalized how Lawton could therefore be considered an accomplice.

Lawton turned and looked out across the Bailey property. With the sky now clearing, he saw a portion of Lake Minnewaska, like a dark hole with some cabin lights acting as a frame to the large body of water below the bluff.

His mind then returned to his curiosity about the next morning's golf event being played somewhere down by that huge lake. It was eating at him…Bailey's description of the questionable skill level of the golfers and the amount of money being wagered. He kept whispering to himself, 'Like picking daisies in a meadow.' It was just too damned bad his timing was so late to enter the tournament.'

Then he countered his enthusiasm thinking about Bailey's warning. Some of the players were not only a bit rowdy, but they might live on the wrong side of the law. Even then, he contemplated how that factor shouldn't be a knock out factor for playing. He'd played in plenty of golf tournaments with players being anything but pure. If there were a few publicized lawbreakers in the next day's competition, who would care? On the golf course everyone competed and the best golfer won… not the nicest….or most moral…or the most law abiding…just the best score. Besides, the participants couldn't be that felonious or they'd already be incarcerated. The purpose of any tournament was for the joy of competition, not just a sporting event based on greed. He wished that wholesome thought would rule his mind…but it didn't. Finally he was able to scoff at himself. 'For Christ's sake, Lawton, who am I kidding? This thing is a private affair anyway.'

He decided it was something he needed to forget. The next morning he'd ask the Baileys to patrol Hwy. #28 for a few moments so he could take off from the state highway. He could be up at Charlie Davis' lake home in less than a half hour. He pictured himself waving to the two Baileys as he went skyward at daybreak. They would return his wave and then they'd begin wandering back to their farmhouse as his biplane rose higher. There would be no reason for the Baileys and him to ever see each other again. Their memory of his visit would fade to nothing by the end of the weekend. As for Lawton, he would make the 9:30 tee time at the Alexandria municipal golf club Saturday morning and his life would continue with nary a thought of the Baileys again.

Lawton's dreamy state of mind was interrupted by the screen door opening. Having finished dinner, the father and son were emerging to sit out on the porch. Both of them stared across the farm yard at the biplane. Adam had finally been made aware of the houseguest standing outside on the porch. The young man stuck out his hand and approached Lawton with a broad smile. "Mr. Lawton, my name's Adam. My Dad tells me you had to make an emergency landing on the state highway just as the storm hit. I wished I would have seen that little act. It had to be kind of a thrill...maybe not for you, but certainly for anyone watching."

He paused realizing his entertainment would have been at Lawton's expense, but behaved neither embarrassed nor sorry for his wording. "Anyway, you seem all right. Did your plane make it through the storm with no damage?"

Reciprocating the handshake, Lawton took note of the strong hand and forearm of the teen-aged young man...something golfers always took note. Lawton guessed the strength was likely buoyed by the work on the farm.

He returned the smile. "Adam, yes, the air machine made it through the storm all right. I've been appreciating your Dad's nice hospitality while we waited out the storm. I guess I proved myself a rather clumsy aviator. I was trying to make it from Minneapolis to a friend's place up at Alexandria and I pushed my luck a bit too far. I barely made it down to the ground before the storm hit like a sledgehammer. In fact, I damn near collided with your father as he was driving home."

Adam apologized, "Mr. Lawton, I'm sorry for not noticing you on the porch. I was so excited about what went on at the golf course today and wanted to tell my father. I wasn't aware of much of anything when I got home...not even your biplane. You must have thought I was about as dull-witted as one can get."

Lawton would recall that statement many times in the future regarding the first time the two of them met. Dull-witted would never be a word describing Adam Bailey. Just in those few minutes of observing Adam Bailey, Lawton could sense this young man was destined for something much more than trying to make a barren farm productive.

The three of them sat out on that porch appreciating the vision of the black hole below the bluff that was peaceful Lake Minnewaska and the occasional broad flashes of lightning to the east. Except for the slight breeze, the only noise that night was the moisture still dripping off the house and trees...and the frogs croaking in the distance. Their conversation drifted from the town celebration to the hard life in the rural areas. That subject was always like an albatross hanging in the atmosphere.

Bailey lamented how he and his son had practically returned to subsistent farming in the past year. What produce they didn't eat they traded merchants in town for other needs and services. Hardly any money was changing hands.

Lawton did learn that their life on the farm consisted of just the two of them...and had been that way for a number of years. He noticed when Adam told his father about a family in town whose mother was quite ill, John's face showed grave concern.

He quietly responded, "Son, let's get over to their house Sunday after the golf tournament to see how we can help." Adam simply nodded as if not expecting any other statement from his father.

To break the melancholy Lawton changed the subject to that weekend's charity golf tournament. That subject immediately picked up the pace and energy in the conversation.

He also learned that Adam played the game well. The young man explained he picked up golf at the Lake Minnewaska Municipal Club atop the bluff overlooking the town and the lake. However, in recent summers he told how he was now being allowed to play at the Chippewa Lodge resort golf course for no charge.

Compared to his father, the young man showed surprising candor about the players who would be participating in the golf event. Smiling, he said, "I've been caddying for this really nice fellow since the first tournament four years ago. His name is Loni. He works in Chicago although he spends a lot of time here during the summer months. With the festival going on in town, he's been here for the last eight days. I've known this man since I was thirteen. We met one day when he was playing over at the municipal golf course. Somehow he got a kick out of me and liked the way I could hit the ball. He bought me a sandwich after we finished playing and then invited me the next day to play at the Chippewa Lodge golf course if it was all right with my Dad and I didn't have farm chores to do. He was even considerate enough to ask if I had a ride out to the Lodge. Heck, by then I'd been driving my Dad's old Plymouth truck for almost two years.

I remember telling Loni that I couldn't afford to play the resort golf course. His eyes sparkled and he told me it would be his treat. That was the first time I'd ever played at the resort golf course. Loni said he had made some deal with the Lodge manager so a bunch of his friends could play there...and included me in the deal. Ever since then I've caddied for him in the charity tournament and on weekends when he's in town. In the last couple summers, I even do errands for him, like running into town to Big Bud's General Store for various supplies to bring back to the Lodge. The real fun, though, is golfing with him and his friends. They are the craziest guys. They kid each other constantly. I laugh so hard sometimes it's hard to swing. But, you know, it's funny...they always remind me to keep my nose clean and not be like them...whatever that's supposed to mean."

Lawton glanced over at Adam's father. John shrugged as if he was used to hearing that kind of innocent observation whether from his son or others in the community.

Adam continued, "Most of them aren't that good at golf like Loni and a few other guys. There is one talented golfer named "Willie". He's thin as a rail and not very friendly, but he can really play the game. He's one of Loni's closer friends. There's also a fancy guy named "Vinnie" and another really gruff fellow named "Danny". These guys say the worst things to each other and then turn to me and wink. I know they don't mean it. They're just trying to get under the skin of their opponent."

Through all these yarns, John sat there neither smiling nor shaking his head. It was as if he accepted that he couldn't keep his son young and innocent forever. Lawton guessed Adam's experience at the Lodge golf course was like a test. John could discern if his lessons on right and wrong were still clear in his son's mind. Lawton wondered if his own father would have been so broad-minded.

As Adam was mentioning some of the first names of these players, Lawton couldn't help but associate these men being described as possible crime figures occasionally in the news. While the practice of criminal law was not his specialty, a professional attention to newspaper reports of gangster activity couldn't be helped. When Adam said 'Willie', or 'Danny' or 'Vinnie', Lawton wondered about their surnames.

He queried Adam a bit further. "So, Adam, do you know any of these guy's last names or what they do for a living?"

Adam shook his head. "Nah...we mostly talk about golf when we're out on the course. No one uses last names. I just hear first names or nicknames."

Lawton chuckled to himself wondering if these fellows could be individuals like Vinnie Spagatini or Danny A'Motta'. Those names had been in the newspapers recently. If it was the same 'Vinnie', this man could be the notorious hit man operating as a local machinist union representative out of the west side of Chicago. His name had been in the newspaper so often Lawton figured the guy had a press agent. He shook his head thinking, 'it couldn't be.'

The other name 'Danny' of course could be anybody. But when Adam described him as a large gruff man who snarled at people Lawton wondered if the guy could actually be 'A'Motta'. He was another infamous Chicago mobster. His name and picture had been popping up quite often in the newspapers as well. A'Motta had been tried for murder not once, not twice, but four times in the last ten years...and acquitted each time. Lawton again doubted the coincidence. How could two men from Chicago of the mob caliber of Spagatini and A'Motta ever sequester themselves to a small lake resort in central Minnesota? It was just too fanciful to believe.

However, when Adam described the third man named 'Willie' as wiry and unfriendly, Lawton couldn't help but think of a purported gangster living and operating right there in the Twin Cities. Lawton knew more about a man named 'Willie LaCurso'. LaCurso was the head of the Grainmiller's Union. In itself that was fine. However, he was also suspected of being the leader of other more nefarious activities occurring in and around the Twin Cities area. There had been a recent report in the *Minneapolis Star* about a group of Grainmiller union members charged with grand theft. It seemed the law frowned on trucks owned by the Grainmiller's Union being backed up to the meat processing plant in South St. Paul. Yet, there were other factors indicating real guilt. Meat was being thrown into the trucks after closing time...like 2:00 in the morning! Most damning was the small issue of having no record of payment. It was an open and shut case of breaking and entering and theft. LaCurso's lawyers got the union members acquitted. The claim was that the trucks had been stolen and the poor union fellows were just there to recover the trucks. That there was meat in the backs of the truck was shear happenstance.

Again, Lawton shook his head. It was unlikely the Twin Cities mobster could be the same Willie portrayed by Adam Bailey.

Then Adam made an off-handed comment that jolted Lawton's attention. "Dad, one of the players in the tournament had to withdraw today. He had some important business matters back in Omaha. Now there is an odd number of players...only nineteen. When I was leaving, Loni was calling some people trying to get one of them to drive to the resort in time for tomorrow morning's tee-time. When I left an hour ago, he was calling but not having too much luck in finding a low handicapper to accept an invitation."

Lawton jumped in. "Why don't they just ask a local guy to play? Certainly there are some good golfers around this area."

Adam looked at his father and they both choked back a snicker. Adam finally responded. "It's difficult, Mr. Lawton. Loni can't invite one of the locals...for a number of reasons. First, some local guy likely would be bothered by the hijinks that goes on during the tournament. He'd be so intimidated; the hometown player would likely play his worst round of the year. But, that's not the real problem. It comes down to the money. No one in these parts could afford the entry fee or the huge side bets."

Lawton nodded while sensing his own interest in the tournament being re-ignited. His competitive fervor began to grind. His brain was reverting to his barnstorming, cavalier days during college. At that age he didn't have a lot to lose besides a little money. He found himself wanting a taste of those days again as he smelled opportunity knocking. Despite there being some disreputable players among the competitors, he didn't believe his reputation could be tarnished as a player in this tournament. Besides, it was a charity tournament with proceeds going to some good cause. Furthermore, young Bailey had indicated most of the players were from out of state. They wouldn't know Lawton or care who he was...just so he had the means to pay off losing wagers.

His inner fight went back and forth. What if he actually won the tournament...and a bulk of the money? What kind of trouble might that cause? For that matter, what if a couple of the competitors were highwaymen. Lawton didn't like the idea of being paid with possible 'dirty' money. On the other hand he liked the chance of fleecing a few high-rollers at Chippewa Lodge. Besides, how much money was really being played for? It was probably in the hundreds of dollars. If he lost, he lost. A couple hundred dollars was not going to break him. And, if he won and decided the cash was somehow ill begotten by his opponents, he promised himself he'd give the money away to some worthy cause. Folks more in need could be helped and he'd still have the satisfaction of having his golf game tested...and winning.

Lawton eyed the young man. If he was to wrangle an invitation, he'd need some help. He had to somehow convince Adam that a very capable replacement player was sitting right there on the porch.

John Bailey interrupted Lawton's sly thinking. "You'll stay the night of course. You'll find the couch in the house quite comfortable. Sorry we can't be more accommodating, but Adam and I have to start our day tomorrow morning especially early. He's caddying and I said I'd volunteer as a scorer. If you need our help getting your air machine back out onto the road, we'll have to do it at dawn."

The matter-of-fact invitation to stay the night brought Lawton's memory of his barnstorming pilot days. How often was he put up for the night by some generous Minnesotans. Whatever the season or the vagaries of weather, people would extend their hospitality. Sleeping on the ground under the wing of his biplane sounded adventurous; however, he found a roof over his head was always preferred.

With the two Baileys ready to end the day, Lawton couldn't waste anymore time. Either he had to solicit some help from Adam or throw away the possibility. He went back in the house to get his golf bag. He pulled out his latest addition …that new-fangled Gene Sarazen sand wedge he was going to use for the first time the next day against his friends. The new club was the talk of the golf world. If Adam Bailey was any kind of a golfer, he'd want to examine it.

Returning to the porch, young Bailey took the bait. His eyes glazed as he asked to hold the club. He then looked over at the rest of Lawton's golf equipment propped up against the wall just inside the house and nodded his head. He began having the realization that the 'guest' staying at his home might just be a golfer, maybe even of some prominence.

Adam then asked the question one good golfer can say to another where both know the true depth of the query. He merely inquired, "Can you play?"

The less skilled golfer might nod but then mollify the claim by assessing how poorly he plays. The more skilled golfer modestly shrugs and makes some non-committal statement like, 'Yeh, I play' or 'Yeh, I can hold my own'. In Lawton's case he didn't say anything. He just grinned while polishing the head of the sand wedge with a handkerchief.

Lawton then responded with a return question. "Adam, have you seen the new metal shafts. I got a set last summer before I qualified for the state amateur. Have you played this latest kind of shaft yet?"

Ignoring the question, the young man stared at him. "So, did you qualify or not?"

This was not the time for Lawton to be modest. He had to use the edge he had to continue baiting the hook. "Damn right I qualified, but I didn't finish well. I haven't won the state amateur yet, but I got 3rd place a couple years ago at the Minnekahda Golf Club in Minneapolis. That was my best finish so far. How about you? Have you played any big amateur tournaments down in the Cities?"

The young Bailey shook his head but his eyes gave away the new respect he held for Lawton. Having Adam's attention, he now had to tweak the conversation around to the weekend charity tournament. "So Adam, what kind of game do you have? I mean…where's your skill level at?" That type of question normally appealed to a better golfer's ego.

But, Adam ignored the question. He looked Lawton straight in the eye and asked incredulously, "You got 3rd in the state amateur a couple years ago?"

Lawton nodded, "Yeh, I was lucky." Then in a more disappointing tone, he added, "However, I guess I'm not so lucky this weekend. I was planning on playing golf with some friends this weekend up in Alexandria. This storm could have caused enough damage up there to possibly close the golf course until it gets cleaned up. So, there's likely going to be no golf this weekend…just fishing, eating, and seeing friends. I guess that wouldn't be all bad."

Lawton wasn't certain if he was being too obvious in luring young Bailey, but he decided not to waste anymore time. "Adam, you might just have an option for me. You mentioned this guy you know out at this resort possibly needing another player for his charity tournament. That sounds kind of interesting. I might fit his dance card."

The reaction wasn't quite what Lawton had hoped. Instead of taking the suggestion seriously, Adam howled with laughter. The lad spat out, "Interesting!!!! Mr. Lawton, this tournament is far beyond that word. It's like nothing you've ever seen. The stakes are unbelievably high. The actual playing of golf is at times downright dangerous. You have to understand, the players show little or no sportsmanship. They'll do anything to rile an opponent. My God, I've seen them on purpose hit shots at one another. And all this goes on while they're all playing for a ridiculous amount of money. I've never laughed harder or seen more intense play. Your concentration would be destroyed. You wouldn't find this to be anything like other tournaments you've competed in."

Lawton didn't react. In fact, he didn't blink. He only responded, "You said a couple of the players are pretty good. Can any of these players match par?"

Adam looked surprised with his house guest's placid reaction. He thought for a moment. "There are a few guys who can play pretty well.

But, they get so mad with all the antics that even they get rattled. I've played with some of them and can usually beat them handily. However, this year Loni is bringing in a couple new participants. I hear they're pretty good players. One of them played with Loni this afternoon for an amount of money I still don't believe. I have to tell you these new fellows...well, I don't think I'd want to play with them. The guy this afternoon was none too friendly. He probably wouldn't want to play with a kid anyway."

Now the conversation was progressing better. Adam's additional warnings were not intimidating Lawton in the least. Making it sound like Adam's idea, Lawton assumed Adam's support. "You know, this could work out if I chose to play. Your friend needs a lower handicap player...and I've got some time tomorrow if I chose to stay around. Tell me, how do I get in contact with this fellow running the tournament?"

Adam looked skeptical. "Mr. Lawton...really...I don't recommend doing what you're suggesting. You probably have the game to do fairly well in this competition, if it were a normal tournament. But, again, it's quite abnormal. I don't want you throwing away what money you might have. What'll happen is that you'll be assigned to a team with three other guys. The best two scores of the four players on your team count for the team total on each hole. So, it's not just how you play. It's also how your teammates stand up to the pressure."

Young Bailey let that statement brew for a moment and then added, "Also, you're going to need some money. Unless Loni knows you can afford to play, you wouldn't get to first base. I don't know the actual entry fee, but it's expensive. Also, the rest of the players except the guys on your team expect you to play individual games so they can soak you out of as much of your remaining cash as possible."

Again, Lawton only shrugged. His attitude was not lost on Adam. Still, he kept shaking his head as if not wanting to get Lawton into something where he'd be defenseless and lose an extraordinary amount of cash. Experience had proven to Adam that anyone not familiar with the players or the format in this golf tournament had most always lost their concentration and their money while undergoing the unusual verbal heat and gibberish from the other participants.

Lawton sensed he had to ease the young man's concern. "Adam, I appreciate you being concerned about my welfare, but let me tell you a little story. It might relax you."

Both Adam and his father leaned back in their chairs not knowing where Lawton was going next. "Adam, have you or your father ever heard of a few fellows who fly their biplanes into county fairs and put on air shows?"

John, who had been mostly quiet while resting his head on the back of the rocker opened his eyes and stopped rocking. Adam nodded still wondering what point Lawton was about to make.

John chuckled, "Yep, I've seen or heard plenty about those lunatics who fly upside down or put their air machines into a deathly spin and recover just before making contact with the ground. Hell, those guys must be nuts...that is, if they're still alive."

"Well," Lawton grinned, "did you ever hear of the guy who stood on the wing of his biplane and hit a golf ball while it flew low over the audience?"

John began to gander at Lawton in disbelief. Adam looked at Lawton vaguely and said, "Yeh, it's been quite a few years, but I've heard of someone performing that feat. I don't know if it's really a true story."

Lawton got up and began walking through the front door of the farmhouse and flashed a big grin toward the two Baileys. Halfway through the doorway, he leaned back and blandly stated, "Gentlemen, I've hit more balls off the wing of that biplane parked out by your barn than I care to think about. Do you really think I'm going to be scared of a few blow-hard amateur golfers who behave poorly on the golf course?"

Before the screen door slammed shut, he'd made his point. As Adam and his father stared at each other in disbelief, Lawton's voice echoed from within the house. "Adam, you get me a meeting with your friend Loni tomorrow morning. If I get into that tournament, 10% of any of my winnings go into your pocket!"

Then Lawton appeared back at the screen door. "And call me Jamie. My father's name is Mr. Lawton." Then he walked back away from the door.

In the following seconds all Lawton could hear was the buzz of talk between the son and his father out on the porch. The hook had been baited. The fish was nibbling. It was now only a question how long it would take for the fish to take the hook.

The screen door was opened and slammed shut once again as Adam suddenly was standing next to Lawton in the small living room. His manner was surprisingly cunning for a kid his age. "O.K.... Jamie....let's pretend I could help you get a meeting with Loni. Is that ten percent for both days plus ten percent on the side bets?"

Lawton chortled. The kid was sharper than Lawton had given him credit. Young Bailey had just proved he was no beginner when it came to negotiating. Lawton smiled ruefully realizing he may have just run into the devil in kid's clothing who just happened to be living incognito on a Pope County farm. If anything, that possibility made the thought of Adam's help even more inviting. Lawton stuck out his hand toward his new partner. They cemented their deal with a smile and a firm handshake.

Their next breaths were barely completed when Adam had to offer his ultimate concern. "Jamie, I can probably get you a short introduction with Loni, but I'll be surprised if he'll allow you to play. You'll just be another local hack. Plus, he'll have to see your money. Hell, we'll be lucky just to slip you through the gates of the resort past the guards. But, we may as well give it a chance. Who knows how desperate Loni might be for that twentieth player."

John then came into the house and joined the two new business partners silently mulling over the challenges of the next morning. Lawton looked at the two Baileys with whom in just a few short hours he'd come to enjoy their company while forging a kind of conspiracy for the fun of it. Here they were...a discontented 38-year old farmer, an opportunistic 31-year-old aviator/lawyer and a 17-year-old entrepreneur...now straining to come up with some idea how to get Lawton into a closed invitation golf tournament.

In the next ten minutes, they surprisingly did agree on one key factor. Lawton had to somehow display his golfing skills. The likely spot would be at the practice range at the Chippewa Lodge golf course prior to the start of the event. Adam could help by getting Loni out on the range. As the caddy, Adam could position Loni as close to Lawton as possible. It would then be up to Lawton win the attention by showing his golfing talents.

At best it was a very loose plan, but it was the only one they had. Success seemed questionable, but they agreed how no worthwhile risk-taking, potential money-making endeavor was ever guaranteed?

The other problem that Lawton didn't bring up to the two Baileys was the question of the entry fee. But, before they left the living room, both Baileys repeated the subject. Both were surprised at Lawton's confident response, "Gentlemen, don't worry...I'll get the money. Let's just concentrate on getting me into the event."

The father and son were pleasantly surprised. With the whimsical plan set, the two Baileys headed for bed happy that the entry fee was apparently not a setback and looking forward to the adventure the next morning.

Lawton watched them go upstairs realizing the required money was indeed going to be a challenge. It was safe to assume the $3.59 he had in his pocket was going to be a bit short of the needed entry fee. Yet, he wasn't completely desperate. This was one of the many times it was good to have a loyal friend. Charlie Davis lived only a half hour away in Alexandria. The two of them had established a fund a few years before. The intention was to have money needed when desperate times or a surprising mutual opportunity came into focus. Lawton had only to convince Davis this golfing enterprise with Adam Bailey was one of those opportunities. Besides, Lawton truly didn't believe he'd need more than a couple hundred dollars...maybe $500 tops to cover the entry fee and individual bets. If he somehow got into the tournament, it would be nothing more than calling Davis and having him bring the few hundred dollars from their combined fund stored in a leather packet under one of Davis' beds.

Lawton strolled out to his biplane to check its condition after the storm. It had survived the storm in fine shape...of course, only relative to its normal decrepit and depreciated spectacle. If all else failed the next morning to get into the charity golf tournament, there was still the chance for golf with his friends up in Alexandria. There would be some money won and lost in that small contest as well. Either way he figured he was in store for a sporting weekend.

Strolling back to the house with suitcase in hand, the post-storm air was crisp and the sky was clear. The toads were croaking and the crickets were chirping. The vast blackness of Lake Minnewaska off in the distance below the bluff looked like it never ended. Quietly entering the house, the smell was neither fresh nor bothersome. The odor was that of the outdoors. There were no flowers or noticeable decoration to make the place more inviting. It was obviously a place where two males were satisfied with their surroundings. The home was still missing something without the impact of a woman. As great as the father-son relationship was, the house felt empty.

Lawton eased into a fitful position on the Bailey's living room scratchy, brown couch. The blanket smelled stale, but it kept him warm. He'd slept in less comfortable conditions...and not that long ago. He lay pondering the next morning and wondering how much the Baileys could be exaggerating the behaviors of the players in this unusual golf tournament. He kept telling himself one or two golfers might have a checkered past, but that was nothing. Even at his own private golf course, Midland Hill Country Club, there were some less than honorable men who were members. .

Finally he took a deep breath. It had been a long day. He disappeared into a deep sleep.

Charlie Davis had been more than a bit antsy watching a major summertime storm whip itself into a frenzy that Friday evening at his Lake Ida home near Alexandria. The wind and rain were relentless. Looking out his picture window to the west and north, Davis watched sheets of rain pummel the huge lake. Lakeside trees bent with the blustery winds. The gusts caused waves to flow over his dock and fill the hull of his small sailboat.

While agitated having not put a cover over his sailboat, his thoughts never left his true concern about his friend Jamie Lawton's situation in the storm. Experience told him Lawton was someplace on the ground. The hope was that the pilot was in one piece.

Davis had planned a pre-golf bash for twelve friends that evening. They were coming from as far away as Fargo from one direction and the Twin Cities from the other. It would be a weekend full of food, drink, bantering and golf. However, the widespread storm had thrown a damper on that entire first night...and likely the weekend. At least he had a few local friends who were going to make it over to his home later for some cards and beer.

As the wind and rain continued, he did grow apprehensive. Being more fun-loving and crazy, it was rare that Davis showed worry. This cloudburst, however, was strong. Maybe if he wasn't standing in his house alone watching the horrendous weather conditions out his picture window, he might have been less anxious. Then again, he always exhibited some unease when he saw Lawton take off or land in his beat-up biplane even in reasonable weather conditions. He questioned how a rusty machine like that biplane could even get off the ground. He'd said to Lawton repeatedly that the two of them would never fly together again until that 'damned plane was finally buried'. The hope was obvious that Lawton wouldn't get buried with it.

Yet, by 1931 his friend had flown up to Alexandria from the Twin Cities enough times that Davis had gotten used to Lawton dealing with weather emergencies. He knew Lawton had landed on so many roadways just previous to inclement weather that his friend knew the towns in the area as well as Davis did. He recalled Lawton once landing on the main avenue in a small town called Long Prairie just before a black cloud encapsulated the village. Conveniently, he touched ground close to a big open-door garage on one side of the street and the local police station on the other side.

Lawton promptly drove his plane into the large open shelter and ran over to the police station to ask for use of the telephone. The local police chief actually had Davis' phone number. After making contact, Davis drove his old sports car over to the town. Until the overcast skies passed, the two of them frittered the time away in the backroom of a local café playing cards with some of the locals including the police chief. When the weather disturbance ended, Lawton gave his winnings to the café's proprietor to buy dinner for the small group of card players. It was a typical gesture by Lawton. He knew the next time he needed help in the vicinity of Long Prairie, he now had some friends to give him some assistance. Lawton and Davis then had taken off in their respective forms of transportation towards Lake Ida with the biplane beating Charlie's roadster to the lake home by a good half hour.

Except for flying, there was almost nothing the two friends didn't enjoy doing together....especially playing golf. While Lawton was the better striker of the ball and a scratch golfer, Davis was the better negotiator for being given strokes on the first tee box. Charlie's game was on the wild side. The golf ball tended to stray a bit...like to the next county. Nonetheless, their golf matches were legendary at Midland Hills Country Club, especially for the ferocity of the competition, the constant jabbering and multiple bets going on between the two of them. Naturally, each of them claimed the lion's share of victories over the other.

While the two men's personalities seemed quite different, whether on the golf course, at a speakeasy, or just lounging at either one's household, there was constant kidding between the two of them. With Davis being the more outgoing one, it was he who knew more halls of shame in Minneapolis or St. Paul than Lawton did...and Lawton had lived in the Twin Cities all his life. Lawton appeared quieter, but his mind was always darting and his comments quick.

The three years in law school had gone too fast for the two of them. What they lacked in dedication to their studies, they made up for in squabbles with various professors during classes. Davis recalled debating a point with a professor...and then with each other in the classroom. While they're grades didn't place them amongst their highly ranked colleagues, it didn't matter. They both had a vision of what they would do after graduation. As far as they were concerned, law school just had to be survived. Then they had to somehow pass the bar exam. Both requirements occurred if just barely.

Since those years in law school, the two of them had matured... somewhat...but it was still a work in progress. With Lawton taking on partners and trying to keep his Twin Cities law firm afloat, he did have to show more responsibility than his sole practitioner, independent friend in Alexandria. Lawton would say often to Davis that at least one of them had made it to adulthood.

As for Lawton it was probably quite true that he did grow up faster because it happened so abruptly. His father passed away within months after Lawton passed the Minnesota bar exam. Immediately he'd taken over the responsibilities for the family house on Lake Johanna. Davis recalled Lawton's admission a couple years later how his sudden maturity had really had been more attributable to one particular weekend golf tournament on the Minnesota-South Dakota border. It was the weekend after passing the bar exam. Davis remembered how the two of them had plans to meet on a Friday night in Ortonville, Minnesota to play a Saturday golf tournament. Lawton had just received word that Thursday he'd passed the bar exam and was still recovering from the festivities and celebration in Minneapolis.

He'd brought along a few left-over beers to be consumed in the cockpit as he flew across the central part of the state. He'd never been to Ortonville but figured he could find the town since it was close to Big Stone Lake. That was as much of a flight plan as he had.

While flying his rickety biplane westward from the Twin Cities he'd consumed the beers and ended up overshooting Ortonville and accidentally landed in Milbank, South Dakota. In his somewhat dissipated condition, he thought he was at his destination. State lines were not exactly visible on land or in the air. Spotting the Milbank golf course, Lawton naturally thought it was the municipal golf course of Ortonville. He landed on one of the fairways and maneuvered his biplane over towards the maintenance shed to keep it safe from errant golf shots. Grabbing his clubs from the fuselage, he strode shakily over to the clubhouse to meet his friends and get something to eat.

Not seeing any of his golfing buddies, he figured he was early. He later admitted he wasn't at his best.

After a sandwich and a bicarbonate of soda, he paid the green fee and went out to practice and play the golf course. When dusk arrived a few hours later, he stayed at the club being enticed by the Friday evening dinner special. Still not seeing anyone he knew, it finally dawned on him he was at the wrong golf course.

As luck would have it, there were a couple ladies at the club that night. They happened to be unattached. He suddenly didn't care that he wasn't in Ortonville, Minnesota.

That night he slept at the Milbank golf club with or without the permission of the clubhouse manager. The next morning he was given directions where to fly to return to Minnesota. In less than a half hour he had flown back across Big Stone Lake and was circling over the green fairways of the Ortonville Municipal Golf Course. He didn't' want to admit to his friends, and especially to Charlie Davis, that he'd overlooked beautiful Big Stone Lake on a crystal clear Friday afternoon and flown beyond it into the neighboring state. He planned on just saying he'd gotten a late start out of Flying Cloud Airfield and landed someplace at dusk to sleep under the fuselage the previous evening.

While his friends would give him the benefit of the doubt, there was no doubt in Lawton's mind that he'd gone too far the previous day in more ways than one. The Thursday night out was bad enough at the speak-easy, but drinking some beers while flying showed disregard for life and limb. He changed his attitude for alcohol from that day forward. He knew he had too much to live for to fritter away his time on earth so carelessly.

With his tee time only ten minutes away while flying about the golf course, he eventually landed on the Ortonville golf course against the wind on the short dogleg Par 4 seventh fairway. It was the only fairway that was open without golfers. His friends having seen the spectacle before acted as if the landing was quite normal. The tournament officials didn't know what to say other than to announce his name for the next tee time. His friends helped him push the plane under the protection of some trees. With minutes to spare he took two practice swings and promptly shot 35 on the first nine holes.

Davis smiled to himself recalling the additional side story that day. During the second nine-hole round of the tournament that Saturday, the two ladies Lawton had met the previous night in Milbank had awoken and driven over to Ortonville to see their flying ace. They found him on Hole #4. With unsteady balance from their intake of booze the previous night coupled with high heels and the same frilly dresses, they began following Lawton's foursome. The ladies shouted and clapped after each of Lawton's shots. Lawton noticed the support but didn't recognize the ladies.

Davis had known something was up and kept pestering Lawton as to where he'd met the two questionable females. Lawton kept shrugging, legitimately not having a full answer. Finally, just to get Davis off his back, Lawton told him one of the ladies worked as a secretary at the University Law School and the other was a waitress at a speak easy in St. Paul. Davis knew his friend was lying and kept razzing him. The ladies ended up walking barefoot with the Lawton and Davis foursome for the remaining nine holes. Lawton scored a 73 and was one shot off the lead after the first day of the two-day tournament. The ladies stayed for dinner and some late night partying at the Ortonville club until they became virtually unconscious. Someone drove the two ladies back to Milbank. The next morning Charlie again prodded Lawton into telling him where he'd met the two ladies. Finally an honest answer was given. Lawton shook his head and admitted, "Charlie, I haven't a clue. I only learned their names last evening after we finished our golf."

Indeed, Lawton was telling the truth despite being with the two gals and other members at the Friday night dinner at the Millbrook, South Dakota golf club. As for Davis, he couldn't debate the point. He'd witnessed often how Lawton could be speaking with a beautiful female and later not recall her name.

As the hours passed during that Friday evening storm, Charlie Davis continued to get more perplexed about the whereabouts of his pilot friend as another huge lightning bolt practically blew a tree out of the ground a half a mile away. He knew there would be no way Lawton would complete his flight that evening. The only question was where he might have landed his plane.....Paynesville....Willmar.....on a grassy field....or had he even taken off from Flying Cloud Airfield in the Twin Cities. Of course Lawton would have called if that had been the case.

Finally about 8:00 he called his friends at the Alexandria police station to check on some other towns in the area in case a wayfaring pilot had been forced to land in their jurisdiction. Davis also made some personal calls. He had a lot of friends and knew a lot of law enforcement people in almost every town along Hwy #55...the normal route Lawton took in flying up to Alexandria.

Davis chuckled to himself after his first few calls. He figured he'd find Lawton's location within the hour given the contacts he had with various city and country law enforcement offices. Forty minutes later he found out from a deputy at the police station in Glenwood that a biplane had been reported parked out by a farmhouse east of town.

Davis relaxed immediately. He knew he'd be getting a call whether that night or in the morning from Lawton. He could now concentrate on playing cards later that evening with some local friends.

—ɯ—

Saturday morning Charlie Davis woke early. The previous night had been late thanks to the poker game played at his home with four local friends. It had lasted well past midnight. There had been much grumbling at the table about how Saturday morning would be taken up with cleaning the refuge from the storm.

In Davis' case, he didn't give two hoots about the extra work. This was one time that money bought privilege. He hadn't said anything, but he knew a high school chum who needed the work and the money. They played football together more than a decade before. Bernard Coyle was now the odd jobs man around area. Charlie had hired him previously for cleaning up or maintaining several properties in his arsenal. Bernard would be over at Davis' place yet that afternoon ready to cut fallen limbs, burn the refuge, and fix any damage. It was work Davis had always promised himself he wouldn't do unless times were really tough. He worked hard so he wouldn't have to experience those kinds of times. Besides, he felt good being able to help out Coyle and his family as times had been hard for that family.

That morning Charlie was surprised he hadn't already gotten a phone call from Lawton. All Davis needed was directions to the Glenwood farm and he'd drive the half hour down to Glenwood to pick up his friend if the biplane was damaged. It would be better that way. Charlie's landing strip might be too saturated for a safe landing. This had happened before. Besides, the conditions gave him a chance to loosen up his favorite car, his 1922 A-68 St. Claire Roadster on the open road.

Impatiently waiting for the call, he gazed out his library room picture window at the now calm, deep bluish green waters of Lake Ida. What a difference twelve hours made. The previous night waves had been churning over his dock. This new morning the sky was clear and the water had returned to a half a foot below the dock just slightly higher than normal. What hadn't changed was the amount of damage to the trees. There were fallen limbs all over his lawn leading down to the lake. His experience told him there would be no golf that morning. Alexandria Golf Club would ask members to come out and help with a daylong clean up process. Charlie wanted to clean up branches and limbs about as much as he wanted to take a spin in Lawton's biplane.

Though it was 7:30 in the morning, he half expected to hear the hum of the World War I vintage biplane circling over his place at anytime. He went out to check the grass landing strip to note whether it was dry and firm enough for a landing. The alternative would be his long driveway leading up to the house. Davis finally called down to the Glenwood police station and this time talked with Police Chief Rich Brey. Brey confirmed his sighting of the biplane parked east of town.

Charlie chuckled thinking 'a biplane parked at a farm. Who else could it be?' The chief identified the farmer almost reverently as John Bailey. Davis didn't know the man and couldn't call him since most rural homes typically didn't have telephones. With no report of injury and the biplane apparently still in one piece, he surmised that Lawton must have survived the evening.

Still impatient, he finally called Bernard Coyle to find out when the man could clean his property. Coyle sounded eager for the work and arrived less than a half hour later with rakes, tools and shovels. There was still no word from Lawton.

Davis had one other thought. It was far-fetched yet consistent with his naturally depraved mind. 'Maybe farmer Bailey had a daughter and Jamie had plenty of reasons not to call.'

Then he shook his head while grinning. No one including Lawton could be that fortunate.

Immediately upon arriving at the Davis lake property, Coyle began cutting up fallen limbs and branches and then started a fire down by the lake. Another thirty minutes went by and still no call. Davis brought some coffee out to Coyle and they chatted. The two were friends so it didn't take much for Coyle to sit down and relax. Another half hour went by.

As Coyle went back to work, Davis made an empty offering. "Bernard, my head still feels a bit thick from last night...too much Canadian beer and too many hands of poker. If I feel better, I'll come out and give you a hand." He had no intention of fulfilling that statement, but made him feel good just to offer that possibility.

As Bernard kept the rubble burning down by the lake, Charlie went into his house and called back the police chief in Glenwood. He wanted to ask if a deputy could drive out to the farm and see what condition the biplane was in...as well as the pilot...so he could decided whether a trip to Glenwood was necessary. The telephone call proved fruitless. The talkative deputy had no idea about any biplane parked out at someone's farm. Chief Brey hadn't mentioned it. Davis was then told Police Chief

Brey with his friend Clarence Petracek, the Pope County Sheriff, would not be back at all that Saturday. They had taken the day to go fishing.

That brought a guffaw from Davis. "Deputy, the whole damned town could be going to the dogs this weekend and the community's two top law enforcement officers are out fishing for walleyes."

The deputy didn't react to the joking. He simply responded, "Yeh, they've been having good luck whether at Lake Amelia or Lake Osakis lately. Anyway, the other deputies and I have got things under control even with the huge annual town celebration going on in Glenwood this weekend."

That comment caught Davis' ear. It was odd that both the Chief of Police and the County Sheriff would schedule themselves out of town during such a big event. It didn't make much sense. There would likely be swarms of visitors in Glenwood bringing with it the potential for a lot of problems. He shrugged and decided the police chief and county sheriff knew what they were doing.

Then he called a couple other contacts he knew in Glenwood who might help him locate Lawton. Those included the mayor Charlie B. Good and a lawyer friend, Logan Nelson. Neither man was home that Saturday morning. Each wife responded that her husband had gotten in late the previous night from festival events in City Park and then left very early that morning for a 'gambling' event at Chippewa Lodge. Both spouses didn't seem pleased that their husbands would be at the Lodge all day…and Sunday as well.

Davis was taken aback. Normally he kept up with activities in the area. Also, he found it curious that each wife described the activity that morning as a 'gambling' event. Normally there would be a euphemism to cover up something that could be construed as illegal or not above board…especially considering the men were a mayor and a local lawyer. Then again, if it was all in fun for the town festival, it was probably all right. If that were the case, the city police chief and the county sheriff were being "good guys" by staying out of town during the weekend. The County Sheriff was an elected official. He was not about to cause a snit if he wanted to be re-elected. A little game of chance never hurt anybody, especially if some of the funds would be directed to various town charities.

As for the police chief, he was hired by the city. He wouldn't want to upset his employers by disallowing this one or two day departure from the rules. A little gambling…wherever in town it was being done… would add just a bit more fun to the festival.

Hanging up the phone, Davis resigned himself to having to wait even longer for Lawton to call. Hearing the name 'Chippewa Lodge' did bring up some unpleasant thoughts. Charlie sat at his kitchen table and recollected his efforts to try and buy the secluded resort south of Glenwood. It had been a bucolic, isolated, and not very successful resort in operation on and off since the turn of the century. He frankly couldn't understand how the property could be solvent much less open with the economic times such as they were. It was virtually an unknown resort compared to the better known lake properties in the Alexandria area.

Before the stock market crash almost two years before, Davis had inquired about buying the entire property. He'd made a ridiculously low bid and expected a counter bid. Instead and rather surprisingly, the owner didn't even acknowledge his offer. That was unusual. When there was a potential buyer for anything in those difficult days, normally the seller would at least show some respect and say 'thanks, but no thanks.' Instead, there had been only silence. Having been ignored had irritated Davis.

As for the Glenwood town celebration, he'd heard about it...and forgotten about it one minute later. It wasn't something that held much interest for him. While he'd gained a certain level of wealth in real estate, he didn't have a fabulous cash flow since he was paying off notes on most of these land and lake property purchases he'd made in the area. In fact, he portrayed himself as a charity case to all his friends...a convenient claim to appeal for a free beer from some of his friends.

Nonetheless, whether he had loose cash or not, the last thing he desired to do was squeeze out some of his capital from his starving billfold to give to some festival in Glenwood. No, as far as Davis was concerned, Glenwood was one community to stay away from that weekend.

Fifteen minutes later, the telephone finally rang. As he hustled up to the telephone he went over all the off-colored remarks he was going to make at Lawton for not calling sooner. Surprisingly, when he got on the line, he could hardly get a word in edgewise. His friend was inordinately animated not just for a Saturday morning, but for any time.

Coincidentally, the call was originating from that very same resort Davis had been thinking about...Chippewa Lodge. The conversation was also surprisingly short and not at all what Davis expected. Lawton just said due to the party line he didn't want to converse until later, but that something hot was going on. He emphasized it was important Davis motor on down to Glenwood and get to the resort as fast as possible ...with some cash. Davis knew exactly what his friend meant regarding the cash, but not why the money was needed. Before he could ask, Lawton had hung up.

It took Davis five minutes to find his unwashed chartreuse golf shirt and his "dressy" casual pants he always wore on the golf course. The pants were larger than needed so he could better camouflage his slight paunch. As far as he was concerned, his weight was fine if his pants still fit.

He threw one other change of clothing into a small bag. He and Lawton were in far too many situations where they'd stayed longer than their original intentions. The additional clothing consisted of his old reliable six-year old off-white golf shirt with the permanent mustard stain on the belly and his favorite boat pants. The boat pants hadn't seen the inside of a washing machine for months, but they were dark, so to him, it didn't matter.

Finally, before he left the house, he reached under a mattress in the guest room and grabbed a leather parcel. There was between $5000 and $6000 in the bag. Both Davis and Lawton stuffed extra cash into that bag from time to time. Their purpose was to have that money available if something important came up where they could partner.

Following that short telephone conversation, he figured that situation had arisen.

Minutes later Charlie was buzzing down State Hwy. #29 toward Glenwood in his 1922 Wills St. Claire A-68 Roadster. He had put the roadsters top down. It was a bright day. He needed only a windshield to keep bugs from hitting his face as he sped along the open roadway. His mind was buzzing with various thoughts both positive and negative. One reoccurring flash was the coincidence between the town festival, which he wanted no part of, and some kind of opportunity at Chippewa Lodge. He hoped the two factors were not related, but he had an ugly feeling they were. He kept repeating to himself, "Damn...that town festival is going to get a piece of my hide yet...I just know it."

If only premonitions could be taken more seriously.

CHAPTER

6

James Lawton had awoken with the sun that Saturday morning. It was minutes before 6:00 AM. He washed up in the kitchen sink quietly so he wouldn't wake the two Baileys sleeping upstairs. Then he glanced out the window and realized silence was no longer necessary. There were John and his son, Adam, walking past his parked biplane toward the house apparently having finished some of their morning farm chores. Life started a bit earlier in rural America.

He watched as the two Baileys stopped and examined the air machine. They seemed amused…a typical response. John pointed out to Hwy. #28 no doubt describing to his son the emergency landing on the roadway. Lawton wondered if Adam was still enthused about trying to get him into that morning's golf tournament out at Chippewa Lodge. The little plan they'd schemed the night before now seemed even more adolescent.

As the two Baileys entered the house, they greeted their guest with some kidding remarks about the condition of the biplane…all comments Lawton had heard repeatedly from his own friends. By their upbeat nature so early in the morning, it appeared the father and son were looking forward to seeing if Lawton was actually going to follow through and seek an invitation into the charity tournament.

Lawton showed them he was serious. He held nothing back. He decided to wear the golf attire he had planned to wear that evening with his friends in Alexandria. The outfit was formal and almost ostentatious. Lawton figured first impressions would be important. He had to get some attention. The more he looked like a high roller, especially to this fellow named 'Loni', the better chance he had. He had to look like he had some money…a lot of money. The purplish shirt and tie combination was better for a social gathering, but he envisioned trying to copy the immaculate look of the amateur golfer, Bobby Jones. He even added suspenders for another touch of class.

John was impressed with Lawton's dapper look and commented, "Jamie, you look just like one of them." The intention was to be complimentary, but the statement didn't give Lawton any particular satisfaction.

Over coffee the three of them agreed on the plan how Lawton would slip by the intimidating guards at the front gate of Chippewa Lodge. That of course would be the least of their problems. The primary challenge was for Lawton to get Loni's attention. While Adam didn't seem daunted by his part in the little sham, it was important he not get himself in trouble with D'Annelli. Adam could help, but Lawton had to close the deal.

At 6:30 they left the farm in Bailey's creaky Plymouth sedan. The sun was rising behind them casting a yawning glow across the pastures. As they were about to descend Hwy #28 into downtown Glenwood, the magnificent sprawl of Lake Minnewaska appeared straight ahead over the crest of the bluff. Driving towards the main downtown intersection, Adam was careful to keep his speed lest the vehicle get stuck in a mud hole from the previous night's rain. There was some damage in town with tree branches and limbs lying all over the streets and yards. Some folks were already out on their properties beginning the clean up. Lawton was impressed. John and Adam waved to their friends as they drove by, but there was no slowing or stopping. All three of them were focused on their little mission. The timing allowed no distractions.

At the main intersection, nothing much was open except the downtown café. Some late model automobiles parked out in front had Illinois license plates. That was Lawton's first hint that the story told to him by John Bailey had some ring of truth. The three of them glanced through the plate glass window of the Glenwood Café. A number of the patrons were dressed in shirts and ties. That seemed out of the ordinary to Lawton for a small town café. Nobody in a rural farm community like Glenwood would be wearing a shirt and tie on a Saturday morning.

Taking a left at the intersection, they headed south out of town along the east side of the massive lake. He'd flown over the lake, but now driving beside it and not seeing the western shoreline gave him more of the impressive size of Lake Minnewaska. Looking back at City Park was a large assemblage of tents and booths reflecting the commitment of the townsfolk to their festival. It was obviously a big deal to the locals.

They drove along the lake shore a few more miles until they began encountering a surprising number of parked cars along the lake's edge. Volunteers and a few spectators were already walking along the lakeside road up to the entrance of Chippewa Lodge. Ahead were more tents offering food and games. Townspeople were also getting set up for various sailing and boating contests that morning.

As planned, Lawton was riding behind the front seat lying under a blanket as the old Plymouth sedan approached the front gate of the Lodge. It was not a very classy way to enter the golf tournament grounds, but expedience was more the rule.

Adam greeted the two guards wearing long coats by their first names. They were not great examples of affability and kindness. Adam had ventured through the gates often enough that he fully expected to be waved through. But, that morning they made him stop. Lawton's throat grew dry from under the blanket. The two men wanted to know who the fellow was in the front passenger seat.

Adam responded unflinchingly, "Guys, he's my Dad. He's volunteering today." Without further word, they motioned the vehicle through the gate.

Once through the gate, the three of them were home free. Pulling the blanket off, Lawton observed the rustic but very inviting surroundings of Chippewa Lodge. It was truly a very quaint resort. The golf course straight ahead looked manicured as did the practice area. Adam parked the sedan behind some trees by the pro shop. The three of them then went their separate ways as agreed upon earlier. Adam went to find Loni. John just strolled seemingly spellbound by all the late model cars parked at the resort. Lawton wasted no time unpacking his golf clubs. He headed straight toward the practice range.

Studying some of the golfers leaving their cabins for the main resort restaurant, he could see this private event was first class. They were dressed as sharply as Lawton. The few spectators who had arrived early wandered around in a seeming daze appreciating the heavenly quality of the Lodge property.

A couple golfers walked by Lawton and nodded. They assumed he was a new guy playing in the charity event for the first time. Lawton made his way to the practice area and continued to be amazed. It was freshly mowed radiating a cut grass smell he always found intoxicating. As he stretched, he saw practice balls stacked in a pyramid ready for use by any golfer. Normally a golfer would have to buy a small container of some low-quality range balls for two bits. The golf balls were often castaways with cuts on their cover. They had little bounce and compression, but they allowed a golfer to hit some shots and limber up before teeing off.

On this practice range, though, it was different. He noticed immediately the Lodge range balls were new! That exuded even more class...like champagne at breakfast. Lawton's immediate impression of the guy named Loni was that this fellow certainly knew how to throw a party. This charity event was in a vastly different league than almost all other tournaments Lawton had played in previously.

Wasting no time, he got to work. He positioned himself on the practice range where his visibility would be obvious. With his purple shirt and tie combination, he'd command additional flash to those ticket holders entering the grounds. Warming up he began hitting some short shots with his new Gene Sarazen sand wedge.

Some spectators walking by slowed as Lawton greeted each of them with a friendly 'Good Morning'. It was the type of gesture golfers about to play in a tournament rarely did. Normally they invented some kind of serious game face that would indicate to everyone they were not to be bothered.

Lawton played it totally the opposite. As he hit some low and high shots with the new club, he kidded with some patrons or asked them from what town they lived. His goal was to create conversation and keep them close. It was all part of his plan to build his own little practice range gallery. He wanted as much attention as possible. In ten minutes he had fifteen to twenty people watching him display his golfing skills. They all showed amazement the way Lawton could chat while in mid-swing.

There were a couple other impeccably dressed golfers that began warming up at the other end of the practice range away from the spectator traffic. They were addressing their practice shots and generally behaving like a regular competitor...that is, hitting shots quietly and giving signs they didn't want to be disturbed. They'd periodically glance over at the dapper purple-shirted golfer with the increasing number of people surrounding him. They couldn't help but wonder why this golfer was taking the time to talk with just a bunch of spectators.

For Lawton what he was doing on that practice tee was unique even for him. He'd never been that outgoing in his entire life. He even stopped swinging a couple times and started relating some humorous golf stories as if he was Will Rogers on stage. The result was an even bigger throng surrounding him. The laughter became somewhat bothersome to some of the golfers warming up. They gave some sharp looks at the dapper golfer entertaining the crowd just to register their disapproval.

Once warmed up and seeing he'd gained the size of crowd he wished, Lawton got more serious with his shot making. His chatter didn't stop; it was non-stop as he pulled out a mashie from his golf bag and started hitting trick shots. He'd explain that golf was a game of balance as he stood on one leg and hit a shot. Then, he'd stand on his other leg and hit a similar shot. Then with the same club, he hit a ball low, then high, another one curving to the left and another curving to the right. With each shot he'd create sounds of awe as well as rounds of applause. His antics were working out even better than he'd hoped.

A highlight to his performance was when he hit two balls simultaneously with one ball popping straight up in the air and the other took its normal flight out onto the practice range. As the second ball that went straight up descended, he caught it in his golf cap. The crowd went nuts on that particular gem of a trick.

He wasn't done. He pulled out an outlandish-looking foot long tee placing the ball unnaturally high off the ground. He then inquired if there were a couple golfers in the crowd who'd like to try and hit the elevated golf ball some twelve inches above the ground. Lawton knew the trick. Invariably the golfer would undercut the ball because his right shoulder would dip. He'd whiff causing the ball to simply fall off the tee. To the delight of the crowd, Lawton then hit the same shot adjusting his swing and shoulders so he could hit it square. All the while he was performing, he was greeting more folks as they strolled up wondering what was going on. Just over a half hour since arriving at the practice area, Lawton had a spectator group of more than a hundred fifty.

Some other tournament players arrived at the practice area and placed themselves as far from Lawton and his audience as possible. He was creating way too much attention and these players didn't seem comfortable in the limelight. However, even those players began whispering among themselves as to who Lawton was. They also stopped and took note of some of his trick shots. A couple of them even applauded when he teed up two balls and hit a mashie and niblick holding both clubs together.

Everything was going fine, but Lawton was beginning to get a little stage weary. He'd gaze hopefully over at the resort restaurant wondering if Adam was bringing the crowd gathering display to the tournament director's attention...the man named Loni. Adam had to drag that fellow out to the practice tee soon or the spectacle of his little act would pass.

With the crowd about ten people deep forming a 'U' around his area of practice, Lawton thought of one last way to create the ultimate attention. There was a chance he might even cause more raucous cheering.

Knowing spectators always liked to see the long ball, he started talking to the crowd about how to swing in order to get more length on their drives. He looked out to the end of the practice area and realized there might not be enough room to carry out his idea. That range was set up to handle mostly shorter shots with irons, not necessarily the longer wood shots. The wire fence at the outer reaches of the range was only 250 yards away. With the poorer practice balls, a golfer would be hard pressed to hit one of them out of the practice area. However, with brand new golf balls as range balls, they likely would fly a lot further. That understanding got Lawton thinking more creatively.

He pulled his driver out of the golf bag with the crowd anticipating something interesting was about to happen. To no one in particular Lawton looked at the spectators and asked, "What do you think, folks, you suppose any of these practice balls could ever get hit beyond that 250-yard fence at the end of the practice range?"

Someone in the gallery answered, "Nah sport, them balls is just too soft to fly that far."

Lawton looked at the rotund fellow, then gazed out to the far reaches of the practice range, then looked back at the voice in the crowd. "My friend, I think those couple houses on the other side of the wire fence might just be in jeopardy?"

Another guy in the crowd laughed derisively and shouted out, "It's not likely. That back fence is some 246 yards away. I know, because one of those houses is mine. My backyard and patio are on the other side of the fence. I've never found a practice ball on my lawn, or for that matter, on my patio."

Lawton smiled at the homeowner, then out at the man's house. Right then, a woman...hopefully the man's wife...walked out of the house onto the patio with a newspaper and what looked like a cup of coffee. She sat peaceably in her robe not knowing that a host of people were staring at her from 270 yards away.

It was a scene reminding Lawton of his grandstanding days as barnstorming pilot. He always had to be quick in reacting to various comments from a crowd. The natural response and idea came to him like it was those days again. He said to the man who owned the house, "Friend, is that your wife.....or...niece...sitting out on your patio?"

The crowd snickered.

The guy quickly responded not enjoying the joke. "That's my wife!"

The crowd laughed knowing if that wasn't his response, he might be in trouble with his actual wife.

When the amusement died down, Lawton didn't miss a beat. Theatrically he made a declaration. "Sir, would you be up for a little wager...especially if the odds favor you?"

The man in the crowd shot back, "If I like the odds, I'll put some money on almost anything."

The guy's response was perfect. Lawton then confidently offered his intentions. "Sir, I'll bet you $50 that I can force your wife off that patio for her own safety...and I'll do it within three shots. If she doesn't get up and go in the house, I lose. If she runs into the house, I win."

The crowd exploded in mocking laughter at Lawton's outlandish wager offer. He could tell the spectators loved his brashness just as they did at the county fairs when he would bet some local guy he could hit a golf ball from the wing of his biplane while flying by the grandstand. What the bettor didn't know was that Lawton had another pair of shoes nailed to the wing and another pilot hunched down in the fuselage ready to take control of the biplane when the plane raced by the grandstand with Lawton standing on the top wing. It was a great trick that eventually ended when Lawton was older and had come a bit more to his senses.

As a result of tricks like that one, Lawton was always looking for the edge in any bet. On the wager he was making with the man in the crowd, he felt he had the slight upper hand. The practice balls were new ones. They'd fly further. Secondly, the wind was in his favor from off the lake.

The man in the gallery didn't consider Lawton's advantages. He guffawed and gladly took the bet appreciating the easy $50 he was expecting to pocket.

Whether the bet worked or not, the whole idea was to rile up the crowd. Lawton figured he could aim at the house; he certainly didn't want to injure the lady on the patio. His hope was that she'd hear the ball slamming against the house and realize remaining on that patio was not advisable.

The crowd had now multiplied by another one hundred as more spectators ventured over to the practice tee to check out all the commotion. Lawton readied his first shot as he noted some of the players were also meandering over from their breakfast at the restaurant to see what was causing all the excitement on the practice range. He could only hope one of them might be Adam with the man named Loni.

Everyone was buzzing about the ludicrous wager that had just been made. As he was about to tee the new practice ball up, Lawton noticed a young lady standing right in front of him. A number of things caught his attention, the first being that she was extremely attractive. Curiously, she was noting something on a pad with one of those scoring pencils with a flat top. When she looked up at him, she had a disapproving gaze as if she was seeing right through his little charade.

With all the merriment going on, her unsmiling face became a kind of immediate challenge. He wondered why she was so serious...almost as if she was at a place she didn't want to be.

Her flat-ended golf scoring pencil gave Lawton an idea, something he'd done numerous times on the golf course. He was surprised he hadn't thought of it already given his penchant for finding the advantage in making bets. He quickly stood tall and asked the crowd for quiet. He shouted, "Ladies and gentlemen, does anyone have a common flat-ended scoring pencil? I have a need for one to carry out my little demonstration of power golf."

Then he stared directly at the young lady...then at her pencil. Standing but fifteen feet from him, she shrugged and without further thought said demurely, "Here...you can have this one."

Lawton liked her voice. He reached for the pencil and continued holding her hand longer than necessary as he explained to the crowd how he was going to use the pencil as an extra tall tee. People in the crowd scoffed in disbelief. Finally letting go of her hand, he stuck the pencil into the ground so that four inches of it stuck upwards from the ground. He then got on his hands and knees and balanced a nice new Spalding golf ball on the top flat end portion of the pencil.

Everyone began whispering not really believing he was going to be able to hit a ball teed up that high...and on a pencil. There was no real trick to the shot. The height of the ball was actually to his advantage. To the more proficient golfer and with a little practice, the ball would be hit on the upswing. Prodigiously long drives could be the result; however, accuracy often times would be sacrificed. With the whipiness of that day's shafts, the golf ball might travel fifty yards right...or left... of his intended aim.

He held his driver up to the elevated ball. Then taking the wooden headed club back very smoothly, he swung with the extra acceleration he wanted. The crack sounded like a shotgun. The wind aided ball flew skyward like a Jules Verne rocket ship. The trajectory was high and surprisingly very straight. He could hear the gasps as the ball flew directly towards the guy's house on the other side of the 246-yard hitting range boundary. It seemed like the ball was still climbing when it went over that fence. The golf ball hit the roof of the house with a thud making the lady sitting on her patio noticeably jump. She stood up and looked around until suddenly a golf ball came rolling off the roof and bounced across the patio past the very chair she had been sitting in.

The gallery went nuts at the sight. They had never seen a golf ball travel so far, at least on this compact practice range.

Not knowing where the golf ball had come from and not believing what she'd just seen, she nervously sat back down returning to her reading material.

Lawton acknowledged the crowds loud cheers but held up two fingers indicating he still had two more shots to win the ridiculous wager. He then placed his eyes back on the pretty female still standing a short distance away. He asked her for another pencil since he'd broken the first one.

The female patiently got another one out of her purse and gave it to him. He then repeated his action…on his hands and knees balancing the ball on the flat end of the pencil…and then addressed the ball once again. This second shot was a bit higher and equally as accurate…but a bit more toward the patio. Lawton gasped hoping the ball would not land near the innocent lady. His heart was in his throat as the ball hit the garage fifteen yards left of where she was sitting.

It must have sounded like a gunshot. The lady jumped out of her chair as the gallery roared. She walked around the patio gazing over toward the club not having any idea what was causing all the crowd noise so far away. She obviously did not believe that someone was able to hit a golf ball onto her property. As her husband had said to Lawton, no one had ever done it…or had the brashness to try it.

After some delay, she finally went back to her patio chair and sat back down. The crowd moaned knowing that she'd have to go into the house to seek safety for the bet to be won by the crazy golfer.

Lawton too showed some disappointment, but it was all an act. He then broke into a smile and held one finger up. He had one more shot at winning his wager. The home owner in the crowd was giving Lawton the needle saying that he was looking forward to an additional $50 in his pocket. That was the first time Lawton remembered he had but $3.59 in his own pocket. He had created the spectacle he'd hoped, but the guy was going to have to accept an IOU if the bet was lost.

It was back to the pretty girl in the gallery for another flat ended pencil. This time she acted a bit peeved. She didn't like being the center of attention. She finally dug into her hand bag and presented him with her last flat-ended pencil. Then she drifted back into the crowd to get herself off the 'stage'.

When that third and last ball whistled off the pencil toward the man's house Lawton knew he had nailed the shot. It was heading directly at the man's house. The woman on the patio was in no danger.

Then something happened that Lawton or anyone in the crowd hadn't considered. The sound of the large upstairs bedroom window shattering echoed back across the practice range. The sudden explosion got the guy's wife off her chair screaming and running into her house before the ball finished rolling around in that upstairs room.

There was a stunned silence followed by the most uproariously loud explosion of laughter and applause from the crowd around him. People were patting Lawton on the back. The guy whose window had been broken had tears in his eyes either from laughter or thinking about the cost of repair. He thrust a $50 dollar bill in Lawton's face and the two of them shook hands...one laughing and enjoying the moment and the other not feeling really good about the sudden inconvenience.

When the shouting and rowdiness had somewhat subsided, Lawton realized he had a chance to really win over the crowd and draw some more attention. He held up his arms and asked the crowd to be silent for a moment. He then held up the $50 he'd just won saying he wanted to pay for the broken window...and then promptly returned the $50 to the home owner. The crowd cheered wildly more for the golfer's magnanimity than his golf prowess. He could have been elected governor on the spot.

Shortly before the practice range episode, Adam Bailey had gone immediately to the Chippewa Lodge restaurant to find Loni D'Annelli, the man in charge of the tournament and the player Adam had been caddying for since the origination of the golf event. Adam wanted to verify if the roster of players was still one golfer short of the twenty players needed to have five four-man teams. Not surprisingly, he found D'Annelli at the breakfast table smoking a big stogie and joking with everyone around him. The pre-made scorecards with the names of the players were lying by his coffee cup. Leaning over, Adam noticed one card with only three players. His heart pounded a bit faster. Another player was still needed.

Adam jumped right into the conversation knowing it wouldn't bother Loni. He could do no wrong as far as Loni was concerned. "Morning, Loni, where are your clubs. I'll get them ready so you can hit some practice shots."

Loni didn't seem interested as he filled his large mouth with sausage, eggs, and toast. Portions of all three food items disappeared into Loni's mouth in one bite. Loni was a larger than life figure with a huge face and a bigger voice. When he talked at regular volume, the folks at the end of the restaurant could hear his every word. At a louder level it seemed his voice could carry to the county boundaries. Most of what he said was constant joking filled with colorful profanity. D'Annelli had an intimidation factor that caused people to listen wide-eyed to his every word.

Loni greeted Adam with a pat on the back, "Adam, my boy" he said, "you've been caddying for me for four years in this tournament and I've walked away a winner each time. And now you're going off to become a damned college student this fall. Maybe I'll need to increase your pay so you'll always come back here in the summers to help me stay on the winning track. Sit down kid and have some breakfast. We got time to hit practice balls later. I want you to be strong today."

That was Loni. He always made those people he liked feel good. Adam had no idea what Loni did or had done to those people he did not like. In fact, he really didn't think about it. He'd never seen Loni really angry...except after a bad golf shot.

There was still plenty of time for Adam to maneuver Loni out to the practice range, but he knew the sooner the better for Lawton's sake. He got some help when restaurant patrons as well as servers began looking out the picture window toward the practice range. There was a lot of crowd commotion out there. Adam figured Lawton was carrying out his part of the deal...doing anything to cause attention.

As for Loni, he showed no interest until folks in the restaurant began leaving to go out and see what the fun was. Loni didn't move from his chair. He relit his cigar and commented, "Christ Almighty, a bunch of people must be desperate for entertainment if they're out there watching some of my boys hitting practice shots."

As more people left the restaurant, he finally turned around and glanced out the window toward the crowd. To no one in particular he growled, "Who the hell are they getting all worked up about?"

Adam slipped over to the window and couldn't help but chuckle. Lawton was doing exactly what he'd intended. He was putting on a show, just like he'd apparently done years before on his barnstorming circuit. From that picture window Adam watched his new friend hit some trick shots and then stop and converse with spectators. The crowd seemed to grow by the minute as more people came through the front gate attracted by the unexpected entertainment.

It would be that moment Adam truly believed Lawton had the moxie necessary to get Loni's attention. More determined, Adam went back to the table and sat down next to D'Annelli. The young man continued to eat heartily the breakfast Loni had just bought him while fingering the pre-made scorecards. Shaking his head he lamented, "Loni, it's too bad that twentieth player had to leave. It makes the teams uneven. I guess you haven't had any luck finding a qualified replacement?"

Loni smiled at Adam and shook his head while blowing a huge cloud of cigar smoke toward the ceiling. Then he gave Adam a light punch on the shoulder knowing Adam understood exactly the type of player who could be 'qualified' to play in the match that day. And 'qualified' meant as much 'financially' as it did regarding the needed golfing skills. Truth be known, Loni would prefer a guy who couldn't hit a ball out of his own shadow as long as the guy had the finances to pay off losing bets.

Another cheer from the throng out at the practice area again got the remaining people's attention in the restaurant. Loni got up and roved over to the window. His voice echoed in the room, "What the Goddamn hell is going on out on that practice range? The crowd is cheering for someone hitting practice shots. What the hell's happening?"

Adam jumped at the chance to tell him. Making up his own little story, he responded, "I believe it's that trick shot artist who travels around the state. He shows up at the darndest places and performs his trick shots. I've seen him at the State Fair and at community celebrations. I've even heard that he hits golf balls while standing on the wing of one of those biplanes!"

That last statement got Loni's attention. It was the only comment made by Adam that was actually true. He just made up the parts about the State Fair and the community celebrations.

Loni went back to the table and sat back down. "Can the guy play golf or does he just do trick shots?"

Adam replied, "I don't know how well he plays but he has a set of clubs. And something else...if he's the guy I'm thinking of, people say he comes from family money. He doesn't depend on any money he gets from trick shot performances." Again, Adam was lying through his teeth.

Loni scoffed, "Well, I hope he hits a lot of trick shots during the summer, cause in the winter up here, he's gonna have slim pickings for any kind of an audience."

Adam added another untruth. "I heard he runs his father's business in the winter."

After pausing, Adam then put the clincher on Loni. It was a line Lawton had suggested Adam use when the time was right. The time was right. "Loni, if he's the guy I've heard about, he's got plenty of money."

Loni eyed Adam and pushed his chair back from the table. "I've got to see this character."

Adam held back his smile. Bang..... the bait was on the hook. It was time for Loni to meet the trick shot artist. Adam had new found energy as he helped Loni up from the table. The big man had just engulfed six sausages, four eggs, and four pancakes.

Loni arrived at the practice range in time to observe Lawton almost being raised on two peoples' shoulders after he'd just won a bet by apparently hitting a golf ball out of the practice range and shattering a window on a house. Loni didn't understand what had happened but he was taking in the whole scene with a satisfied smile on his face. He couldn't help it. Everyone was reacting in disbelief about the golf shot. Loni took note that the ball had to have traveled over 270 yards from the practice tee box to reach that house.

Loni and Adam then stood together as the 'trick-shot' artist added to the fun by holding up his arms, quieting the crowd and then returning the man's $50. Loni actually began wheezing he laughed so hard when he heard it was the loser's house whose window had been broken.

Loni eyes were dancing as he leaned over to Adam commenting, "That fella's got some class returning the $50 the way he just did. It tells me a lot about the guy...in particular that the $50 isn't that important to him."

Adam could see Loni's brain working, so he added some grease to the frying pan. "Hey Loni, why not talk to that guy. If he can play as well as he hits trick shots, he could be the replacement player you're looking for."

Loni scratched his chin and gave Adam a nod in agreement. So as not to appear too forceful, Adam added, "Of course, the guy might not want to play in the tournament."

As if written from a script, Loni began sauntering over toward the showman. Adam couldn't believe what was happening. This huge man...this larger than life figure responsible for this huge charity tournament had just taken the bait and the hook Lawton and Adam had concocted the night before.

As Loni approached, it was the first time Lawton got a good face to face look at the man named 'Loni'. Adam was walking behind the big man pointing at the larger than life character with a stogie in his mouth. The young man needn't have pointed. It was pretty obvious.

The man named 'Loni' had been delivered. It was up to Lawton to now take over and win an invitation.

As Loni bulled his way through the crowd, Lawton continued to accept congratulations and back slaps from various spectators with only half attention. His eyes were now pegged on Loni. The man's sheer size was unbelievable. More significant was that Lawton realized he knew this man. He'd never met him, but he'd seen stories and pictures in the *Minneapolis Star*. There was no doubt in his mind. The fellow was the notorious Loni D'Annelli. In the reports and newspaper accounts of this man's activities, the descriptions were generally not complimentary. It occurred to him that he'd not seen or heard of this man in recent times...as if he'd disappeared from the lime light of underworld activity.

As D'Annelli approached, Lawton could tell he was being examined very closely. Loni had already taken note of Lawton's returning of the $50 and the crowd's favorable response. There was no doubt he was curious. His left hand reached for the stogie in his mouth as he raised his right hand in introduction. To Lawton it looked as if that one hand could crush his skull. There was no question both hands could do the maneuver with ease.

When D'Annelli stuck out his cigar stained right hand, Lawton seriously thought he'd gone too far. He had barged out onto the stage and Loni D'Annelli owned the theatre. Now the 'theatre manager' was either going to throw him out on his ear...or give him a part in the 'production'.

D'Annelli simply introduced himself. "My name is Loni". The surname was not mentioned...not that it was needed. The innocent description of this man by John Bailey and Adam by naively calling him just 'Loni' left Lawton somewhat shaken. The deep tan on Lawton's face faded a bit, but he recovered enough to reciprocate the handshake and mumble his own first name.

Adam immediately took note that Lawton was beginning to choke. He'd known Lawton for about twelve hours but could tell the man had become uncharacteristically speechless. Everything had come together surprisingly smooth. It was not the time to let their little sham disintegrate in the final minute...not with the money Adam had riding on Lawton getting into the charity event.

With Adam gritting his teeth at Lawton, the golfer recovered despite his own hand being completely engulfed in the mitt of the notorious Chicago mobster. His brain swarmed as he tried to recall the various details filed in his mind about Loni D'Annelli. The big man was noted for his strong connections with the steel industry on the south side of the city as well as his imperious girth and personality. In his younger days he was reputed to have moved up very quickly in that union. His competitors for union leadership had either decided to support him or had become part of the cement foundation for the steel supports on some of the new construction on Michigan Avenue. Today he was the understood leader of the International Brotherhood of Steel Workers. However, that was only a partial description of his activities. He'd been skirting the law with other nefarious deeds for years. Only well-paid attorneys had kept him out from behind bars.

After his lawyers warned him that he was becoming too popular of a target for the Bureau of Investigation, he'd become a less visible figure. In fact, he'd been so invisible in previous years that Lawton didn't even know the guy was still alive. But there he was...in all his glory! Somehow he had sequestered himself off to Chippewa Lodge running a charity golf event apparently for the good of the local civic and church organizations. There was no question in Lawton's mind the man had more going on in his life than running a golf tournament... and there was also no question the good of the local community was secondary.

Adam stood beside the big man like a proud papa relishing the sight of Lawton and D'Annelli actually meeting. The little diversion Lawton and he had invented had actually worked. Now it was time for Lawton's basic audacity to materialize and win over D'Annelli. Yet, Lawton had no idea what the large man's response was going to be relative to his antics on the practice range.

Loni's gravelly voice sounded like they were in an echo chamber as he challenged Lawton. "So...I see you created quite a stir out here on the practice range."

Then he focused his beady eyes on Lawton and asked, "I got a question for you. Why are you here?"

Lawton appreciated how this man got to the point. The words were spoken like a guy who was actually sizing the trick shot artist up to be included as some material for an upcoming cement shipment. But, Lawton had caught his second wind. He was going to be damned if he was going to let some mob guy try to bully him.

Taking a breath he relaxed his voice and responded, "Well...I'll tell you, Loni,"....as he searched his brain for some kind of acceptable answer... "I've been meaning to play this golf course for a long time. I stopped by early to get a tee time not knowing there was some kind of event going on. Then when all the people start walking by, it brought back memories of some crazy things I did years ago as a barnstorming pilot. I couldn't help myself. I used to put on some trick shot golf shows in order to bring people over for rides in my biplane. I'd take them up in the air for a couple bucks for a ten-minute ride. I'm a bit of a ham and hope I didn't cause you gents any inconvenience."

Loni smiled thinking the story was likely more true than false. Certainly, it wasn't the type of tale that could be made up. D'Annelli had nothing against initiative or someone who recognized opportunity.... as long as it didn't cost him anything.

Lawton and Adam could sense they were winning. When Loni pulled out one of the clubs in the bag Adam was carrying, Adam gave Lawton a very favorable nod. D'Annelli began to warm up by hitting some meaningless practice shots all the while conversing with Lawton. Everything was working well. D'Annelli was listening intently and kept asking Lawton questions. "So, what brought you to Glenwood this particular weekend?"

Lawton was able to be almost honest. "The storm last night forced me to land close to town. Then, since I was here anyway, I got a ride out here from some locals. Like I said, I didn't know about your event when I arrived. I just told the guys at the front gate I was playing today. They saw my golf bag and allowed me in."

Then Lawton threw a question back at D'Annelli. "So, Loni, it looks like you have quite a tournament going on out here given the number of spectators walking through the gates. How does one get into your event?"

D'Annelli played with his response. "It's a charity event. You pay a lot of money to enter."

Adam and Lawton smiled at each other knowing this was the moment. As the two of them had hoped, Lawton was able to say the line, "Well, I was blessed with a father who runs a very profitable business. If it's for a good cause, I'm certain I could find the amount for the entry fee."

Loni grinned at the response. He smiled even larger when Lawton added the flagrant lie, "Yeh...it's been up to me not to run the business into the ground after my father passed a few years back. To date things have been going well enough considering the times. The business is at least solvent, which is better than most people can say nowadays about their businesses."

The huge man had heard what he wanted to hear. He truly wanted to have a twentieth player. For an unknown outsider, Lawton seemed to fit the key qualifications. He had an apparently strong game...and he had the finances. D'Annelli tossed his club to Adam and got closer to Lawton. "So, it's nice that you can perform some trick shots, but I have a key question. Can you play the game competitively as well?"

Lawton didn't answer the question directly, but just said he'd played in a few tournaments around the state. Then he hit a couple shots throwing the ball in the air and hitting the golf ball as if a baseball coach hitting fly balls to his outfielders. Then he hit a shot left-handed...with a right handed club. D'Annelli chuckled knowing the man in front of him could definitely play the game. It was at that point he simply began referring to Lawton as 'Trick-shot'.

For Lawton, that was a blessing. He didn't exactly want to become a friend of this large man and have to share his full name. All he wanted was an invitation to play. There was no question there was going to be a lot of money at stake in this tournament.

Finally D'Annelli looked at his watch. Without skipping a beat, the invitation was offered. Both Lawton and Adam appeared slightly open-mouthed as they listened. "Well, Mr. Trick-shot, I have a little proposal you might want to consider. I happened to be in charge of this little charity golf tournament. I have it for a few of my friends. We've played it annually the past few years right here at this little resort. One of my gang... rather golfing buddies... had to return home for personal business yesterday. We actually have an opening that we'd like to fill. If you're available this weekend, you might get your chance to show off your talents. You'll have to understand that it might be a little different tournament atmosphere than what you're used to at your own club. My boys...rather my friends...like to kid around a lot. And, just as important, they like to make a lot of side bets. So, besides the entry fee, you'll need some extra cash to get into that kind of action.... that is, if you're interested."

The large man eyed Lawton closely for his response.

Not wanting to appear too willing or too greedy...although he was... Lawton forced himself to be patient and not appear to be over eager. He asked, "What type of format are you guys playing...is it a gross or a handicap competition? Do you play as teams or as individuals? And, is it cash or merchandise for prizes?"

With that last question both D'Annelli and his caddy, Adam, almost choked with laughter when the word 'merchandise' was voiced. This question proved Lawton's innocence and his ignorance about the event. Most amateur tournaments offered merchandise and trophies to the winners. That type of prize was the furthest from Loni's mind.

He spoke quickly and made his point very clear to Lawton. "My friend, like I say, this tournament is different. There will be no merchandise as a winner's prize. We play for cash...plain and simple."

Lawton got the answer he expected. Now the only question he had was how much this little excursion on the links was going to cost him to enter. He stood there in front of this giant of a man still thinking that he could mow any player in the field down at will. He considered the entire matter simply an investment with a huge potential return.

D'Annelli was still laughing at Lawton's "merchandise" question as he wiped the sweat from his brow with a towel slung over Adam's shoulder. He then calmly lit his ever present stogie for the fortieth time that morning while looking directly into the eyes of Lawton. He retorted, "Trick-shot, if you have the game and you win this tournament, you can buy the whole stock of golf merchandise and clothing in the clubhouse. All you have to do is win."

Lawton chuckled at the large man's swift appraisal. He had finally come to realize that Lawton had the game to be very competitive in this weekend event.

D'Annelli then added, "Tell you what...the invitation is yours if you want to play. At 9:30 all those who are playing will meet in the Lodge's restaurant. You can meet the rest of the gang...that is, the competitors. We'll go over the tournament rules and establish all bets. I'll need to know how you want to cover the $5000 entry fee. I prefer cash, but we can arrange an IOU if you don't happen to have $5000 on you."

Lawton tried not to flinch when the entry fee amount was mentioned as well as the suggestion of the IOU. He figured D'Annelli had to be thinking a piece of Lawton's fictitious family business would have to be the collateral for the IOU.

Lawton felt the heat build up under his collar. The fee was far beyond what he ever expected. At the same time, he had not observed any other competitor hitting balls on the practice range who could match his skill on the golf course. Adam's warning about mischievous deeds being performed during play had no impact on him at that moment. He was always involved in joking and kidding on the links. That warning by D'Annelli seemed frivolous. No competitive hijinks was going to limit his ability to perform on the golf course.

Loni shook Lawton's hand again and seemed sincere when he repeated about the 9:30 pre-tournament meeting. He then turned and left with Adam following. The young man turned and pumped his fist in glee at Lawton while sprinting to keep up with the big man.

It was only 8:15 in the morning and Lawton...with some help from Adam Bailey...had done it! Now Adam was in for 10% of any winnings. That seemed very possible to Lawton as he hit a few more practice shots with more earnest. If he only realized he'd just committed himself to the ride of his life.

There was no time to pat himself on the back. Lawton gathered up his golf clubs and proceeded to the main lobby of the resort. He had to call his friend, Charlie Davis, and attack the next step. This normally wouldn't be any problem. Both of them were always quite willing to take an investment risk, but that usually meant a piece of real estate would be in the offing. This type of investment would take some convincing. A $5000 entry fee plus more cash for side bets didn't exactly fit the intent of their shared fund. Lawton would understand if his friend might be a bit dubious.

But, in the end, Lawton knew he could convince Davis. His friend would eventually give in just because of Lawton's single-minded determination. If the circumstances seemed that encouraging, Davis would support him. Besides, the two men appreciated a good adventure and a lively game of chance...especially if the opportunity looked favorable.

As he approached the veranda of the Lodge restaurant, John Bailey was lounging on a rocker smoking his pipe. He'd been watching the crowd standing around the practice area from the comfort of that porch. He wasn't following what was going on and fully expected to be driving Lawton back to the farm at any moment.

Lawton recalled vividly Bailey's joking comment the previous evening about caddying for him if the impossible came true and he was allowed into the charity tournament. Bailey had made the offer as if it was as likely as snow in June. However, seeing the excited anticipation that morning on the face of his son, Lawton noticed that Bailey had changed his work pants into something cleaner. That showed Bailey respected there was a chance that snow flurries could form in June after all. Then again, it could have only meant that his work pants needed laundering.

Bailey didn't play the game of golf, but through his son he understood it. As for the idiosyncrasies of this particular tournament, he was well-versed. Strolling up to the restaurant porch, Lawton kept his enthusiasm in check. He gave the relaxed farmer a cheery but pensive look giving Bailey the impression the two of them had about two minutes to leave the premises.

Lawton finally stopped directly in front of the relaxed Bailey. As the farmer awaited the bad news, Lawton put some of his personal items into the golf bag as if he were packing up to go home.

Bailey kept waiting for Lawton to lament how he'd failed to get the invitation. Yet, something wasn't right. There was a gleam in Lawton's eye as he looked up at Bailey on that restaurant porch. Then the man he'd only known since the previous evening blandly retorted, "John, here's my golf bag. We'll be teeing off around 10:00 this morning. Since you'll be caddying for me, I'd appreciate you watching my clubs while I go into the restaurant to get a rules sheet...and make an important telephone call."

Lawton then went up the steps and entered the Lodge peripherally seeing Bailey almost choke on his pipe. He didn't see Bailey's growing grin, but he heard the farmer repeat a phrase he'd heard him say the previous night when Bailey finally noticed the biplane parked by the barn.

Under his breath the farmer said disbelievingly, "I'll be damned'. Then, he repeated it again this time more emphatically.

The outside telephone line in the registration lobby was also a party line. There would be no telling how many people might be listening in. He'd have to somehow camouflage the call. Lawton began chuckling already contemplating the initial response from Charlie Davis. There was no question Davis would think him crazy for entering a golf competition requiring a substantial entry fee. His plan was to be quick and to the point and not let his friend respond. Besides, the less said the better on the party line. He gave the operator the number at Davis' house, told her to reverse charges, and waited.

As he waited for the connection, he cautiously looked around making certain no one was within ear shot. There was an attractive woman fiddling with her purse, but she seemed not to be paying any attention to him. She didn't even seem impressed with his presence despite his purple shirt and tie combination. In fact, there was not even a friendly glance in his direction. After the unbridled attention he'd received out at the practice range, her response was a bit disappointing. His ego at that moment was quite elevated. He thought he might go introduce himself to the young lady after the phone call. Even if she reacted negatively to him, he had enough fuel in his self-image to counteract that unfortunate possibility.

Finally, the operator made the connection. He could hear the familiar clearing of the throat and the typical early morning hoarseness of his friend. With echoing in the line, Lawton smiled when he heard the perturbed voice. "Yeh...this is Charlie Davis...and yeh, I'll accept the reverse charges from the cheapest son-of-a-bitch I've ever known." Even the operator giggled.

That was all Lawton needed to embark on a conversation that would be was unalterably one-sided.

"Charlie, it's Jamie. Are you conscious yet?"

"Jamie boy, it's about damn time. Where the hell have you been? We missed your money at the card table last night."

"Chas, listen to me. Drop whatever you're doing and get your ass down to Chippewa Lodge in Glenwood now. Also, get our sack out from under the mattress and stuff the contents under the seat of your jalopy. I've got some action that's too good to pass up."

"Lawton, for Christ's sake, what type of action would require anywhere near the amount we have in our little fund? What did you do last night, crash into someone's house during the storm? Or, better yet, did some of your hot barnstorming blood bleed into that soft brain of yours? Just tell me her name…maybe I know her."

"Charlie, it's none of that. It's bigger…and better. Kick start that ratty old sports car of yours and peel on down here. When you get to the entrance of the Lodge, tell them 'Loni' sent you. Drive to the front of the pro shop to park. You'll probably find me in the resort restaurant. Now, don't say another word. Remember, we're on a party line. Just bring the cash and bring your golf sticks just in case we need them to defend ourselves."

"My friend, I can tell you're serious. It's probably some kind of golf action. I can tell by your voice you've got some pigeons ready to be skinned. O.K.….O.K.…I'll be down there within the hour. Since it's something special, I'll throw on my eye-catching…if I do say so myself… chartreuse golf shirt rather than the stained rag I normally wear on the golf course."

"Charlie, I don't care if you wear the old shirt you use to wipe down your car engine, just get here fast. Don't forget… at the front gate just tell the two guardsmen that 'Loni' sent for you. Otherwise, you'll never get in."

Lawton hung up to the sound of a few more expletives from Davis, but his purpose had been accomplished. He now had the entry fee and found himself relaxing for the first time that morning. There was time to grab some breakfast. He looked around the lobby for that attractive lady he'd just seen, but she'd disappeared. He had been feeling just audacious enough to ask her to breakfast. He smiled to himself. That would have been a first…inviting a lady to breakfast when they hadn't even gone out the previous night.

Strolling by the guards at the restaurant entrance rustling the $3.59 in his pocket, he was quite surprised by the activity. The place was a madhouse of fun-loving banter. It occurred to him that he was seeing a financially successful resort. It was hard to imagine given the secluded location.

In the eating area, there had to be over sixty people including some very attention getting women. The smell was a mixture of bacon and sausage, cigar smoke, heavy cologne and equally noticeable perfume. It was neither inviting nor unpleasant...just an obvious hangout dominated by men...a typical clubhouse atmosphere.

Lawton looked for a table. A harried waitress pointed to a free table and asked him if he wanted some coffee. He nodded. It was an environment he was normally quite comfortable. However, it didn't take him long to notice there was something quite different about this atmosphere. He'd played a lot of golf tournaments and met a lot of people around Minnesota. In that restaurant that morning, he didn't see one person he'd ever met. In fact, it was as if he was in a different state. He kept panning his eyes around the eating establishment for anyone who looked the least bit familiar.

Then he began to study the individuals, their boisterous behavior, their style of clothing, and the type of women hanging around them. He looked back at the guards by the entrance to the restaurant area. It would have been fair to say that John and Adam Bailey had incompletely described the players and the surroundings to him the night before. He had one certainty at that moment. He'd be better off not getting to know many of the players ready to tee it up in this dubious charity golf affair.

CHAPTER

7

Charlie Davis was speeding down Hwy. #29 toward Glenwood. Only eight minutes had passed since hanging up the telephone with Jamie Lawton. Lake Reno was on his right as he accelerated to some unknown speed. His speedometer had broken about a year before. He figured his 1922 vintage A-68 St. Claire Roadster could outrace any traffic cop on the roadway given the new Ford engine installed by the local garageman. At his rate of speed, his only real concern was any slow moving horse-drawn farm wagons suddenly visible over a hill. He'd faced that situation too many times.

Davis' speed on the roadways was notorious. Through his law practice and a few speeding tickets, he'd become good friends with various city police chiefs and county sheriffs in the area. To ensure a wholesome and forgiving attitude by these various law enforcement offices, Charlie always made certain a good brand of Scotch shipped in from Canada was delivered to those offices each Christmas. Ordering the booze through the neighbor to the north was the legal...or at least...the accepted way to circumvent the U.S. prohibition laws.

The extra cost was well worth it. He found the good public relations helped him stay on the good side of law enforcement. The reduction of arrests, charges, and convictions for some of his friends and clients made the 'Scotch' investment even more worthwhile. Just the mention of Charlie Davis being their lawyer caused many law infractions to be reduced or in some cases even ignored. It wasn't necessarily right, but it was the fact.

Before he'd left his house that Saturday morning, Charlie had stuffed a satchel full of money under the driver's seat of his roadster. He didn't bother to count it. He knew it was around $6000 in small bills. His only curiosity was what type of worthwhile investment would cause Lawton to suggest he bring the entire bag. There had to be a huge potential return. In the back of his mind, he let himself dream that Lawton had actually secured some option to buying Chippewa Lodge. Lawton knew Davis' interest in buying the struggling property along with its nine-hole golf course...for the right price.

The half hour drive was luckily uninterrupted by farm equipment or cows on the roadway. As the road descended down the bluff into the municipality of Glenwood, the most beautiful scene was bestowed. It always made his periodic venture down to the Pope County seat something to look forward to with the view of grand Lake Minnewaska.

For 9:15 on a Saturday morning, the community seemed especially quiet until he got to the intersection in the center of town of the two state highways, #28 and #29. Then the atmosphere changed quite noticeably. Hundreds of people were ambling by the store fronts. As he passed through the intersection, he noticed even larger numbers down at City Park. He was amazed at the apparent success of the community festival.

With no interest in the town event, he touched his accelerator a bit harder. As he drove on, he was impressed with the unusual cleanliness of the streets and even the uncommon sheen to buildings and homes. The community knew how to do it up right for their festival.

He drove slowly by the sandy beach on the south side of City Park and saw more people already enjoying the day. On that end of the park, booths were set up with food, games, home-made clothing items for sale, and animal pens. His eye then caught a large tent with a scoreboard in front of it. It was something normally not seen at a town festival. The huge scoreboard had first names or nicknames along with dollar amounts apparently bet on them. There were also five team names with even bigger figures by each one.

Davis slowed and glanced twice. Unless he was not yet sober, he sensed he was observing an obvious game of chance. He wasn't certain if the wagers were on horses or boat races, but there was every indication some kind of large scale, and probably questionable betting, was going on. He wanted to believe the wagering was for the benefit of some church groups or civic organizations. That would be the excuse for local law enforcement to look the other way. But, the scoreboard with the names seemed too public. He wondered how the town got away with it. Even if outside authorities were unaware, there were enough prudish people living in any town, including Glenwood, to produce complaints to the local town fathers.

As Davis drove on along the lake shore and neared Chippewa Lodge, he became even more surprised. A sizable number of cars, horses, and horse led wagons were parked along the lake front road. He saw one larger horseback wagon with a Lutheran Church sign on the back taking a group of people toward the resort. There were civic clubs selling lemonade, fruit, and fresh rolls at small tents next to the lake. He saw fishing contests, sailing competitions and boat races being organized or already taking place out on Lake Minnewaska.

A few blocks from the Lodge, the walking traffic thickened. Davis had to honk his horn so his sporty roadster could slip by all the people walking on the single lane lakeside road. Fifty yards from the front entrance to the resort, he was no longer able to move forward. There was a line of cars trying to enter the resort. Most were being turned away by two imperious looking guys in long overcoats at the front gate. People seemed not to question or argue with the two gatekeepers. They backed their cars up and retreated back down the lake roadway creating a worse traffic jam.

As busy as the activities were on the lake, there was obviously some kind of major event going on at the resort as well. The golf course looked especially green and inviting. Davis knew right then this would not be the day he'd be buying the Chippewa Lodge resort. It appeared in too good of shape for him to make any 'steal'.

With no movement of the traffic, Charlie immediately became edgy. He asked a fellow walking along the road what was going on at the Lodge.

The guy looked at Charlie like he was crazy. "Buddy," he said, "there's more money going to be blowing around this golf course today than most people will see in the next twenty years. We've got some real high rollers teeing it up at 10:00 and they're playing for some serious money. If you turnaround and go back to the park you can put some bets down on some of the players, but you have to have at least $10 to play. Or, if you can find someplace to park, there's a betting booth right across from the entrance to the Lodge. But, that booth is always busy."

Charlie thanked the guy for the information and smiled at the thought of $10 when he had $6000 under his driver's seat. $10 was nothing. But, $10 was hell of a lot for most people living around Pope County to wager.

Another minute went by and the delay had become too much. Davis had promised to get to the resort as soon as possible. He was not about to sit in his roadster for another half hour waiting for a long line of vehicles whose drivers were trying to talk their way into the resort property. It was time to get creative, get through the gates and find Lawton.

Never having faced the curse of shyness, Charlie honked his horn and began bellowing, "Tournament official, let me through...move out of the way....tournament official...let me through!!!" Within ten seconds, it was like the parting of the Red Sea. Charlie drove right up to the gate and announced to the two rather daunting gents in the long coats that 'Loni sent for him'. The two guys did not raise an eyebrow but simply waved him through.

There were plenty of parking spots by the golf shop. He got out of his roadster, making certain the satchel was securely hidden under the driver's seat. He pulled his money belt above his slight paunch, shoved a new cigar in his mouth for luck, and sauntered into a very noisy restaurant inside the main building.

Approaching yet another set of guards at the entrance, he repeated the line, 'Loni sent for me' to the gruff looking burly men. They nodded and allowed him entrance. Once in the knotty pine walled restaurant, he took note of an enormous fellow with an even bigger stogie in his mouth talking to the group. The man was laying out some rules for a golf match. His booming voice sounded like he could make up whatever rules he wanted and he'd get no argument from the participants.

Davis figured Lawton had to be somewhere in the throng. He wandered over toward the kitchen while perusing the entire eating area. He found his recently laundered chartreuse golf shirt fit in well with the equally loud clothing of the players. As he floated virtually unnoticed around that restaurant, he took a cup of coffee off a tray as a waitress walked by. Not to be too conspicuous, he finally planted himself on a convenient stool at the side of the kitchen and quietly listened to the gravelly voiced tournament organizer.

Although not thinking it important at the time, he found himself sitting next to a very nice looking waitress intently listening to the same large man. She seemed far too classy to be walking around filling coffee cups. To that end, she showed little interest in leaving her post. He also noticed how ill-fitted the waitress uniform was on her. The skirt was cut a bit too high showing more leg than the other waitresses. Of course, it didn't matter on the other waitresses. They didn't have this female's legs. He figured she was wise remaining back by the kitchen. With this crowd she'd probably get more pinches on her rear than tips.

Davis finally spotted Lawton sitting with a younger kid right in front of the big man speaking to the crowd. He found it interesting his friend had chosen to dress so sportingly in his light purple shirt with matching tie. The last time he'd seen Lawton in that get-up was not on the golf course but at a bar association dinner in Minneapolis. That was the last time Davis had worn a tie...period. He recalled he had to have Lawton tie the Windsor knot for him.

Seeing Jamie so fancily clothed said volumes. He wouldn't be wearing his best clothing unless the event warranted it. That was the puzzle. Davis couldn't imagine how this little resort tournament could earn such a tournament. He also had the sinking feeling that a portion of their money in the satchel was going to be invested in some kind of high roller golf match.

As Davis continued scoping the room, something else occurred to him about the assembled group. They were unusually crass for an entourage of fancily dressed golfers. Waitresses were taking their life in their hands serving the tables. Some of the players spit tobacco juice on the floor. Normally a country club or golf club atmosphere displayed quite a bit more class both for the location and for the venerable game they were about to play.

He was about to lean over and comment about the group to the young waitress beside him, when he saw the cold look in her eye. She was staring at one particular individual sitting in the crowd. He swore if she had a gun, that person would no longer be alive.

He was becoming aware how this waitress did not fit into this atmosphere. There was an air about her...a confidence...an intelligence...even a disdain for what was going on. Waiting on tables appeared to be the last thing on her mind. There was no approval in her look whatsoever. Davis wondered how beautiful she'd be if her tense face changed to a smile. It was a challenge he figured he might try, but another day. At the moment she had other things on her mind. Ever the romantic, he smirked thinking it was her loss for not looking his way.

Giving up on the young waitress, Davis stared at Lawton until he got his friend's attention. Lawton was definitely out-of-place with this assortment of loud, profane men and scantily dressed females. He seemed almost apologetic as he gave Davis a regretful shrug. Davis returned a response giving his friend the wide-eyed look as if to be asking, "what the hell have you got us into this time?"

Prior to Davis' arrival at the Lodge restaurant, Lawton had casually walked into the restaurant just before 9:30. Loni D'Annelli had not been hard to find. Wherever he went there was laughter and loud voices. Lawton's stealthy compatriot, Adam Bailey, naturally was at the big man's side simply enjoying the scene. Hoping Davis would soon arrive with the money for the entry fee, Lawton still had to officially commit to the 20th and last spot in the tournament. He didn't look forward to having to sign a temporary IOU. His preference was not having to sign his name to anything.

As he strolled to the back of the restaurant toward Loni and his entourage, Lawton glanced from side to side at the interesting group of participants. There were some nattily dressed gentlemen who looked like the last place they'd spend their time was at a golf course. He couldn't help but be impressed by the number of eye-catching females with some a style of dress that covered 'some' parts of their bodies. He'd never seen so many semi-exposed breasts.

Despite the show of anatomy, he was able to focus on a few of the players relaxing at their tables. Strangely, he felt he'd seen some of them. They were laughing and joking and moving around the room making bets. It was hard to get a bead on any of them.

Approaching D'Annelli, the big man broke out into a legitimately sincere smile. Wasting no time, he bellowed, "So Trick Shot, if you're here, you must be in. That's just great!" He rubbed his hands together like he'd just pulled off his own triumph. Lawton felt momentarily uncomfortable. By nodding his head at D'Annelli in response, Lawton felt like he was about to go ahead with the bank job and personally blow up the vault.

It was not, however, the time to show timidity; he had to maintain a confident air. He said nothing about the IOU for the entry fee. Lawton said simply, "I'd be pleased to accept your invitation. The entry fee will be in your hands before we finish the first nine. It will come to you in cash."

Loni slapped him on the back with pure delight like they were old friends. Lawton felt like his larynx had just been dislodged. Unconsciously he rolled his tongue over his teeth just to make certain they hadn't been disengaged.

While Lawton regained his breath and voice, D'Annelli raised his hand for attention. The crowd quieted as if their eyes had been on him every second. "Gentlemen, we have our 20th player and he has qualified in the most important way....in cash!"

There were cheers and laughter in the room for the next ten seconds. Then, just as quickly, D'Annelli raised his hand again and quieted the group. "Since we have no tournament history on our new player, I'll declare him an 'A' player...and I'll put him on my team."

Everyone around the room nodded their heads and seemed to accept the proposal. It didn't seem to matter to them. They all looked at Lawton like he was a pigeon about to be plucked. He was not used to that type of mocking look...and he didn't like it. The golf course was his environment. He normally enjoyed an intimidation factor against his opponents. It raised his ire enough that his competitive juices began to flow.

Loni continued, "Now that we have an even number of players on each team, let's go over the rules of today's first eighteen holes of our two-day tournament."

With that Loni uncovered a giant scoreboard with the first name and only the initial of the last name. In some cases there was only a nickname. That was enough. Everybody knew everybody...except of course Lawton.

As D'Annelli talked on, Lawton could hear the whispers of 'trick shot artist' float around the room. He sensed the general surprise that D'Annelli was gambling on the 'visitor' being a teammate. To the players it looked like D'Annelli was truly sticking his neck out, apparently for the good of the event. Betting began to increase at D'Annelli's table. Even if the trick shot artist could play the game, the other players knew an innocent newcomer had no idea about the perils waiting for him on the golf course. The general feeling was that this blondish fellow would crack under the stress created by the players. As a result, credentials didn't much matter for any innocent new competitor. All they really cared about was that he had the financial backing to pay the entry fee and pay off the side bets that he was very likely to lose.

Lawton noticed there was a blank spot on the huge scoreboard with the other nineteen names. One of D'Annelli's men took care of that once he heard the twentieth invitation had been accepted. Keeping with the general anonymity of the other players, Lawton's name was mercifully printed on the board as simply "Trick Shot". Lawton breathed a sigh of relief given that no one asked or really cared about his actual name.

It was then that reality hit him like a sudden infusion of caffeine. He began to compare the singular nickname or first name with the player seated in the raucous restaurant. It was difficult to keep his eyes from bulging as they jumped from scoreboard to person, person to scoreboard, and so on.

He saw the name 'Willie'. John and Adam Bailey had alluded briefly to this man. Lawton had momentarily envisioned a hoodlum he knew about who lived high in the Twin Cities. It wasn't probable. What would a mobster like Willie LaCurso be doing spending his time at an isolated lake resort in the middle of Minnesota?

Then he saw the wispy, intense fellow up close and Lawton felt his stomach gurgle. He'd not only seen this man's picture in newspapers but he'd seen him at some swanky private affairs around the Twin Cities. The man was definitely Willie LaCurso...the Grainmiller's union president and a purported Minneapolis racketeer. LaCurso's reputation was that of a picture of decorum as long as no one tried to compete in his little empire. If anyone did, Willie "sent these people to Iowa" as was the joke Lawton had heard. In other words, who would go to Iowa by choice? That person either then changed his mind about contending with Willie or his life would change...sometimes permanently. Willie obviously didn't believe the law against monopolies applied to him. Though frequently arrested, he'd never been convicted as far as Lawton was aware.

Now Lawton faced the discomfort of possibly having to be friendly to this hooligan. He didn't want to talk to this man much less exchange glances. While he knew LaCurso lived in one of the stately secured mansions off River Road close to St. Thomas College and Town & Country Golf Club in St. Paul, Lawton didn't want this gangster to have any idea that 'Trick Shot' even lived in the same state.

Lawton watched the unsmiling small man interact with other players. With that burning look in his eyes, LaCurso looked right through another man's head as if x-raying the player's mind. The wiry guy was so intense Lawton figured this man could finish a cigarette in one drag.

Lawton panned over to another guy by the name of "Vinnie" on the scoreboard...yet another person described by the Baileys the night before. Sure enough, there was Vinnie Spagatini sitting at an adjacent table...a purported hitman from Chicago. Although not a criminal law attorney, Lawton couldn't help but pay attention to gangster related crimes. These types of felonies more than occasionally drifted over to Lawton's legal specialty of corporate law. Lawton began to count the number of times this thug had been arraigned for murder, not counting the totals accumulated by his own gang of heavies. Rumor had it that he had his former mother-in-law murdered solely because she was responsible for having given birth to his ex-wife.

And sitting next to 'Vinnie' was Bert Bertinelli, one of the right-hand guys to Capone himself. Bert had a twitch. He kept moving his head to the right, like he was perpetually looking for someone over his shoulder. Based on his reputation, there was every reason to believe he should keep that twitch permanent for his own safety.

Lawton cautiously moved his feet as another gruff looking man lumbered by his table. He again gulped as he recognized Danny A'Motta. Just by his look, A'Motta personified evil. Newspapers had reported this hoodlum being paroled out of Leavenworth the previous Christmas after serving two years of a five-year sentence for tax evasion. Lawton muffled an unconscious and cynical smile as he mumbled to himself, "Yeh...tax evasion!" Relatively speaking, that conviction was like putting Billy the Kid behind bars for underage drinking.'

A'Motta gave Lawton an odious look and then in a quasi-friendly sort of way snarled, "Let's see if you got the cohunes to hit a ball off a pencil when you got $80,000 dollars on the line. You'll be sweating all over that pretty tie of yours."

Lawton hadn't heard the word "cohunes" often, but he understood the meaning. A'Motta then gave a throaty laugh that sounded like the rasp of a northern Minnesota bear in heat...only more fierce. Lawton could not remember meeting a more daunting human being...ever!

The names in that restaurant went on and on. While recognizing some, others looked familiar, and still others looked shady. Lawton didn't see one person he really wanted to meet.

One thing for certain....while Lawton had expected a few questionable characters playing in the event, it had become quite clear that this little Minnesota resort restaurant had more Midwest mobsters in one place than a skybox at the Arlington Park racetrack on Labor Day. He was way over his head with no real way to escape. He'd committed because he'd been blinded by his desire to compete. And, as far as the men in the room were concerned, the only thing that made him the least bit acceptable...besides having the money to be in the field of players...was that he was Loni's guest.

As D'Annelli railed on about the various rules regarding the tournament play...something that seemed completely superfluous in this group of lawbreakers...Lawton could feel the eyes of the group staring menacingly at him. He knew he was being considered easy pickings...like they'd clean every penny out of his trousers as well as winning the very purple shirt and tie of his body.

When D'Annelli finally completed the rules and format of the tournament, Lawton learned the shear fortune the eventual winning team was going to pocket. It was mind boggling. The amount was far beyond anything Lawton had ever played for on the golf course. With twenty players tossing the $5000 entry fee apiece into the kitty, there was $100,000 in the Saturday pot alone...heavy money given the economic times. There were five foursomes with each team predetermined by the previous history of their scores in the last three Chippewa Lodge tournaments. Each team had an 'A' player or a more skilled golfer as well as supposedly a weaker player designated as the 'D' player. The other two members of the team were supposed to have a skill level somewhere in between.

As for the format, D'Annelli had explained that the best two scores of the four-man team on each hole would count for the team total. The low scoring two teams after eighteen holes would earn the pot after the first day of the two-day tournament. The first place team got to split $80,000 or $20,000 apiece to each of the four players on the team. The second place team would split the remaining $20,000 four ways.....in other words these players would get their entry fee money back. All the other players would wave good-by to their $5000 entry fee. However, there was still plenty of other money to be won or lost with individual bets between players and teams.

D'Annelli had shouted out to the group when he'd finished. "O.K., you bums, any questions?"

Vinnie Spagatini yelled out asking if automatic weapons were still outlawed by the tournament chairman like the previous year since the noise had become too bothersome on player's backswings. As the group laughed openly, D'Annelli took the question seriously. He said, "Vinnie, same rule is in effect this year." Then he added, "But tomorrow's another day."

The whole place again exploded with laughter while Lawton sat there concentrating hard not to soil his pants.

Loni then informed the group to finish their side bets since the first foursome was scheduled to tee off at 10:00. Immediately fellow competitors sidled up to Lawton wanting to make a 'grand' bet with him individually on the front nine. Lawton knew he'd better forgo these individual bets until he talked it over with Charlie Davis. He nervously assured them, 'Fellas, I have to wait for my financier. I want to have the money in hand just in the small chance that I might lose a bet with you. But, I'll be ready to make some bets on the back nine once my money arrives."

The players around him chortled...some derisively. What surprised Lawton was the general acceptance of his delay in betting. They appreciated his decision not to wager until he felt comfortable he had the ability to pay lost bets. In truth, Lawton was chomping at the bit to make a healthy wager with each player. He'd still seen no one out on the practice range with the ability to compete with him head-on-head.

The players began to step away from him. Some of them were even cordial and offered a generous comment of 'play well'. They were crooks, but they seemed to have a sporting sense. A couple guys, like 'Vinnie' and 'Bert' seemed especially determined to make a substantial personal wager with Lawton. They both said they'd for certain catch up with him before the second nine-hole competition. Lawton didn't exactly like the sound of the phrase 'catch up with him'.

As the room began to clear, Lawton was more than ready to tiptoe out of the restaurant and catch his breath. Whatever swagger he'd had upon entering the resort earlier that morning had all but melted.

It was then that he heard a loud voice across the emptying room. It had a familiar husky tone. He'd heard the tell tale crusty echo too many times to count. There in all his glory was his friend, Charlie Davis, giving one of his pathetic drunken performances...and it was only 9:45 in the morning. It was Davis' attempt at getting Lawton's attention without the two of them having to admit that they knew each other.

Davis obviously wanted to talk. His act was his proven way of cleaning out a room quickly. No one wanted to be around an obviously out-of-control dipsomaniac.

As the golfers and other guest left the restaurant looking disgustedly at Davis, Lawton remained behind. He'd wait until he and Davis were alone.

Willie LaCurso and his entourage were among the last to leave. Davis was at his blustering best. Lawton closed his eyes knowing his friend likely didn't know the short, grim-faced Twin Cities mobster. He watched as Davis gave a slurring offer to the wiry fellow to play one hole and the winner gets enough money to buy the 'whole damned resort'. Lawton had seen his friend make many a staged drunken wagers which no one would remember, but this one was way out of bounds. Lawton began to move forward to somehow stop the probable death of his friend when LaCurso gave Davis an evil smile and moved on out of the restaurant. Luckily LaCurso had other things on his mind. Had it been another occasion, Davis would likely have gotten a much worse response.

Finally only the restaurant staff remained. Davis had effectively cleared the room as efficiently as a fire alarm. What Lawton always appreciated about his friend was his complete disregard of personal embarrassment. Davis had no problem making a complete ass out of himself...if the need arose. Of course Lawton had often reminded Davis that he didn't have to pretend to be drunk to have such a revolting effect on people.

As the last of the guests made it outside, Charlie then feigned an alcoholic seizure and fell over a table and onto the floor. Lawton patiently nodded appreciating the final act. This routine of Davis' had definitely compared favorably with the one he'd performed one night in St. Paul the previous winter. Lawton recalled the two of them had wanted to ditch some ladies they'd met at a speak-easy. That night Davis lay shaking on the floor looking pathetic. All four ladies thought he was wretched and left the scene. Once gone, Davis miraculously 'recovered' within seconds. The two of them had then headed on to a more proven speak-easy in Minneapolis...where they had better luck.

Lawton was well-tuned to Charlie's game. It was now his turn to participate in the charade. Showing phony concern for Davis' condition, he rushed over as if to offer some aid. Lawton ordered restaurant workers away declaring the intoxicated man needed room to breathe.

Most everyone seemed relieved they didn't have to deal with this piece of human humiliation.

Lawton giving the impression he had some medical background called for some cold towels and strong coffee. While the remaining staff then went about their duties, Lawton and Davis finally had a chance for a brief interchange…except for one waitress who was cleaning tables too close to them.

Motioning her away, she moved but a few feet back. The two men couldn't be as straight-forward with one another with her so nearby. Charlie was aware of her presence as well and just lay there in his feigned stupor.

Lawton gazed at her again and repeated his waving motion. "Ma'am, you can get back to work. I've got this matter under control."

She stepped back further and began slowly picking up more dirty dishes, but her eyes kept glancing toward them.

Time was wasting. Lawton had to get to the first tee box. He leaned down toward Davis and whispered, "Nice entrance, Chas. You've made a lot of close friends once again these last five minutes."

Charlie grinned slightly with his eyes still half-closed. Then he showed a very pained expression as he gurgled, "Jamie boy, I'll look forward to hearing how you got yourself into this mess. I swear to Christ there were more criminals in this restaurant than are currently residing at Stillwater State Penitentiary. I've been here fifteen minutes and watched the whole unbelievable circus from the kitchen door."

He then paused before opening his eyes fully. "Somehow my memory is slipping. I can't remember if I brought along our satchel of cash or not. In fact, if you've gotten yourself into this adventure on purpose, counselor, I may forget that I ever met you. Please tell me we're going to have some great laughs sometime in the future because right now I don't see a lot of humor or value in this little endeavor."

Then he lifted his head slightly. Noticing the waitress just a few yards away, he whispered to Lawton, "Just tell me one thing…what the hell are we investing our money in?"

Knowing how he was going to react, Lawton had to turn his face away from his friend preparing himself for an outburst of laughter. He once again leaned in closer to Davis' ear and calmly admitted, "It's the entry fee for this tournament."

The gray look in Davis' eyes was no longer factitious, but authentic. Lawton was afraid his friend was truly going into cardiac arrest. The two of them tried to stifle their laughter but were failing miserably… as if being two youngsters coming upon a male and female skinny dipping in a creek.....and realizing it was the principal of the school and the minister's wife.

The few people who remained in the restaurant, the waiters and waitresses, looked at the two of them like they were out of their minds. They just shook their heads and went about cleaning the restaurant. Given the strange people staying at the resort, they'd seen many odd happenings. This was just another chapter.

Unfortunately, there was one person paying much closer attention. That same waitress who'd positioned herself closely to Davis at the back of the restaurant now stood by the two of them looking disgusted but holding back her own laughter. It was as if she had come to realize the two of them were different than the rest of that corrupt crowd in the restaurant that morning. She moved away, but kept her attention on the bizarre antics of the two males.

Finally recovering, Lawton stood up and continued the act. He proclaimed to no one in particular, "I think he's going to make it. There's no reason to send for a doctor."

Lawton assisted Davis to his feet and then sat down with him at a nearby table applying a wet towel to his friend's neck and shoulders. With his tee-time fast approaching, he spoke low and gave Davis as much of the story as he had time.

Davis occasionally grinned, but mostly shook his head. Lawton had rarely seen his friend as exasperated.

Finally Davis responded. "Jamie, we both appreciate a good competition, but you know as well as I do the type of people in this crowd. Hell, the money in their pockets is dirty. You want to win that kind of money? And, if you lose to these hooligans, I hope we're only out $5000. I don't get it. Why are we doing this?"

Lawton's response was quick. "Charlie, I thought there might be some scalawags in this group when I first learned of this tournament last night. I had no idea the level of lowlife playing in this event. I was ready to pull up stakes and run when I saw some of the hoodlums in this restaurant. Then as I got thinking about it, when else would I ever have a chance to fleece a group of gangsters and have no apparent repercussions? What an opportunity! I tell you these guys can't play to my skill level. I can win...and I don't want the money for myself. Hell, whatever money I might make beyond our $5000 entry fee I plan on just giving it away. Besides, this is supposed to be a charity event. I'm certain I could find some deserving charitable organization who might appreciate a sizeable monetary gift.

Charlie nodded but was still not sold.

Lawton continued. "Chas, there's another factor. I've got clients getting their butts burned by lugs like these guys. You and I might know a few other legitimate business people on the receiving end of various organized crime activities. I have no doubt a couple of these jokers in this very tournament work against my very clients. It would give me great satisfaction to pin these bastards' ears back."

Then he leaned closer and whispered even quieter, "Charlie, I'm not trying for the Good Samaritan award. I simply fell into this opportunity. If I'm on my game today, this could be a milk run. If I'm not on my game, well, I'll have to play some really poor golf not to cover our entry fee from side bets. Judging by what I've been hearing, I can make some individual bets to make up some or all of the entry fee if my team doesn't finish in the top two places out of five teams. And, if my four-man team wins, we split $80,000 four ways. That's some good money to fleece out of these bums."

"Or, an interesting expenditure," Charlie mumbled.

Lawton smiled and looked at the time. It was time to warm up once again. He'd be teeing off shortly. The restaurant manager strolled over to the two of them. Noticing Charlie's chalky complexion…now legitimate… the concerned manager murmured to Lawton, "Is this guy O.K.?"

Lawton looked at his ashen-faced friend and answered quite honestly, "No, not yet…but he'll come around." Then in his most serious tone, he said to the manager, "You know, I believe he needs a big breakfast to balance out the inappropriate amount of liquor he's consumed."

Davis rolled his eyes skyward. His drunken act was over. His current mental anguish was genuine. He didn't really feel like eating anything….that is until Lawton added, "….and put it on Loni's tab."

That relieved both the manager and Charlie Davis. The manager's thumb snapped toward his kitchen cook for one more breakfast order. Davis still looked at his friend as if Lawton was minus a few screws. Yet, before Lawton walked out the exit, Davis called out, "Oh, what the hell, Jamie. That money was meant for risks and by God this is a big one. Play well, my friend, play well."

Lawton was relieved. It was important to have Davis' support. They'd done some crazy things during the course of their friendship. This was just another one. He was about to play golf for the largest amount of money he'd ever played for on any golf course. There wasn't even a close second. He had no idea what the next few hours were going to offer, but he was looking forward to the challenge. He knew it would be a day he'd never forget.

He marched over toward the first tee box very relieved and with renewed confidence. He was ready to take on this gaggle of mobsters and skin them for whatever dollars he could win. He felt a sense of satisfaction that this was a special opportunity to test his competitive fervor...something every skilled golfer wanted.

As he looked around for John Bailey who was going to be carrying his golf clubs that day, Lawton flashed back to that waitress who had located herself so close to the two of them. The thought occurred to him that she certainly didn't seem like a waitress. Her behavior had been so....so different...compared to the rest of the staff. She seemed so uninterested in her work and more interested in what Davis and he had been saying. Scratching his head, Lawton's mind moved over to how she was dressed. The clothing was so ill-fitting. It seemed like he'd seen her someplace before.

After Lawton had left the restaurant, Davis had turned his sights on the same attractive waitress with the ill-fitting uniform. As she filled his coffee cup, he conversed with her as if nothing had happened. He asked her questions relating to how long she'd worked at the Lodge and if she was a local. She answered evasively. Mostly she had a smirk on her face as they talked.

As for the young lady, she had a good idea what was going on at that resort and the backgrounds of many of the tournament participants. She had gathered the two men she'd just witnessed whispering to each other on the floor of the restaurant were definitely not part of the group of mobsters. They were not cut out of the same material. She wondered why they had even gotten involved with a bunch of gangsters. She was convinced they were up to something and chances were good the ending would not be happy. They were just two ignorant dolts involved in something way over their heads. She actually felt sorry for them.

For Lindy MacPherson having been working undercover for the Minneapolis branch of the U.S. Attorney's office for the previous two weeks, she now had an additional quandary...one that involved simple humanity. She had to warn them somehow about the big mistake they were making...or else they might not live through the weekend.

There was something else. Whatever they did have planned, she didn't want them to get in the way of her own plans. Sunday was going to be an important day. Nothing could interrupt the raid on Chippewa Lodge.

CHAPTER

8

Lindy MacPherson was a woman ahead of the times. At twenty-eight years of age in the spring of 1931, she had completed her undergraduate studies in Switzerland and her law degree at the University of Minnesota. She'd also been engaged. Unfortunately, that relationship had ended with the dreadful death of her fiancé a few years before. Immediately upon leaving law school, she was hired by the U.S. Attorney's office in Minneapolis because of her strong interest in investigative work. It was a very choice job especially for a person…male or female…just out of law school.

She'd certainly earned consideration for the job as she graduated in the top five of her law school class. It also didn't work against her that her father was a current Justice on the Minnesota Supreme Court and a personal friend of the head of that U.S. Attorney's Minneapolis branch office, Ernest Lundquist. Her beauty from her mother's side of the family wasn't supposed to matter either…but that didn't hurt her chances of gaining that job either.

Regarding her mother, tragically she had passed while MacPherson was yet in high school. Her father did his best helping his daughter through the process of young womanhood. With the Judge's busy court and social schedule, he often wondered if his parenting effort had any real impact on his daughter. She had a mind of her own and eventually a social and travel schedule that rivaled her father's.

By the spring quarter of her first year at the University of Minnesota, she had persuaded her father into allowing her to continue her schooling in Zurich, Switzerland. Her remaining three years of undergraduate studies kept her in Europe with her father having extended visits overseas during the summers before her junior and senior years.

Upon her return to the U.S., she had little direction to her life. She missed the other side of the water. MacPherson took on insignificant jobs in retail sales in downtown Minneapolis which allowed her plenty of evening social time. She became one of the hot 'Roaring Twenties' females in the Twin Cities social circles often cavorting until odd hours even during the work week. Nonetheless, she was legend in the way she answered the bell each work morning no matter how bleary-eyed she might have been.

In her second year since returning from overseas, she began dating a young man whose father was a prominent agricultural storage contractor responsible for storing and shipping grains from around the Midwest. The young man was twenty-nine and had been moving up regularly and deservedly in his father's business. He and Lindy became engaged during the summer of 1926 but gave no indication of any specific dates for a wedding. It wasn't the love affair of the decade, but the two of them were good friends with well-known, prosperous, and respected family names. Neither of them admitted it, but it was more a covenant of convenience and logic than emotion.

From her time in Switzerland, MacPherson had become fluent in French and could communicate adequately in German and Italian. After her engagement she became more grounded landing some higher quality interviews and meeting prominent business people in the Twin Cities. Her language skills and international experience gave her an edge against other candidates. She was about to accept a job in the fashion industry when a bombshell was dropped in her lap. She knew something was wrong when her father was waiting for her at their family home. He never got home before 7:00. It was almost two hours earlier than his normal schedule.

His words echoed in her head and she felt faint. Her fiancé had been gunned down following a secret union meeting he was asked to attend.

Lindy had known about the problems her fiancé's company was having with the trucker's union and the grainmiller's union. He had been given the responsibility of dealing with the union bosses by his father. Despite the son gaining respect with the union hierarchy, a messy strike ensued. Emotions had been running high. There was plenty of talk that the union bosses were deeply involved with organized crime. That only added fuel to the already incendiary affair.

Her fiancé's body had been found in an alley that morning in north Minneapolis. The strike ended peaceably two days later. He was given much post-mortem credit, although his death was generally lost in the good news regarding the end of the labor dispute. It made his death that much more wasteful and hurtful. There never was anyone indicted for the crime.

When she learned of the death of her husband-to-be, it changed her entire career focus...indeed her very life. Almost overnight the party girl within her disappeared as if medicated. She developed a deep enmity and focus against organized crime. She enrolled in law school that very fall at the University of Minnesota. With her aim to prosecute, her unerring motivation helped her graduate with top honors.

In late 1928 she became the first woman attorney hired at the regional U.S. Attorney's office in Minneapolis. She did not share the initial discomfort in her office that her male counterparts felt. In time she became known for her fearlessness, her attention to detail, and her sound thinking. In her two and a half years on the job, she would gain the respect of her contemporaries as well in the law enforcement community around the Twin Cities.

Most of MacPherson's work was investigations in Minneapolis and St. Paul. She had a couple cases in Duluth on mostly shipping and transportation issues relating to illegal bootleg whiskey. She also was involved in some corporate tax evasion matters. All these cases were of some importance, but they weren't the real high profile cases against organized crime she was hoping to probe.

Her frustration had become quite evident to her boss, Ernest Lundquist. Unfortunately, he was from the very old school. He had acquiesced to Judge MacPherson's subtle request to at least give Lindy an interview. Lundquist had no belief that Lindy would be cut out for the type of work handled by his office. However, in a couple meetings with her, even he couldn't help but be impressed. Her intensity could not be ignored. He sensed not only was she qualified, but her high drive would bring an energy to his office. There was another factor in her being hired. Lundquist was like an uncle; he'd know her since she was a child.

Nonetheless, Lundquist soon learned he had a handful in MacPherson. She was neither the cute little girl he'd know in her formative years nor the frivolous debutante in her college years. He kept trying to define her from the past, but that was no longer valid. He was very uncomfortable assigning any jobs that would put her out on the road. Any cases in the Twin Cities he considered too dangerous would be assigned to others.

Through all this initial adaptation between the older man and the younger woman, she bristled, but remained patient. With the death of her fiancé still aching in her mind, she always volunteered to be involved in any way with gangster investigations. While Lundquist patiently directed her away from these types of cases, she invariably found ways to support her colleagues even without her boss' permission. Lundquist would mutter often that controlling her actions was like steering a horse drawn carriage without the reins.

After a year on the job, she changed her tactics...or at least she'd lost her patience. She became more insistent about getting better assignments...jobs that would give her more worthwhile experience. She argued with him. She sweet-talked him. But, nothing would work to get him to allow her to take on any assignment that smelled hazardous. It was a constant fight between a man approaching retirement age and an energetic, determined young woman biting at the bit to take on larger cases.

It was in the spring of 1931 that Lundquist began receiving information confidentially from an anonymous source about an apparent gambling ring operating in the Lake Minnewaska area near Glenwood, Minnesota. Lundquist didn't think too much about it. In fact, he was inclined to ignore the whole thing. Most definitely he didn't want to waste his staff's time on what he considered some 'sod religious fanatic out in farm country wanting to close down a bingo game at a local church'.

Hearing Lundquist's derisive jokes about the suggested criminal activity with the local and state law enforcement supposedly doing nothing about it, MacPherson chose this to be her case. She emphasized to Lundquist the complete lack of danger in an investigation like this one. She even proposed he let her go undercover to ensure her own safety. Her winning argument was that it would be an easy training mission with not much risk.

Lundquist of course didn't want to send anyone. She persisted. He finally gave in more to get her out of what remained of his hair. He considered it to be a boondoggle for her and a vacation for him from her persistent haggling for better assignments. He agreed to let her set up her own cover for five to seven days during the fourth week of May and find out what she could. He was adamant, however, that she then return to the Minneapolis office.

In his phony rage, he insisted, "God dammit, Lindy, I don't give a flying shit if you find something or not. If you do, call me. I'll call the state patrol and we'll arrest the minister of the God damned church where the bingo games are being played. We've got too many things going on in this city to be wasting time on small cases. So, just go...and for the love of Christ, keep me informed. Now get the hell out of my office."

Normally she would have told her boss she was going to call his wife about his salty language...something she threatened to do since childhood in order to get him to do something for her. It was still part of their personal relationship even at the office, except that MacPherson could belt out some invectives of her own if provoked. More than once Lundquist good-naturedly returned her threats by saying he was going to tell her father about her salty language.

There was another reason Lundquist had decided to give in and let her go on this lesser significant assignment. She hadn't taken a break from office endeavors in over two years. He figured it was a way of forcing her to take a short break.

Within days MacPherson had planned out the cover up she was going to use out in the Lake Minnewaska area as if she was about to meet up with and undermine the entire Midwest mafia organization. Had she known what she was going to find, she may have strategized even more conscientiously. She called on a favor from a local publisher friend. She wanted to represent his travel magazine as her cover story. She rationalized that any resort community like Glenwood would accept free publicity anytime, especially during the tough financial times of the early 1930's. She could ask a lot of questions and not raise many eyebrows.

She left for Glenwood on Friday, May 22 wanting the full weekend to establish her name and cover. Typically, weekends brought rural folks into town to pick up supplies, greet friends and neighbors, attend church, and generally try to seek some enjoyment from their discouraging and hard farm life. It would be a good time to get people talking.

She hadn't realized what Lundquist had made her promise about checking in with him daily. With rural phone coverage being what it was, party lines would destroy any confidentiality in their conversations. What it really showed was how little her boss expected from this investigation.

Arriving late Friday afternoon, Lindy MacPherson checked into a small cabin resort along the lakeshore of Lake Minnewaska adjacent to a place called City Park. Her first impression of the town was frankly quite favorable. She was surprised to see so much activity in the community for being in such a rural, browbeaten area. Instead, there seemed to be a spirit amongst the citizenry. It was as if Glenwood had missed the news about the bad economy.

Another unexpected pleasure was the beauty of the town. The bluffs around the community overlooking the large lake combined for a stunning vista. That first evening as the sun disappeared behind the billowing clouds, she sat on her cabin porch transfixed with the smells and sights around the lake. It made her realize she hadn't taken a full breath of pure life for a long, long time. She laid her head back on the rocker and made a decision right then to do her work, but to take a bit of a break as well. Certainly, Ernest Lundquist wouldn't care. She laughed thinking what a relief it must be for him to have her out of the office for a week.

Saturday morning she strolled through City Park toward the downtown businesses. As she passed, citizens were scurrying about cleaning the grounds. They were obviously preparing for something. One person was repairing the roof of the park gazebo. She figured there was going to be some kind of small band concert that evening. Walking leisurely up to the main intersection, she discovered the Glenwood Café, an obvious spot for local gossip and small talk. Stopping in at the old eating establishment for breakfast, she found that half of Glenwood had the same idea.

A vacant bar stool at the counter gave her a place to order a roll and a cup of coffee. There was a section of the *Minneapolis Star* lying next to her. She was perusing it until she felt a strange silence in the café. She looked up from the newspaper and realized almost every eye in the place was on her. She wondered if she'd forgotten to zip up her skirt. Her hand slipped to that object on her right hip while also checking to see if she'd missed a button on her blouse. Finding her apparel dutifully covering her body, she finally realized the reason for all the stares. She was the only woman in the restaurant except for the waitresses. She'd been eyed before, but not so obviously.

A bit nervous, she discarded the Minneapolis paper and switched to the local rag. It was only eight pages with most of the reports covering the activities planned for the week long annual town celebration beginning the following Saturday, May 30. She was surprised at the length of the festival. This was not one day of gaiety. The affair was to last ten days concluding with something called a 'charity golf tournament' on the weekend of June 6-7. The gala included everything from games and carnival rides, boat races, fishing contests, swimming competitions, food booths, dance contests, band concerts, and various contests relating to pies, cakes, and cookies. It culminated with a Saturday night beauty contest and dance.

MacPherson was impressed. There were plenty of lake communities in the land of 10,000 lakes. She wondered why other towns were not as assertive or progressive as Glenwood. She was amazed that the local townsfolk would take on such a large community project.

Looking up from her concentrated reading, she found the flock of men had finally returned to their own breakfasts and conversations. It was then her turn to examine the people in the café. There was quite an assortment. She gauged that the locals wearing the bibbed overalls were the area farmers and the regular jeans worn by other folks were those who lived in town. Very oddly, there were also six patrons dressed in suits. These six men were huddled in a corner booth. They were the only ones who had given her only a brief overview and then returned to their own private conversation. These men seemed totally out of their element. They were dressed like downtown businessmen seen daily in Minneapolis. Yet, there was still a difference. They behaved slovenly, laughed loudly and didn't care about their noise level. Cigar smoke belched out of that corner booth like a fire had just broken out. They exuded little if any class.

MacPherson found herself repeatedly staring over at this group of men until she realized two of them shot her a wink. She looked back at her newspaper immediately without changing facial expression. That's something she hadn't planned on while under cover. She was a single female in a resort community. There might be various men... whether married or not... who might take an interest in her. She had to do everything to thwart that type of attention. She had a job to do.

She initiated her charade immediately after breakfast. The sooner she got known as a free lance writer for a travel magazine the sooner she could begin her investigation. The mayor's office and the Chamber of Commerce office were her first stops. She wanted to find out where the key resorts in the area were located. From this list she figured to begin finding more information about the purported illegal gambling ring. From there she could assess the severity and decide whether bringing in the state patrol was necessary. For certain, however, she was not going to hurry her investigation. She found herself enjoying the activity in town, the beauty of Lake Minnewaska, and the relaxed accommodations by the water.

Leaving the café she felt naked as she sensed the eyes of every male patron staring at her shape. Her first stop up the street was at the Mayor's office. The Chamber of Commerce office happened to be in the same building. Both secretaries were doing their nails and reading a book. Saturday was obviously a slow day at both offices. She wondered if the weekdays were likely the same.

MacPherson learned that Mayor Charlie B. Good and Bud Bunsen, the head of the Chamber of Commerce, were attending meetings that morning. The secretaries brightened up when she explained her purpose for being in town...that is, to write articles on the resorts around Lake Minnewaska. They were frustrated that neither Mayor Good nor Bunsen was available right then, but implored her to return at lunch time. The Chamber secretary told her, "I've never seen Big Bud miss a meal yet. He'll be back here for lunch before going over to the café."

As for the Mayor's secretary, she also urged MacPherson to return. "Mayor Good would be horrified not to get some quotes in your articles. He never misses a chance to promote our town and our huge ten-day celebration. I hope you'll be able to stick around town for a few days during the festival. People come in from all over."

MacPherson was getting the feeling the long event was bigger than the Minnesota State Fair to these local folks. She asked for and received a list of local resorts. The Chamber secretary, Miss Beatrice Bean, also suggested Lindy talk with the general manager of the local Feed & Grain Mill.

Miss Bean was trying to be overly helpful in her boss' absence. "Miss MacPherson, this man is also our festival chairman. His name is Henry Hanson. He's difficult to track down especially with the celebration being so close and the booth construction beginning this morning down at City Park. He's acquainted with most everybody and everything going on in this town. I don't know a busier man. He also knows all the resorts and can help recommend more people who might be good to interview for your articles."

MacPherson wrote Hanson's name down, but didn't think much about it. She didn't need to talk to some gung ho civil servant about how great this 'festival' was going to be. She was there to find out if any laws were being broken.

Leaving the building, she strolled back down the street towards City Park. It had been just over an hour since she first walked through the park. It was busy then. Suddenly it was buzzing with workers putting up tents and constructing various platforms for booths. Staging was being constructed in front of the gazebo as well.

It was pretty obvious the way into the hearts of the locals was to ask them about their upcoming town festival. She figured no one would be shy conversing about that subject. She approached some workers at one of the church booths and told them about the articles she was writing. They seemed delighted. One of them emphasized how the upcoming gala should be part of her article.

Feeling some comfort with the booth builders, MacPherson tried to stray over to asking about the golf tournament. She queried, "So, what about this charity golf tournament? What's that all about? What's the charity?"

Suddenly the workers showed a greater interest in getting back to work.

She got one answer. One man just looked at his fellow workers and then back at her finally responding curtly, "Yeh, it's quite an event."

That was it. There was no further comment as the men started pounding and sawing. She gave them a friendly wave and moved on not wanting to destroy whatever charisma she was beginning to build in the community.

Thirty yards away she spotted a young man working alone on the roofing materials for the gazebo. She knew at times men were intimidated by her forward manner, but she greeted him nonetheless. In this case, the man on the roof, Nate Morrison, gave her a very pleasant hello. He even came down the ladder to greet her. He'd already heard about the magazine writer in town and that she was a 'good-looker'. It didn't take much for him to guess she was the one.

He seemed quite interested in the magazine she was representing. As they talked, she was impressed how well spoken he was. Morrison was obviously educated, though, dressed as if he was just another farm hand. He was a taller, bonier and she guessed a few years younger than her.

As affable as he was, she found herself feeling uncomfortable. Morrison was asking her more questions about her and her travel magazine than she was prepared to answer.

He then added, "You're darned lucky. A travel magazine...that sounds pretty exciting to me. You've probably been a lot of places."

Lindy nodded, "Yes, I guess it helped that I went to school over in Switzerland. That got my interest in travel."

Nate grabbed a few boards and placed them by his ladder. "So, were you on the Lake Geneva side or the Lucerne and Lugano areas of that country?"

Lindy was slightly awed by his question. "Nate, you sound like you've traveled as well. When were you over in Europe?"

He put one foot on the first rung of the ladder and turned toward her smiling, "Me...travel a lot? Don't I wish? No, I just read a lot and have a good memory. Some day, though, I'll have the time and money to travel in Europe."

Then his voice trailed off and his face got momentarily somber. "Yeh...some day."

She found herself intrigued by this young fellow. She didn't expect to stumble upon someone like him in a small town. She watched Morrison throw the lumber on his shoulder and ease up the ladder. He didn't look strong enough to handle the climb with the wood on his shoulders, but he did it. She caught herself momentarily wondering what it would be like to go out with a person like him brought up out in farm country. There was just something quite natural about him that she liked. She calculated that while he hadn't made too much of a success out of his life so far, she recognized that he had the intelligence and personality to pursue and accomplish some of his dreams.

From the roof he continued inquiring more about her writings and her work for the travel magazine. Though only innocently asking, she found herself having to make up some lies to satisfy his curiosity. To get him off being the interviewer, she switched the subject to that of the charity golf tournament. His tone or manner remained unchanged. He shrugged and told her what he knew...which was not much. Then she found out why.

Morrison explained, "You have to understand that I might not be a fountain of information about the resorts or this charity golf event. I've only been in town since early April to help my aunt out on her farm. I've never experienced this town festival nor do I really know that much about the town. I guess I'm like you. Everything I see and hear about this town is mostly for the first time."

Then he too mentioned Henry Hanson. "Lindy, I do some odd jobs... like this one...for a guy who's in charge of the entire festival. His name is Henry Hanson. Be sure to meet him. He seems to have his hand on the pulse of this community. Besides, he's a real nice guy. The problem is that you have to catch up with him. He'll no doubt be able to give you some background to a lot of these vacation spots around the lake."

She threw a more profound question at the articulate young man just to see if he was playing it straight. "Nate, what makes Glenwood so special? There're a lot of lakes and lake communities around Minnesota. This town seems to have an unusual enthusiasm. It's great to see, especially in these tough times. But, why here?"

Nate just nodded. "You're right. I got the same impression when I arrived in town. I've thought about that question myself. The townsfolk seem to appreciate the special location they have with the beautiful lake and surrounding bluffs. But, I'm seeing certain people in town who step up and get things done. Henry Hanson is one. Mayor Good is another. The minister over at the First Presbyterian Church is another. Even Big Bud Bunsen who doesn't miss a chance to make a buck does a lot of good for the town. All these men seem to spark the citizens to take pride in their community...and get behind this upcoming festival. Everyone hopes the bubble never bursts."

She was about to follow up his last statement with a question about 'what bubble bursting' when a flat bed truck drove up with some more construction material. Nate had to cut the conversation, come down off the roof and unload the truck. His smile was very genuine. "I'll no doubt be seeing you around town, Lindy, if you're going to be here for awhile. I think you'll enjoy your stay. I sure have."

It was refreshing to meet someone close to her age who seemed both civil and intelligent. He was just another example that all the smart people didn't have to live in the city. She then ambled back through the downtown area to buy a sun hat. She stopped by quite a few shops and introduced herself as a travel magazine writer. Again everyone spoke animatedly about the upcoming celebration. Talk of anything else was muted.

By the afternoon she had introduced her 'cover' around town but gotten little information about anything else but the festival. It was only the first day playing her role. She wasn't discouraged. The local folk were approachable and generally pleased she would be writing about their town and resorts. Her last stop that afternoon was to return to the courthouse. She thought it wise to meet the County Sheriff and Police Chief in case she ever needed their help. Besides, maybe they'd be more open about any curious developments in their community.

The Polk County Sheriff had his office adjoining the city police chief's office. The police chief's desk was vacant but someone was dozing in the sheriff's office. She looked in. County Sheriff Clarence Petracek had fallen asleep while playing with what appeared to be a new fishing pole. His feet were propped on a desk full of papers. There was a picture of an alluring girl smoking a cigarette on the wall by his desk. A half-smoked cigar was sitting unlit on a clay ashtray.

McPherson backed up and knocked on the outside door to give him a chance to wake up and recover. "Is anyone in?" she yelled. She could hear the man gasp as he simultaneously got his feet off the desk and his fishing rod leaned back against the cabinet. This move was well practiced.

When the noisy moment transpired, she heard a sonorous voice announce, "Ah....yeh, my deputy must have stepped out. Come on in, ma'am. What can I do for you?"

When Lindy walked in, the County Sheriff stood up and tried unsuccessfully to tuck the front of his shirt into his trousers while offering her a chair.

She ignored his discomfort, sat down and introduced herself. "Sheriff, my name is Lindy MacPherson. I'm a writer for a travel magazine from Minneapolis. I'm here for a couple days to visit some resorts and write about your town. This upcoming celebration seems to be keeping everyone pretty busy."

Sheriff Petracek, listening intently, sat back down and smiled. Though not having expected to see such an attractive female walk into his office, he eventually got his eyes back in their sockets and politely asked if she'd like some water.

She smiled and accepted the offer. Giving her a paper cup with tepid water, he scrunched back into his chair. It fit him like he'd been born in it. Petracek was at least the age of her own father but about forty pounds heavier with most of the weight hanging over his belt.

He comforted himself as if hoping he was about to have a very pleasant conversation for as long as he could stretch it. "Well, welcome, Miss...MacPherson...you say? He looked at her for acknowledgement.

She nodded politely waiting for him to fully recover and get comfortable.

With his posterior finally just right in his chair while fending off a determined fart, he responded, "Yes ma'am. You're down tootin'. The whole town is bustling. The ten-day event actually begins next Friday night and goes through the following Sunday. We attract a lot of people. This has been going on for four or five years. I can't even remember. It keeps getting bigger and bigger."

She smiled hoping to have found someone willing to open up a bit. She stayed away from anything controversial...like the golf tournament...mostly talking about the lake, the farming conditions, and of course the omnipresent festival atmosphere.

Petracek chatted on. "Thank goodness Glenwood has another source of attracting trade besides farmers bringing in their crops to town. Our lake and the resorts still bring in a lot of people during the summer, even in these kinds of times."

She took a chance and asked him a non-travel magazine question. "Sheriff, when you talk about a lot of people, it seems you're already getting some of them coming into town. I wouldn't think many local people would show up in their Sunday best on a Saturday morning to eat a casual breakfast at the local café. You must have some pretty important gentlemen who stay at your resorts."

Petracek repositioned his rear end on the old leather chair hoping that nothing inadvertent might occur. Showing obvious relief that he'd held it, he proceeded to talk around the subject of the well-dressed 'gentlemen' down at the Glenwood Café. "Oh yes, those are just some businessmen in town for some meetings out at Chippewa Lodge. It's one of our nicer properties complete with a nine-hole golf course. I'm certain it'll be one resort you'll hear about again and again during your stay in Glenwood."

MacPherson made yet another note. She had heard of this resort three times already that day. Then she hit the county sheriff with what had become a conversation stopping point. "Sheriff, I heard something about a charity golf tournament on the last weekend of the town celebration. Is that activity held out at the Chippewa Lodge golf course?"

She noted Petracek's eyes beaded on her for just a moment before responding. Then he allowed his face to relax again. After all, he was just talking to a magazine writer who was trying to write a positive article about his community.

"Oh yes, and you should know that there is a small Calcutta that allows players and outsiders alike to put a little money on the outcome. My friend, the local police chief, Rich Brey, and I look the other way because the aim is for the Calcutta to be for charitable purposes. In fact, the First Presbyterian Church Men's Club actually manages it so everything is on the up and up. The Calcutta is a bit more than bingo, but we're allowing it within the broad boundaries of the law."

Then as if to further defend his decision, he scratched his belly and added, "Besides, it's just a once a year event. We don't think we have to raid the First Presbyterian Church or anything like that."

Then he chuckled nervously causing his entire body to shake like a jelly dessert. He was hoping Miss MacPherson might think him witty as well.

She let her eyes light up and flashed her smile. It would make him feel safer talking with her. "Well, that's great, Sheriff. It sounds like the celebration and even your innocent little charity golf tournament bring in people, trade, and money. What a great idea!"

Petracek looked relieved for the third time. MacPherson then changed the subject of the charity golf tournament and asked him some benign questions about some other resorts in the immediate area. That took less than two minutes. She had what she wanted. It made sense that the first resort she was going to visit was the very place this charity golf tournament was taking place. If the gambling accusation was real, she guessed that it could be connected to this 'Calcutta' the Sheriff had just mentioned. It might be innocent enough that her job might be over in a hurry. Yet there was something about the secrecy surrounding the charity golf tournament that sustained her attention.

"Well, Sheriff, you've been very helpful. If the President of the Chamber of Commerce ever resigns, you'd be a perfect replacement. You seem to know a lot about the town. Thanks for your time."

She got up quickly to leave, shook his hand, and marched out the door.

Petracek sat back in his chair going over the entire conversation with the young lady. A local friend had tipped him off confidentially how there might be an investigator in town asking questions about the charity golf tournament. He just didn't expect the questioner to be undercover...and so attractive. He nodded his approval as he watched her walk down the street. Her cover as a travel magazine writer was a masterful idea. Yet, once she made it out to Chippewa Lodge, her safety might come into question. He figured he'd better keep her under surveillance as much as possible by his deputies and the city police force. Even if he was mistaken and she was legitimately just a magazine writer, she being alone as she was would likely need some protection.

The Sheriff looked at his watch. He'd be seeing Chief Rich Brey shortly after he returned from patrol. They were going fishing the next day at Lake Osakis. The police chief would be very interested in hearing that a so-called 'travel magazine writer' had arrived incognito in Glenwood. Petracek also had another person he wanted to pass along this information...that same friend who'd foreseen that an investigator might be coming into Glenwood. Petracek would be seeing Henry Hanson over coffee the next evening over at the Feed & Grain Mill office.

Petracek again scratched his belly and grabbed a snort out of his desk drawer. He looked hopefully again out the window as Lindy MacPherson stopped to talk with some church worker who seemed self-conscious talking to such an attractive lady. The worker heading toward City Park kept looking around to see if anyone was noticing his unbelievable good fortune.

Petracek took a deep swallow out of his desk drawer bottle and wondered if it was happening...that maybe, just maybe, he might be witnessing the first stage of the long nightmare that might be coming to an end. He hoped she'd be as curious as she seemed in his office. Certainly if she had any investigatory skills at all, it would be just a question of time before she made it out to Chippewa Lodge. Once there she would have to notice the odd assortment of 'guests' and their rough, adolescent behaviors. She hopefully might even notice the identities of some of those ruffians and realize the 'guest' list at the Lodge was full of individuals wanted by the law. He would expect her then to take the proper steps to obtain their arrests.

Petracek slowly shook his head once again gritting his teeth over the circumstances he and Police Chief Brey had put themselves in years before. They both rued the day they had gotten themselves too close with the leader of the questionable activities out at the Lodge. They were now vulnerable to both sides of the law...certain reprisal from the underworld if they made any arrests out at the Lodge; certain accusations against the two of them from state authorities for negligence of their duty.

He thought back to how he and Brey had gotten themselves into this no-win situation. The man had walked into the County Sheriff's office just as Lindy MacPherson had just done minutes before. It had been over four years since that meeting. Loni D'Annelli had seemed so friendly and straight up the way he was so complimentary about the town and its natural beauty. He and Brey had coffee with the man only twice when D'Annelli mentioned that he was renting some cabins on a more permanent basis out at Chippewa Lodge. He'd said as president of a union in Chicago he was sending some of his union members out to the Lodge for vacations and to do some work in the area as part of a government contract. While he didn't go into the specifics of the contract, the two officers of the law had already heard about the stroke of luck that had hit the isolated resort south of town. They knew the apparent presence of this Mr. D'Annelli and his 'guests' was not only good for the Lodge, but for the town as well.

When D'Annelli asked them if they'd be willing to be hired for off-hours routine security work out at Chippewa Resort, they saw no reason to decline the offer, especially when the work would not overlap with their normal county and town duties. D'Annelli asked that their employment with him remain confidential. All he wanted was for them to drive by the resort periodically just to make a presence and assure nothing out of the ordinary was happening.

They'd checked him out hoping his story was true, especially given the money he'd offered them to perform the security work. Their investigation on D'Annelli was not as thorough as it should have been. They were blinded by the sound of 'government contract' and the good his long-term rental of cabins at the Lodge was already doing for the town. The clincher was when they'd learned that D'Annelli was talking with certain town leaders and church organizations about helping out with a charity golf tournament being planned at the Lodge nine-hole golf course. The man from Chicago was displaying legitimate interest in the community at large. In short order both Brey and Petracek had enthusiastically accepted the after-hours security job.

The outline of the job had been so easy to handle during their off-hours. They only had to patrol from outside the resort...never having to enter the property. As a result, they heard rowdiness, but they never saw real problems. In time when there were problems stemming from some of the 'guests', the County Sheriff and City Police Chief either looked the other way or brought it to the attention of their employer,

Loni D'Annelli. It was the best course of action. They found D'Annelli dealt with the inconvenience immediately. It made Petracek's and Brey's security job even more uncomplicated...especially as D'Annelli had become such a positive figure in the community.

Over the years since 1927, the two officers of the law tended to relax their surveillances of Chippewa Lodge. They actually didn't want to discover any improprieties. Either way they would receive their monthly paycheck from D'Annelli. It was money they had come to appreciate given their low paying county and city government jobs. In time their job became more of keeping townsfolk from seeing or hearing of anything problematic at the Lodge. They discerned it was in the best interest of the community to minimize difficulties caused by the growing number of D'Annelli 'guests' living at the resort.

Within that first year as private surveillance officers employed by D'Annelli, it didn't take much for them to realize the Lodge had become nothing more than a temporary if not permanent recluse for the mob element. They didn't even want to know the true name of some of the 'guests'.

Both Petracek and Brey had often discussed if they should continue allowing the 'safehouse' to endure at the Chippewa Lodge. They would always end up rationalizing the impact on the town and even on them if they did clamp down. With the hoods sequestered out at the Lodge, the two primary officers of the county and town talked themselves into believing these gangsters were in effect incarcerating themselves and thereby keeping themselves from being a threat to society as long as they remained at the Lodge.

As rationalizations went, this one was as creative and dubious as one could get. It was also self-serving. It was not hard to choose between the monthly check from D'Annelli for performing an empty task of patrolling the Lodge versus facing retribution from both the 'guests' at the resort and the state authorities for not doing their jobs.

In the last two years, Brey and Petracek had come to realize the safe harboring of criminals was only one of many unlawful actions taking place at Chippewa Lodge. They had become aware of the on-going gambling operation at the Lodge, but stayed quiet hoping it wasn't that organized or big time. They trusted Loni D'Annelli not to make the gambling business too obvious.

That discovery left them completely disinterested in patrolling the Lodge area. By the end of 1930, they began to purposely maintain a distance from the resort. Petracek and Brey talked themselves into the belief that by remaining broadly ignorant of the Lodge affairs, though embarrassing, they could claim they simply weren't aware of anything going on at the resort...especially since it was either out of their jurisdiction or their regular patrol area.

When Lindy MacPherson left the Sheriff's office that Saturday afternoon she felt she was making some progress. Chippewa Lodge was the obvious next place she had to explore. As a magazine writer she planned to call the resort manager and arrange an appointment. It would be the professional way to initiate contact.

She wandered back across City Park to her cabin returning friendly greetings from townsfolk as she walked. She stopped for awhile and commented on the progress Nate Morrison had made on the roof of the park gazebo. Word had been spreading about why she was in town. While her effort was considered quite favorable to the town, she also sensed a few looks of concern in the eyes of some of the townsfolk.

By the time she arrived back at her cabin, she noticed a city police vehicle sitting out in front of the rental office. As she stepped up to her cabin door, a much younger and only slightly skinnier rendition of Sheriff Petracek waved at her from the cabin office. He hitched up his pants and approached her. The pants returned to the exact position on his slightly protruding tummy they'd just been. He had a very friendly smile...and sincere. Lindy knew the difference.

"Miss MacPherson....hello....my name is Rich Brey. I'm the police chief of Glenwood. Sheriff Petracek just radioed me and told me about your arrival. To save you time we called the resort manager out at Chippewa Lodge to let him know a travel magazine writer is in town. We knew he'd want to meet you. His name is Darrell O'Donnell."

Lindy thought their contacting the resort manager for her was rather odd, but she showed no annoyance "Well, that's certainly service. Thank you Chief."

He sheepishly grinned at her. "Please...call me Rich. Darrell said he'd be glad to set you up with a room at no cost while your doing your... ah....work in our community."

"You mean writing my article about Glenwood resorts," she said emphatically. The police chief seemed to have hesitated at the wrong time while completing his sentence.

"Of course...your article. He said if you even wanted to stop out late this afternoon he'd be glad to meet with you. You can have the cabin he'd set up for you or stay here in town...whatever suits you."

She shook his hand in appreciation. Brey was surprisingly awkward with her as if he wasn't used to being alone with a pretty woman. He retreated to his patrol car again offering her any assistance she might want.

MacPherson calmly thanked him. As his patrol car whipped up dust, he pulled away with a smile and a wave. She wasn't certain why the Sheriff and the Chief of Police were being so accommodating, but it was nice to be so well received by the law enforcement team in town.

For a brief moment MacPherson wondered if her boss had contacted the local authorities just to keep an eye on her. She wouldn't put it past old Lundquist. But, he didn't know she was going to be in Glenwood until Monday. She doubted he would have contacted anyone until then. Presently it was only Saturday. How would anyone know she was in Glenwood incognito taking on an investigation? She also believed Lundquist wouldn't entrust her cover with anyone...especially the local police. The two officers she'd just met could be involved if there really was an illegal gambling scheme going on.

After the Chief had taken off, she threw off her shoes and sat out on rocker on the small cabin porch. It had become a favorite perch. Being twenty feet from the lake's edge, she had a panoramic vision of the massive lake. Sailboats floated lazily by the shore. A young boy and girl rowed by oblivious to her watching them. They were engrossed in themselves. Down the shore a few children were playing in the lake under the watchful eye of their mothers. The entire picture was that of tranquility.

Lindy MacPherson found the entire scene very inviting. The fresh air off the lake relaxed her body, but not necessarily her mind. It still was on full alert. She'd been in town less than twenty-four hours and already she sensed there was far more happening in this town than a minor gambling ring. Surely local citizens could see it. Why else did their words become very measured if asked about anything beyond the town festival? The two top law authorities in town didn't appear concerned if anything illicit was happening in their community. Yet, some person in town had written an anonymous letter to Ernest Lundquist about some kind of gambling ring. It had to be big enough or bothersome enough to warrant a confidential note.

The other question that had bothered her since breakfast was those fancy suits sitting in the Glenwood Café that morning. They seemed out of place. They drove fancy cars...and they weren't going to any funerals. Somehow those 'gentlemen' had to make enough money to buy those expensive vehicles. As nice as the town of Glenwood was, she hadn't seen any businesses that could support such a life style.

After a short rest, MacPherson traveled out to Chippewa Lodge to see the resort manager, Darrell O'Donnell. She didn't want him to be prepared for their meeting. She wanted to see the resort in its normal routine.

MacPherson, in her government issued Model 'A' Ford, rounded a lake side corner and came upon the isolated Chippewa Lodge property. She noticed the golf course was surprisingly busy for the end of the day on the three holes she could see.

Arriving, she was immediately impressed with the grounds. The landscape was manicured nicely. Though it was a Saturday, there was a grounds crew working out on the golf course.

She drove up and parked in front of the resort office and restaurant. Rather than enter the office, she decided to stroll around the property. Right away she observed the imposing display of the latest automobile models, the likes of which might be seen more at the Minneapolis Golf Club where her father was a member. Walking behind the restaurant to a patio overlooking the ninth green, she found some guests lounging under what was left of the sunlight. Three buxomed women were lying next to some fellows who were decidedly whiter, older, and overweight compared to the shapely females. A few other men were cooking steaks on an outside grill. As she wandered by, one of the guys grilling steaks waved and whistled at her. He yelled out, "Hey babe, come on over and join us. We got some extra meat."

Then he leaned over to one of his friends and said something that made both of them laugh uproariously. MacPherson didn't need any coaching to know his inference. They were the kind of guys who would expect some kind of payment for their generosity.

She ignored the comments and meandered back toward the Lodge office. So far she wasn't awed with the clientele at this resort. She also made note that she saw no families or young kids anywhere.

Entering the foyer of the Lodge, the rustic surroundings included various animal heads hung on the wall. There were also some Native American Indian blankets covering the knotty pine décor along the stairs leading to the second floor. Very comfortable looking animal skin covered chairs and sofas filled the lobby. All of it looked newly decorated. She wondered if this O'Donnell had heard about the seriously depressed economy. Many resorts had to close around the state. Chippewa Lodge seemed to have missed that bit of news.

She strolled into the restaurant where she noted a number of guests playing cards and drinking Canadian whiskey. Still others were just drinking and talking. Again it was mostly middle-aged men with much younger good-looking females either laughing too loudly or sitting quietly by their man. Some of the patrons still wore their ties with suit coats hung over the back of their chair...as if they didn't know how to relax...or they were about to attend a funeral.

Three of the men waved at her as she passed through the restaurant. They didn't make any comments; they just waved as if they knew her but couldn't place her. Then they continued their conversation or returned to their card game.

She circled back toward the lobby when she suddenly heard a female voice from the foyer. It was the desk clerk. She was working the slower Saturday afternoon shift. "You must be Miss MacPherson. Mr. O'Donnell said you might stop out this afternoon. How's your article going?"

MacPherson found herself at a loss for words. She was becoming well known and she'd only been in Glenwood less than a day.

The clerk continued, "I'll let Mr. O'Donnell know you're in the lobby. Please have a chair wherever you'd like. Would you like some lemonade?"

MacPherson shook her head, but thanked the polite desk clerk. "I'll wait for him in the restaurant."

That decision became a mistake within seconds of taking a chair. No less than four slick-haired, well-dressed but sleazy looking men came up to her and introduced themselves.....by their first name only. They were polite, but they got right to the point. Each wondered if she'd like to have a drink in the bar before dinner. Only one of the four men looked her in the face when he offered her the drink. The other three were checking her out from head to toe as they spoke to her.

She declined each one politely saying to them she already had plans. They didn't appear bothered by her rebuff...only that it was just a matter of time. Their brash confidence was almost frightening.

O'Donnell finally came into the restaurant and greeted her causing the wolves to retreat. He was immaculately dressed and pudgy. His manner initially made her uncomfortable as he appeared as nervous as she had become. His handshake felt like she was holding on to a freshly caught walleye. Something told her he would behave. Her body was of little interest to this man. He seemed more concerned about her being legitimately amazed with his resort.

He offered her a drink and again she declined. She wasn't interested in staying another second in that restaurant. Guessing her discomfort, O'Donnell respectfully placed her hand on his arm as he got up from the table. "Well, Miss MacPherson, I'm so happy you could fit our property into your schedule. Shall we take a tour and then I'll give you some brochures about our lovely lakeside resort. Let me show you the main building first and then you can see an example of one of our redecorated cabins."

MacPherson smiled over the formal way the resort manager was taking control of the situation. She allowed herself to be led through the bar area of the restaurant. While O'Donnell was pontificating about the wonderful selections on the menu and the restaurant hours, the eyes of the males in the bar were on her like waves on water. MacPherson felt as naked as the day she was born. She knew they wished she was.

O'Donnell wisely began to speed up his tour through the bar. Lindy tried not to pay attention to the lascivious looks, but she found herself holding O'Donnell's arm more tightly. The aggressive men slacked off as long as O'Donnell seemed to be having business with her.

As the two of them were about to exit the restaurant she did recognize one man. She couldn't help it. His appearance was unquestionable. He was playing cribbage with another man off in the corner. He was concentrating on the game and not on her. When she saw Willie LaCurso play a card, smile cattily, and take a drink, her blood literally boiled. LaCurso had just beaten his opponent. He was used to that experience. She knew him as one of the well-known leaders of the Grain Millers union in Minneapolis. If he hadn't been directly involved in her fiancée's death a couple years before, she figured he knew who was responsible. Her eyes were like daggers as she watched him relax and take another swig of his Canadian beer. For two cents she'd pull the 45-caliber revolver she kept in her purse and shoot the beer glass right out of his hand. With any luck she'd miss and take him out. Her hatred was without boundary. As a professional and very successful gangster, LaCurso was a prime example of the reason Lindy had invested her time in going to law school and why she wanted to work for the U.S. Attorney's office.

The manager of the resort was surprised by the dark look in her eyes as he held the door for her to leave the bar. He expressed concern. "Miss MacPherson, is everything all right, ma'am?

Lindy blinked away her evil stare at LaCurso and altered her look immediately. Smiling radiantly, she responded, "Oh, I'm quite well, Mr. O'Donnell. I was just admiring the glassware in your restaurant."

O'Donnell took the compliment like a young debutante. He was pleased but hadn't ever considered the glasses in the bar to be that special. He shrugged and continued the tour.

As they walked out onto the parking area on their way to the resort golf club, she was greeted with some whistles and a "Hi ya, toots" from some men getting ready to tee off on the first hole. She pretended not to hear concentrating on what O'Donnell was saying about the golf course.

As they passed another group of wolves, she stayed close to the Lodge owner and manager. He seemed very satisfied but showed no inclination to make any move on her. She continued to perceive he was non-threatening especially after he'd gone into detail about the wallpaper, napkin, and tablecloth designs in the restaurant.

She noticed O'Donnell generally behaved obsequiously to the sights and sounds of his guests. He had 'puppet'" written all over his face and behavior. She began to understand why. He was making a lot of money offering his rural lake resort to the likes of the domineering clientele he seemed to be serving. Being insensible to the low-grade characters at his Lodge was a highly profitable method of handling his business. His big spender, no-class clientele had gotten used to his unawareness.

O'Donnell's pride in his business was obvious. He wanted to show her the best of his property because as a travel magazine writer, she could influence potential vacationers. He had to plan ahead in case his present clientele suddenly left his secluded resort with a bunch of unpaid rooms and future vacancies.

As they continued the tour, the resort manager showed relief that she took no apparent offense to the insufferable 'guests' at his Lodge. He just trusted that as an attractive woman, she was used to the whistles, loose talk, and male advances.

She saw a few more 'guests' as O'Donnell and she walked out onto the beautiful golf course. While O'Donnell gave a short history of the golf course, she paid no attention to him. A few of the men she saw in the bar were on the 'rap' sheet that was passed around her office each week. She swore a man marching down the first fairway was Bobby 'The Noose' Lewis, a murderer and escaped convict from Stillwater Penitentiary. He hadn't been seen since he was missing from roll call six months before. Playing with him in the same group was Eddy Marina, a right hand man to Willie LaCurso. Marina was known for doing a lot of LaCurso's dirty work. He'd never been convicted of anything, but the skin on his hands seemed to have a blood red tinge.

Seeing these 'guests' exchanging pleasantries with one another turned Lindy's stomach. They were behaving like any normal law abiding citizen as well as enjoying the good life at the secluded, bucolic resort.

MacPherson thought how she could make one telephone call to Ernest Lundquist in the Twin Cities and he'd have the state authorities surround Chippewa Lodge by nightfall. She could make this resort into a ghost town before the church bells rang the next morning.

Yet, she kept her patience. If Lewis and Marina rented cabins at Chippewa Lodge, no telling what other things she might discover. An even greater number of arrests and convictions might be at stake. She had another week in Glenwood. Why not use it to gain more needed evidence.

O'Donnell was talking on…something about the collaborative efforts between the townsfolk and the Lodge. She tried to re-connect, but ended up only staring at the easily deceived owner of the resort. She wondered if he had any idea of the potential charges that could be brought against him by the Bureau of Investigation. She had a feeling harboring criminals was not his worst offense. Somewhere along the line in the previous couple years he'd had to decide if the revenue was worth running a safe house for this type of clientele. By the surroundings, the answer was pretty clear.

She kept reminding herself that her purpose for coming to Glenwood was to settle the issue of possible illegal gambling. From what she'd gathered in just one day of minor investigation work, if there was illegal gaming going on, it would likely be at this very site. Yet, except for the private card games with money on the table, she saw no hint of serious gambling going on, even though she wished that bastard LaCurso could be arrested playing cribbage with another gangster for two-bits a game.

Nonetheless, she sensed she was on the right track. It meant she now faced another problem. If Ernest Lundquist had any idea his young upstart might be uncovering something big enough to involve the underworld, he'd pull her away from Glenwood faster than his follow-up call to the state police or Bureau of Investigation. Lundquist would have law enforcement people at the resort in the next hour. They would likely catch some outlaws, but miss out on what she considered was the bigger picture. There were larger fish in the pond. She just knew it. It left her little choice but to be coy. She wasn't ready to give up her investigation. She was finally doing something she'd been intending to do since she joined the U.S. Attorney's office.

By the end of O'Donnell's tour, he'd persuaded her to stay free of charge in one of the newly renovated cabins away from the noise and hubbub surrounding the patio. He admitted to her that she might want to stay clear of the patio that evening. As he said, "Things can get unruly out there on a Saturday night."

MacPherson accepted the invitation with only slight concern about her safety. She was more focused on the opportunity to gain more evidence. Besides, if she felt at any time her welfare was in question, she had a weapon in her purs, and a history of being able to take care of herself. She could head back to her lakeside cabin by City Park at any time.

She drove back into Glenwood to gather some clothing and beauty aides for her night at the Lodge. There would be dinner at the restaurant with O'Donnell. She could then observe more of the 'guests'. Never did she consider she was being too cavalier in her role as a writer for a travel magazine.

At 7:30 she returned to the Lodge and checked in. She was in her cabin less than five minutes when there was a knock on her door. A messenger was there offering her dinner at whatever time she found convenient. The message was from someone called Sammy. He failed to mention his last name. The pure brazenness of the invitation was appalling to her. She controlled her irritation and told the messenger she already had a dinner engagement that evening. Upon further consideration, she realized she should have been more graphic in her rejection. She wasn't prepared for what happened in the next twenty minutes. Apparently word had spread about her staying at the resort. What ensued was the largest supply of attack wolves she'd been around since her last regional law enforcement national conference two years before.

Some of the men sent the same messenger inviting her to a round of golf the next morning, drinks in the bar, and one blatant suggestion at 11:00 that evening that left no question as to the preferred result. Her denials got more pointed and less patient with each response. She finally stated 'no'...plain and simple... before other offers were introduced to her.

Still another messenger tapped at her door. Her patience gone, she told the poor victim at the door if he knocked one more time with one more invitation, she'd blow his hand off his arm with the revolver she had in her purse. That curtailed any further pursuits from the various male 'guests' until she left for dinner at the Lodge.

At 8:15 she called O'Donnell's office and asked if they could move up their 9:00 dinner engagement to 8:30. He was momentarily perplexed like any high-strung person might be, but he recovered enough to agree to the new time. They met in the foyer lobby ten minutes later and he escorted her into the restaurant. They took a corner table away from the people singing around the piano and the drunks at the bar.

The two of them were barely seated when she began receiving unordered drinks. O'Donnell behaved as if he wasn't surprised and said or did nothing to reduce the pesky attempts to win her favor by the many males in that restaurant. O'Donnell's unwillingness to do anything about the blatant interruptions only served to reduce whatever limited respect she'd had for the resort owner. Hurrying through dinner, she gained little worthwhile information about the activities at the Lodge between the continued interruptions and her interest in getting away from the pusillanimous O'Donnell.

After dinner, Lindy had O'Donnell accompany her to her cabin as if it was expected. However, the expectation was not for after dinner drinks at her cabin, but more for her safety. O'Donnell seemed to understand. He politely wished her a good evening, shook her hand, and departed.

Upon entering her cabin she immediately felt uncomfortable. She pulled her revolver out of her purse and checked the bathroom, window latches, and front door bolt before readying herself with a pillow and a book. She placed her revolver under her pillow and began to relax as a light rain began to pelt the roof. She was about to fall asleep when she heard gruff voices in the parking lot outside her cabin. It sounded like a fight was breaking out. She grabbed her revolver just as an urgent knock at her front door echoed within the cabin. Throwing on her robe and with her gun camouflaged, she opened her cabin door slightly to the smiling bloody face of one of her intoxicated paramours. He grinned at her like he was the winning lion. That was the point she'd had enough. She brought her weapon out from behind her body and placed it two inches from the man's face right between the eyes. His eyes actually crossed looking at the barrel.

She said to him, "Cowboy, put your thoughts back in your pants or part of your brain will be lying out on the parking lot."

The drunken suitor didn't say a word. He just turned around and yelled drunkenly, "Manny, you son of a bitch, you said she liked me!"

Then he disappeared into the night.

The other man appeared out in the parking lot. His voice was heavy. He was half in the bag as well. He said, "Ma'am, my friend won't be bothering you anymore this evening. He was not your type anyway. How's about you and me getting a little drink together and get to know each other."

The bruised man had come in second in the fight for the right to seek her favor. She gave the man credit for audacity. She could see some humor in the situation, but it was getting out of hand. She walked outside with her gun pointed right at the chest of the drunken hooligan and laid into the dazed romantic with a verbal onslaught that made his eyes widen. MacPherson could not believe the words she was using that flowed so freely from her lips. The man named Manny was so dazed, he turned immediately and shuffled back toward the restaurant.

As he left, the wasted bum showed no resentment toward her. He just called back, "From what you just said, I guess that meant 'no' for tonight. Is that right?"

Getting no response from her, he added, "Don't be disappointed, sweetheart, I'll try again tomorrow when you're in a better mood."

A confident man to the end thought Lindy. But, she was at wit's end. The man named Manny and every other lowlife at the resort were not going to get any more chances. She was through with Chippewa Lodge for that night and any other night.

MacPherson went back into her cabin and gathered her belongings in less than a minute. She'd had enough of this out of control fraternity party. Carrying her small suitcase in her left hand, she crept out of her cabin literally with her revolver drawn in her right hand. She was going to shoot her way out of the Chippewa Lodge property if required.

The rain was still dripping as she marched towards her Model 'A' Ford. The sound played with her mind…as if there were many footsteps approaching her. She stopped suddenly and glanced in all four directions. It was too quiet. Suddenly she was scared. She was vulnerable beyond anything she'd ever faced. There was a recklessness and lawlessness at this small resort. Bodily harm was one thing, but somehow she felt her very life was not that important to the guests at the resort.

Just that thought made her seethe with anger. She took her weapon and began shooting at random. When she ran out of shells, she re-loaded as fast as she had been trained. She emptied her revolver again as she swore a blue streak into the night air. Any male within a quarter mile of her was either on the ground protecting himself or no longer interested in the crazy female shooting her pistol at random out in the rain.

Then all was quiet again. For one brief moment she felt safe. Checking out the backseat and finding it empty, she scrambled into her car. She peeled out of Chippewa Lodge knowing there were more than a few eyes on her. However, those eyes were likely so inebriated she wouldn't be recognized if they saw her the next day. She raced down the lake side road and made it back to town in half the time it took her to get to the resort. She was literally shaking…and still red with anger. She would remember that night for a long time. Whatever was behind the free-for-all at that resort, she was more determined than ever to find it.

Back at the safety of her cabin, she felt as if she was in a different world…and a preferred one at that. She sat on her small cabin porch next to City Park and the large dark and peaceful lake listening to the din of people conversing within a two block radius of her location. The rain had curtailed the usual Saturday night street dance, but no one wanted to go back to their homes...especially the younger people. They weren't about to end a Saturday night so early. She could relate to that feeling, but felt strangely older. It was as if her own time to enjoy innocent conversations with eligible males was long past. She tried to remember the last time she'd placed herself in that type of social situation. She couldn't recall.

MacPherson laid her head back on the rocker and just watched the light rain. She was alone and content, but still slightly on edge. The revolver was still in her lap. If anyone had approached her while she sat on that cabin porch, her nerves were frayed just enough that they might be staring down the barrel of a still smoking gun.

A half hour later the soft rain had stopped and the moon was peaking through the clouds. She'd fallen asleep on that rocker and had become chilled. Leaving her rocker, she went inside her cabin and bolted the door before going to bed. She made certain the safety was on before slipping the 357 magnum under her pillow. She found herself needing to remain in contact with the weapon as she lay there in the bed. Eventually the fresh smell from the lake atmosphere calmed her and she fell asleep.

Police Chief Brey was patrolling the town that Saturday night... especially paying attention to the young folks disappointed that the street dance had to be cancelled at City Park because of the rain. With time on their hands, mischief could break out. Brey had called for more deputy reinforcement. The more police on duty, the less likely any tomfoolery might break out. He also made certain he or one of his deputies drove by the young lady's cabin at least hourly. He was relieved to see MacPherson's vehicle parked by her cabin at 10:30 as well as her sitting out on the porch enjoying a relaxed evening.

Henry Hanson upon hearing about the young magazine writer earlier that afternoon had re-emphasized to Brey and Sheriff Petracek the need to make certain her safety was never in question. Hanson made it sound like he didn't want any bad public relations to be the result of her running into the wrong type of people. The police chief and county sheriff knew exactly his meaning.

The next morning MacPherson awoke much later than normal. Her hand was stiff from being clamped around the revolver under her pillow. It was 8:00 and already she was hearing the church bells chiming at various locations in the community. She arose and opened her patio door to a rising sun shining on the blue-green lake. The water was so calm walking on the water seemed possible. The atmosphere was so unlike the uproarious previous evening.

She slipped out the door to the rocker...hoping no one would see her in her nightclothes. It seemed worth the gamble. She snuggled into the rocker letting the warmth of the morning sun cover her like a blanket. She had to be careful she didn't fall back asleep. Rocking on her chair she watched the last of a light surface fog across the east side of the lake gradually disappear.

There was something very intoxicating about the town and the beauty of Lake Minnewaska. While she couldn't quite imagine living in Glenwood, there were parts of it...even after just a day...that were quite appealing. She thought back to the previous day pondering how well her 'cover' was working out. It was giving her great access to people, but she was also becoming too visible. She pondered whether she was being too friendly. She blamed the locals; they were so approachable. Yet, like dousing a candle, she knew she could shut down a friendly conversation instantly with mention of the charity golf tournament.

MacPherson was already being called 'Lindy' by many of the people setting up tents or otherwise working in City Park. She looked forward to another week and judged that she needed to use her short term notoriety to more advantage. There were plenty of people needing help to get ready for the festival. It played into her hand to get closer to the locals. More information might slip out. 'Besides,' she thought, 'helping out might be kind of fun.'

And that's what she did. She started that Sunday morning and each morning after having breakfast at the Glenwood Café. Then she strolled over and got involved in helping church groups set up their booths in City Park. She typically found the industrious Nate Morrison working on the gazebo roof or staging area. Between covering for Henry Hanson at the Feed & Grain Mill and committing to the repair work on the gazebo, he was running behind. That Sunday noon, people in the park saw her chatting away and standing on the ladder handing some tools back and forth for Morrison as he completed his work.

In the early afternoon, a flattop truck from Big Bud Bunsen's General Store drove up into the middle of City Park. On the truck were refreshments supplied by the store owner...coffee, coke, water, and cinnamon rolls. She accepted a coke and roll and sat down by two ladies she'd not met. They were sewing quilts while their children played near by. The ladies expressed appreciation for her getting her hands dirty for the good of the town, though as one of them commented, "Hope you don't smudge the paper for your articles."

MacPherson smiled still struck by her relative celebrity since arriving in town. She sat on a park bench with the ladies avoiding any controversial issues until a 1930 Bugatti Drophead Coupe drove by City Park. Absent-mindedly she commented, "My, I surely see a lot of fancy cars driving around Glenwood. That's very impressive for such a small town."

Immediately she sensed she'd gone too far. The two ladies appeared flustered. Both suddenly got up saying they needed to go check on their children. Suddenly, MacPherson found herself sitting on that park bench alone.

The remainder of the afternoon she divided her time between lounging on the lake by her cabin, going for a swim, and periodically sauntering back through City Park to talk with more people. She made no comments about anything relating to Chippewa Lodge. Some folks working on the Methodist food booth invited her out on one member's sailboat later that afternoon. The folks working on the Church of Christ booth prepared her a small basket of food for the evening. People seemed to bend over backwards being friendly to her as they'd heard she was alone while working on her magazine article.

She didn't get back to her cabin until after seven o'clock from sailing on Lake Minnewaska. At dusk she had dinner alone at the Glenwood Café and then returned to the comforting arms of her porch rocker. She read and watched the lake become quiet as a love poem. Sunday had been quite the opposite of the previous day. She'd been in Glenwood two days and was falling in love with the lake lifestyle despite her experience at the Lodge.

She slept like a lamb that night still with the revolver under her pillow. She was relieved none of the wolves from the resort had come prowling for her. She needn't have worried. With Sheriff Petracek, Chief Brey or their deputies making periodic checks on her cabin day and night, most of those 'guests' knew better than to cause any potential problems in town by stalking any young woman. Besides, there were other women out at the Lodge.

By Monday morning Lindy MacPherson's pathway over to the Glenwood Café for breakfast felt as comfortable as a habit. People greeted her on the street like she was a local. The big festival was but five days away... as was her assigned time in Glenwood. It suddenly felt like her investigation would fall behind if she let herself relax too much. Furthermore, she had another challenge to handle that day. She had to decide what if anything she wanted to report to her boss. If Ernest Lundquist thought for one moment she might be in danger, her assignment would be over and he would order her back to the Twin Cities.

It was obvious to her she had to mitigate any findings she had so far. While she might be moving closer to the mystery surrounding the illegal gambling rumor, much more evidence was needed if arrests were going to be secured. She shrugged. Lundquist didn't expect much from her investigation anyway.

That morning she decided her next target was going to be the one man the townsfolk held in such high esteem...the chairman of the festival, Henry Hanson. His name was written at least ten times in her notes since she arrived. She had figured to run into him sometime Sunday, but no one could point him out...almost as if they didn't expect to see him on the weekend. That seemed strange to her. Why would such an important man in town not be in town with the big event only days away?

The café was not as busy that Monday morning as it had been on the weekend mornings. People were involved in their normal week day schedules. She took a seat on a stool at the bar as one of the waitresses greeted her. "Morning Lindy, how's your article going?" MacPherson had never seen the woman before.

Her response had become routine. "Fine...thanks for asking." Coffee was put in front of her and the waitress waited for her order and apparently a more complete response. MacPherson tried to be pleasant. She added, "I wrote a bit more last night. It's going just swell, thank you. I don't want to go too fast. It'll just mean I have to leave too soon."

The waitress was pleased that such an apparent well-traveled travel magazine writer would admit to liking the town. MacPherson's order was given to the cook and then the waitress brought over the newspaper. A little kindness went both ways. MacPherson wondered how the people would feel if they knew her true purpose in town.

Sipping her coffee and reading the headlines, she hardly noticed a quiet man with clean overalls and a collared shirt strolling into the now mostly empty Glenwood Café. One of the waitresses addressed him. "Morning John....you want the usual."

He nodded and gave her a sincere but short nod while she poured him a cup of coffee as he sat at the counter. The waitress didn't bother to ask what he wanted. She just wrote his order down and slung it at the cook. Then she added, "Didn't see you this weekend. You missed all the building going on out at City Park. There was a lot of food. I figured you and Adam would be there."

The man cleared his throat and offered what sounded like a lame excuse. "Too busy...couldn't get off the farm." Then he took his coffee and moved over to a booth away from the talkative waitress at the counter.

Lindy noticed he didn't wear bib overalls. He admitted to being a farmer yet he was dressed in clean jeans and a collared shirt. He also spoke and carried himself with a bearing gained from people respecting him. There was something about this man that was more impressive than other men in town. This man was just a bit taller...or at least he stood more erect. She watched as he accepted some cream and sugar for his coffee from the waitress. He was cordial and made her feel comfortable with a few quiet words. They both smiled as she walked away. All indications were they'd known each other for a long time.

The local man named John looked to be older than MacPherson. She suspected him to be about forty given the lines on his face and his brown-tanned skin. He might have been younger, but she was used to people looking older than their years given the troubled times.

But, there was something else about him. There was an attentive flicker in his eye as he rapidly read over the headlines of the newspaper, then slowed when an article caught his attention. While low-keyed, he seemed like a very intelligent...and pleasant...man. She couldn't remember describing any male as pleasant.

He read the paper with intense concentration. He rarely looked up except to find his coffee cup. When he finished his newspaper and breakfast, he didn't waste anymore time sitting. He slipped out of the booth and reached into his pants pocket unconsciously for a tip and some money to pay his check. MacPherson was almost disappointed as the man hardly noticed her as he passed her on the way to the cash register. While waiting for the cashier, he looked around nodding his head at some people in another far booth. When he finally saw her, he didn't give her the once over like most males. Instead he touched the brim of his cap and said, "Good morning." That was it. She figured he was the first person in the town who didn't know she was a magazine writer.

He paid his bill and left the café without looking back. She decided he was a man she would classify as ruggedly handsome. He looked like he wouldn't make a disrespectful move on a female in a million years.

Meandering over to City Park ten minutes later, MacPherson began talking to some Presbyterians building something called the First Presbyterian Church Men's Club 'Calcutta' stand. She should have been paying more attention, but her thoughts were on other things. She asked one of the workers about the man she saw that morning at the café. She described him as a taller man with a very pleasing manner. She added, "I never saw him this weekend, but he seemed to be well known in the café. I believe his name was 'John'.

A local grocer named Hornbacher working on the booth shook his head and put his hammer down while wiping the sweat from his brow. "Miss MacPherson, I believe I know who you mean. You'll hear nothing but good things regarding that man from anyone in town. He put our town on the map after the 'Big War'."

Then Mr. Hornbacher's voice lowered. "He also had something very tragic happen in his life a few years back."

The man paused again without disclosing the tragedy. Then he continued haltingly, "Anyway, John and his son Adam are highly regarded in this community. His full name is John Bailey. He has a farm on top of the bluff east of town. He is one man who is always there for any person when they are down on their luck. He's not a rich man, but he's one of most generous men I know. And that's all I want to say."

Then Mr. Hornbacher frowned sadly and went back to pounding nails.

Lindy stayed quiet and moved on. A warm compliment followed by a dreadful and brief comment left no doubt there was a lot more to the John Bailey story. She tried two other locals working in the park and got a similar response. The way people's faces went from warmth and respect to melancholy when commenting about Bailey made her stop inquiring. She had her investigation to concentrate upon.

Her quest that morning was to find Henry Hanson. Everyone claimed they had seen him, but couldn't recall where. It fully amazed her that so prominent a local man could be so ghost-like in such a small town. Some guaranteed the Mill was a sure fire way to find him if she was willing to wait for an undisclosed amount of time. His car was described to her. When she didn't see it in the Mill parking lot, she changed her plans to travel to a few other Lake Minnewaska resorts... just in case they could be the center for any illegal gambling.

What she found were properties barely surviving. Not one resort was even close to solvency compared to the more prosperous Chippewa Lodge. Not one property had even one 'fancy' vehicle in its parking lot... to say nothing of harboring criminals or selling possible illegal bootleg whiskey on the premises. By the latter afternoon she was back at her Lake Minnewaska cabin. She saw no reason to focus her efforts on anything but Chippewa Lodge. She had to figure a way to get under the mysterious silence surrounding the upcoming charity golf event.

Before dinner she gave one more attempt at locating Henry Hanson. She'd already heard some kidding remarks about Hanson...but all said with respect. The standard joke was how Henry managed the Mill in his spare time and never on the weekends. She learned that the man was out of town most every weekend. In the words of the locals, "he was likely answering his voracious appetite for travel and to see some female friend."

MacPherson heard some women in the park with crinkled foreheads comment about his missed appearances at the Sunday worship service at the First Presbyterian Church. Those same ladies fretted that it just wasn't right that he didn't attend his own church services since he was a deacon and treasurer of the church Men's Club.

MacPherson had to walk away from those nosy, small town minds. Classic small town observations...like someone missing church... made Lindy roll her eyes and accept that there was good and bad no matter where one lived. Glenwood had its share of people with vapid prejudices as well.

She made her way across the main highway to the Feed and Grain Mill. It looked no more unique than any other grain elevator in Minnesota. Opening the office door quietly, she slipped through the door opening so as not to scare the ghost-like Henry Hanson if he was in. Her heart leaped for a second as she saw a person sitting by an unneeded wood stove with his legs propped up reading a travel magazine. Then she saw it was Nate Morrison. She'd heard he watched the Mill in Hanson's absence. MacPherson let out a disappointed sigh.

Morrison was nonetheless pleased to see her. "Hey...how are you doing this afternoon, Lindy? How's the article going?"

That question was going to follow her around throughout her stay in Glenwood like a bad cold. Forcing herself not to roll her eyes, she patiently nodded. "Just fine, Nate. You finished with the gazebo or you just taking a break?"

He was comfortable with her. "Nah...I'll be working on that gazebo right up until this Friday night as I find the time. I do have to do some work for pay here at the Mill. I'm not independently wealthy like you magazine writers.

The teasing comment made her smile. She thought, 'If he wasn't five years younger maybe' But, he was destined just to be her friend.

Unfazed by her silence, he added, "Actually, you're right. I guess I am taking a break. I like reading all of Henry's travel magazines. Someday I'll go to some of these places."

She smiled again. It was the third time he'd mentioned his dream of travel in the short time they'd met. "Nate, I'm looking for Mr. Hanson. Have you seen him around town?"

"Lindy, you'll be lucky to find him. And call him 'Henry' or no one will know who you're talking about. As to where he is, it could be a number of places. He told me he got in late last night. I've got a feeling he's out at the Lodge. The Presbyterian group is building a 'Calcutta' booth out there as well and he has to train his volunteers how to take the wagers. I know he also has a meeting with some friends of his, the Sheriff and the Chief of Police. Those three guys seem to spend a lot of time together early in the morning or in the evening. The two law officers plus John Bailey are by far his best friends in town."

Morrison thought for a moment. "You know, based on the way he looked this noon, Henry could just be home taking a nap. He's been pretty tired lately...apparently a lot on his mind."

Lindy was unexpectedly learning a lot about Hanson. The connection amongst the four men Morrison had just referred piqued her attention. Petracek, Brey, Hanson, and Bailey were four well-known men in the community...literally leaders by virtue of their position or reputation...and they knew each other very well. Any of the four,' she thought, 'would likely have a very in-depth perspective.'

She interrupted, "So, Nate, is Henry going to be back at the Mill at all today?"

"Nah. If there is any paper work, he'll do it late at night when he can't be interrupted. He's kind of relying on John Bailey and me to handle some of the day to day stuff at the Mill until the festival is over. Of course, then he plans on taking one of his extended vacations like he does every June. There's no question this guy keeps a hell of a timetable for a small town Mill manager."

It was a statement that got MacPherson's mind working overtime. After dinner at the café, she wandered over to City Park where people were only pretending to be working on various festival projects. They looked tired. The pre-construction for the upcoming festival also acted as a social center for the volunteers. People were milling around enjoying some refreshments that seemed to just appear thanks to Big Bud Bunsen.

That Monday evening, she ended up helping the Lutheran's pitch two tents. Mostly she just talked with them about their lives in the town and their attitudes about the politics and economic woes across the country. She didn't press them on anything related to the Lodge.

Back at the cabin later, she squirmed into her rocker on the porch watching the sun fade below the horizon. She hadn't felt this free since her student days in Switzerland. Coincidentally, that was the last time she'd been truly on her own. While sitting on the porch she observed a county or city police vehicle drive by her cabin. The deputy simply waved and moved on. It gave her a sense of safety. She slept that night with the revolver in her suitcase.

MacPherson awoke Tuesday not believing she'd been in Glenwood for three full days. It seemed longer. With four days before the opening of the town's lengthy festival, she found herself caught up in the town's excitement. Yet, she'd forgotten to check in with Ernest Lundquist the previous day. He'd give her hell even though his furor would be all an act. He'd argue that she'd promised...his only real concern was for her safety on this lone assignment. Certainly her report could not be detailed, but she had to concoct some story that would elevate the importance of her remaining at Lake Minnewaska.

Arriving at the Glenwood Café that morning, MacPherson was greeted by the same waitress. Doris brought her coffee and the newspaper including a thoughtful welcome. "Good Morning, Lindy, I hope you're enjoying your stay in town...and your article is moving along."

Lindy responded good-naturedly, "Well, good morning to you, Doris. Yes, folks in the town are great and my work is coming along. Thanks for asking."

Relying on her memory, Doris asked, "Sweetie, you want the same order... two eggs over easy and wheat toast like you had yesterday?"

Lindy was impressed and even gratified with the waitress's recall. "Yes, Doris, that would be just fine."

Then, as if on cue, in walked John Bailey with his copy of the *Minneapolis Star* under his arm. Doris called out to him, "Morning John, honey. I'll get your coffee in just a second."

He nodded and took a seat at the counter with the booths mostly filled. There were a few more people seated at the bar, so he was forced to sit next to MacPherson.

She said sweetly, "I'll move my newspaper so you have some room."

He acknowledged her friendliness with a nod. "Thank you, Miss." Then he spread out his own paper and got lost in the front page.

Lindy stared at her coffee. John Bailey was difficult to break into his mold. She wondered if a hammer would work, since the man certainly didn't need another friend.

The silence was uncomfortable…at least for her…until John Bailey put down his newspaper and put some cream in his coffee. He turned slightly toward her and gave her another affable smile. His first words floored her. He said calmly, "So, you want to talk to me, but you don't know where to begin…is that the deal?"

She laughed. He smiled. "Mr. Bailey, how did you know?"

Without an introduction John continued, "Miss MacPherson, the talk around town is that you'll be writing a very nice article about our lake community. You're talking with everyone you can. So far, you've missed me. So I figured you wanted to break the ice at some point. Now's as good as later. So, go ahead. Let's talk…but call me John."

His warmth and straightforward manner were disarming and refreshing. She dispensed with a formal introduction and replied, "Thank you… John…and my name is Lindy. I did want to talk with you. I understand you've lived here for quite a few years. You have some background on some of the resorts around the lake…and no doubt how the festival got started as well. Can you give me some of your thoughts and how you've seen the town change?"

She congratulated herself. Nothing she'd just said should cause him to hesitate.

He didn't respond directly but went off on his own track "So, Lindy, I've been hearing you've been busy helping folks down at City Park. You probably know more than you're admitting, but I'll offer you a few tales of our town. Maybe that'll help you."

For the next twenty minutes, he contributed stories about the community that were both interesting and funny. He told of how Big Bud Bunsen started his General Store and had built it into one of the better businesses in the area. He also added some yarns about a couple other resorts including the small one she was staying a couple blocks away. But, he never brought up anything regarding Chippewa Lodge.

When she did ask him about the Lodge, he did get quieter. "I don't go out there much, but my son caddies for one of the big wigs at the charity golf tournament. It's a good week for my boy. He does some odd jobs out there as well. Sometimes I can't believe the money he brings home for the work he does. He can hardly wait for the ten-day festival to begin. That's when that big wig stays the whole week along with a lot of his friends. I swear Adam will make enough to pay for his first year of college because of his work at the Lodge."

Then John stopped talking. She asked him a follow-up question about the charity golf tournament. The silence continued as he looked at his watch and mumbled, "Yeh, I guess some folks have fun betting a little money on the golf tournament, but I don't go in for that type of stuff."

Then he shut down and appeared ready to end the discussion.

Lindy had learned. She promptly changed the conversation to talk of his son, Adam. The maneuver worked. Bailey talked generally about his son even though he knew he'd been tricked. "Miss MacPherson, you'll probably want to talk with my son as well for your magazine article. He spends more time out at the Lodge than almost any other local citizen. The problem you'll have is finding him this week, or even next week. He leaves the farmhouse for Chippewa Lodge daily as early as 6:00 now that he's done with high school. There will be nights he won't be getting home until close to midnight. When he's not caddying at the Lodge golf course, he tells me he's being constantly asked to do favors for many of the 'guests'. They don't want to come into town, so they send Adam for supplies at Big Bud's place. Those fellows throw my son their keys and give him money. They tell him to keep the change. I saw him last evening driving through town in a new 1930 Packard. He waved at me and started laughing as he drove by. In his hand he was holding some medication from the apothecary. Somebody out at the Lodge must have gotten ill...or had too big of a previous night."

Lindy grinned at his quip. She found John Bailey to be an intriguing man. There was a quiet stature about him that made him a typical Minnesota farmer. Yet, he had a comfort and confidence in his bearing... as well as a gift for telling a story. She could tell when he was coming to the punch line because his eyes carried a mischievous glint. She couldn't help but laugh. He seemed pleased he could get that reaction from her. Yet, when he waited for her next question, there was a slight melancholy in those same eyes.

She sensed a valued friendship with self-styled Bailey while she was in town. His experience and knowledge of the community could be helpful. With her budding friendship with Nate Morrison, she figured she had at least two males who were comfortable around her...maybe four counting Sheriff Petracek and Police Chief Brey. Most other men in the community behaved nervously with her as if she might ask them some questions they didn't want to answer.

Bailey finally slurped the last drop of his coffee and announced he had to get back to the farm. Tipping his cap, he wished her a good day. There was no attempt at suggesting any further contact. He showed her the utmost of respect. She momentarily smirked at herself. If she was the sensitive type, she might have been disappointed with his lack of interest. It occurred to her she hadn't met very many matter-of-fact and self-assured fellows back in the Twin Cities compared to John Bailey.

Again she centered herself that Tuesday at City Park working with people and generally just conversing with them. For an investigator it was a wasted day. For one who needed a break from her work, it was another shot of fresh air. The day ended with her reading and relaxing on her cabin porch enjoying the view of the lake. There was a small part of her that felt guilty for not being more assertive in her investigation. That day it was a very small part.

The next morning was similar to the previous one. She was one day more comfortable with the locals. She called many by name as she passed them on the street. At breakfast, John Bailey was already there hunched over his newspaper at a café booth when she'd arrived. She felt very comfortable approaching him with a greeting. She asked, "Morning, John, can I join you."

He seemed pleasantly surprised and perfectly agreeable as he set aside his newspaper. Doris brought Lindy some coffee and walked away saying not a word. MacPherson was talking to Bailey as if she'd known him for years. His eyes lit up with laughter hearing her kid about the Lutherans wanting a bigger booth than the Methodists. When Doris stopped by to get the breakfast order, Bailey was interjecting a story of his own of past festivals. She just re-filled both coffee cups and mumbled, "Same thing as yesterday, Lindy?"

MacPherson nodded without losing any of Bailey's words. That morning she found herself rattling on about her schooling and travels in Europe, something she hadn't discussed with anyone for such a long time. It was refreshing. Bailey admitted he'd been overseas during the war, but mentioned nothing about his role. Yet, he did smile and nod at her remembrances about Paris, London, and Copenhagen…places they'd both visited.

It was Bailey who again had to end the satisfying conversation. He almost seemed disappointed. "Well, the farm's calling for me. With Adam working out at the Lodge, I've taken over a few more farm chores."

She saw a sudden sadness in his eyes as he added, "I may as well get used to doing the farm chores by myself. Adam's going to college this fall even if I have to mortgage the last third of the farm. God knows I'll miss him more than I can tell you."

A moment of emotion almost overtook him until he snapped out of his brief malaise. "I guess I'm not the only man who's had to say good-by to his son."

He got up to leave offering a handshake to MacPherson. She'd been hugged by many males for much less conversation. The handshake seemed awkward to her, though it was Bailey's way of securing their friendship. He told her, "Lindy, while you're in town, you just call on me if you need help in any way."

The purity of the offer was so genuine. He was not coming onto her at all. She watched him pay his bill and stroll out of the restaurant tipping his hat silently to some people on the street. She wished she had one male friend...just one...like John Bailey back in Minneapolis.

She had procrastinated calling her boss the previous two days. She knew Lundquist would have her head if she didn't check in that morning. She could already hear his contrived but legitimate anger over her not calling him as she'd guaranteed. She still hadn't decided how much to tell him. Not only did she have more evidence to gain, but she had a new concern now about the festival and the townsfolk. Any type of police raid on the Lodge would likely bring a probable death stroke on the charity golf event and the town celebration. She promised herself she couldn't allow that to happen until at least the completion of the ten-day event. In fact, she'd already decided that somehow she wanted to stick around for at least part of the festival. Remaining in town for another week-and-a-half through Sunday, June 7 didn't seem possible. Lundquist had authorized her to be in Glenwood only two more days.

By Wednesday noon she could put off the call no longer. She marched over to the County Sheriff's office and asked Petracek if she could use his private line to check in with her boss. She offered to pay for the long distance call. Petracek, ever the gentleman, gave her a 'don't be silly' look and left his office saying he had to go out on patrol. Again, she couldn't get over the kindness and hospitality she was receiving from the local law enforcement.

When MacPherson got her boss on the line, he was even more furious than she expected. Either that or she couldn't see his eyes. They twinkled when he argued with her.

Ignoring his wrath, she pleasantly stated, "And good morning to you, Mr. Lundquist. How are you doing this fine day?"

He grumbled without acknowledging her sweetness. She knew she'd made him smile. It took him a couple seconds to get back into character as he bellowed, "Lindy, don't give me that crap about a 'good morning'. If you really want to know, it's hot as hell in this office despite my fan and it's only mid-day."

Then getting back on the subject, he hollered, "God dammit, Lindy, you promised you were going to call me everyday you were in Glenwood.

Hell, you could have been thrown in that lake up there in Glenwood and been drowned for trying to end some church's bingo night."

She giggled. He couldn't control his disregard for the assignment he'd given her. It was going to be a tough balancing act between building up her case and not inadvertently raising his unease for her safety.

MacPherson waited for his fake furor to cool before responding sardonically, "Ah, my dear Mr. Lundquist, you're always so concerned about me. That's what makes you so loveable."

She could hear his grumble once again even though he didn't say anything. She could picture him trying to hold back a smile.

Then she spoke as if nothing was wrong. "I was just calling in like I said I would. I started the assignment on Monday....ah...the day before yesterday. And today's the next day after yesterday...so, I'm keeping my word and calling you like I said I would."

She liked to talk in circles with Lundquist just to exasperate him. She had to stifle a laugh knowing she'd just agitated him once again. But, Lundquist knew her games. He hadn't gotten to be head of the Minneapolis Federal Attorney's office by being brain dead. And, he knew her tricks. She was just trying to mix him up.

He kept up his irascible act. "Oh, bullcrap, Lindy, you and I know damn well you left early on Friday so you could get to Glenwood by Friday night. You probably have the article for the magazine completed as well as the people arrested who were playing canasta at the local Baptist Church."

She tried to muffle her laugh. Not only did he know her, but he was convinced her 'milk run' would be done within a day or two. 'Milk run' was Lundquist's terminology for wasting time on a weak case. She knew she had to say something meaningful or he'd insist she cut her investigation short.

She continued equivocating. "Yes sir, I did get up here a bit earlier. But, Mr. Lundquist, I think I'm onto something. My cover is perfect. I believe if you could give me another week and a half, I'll have the evidence I need."

She had to remove the ear piece from her ear for the howling that ensued. He screeched, "A week and a half! Holy Christ, Lindy, I need you back here. I can't afford you taking time looking for some lawless hooligans involved in bingo games."

His scorn was playful but pointed as he shouted, "What kind of lawlessness are you finding? For that matter, what kind of warrants should be prepared...maybe vacationing without a license?"

She let him moan and rattle on about how busy the office was. His ranting was his way of giving her a chance to substantiate why she needed to remain at Lake Minnewaska, especially for as long as she was apparently requesting. It was his way.

He finally got semi-serious and inquired in a rather disinterested tone, "O.K., Lindy, so what have you got?"

"Well, sir, as I said, my cover is working out well. I'm finding out there really might be some kind of gambling operation going on out here. I've won over a lot of the locals. They've been pretty closed mouthed, but each day I seem to find more people willing to talk. I'll have a better chance to pin this down if I can somehow get more people to loosen up. Something that will help is that the town is having a big time festival starting this Friday evening. I have to believe I'll be seeing more possible evidence. I'm already seeing enough booze... mostly shipped in from Canada...to lubricate even the quietest mouths in town. I think there's a serious case involving the booze as well. That's why I need just a little more time."

She knew she was talking in generalities, but there was a passion in her voice she knew even Lundquist would notice. She was right. His voice lowered and he asked her seriously, "Lindy, you're not in any danger out there, are you? Your father would have me drawn and quartered if you were."

"Absolutely not!" She hoped her lie would not be detected over the scratchy telephone line. "In fact, I should have a complete report by early next week if you can give me the extra time. Then you can decide what next steps should be taken."

Again she hoped her comments weren't too patronizing. He wasn't a dolt after all.

Amazingly, Lundquist was reluctantly beginning to bend...but not for the reasons she thought. Lundquist detected a more relaxed tone in her voice. As he hoped, it appeared she was taking advantage of some free time from her undercover work and enjoying a small vacation as well. He was coming to realize that in the future to force this young woman to take a break, all he had to do was assign her to some nowhere assignment. He'd then give her some extra time to find some unimportant evidence for a minor case.

Trying not to let her hear the self-satisfaction in his voice, he made his voice sound beaten. "O.K., if you promise to call me the moment you find any trouble, I'll give you through the weekend. But, you call the office every day. God knows your father will be asking me about this 'undercover' assignment. I'll see him at the club this Friday night. I want him to understand you're just doing a routine investigation at some small town in western Minnesota."

Lindy had gotten her O.K. She didn't need to sell her boss anymore. It was time to get off the telephone. She replied quickly "Yes sir... anything you say. I'll call you this weekend...like next Monday or Tuesday...or maybe sooner if I have anything!"

Then she made a horrible sound like static in the receiver. The last thing she heard from him was his shouting, "No Lindy, I said daily for the love of God!" She smiled as she allowed the line to disconnect. She had at least another five days and had held back telling her boss about the gangster activity out at Chippewa Lodge. She knew the danger; it was important Lundquist did not for the time being. Besides the personal peril she faced just being out at the Lodge alone, that was a more dramatic added hazard. If any of the hoodlums knew she was spying on them, they'd snuff her life out like a cheap Edison bulb.

That Wednesday afternoon, a rejuvenated Lindy MacPherson stayed around City Park. All the booths were completed. The gazebo Nate Morrison had been working on looked like new. Arts and crafts were already being displayed in some booths. Ropes, buoys, and large blue banners were being secured out on the lake for the various boating and swimming races. Even the town dock had been repaired at the main beach. The preparations were such that the town festival could have started three days early.

Her alias was working better than she could have ever imagined. Her questions were not considered prying. That Wednesday afternoon, she assisted in preparing signs for a Lutheran church food stand and more signs for the hayrides sponsored by the Catholics. She had become like a local. People stopped by as she worked just to talk to her. She found some of the younger boys in town had even begun walking by her cabin in the previous evenings just to see her sitting on her cabin porch. They were spellbound having a pretty female living in their midst. Some of them were as young as ten years old. Wednesday night three young boys with stars in their eyes even stopped by and just chatted with her.

Surprising to MacPherson were the additional details she was learning from these innocent, young admirerers. They were so open as they joked about the strange things going on in town. She heard replays from their perspective about the mayhem that happened during the week of previous town festivals. A few of the boys also kidded about the money being bet in the 'Calcutta'. One of the boys had a father on the Men's club committee that managed the betting booths. He told Lindy excitedly that the church got a 10% cut from all the gambling dollars. That's why the church had a new steeple and an addition for Sunday school classes built in the last two years.

It didn't take a lot of mathematics for Lindy to calculate the cost of a new steeple and an addition to a church. The church Men's Club had to gain quite a sum at 10% to afford the projects. The question to her was who got the other 90%.

Thursday morning she rose early to watch a regatta of sailboats before heading over to the Glenwood Café. That morning she again had breakfast with John Bailey. On top of her list for days had been to meet Henry Hanson. She'd just not put her mind to it. She couldn't believe anyone could be that busy.

Bailey was already at a booth reading the paper when MacPherson arrived. After almost a week, she simply had to wave to Doris to get her breakfast ordered. If anything, that made her feel accepted in the community. Except for Henry Hanson, she had gotten close to various key people in the community. The County Sheriff and Chief of Police stopped and talked with her every time they saw her. Mayor Charlie B. Good made certain he strolled through City Park and greeted her during the day. Folks called her by name when passing her. The little boys continued to look at her with adoring eyes. And, just in the previous two days with the questions she'd been getting from various women in town, she sensed she was even getting sized up as a potential mate for their eldest sons.

John Bailey greeted her with his warm smile. She no longer even asked if she could join him at his booth. She just sat down and began conversing as if they'd been friends for years. They hadn't been talking five minutes when Bailey's attention was interrupted as his eyes flicked over to the café entrance. MacPherson glanced over toward the door and saw another taller, slightly gray-haired man standing and then smiling toward Doris behind the cash register. Though she'd never laid eyes on him, MacPherson knew she was looking at the mystery man himself...Henry Hanson.

At first glance she was disappointed. She expected someone different. This man was not impressive looking. His shoulders seemed not as broad for his height. His skin was whiter than the tanned Bailey. He frankly didn't look altogether healthy. His hair needed a trim and his beard needed to be either shaved or tidied up. He wore tan pants and shirt, an outfit that might be good camouflage in some dried out forest.

Yet, it was his face and eyes that MacPherson eventually focused. It was a very thoughtful, intelligent face, despite his eyes showing exhaustion. He didn't acknowledge anyone, but almost everybody greeted him. He nodded at each one as if his head was a fisherman's bobber. His movements were slow, but his posture was quite noticeably erect. This man was definitely not a downtrodden farmer of the times.

As he sat momentarily on a booth stool, Doris served him coffee and called out to the cook, "It's Henry. Make him the usual."

As he carefully slurped his coffee, the man continued looking around the café. His eyes stopped when he saw the two primary law enforcement men who were deep in conversation in a far booth. MacPherson knew from conversing with Nate Morrison that Henry was good friends with Chief Rich Brey and Sheriff Clarence Petracek. Hanson said in a strong baritone voice, "Morning Rich...morning Clarence." They waved back.

That's all he said until his eyes panned around and he saw John Bailey. Then his face showed more life as he called out, "Morning John."

Bailey waved him to come over to the table. The two of them were quite obviously very close friends.

John took over with the introduction. "Henry, I'd like you to meet Miss Lindy MacPherson. Lindy, this is a friend of mine, Henry Hanson. Though he manages the local Feed & Grain Mill down the street, he's really one of the big wigs in charge of our town celebration. I'm surprised he's taking time to eat.

Hanson grinned at John's remarks, but said nothing in response as he shook MacPherson's hand.

John continued, "Henry, Miss MacPherson is visiting from the 'Cities' writing a magazine article about our town and resorts around the lake area. She'd no doubt want to talk to you if you could spare time in your delicate schedule."

Hanson's grip was strong. It belied his rather weaker looking frame. In itself, that contrast added more mystery to this man who seemed more a phantom. But, whether apparition or not, she had become highly aware how nothing got done relative to the festival without this man's approval...and everyone in town was fine with that procedure. Hanson made certain all the volunteers had food and drink supplied to them daily from Big Bud Bunsen's General Store. She'd heard how suppliers got paid within days of sending their billings.

Hanson had been described to her as a very quiet, decent man who liked to travel. That had been a surprise. Most small town people didn't have enough money to travel anywhere during those economic times. That factor had certainly triggered her inclination that Hanson might be mixed up in the very situation she was investigating. She had been living the previous couple days pondering whether the nickname attributed to this man...Honest Henry Hanson...was more a misnomer. It was entirely possible he could be siphoning funds to run some kind of gambling operation. She had no proof, but she had to count her thought as a possibility. Even worse, hearing that he was Secretary-Treasurer of the First Presbyterian Men's club, he might even be drawing from the very church funds he was being trusted to protect.

As the haggard looking man sat down in the booth, her instincts told her not to trust him. She had no doubt he knew more about everything happening at Chippewa Lodge than any other citizen in Glenwood. She expected him to be somewhat cold and certainly closed-mouthed. She so wanted to dislike and distrust Henry Hanson.

In less than five minutes, however, these initial convictions melted with each sentence he spoke. Straight-forward in his comments, he came across as genuine as anyone she'd met in the town. She could see immediately why John and Henry were good friends. The things they talked about were not of the tough economic times, the horrible farm prices, the medical problems of people living in Glenwood, or even of the imminent festival. Instead, they talked some politics...some places in Europe they'd both traveled...and then in the next breath about some fishing hole John had found over at Lake Amelia. They seemed to both take joy in that discovery.

Then realizing they were being somewhat impolite talking about fishing in front of their guest, the two men refrained from further gibberish and placed their attention back on the town's temporary guest. It was Henry who asked, "So, Miss MacPherson, how is the article going? Are you gaining the type of information you need?"

Strangely, it was the same wording the two law enforcement officers used whenever they saw her in town.

MacPherson responded generally. "Yes, I'm seeing some really nice resort properties and of course enjoying meeting the local folks as they prepare for the town celebration."

Henry smiled, "Yes, I hear you've been jumping in as a volunteer over at City Park. We really appreciate your interest."

There was something about the tone of that remark. She was uncertain of its sincerity...as if she should have been working on her true purpose for being in Glenwood rather than wasting time doing such other frivolous work. 'But, what would he know about that,' thought MacPherson?

She countered with a question of her own. "So, Henry, are you pleased with the progress? I see most of the booths are up and ready to open tomorrow night...including that interesting booth being run by the First Presbyterian Church."

Hanson gave her a close look. He nodded his head ignoring the specifics of her question. "Yes, in the past some of the church and civic organizations have been able to do rather well financially. We can only hope they have as good a week as last year."

Then he abruptly changed the subject to the weather, a sure fire indicator that the conversation was coming to a close. He turned to Bailey and said, "John, I heard the Dakotas are getting some rain. Hopefully the clouds will move into the area tonight or tomorrow morning so the opening of the festival won't be interrupted tomorrow night. He then smiled and added, "Mayor Good would be especially disappointed."

All three sitting in the booth laughed knowing how much the mayor enjoyed being on center stage.

Lindy marveled at how Henry Hanson had slyly slipped out of answering her direct reference alluding to the Presbyterian Church gambling booth. He was even looking at his watch readying himself to make an excuse for having to get on with the day. Sure enough...as he got up, he again shook hands with MacPherson saying, "I hope you're planning to be in town during a good part of the ten-day festival. I highly recommend it. We get a lot of interesting visitors. It might help...ah...your article."

It was at that moment a very large man walked into the café. He was wearing a fedora and an expensive suit. He was definitely not a local guy. He ordered a cup of coffee and a donut. In a harsh, gravelly voice he said to Doris, as she stood behind the cash register. "I need directions to some resort called the 'Lodge'. You got any idea where this place is?"

Doris showed patience. She'd obviously answered that question many times. Pouring his coffee she pleasantly gave him directions. The gruff-voiced man threw a five-dollar bill on the counter and said, "Tanks"...and walked away without a thought for receiving his change. He was definitely not a local citizen.

The remaining patrons including Henry Hanson, John Bailey, Lindy MacPherson, and the two leading law officers of the county and city saw the whole scene. They all had become painfully quiet when the man walked in. When he left, everyone in the café picked up their conversations where they had been left. MacPherson's face showed disgust. She knew she was the only one in the café who recognized the intimidating looking man as none other than Freddie 'The Fish' Fena, a career criminal from Chicago. The gangster was out on bail while his murder trial was being negotiated behind the scenes. At her office in Minneapolis, Fena's name came up more than a few times for seemingly being involved in crimes where the victim ended up in Lake Michigan. Not only was he a murderer, he had no creativity beyond using one of the great lakes as a dumpster. She was further disappointed how Sheriff Petracek and Police Chief Brey, seated at the other end of the restaurant ignored the man. 'Then again,' she thought, 'maybe they didn't know this fellow. If they did, however, their disinterest would make it even worse.'

It was Hanson who broke the silence and repeated almost inaudibly, "Yes, Miss MacPherson, you could pick up some very useful information for your article when this town gets really busy with visitors from around the five-state area in the upcoming week."

The way he looked at her spoke volumes. While he was showing no interest in talking very specifically with her, he seemed satisfied, even hopeful, she was in town. As he left, he said to her, "Nice to have met you. I hope you'll find your visit to our town successful." Again his choice of words was interesting. He'd said 'successful', not 'enjoyable' or 'pleasant' as would be the normal wish.

Bailey then got up. He professed having a busy day as well. "I'll likely see you around town in the days ahead...and probably tomorrow morning right here at the café. I hopefully will get the chance to introduce my son to you. You've been here a week and you haven't even seen him. He might have a story or two to tell about his experiences out at Chippewa Lodge."

In Bailey's case, his verbiage was not as provoking as Hanson's statements. This local man seemed to have no particular concerns or knowledge about the guest list at the Lodge, or what might be going on out there.

He left giving her a genuine smile. She was thrilled she had Bailey as a friend. He was someone she felt she could depend upon. She didn't have the same confidence in Henry Hanson. She sensed he held a lot of secrets. Despite being a very gracious person, he shared his thoughts sparingly. He gave every indication he had other matters than the festival on his mind.

She watched as Bailey and Hanson stopped outside the café entrance and talked very seriously for a half minute. Then they nodded, shook hands and went their separate ways. Paying her bill, MacPherson changed her loosely planned day and decided to follow Henry Hanson just to see what he did and who he encountered. She was certain her investigation could be revitalized with where he might inadvertently lead her.

It took MacPherson less than two hours to realize she was wasting her time. Hanson wandered through City Park greeting various volunteers. He then trudged over to the Mill for less than a half hour. She sat in her government leased Model 'A' Ford until he left his office later in the morning. She hoped he was going out to the resort. Instead, she followed him to his house. She sat in her car down the block from his house for almost an hour. There was a neighbor lady who brought him over some freshly baked bread. He talked with her for a few minutes and then she returned home. It appeared the busy, industrious and trustworthy Henry Hanson had just gone home for a nap. It made sense. The man had looked exhausted.

Realizing her time had just been wasted, MacPherson then returned to her cabin in disgust. Her investigation was at a standstill. It was plain as ducks on a pond that something uniquely foul was going on in both the town and especially out at Chippewa Lodge. She knew she could always call Lundquist and tell him of her intuition, but that was all it would be. The state patrol could be sent in to make some likely arrests of some wanted convicts out at the resort, but she knew there were far bigger fish to catch. Some of the known mobsters were not currently under arrest. They would simply be questioned. Other than a bunch of known criminals vacationing at the Lodge, she really had not seen anything else illegal at the Lodge. It could be her only hope that as it got closer to the charity golf tournament at the end of the following week, she might see an increased number of gangsters streaming into town and staying out at the resort. For the present, though, she was inclined to remain patient as if letting the case she was building come to her. It was not her normal method of pursuit on an investigation, but it seemed to fit in the environment she was in.

The remainder of that Thursday she stayed in the confines of City Park helping more than fifty volunteers make their final preparations for the festival opening the next night. While she could invest more time out at the Lodge, she figured she'd spend more time fighting off the pests staying in the cabins than actually finding any worthwhile evidence. She sensed that letting her cover ripen even more would eventually loosen the tongues of more citizens. She resolved to slow down and become even more of a local if that was possible. She'd disappear in the sea of volunteerism and keep her eyes and ears open. She had a feeling once the festival opened, that might just be the catalyst she needed for further discoveries.

CHAPTER
10

That opening evening on Friday, May 29 of the town celebration, there was to be some welcoming remarks at the gazebo stage by the Mayor followed by fireworks over the lake and then a huge dance in City Park. With the expected largest opening night audience in the short history of the Glenwood festival, the only fear was the length of Mayor Charlie B. Good's remarks. Locals had joked that since the Mayor was contemplating running for the state legislature in the next election, the extent of his speech would be dictated by the size of the crowd.

MacPherson had been strolling by the growing assemblage in City Park on her way back to her cabin from dinner at the Glenwood Cafe. Not interested in listening to the Mayor's welcome, she was instead becoming concerned how close her cabin was to City Park. With the constant activity, crowd noise, and the late night band music, sleep would likely be interrupted.

In the back of the crowd young couples were only waiting for the dance to begin. They cared little about Good's welcome and only slightly for the fireworks. Watching them behave so irreverently and guiltlessly gave her spasms of melancholy. She remembered acting the same way. How long had it been? Seeing these couples brought back thoughts of her deceased fiancé. She retreated from the crowd not wanting to be seen alone. There was a chance some unattached male or even married male might see her alone and strike up a conversation. She was in no mood to be social. She quickened her pace until she was sitting in the comfort of her porch rocker with the echo of the mayor's staccato and imperceptible comments in the background.

Her cabin turned out to be a safe distance from the noisy crowd. She planned on her partially read book to be her entertainment for the night. But, it wasn't working. Hearing the rumble of noise from the park made her feel like she was missing something. She finally gave up and began re-tracing her steps back toward that main activity of the night. As she passed by the cabin office, Homer Smith, the proprietor of the small group of cabins saw her and came rushing out to intercept her. "Miss MacPherson, this telegram was just delivered here a couple hours ago. He handed it to her with a concerned look in his eye.

Opening the envelope, she rolled her eyes. It was from Ernest Lundquist. The terse message said, 'Call me.' She knew he was again agitated with her. She should have talked to him that day, but there was simply nothing to report. He didn't want to give him a chance of ordering her back to the office. Truth was, while at times feeling lonely, she was enjoying her little escape from Minneapolis. Glenwood wasn't Switzerland. It wasn't other places she'd visited in Europe. But, it offered her a place to regain her perspective. As important as her work was to her, she found she could relax and enjoy some simple things in life again...even if it was just helping a town with its upcoming event.

Poking along the path back toward the gazebo, she countered every creative thought she had on how she might squeeze one more week in Glenwood. None of her ideas sounded convincing. MacPherson sat down on a park bench lost in her own world. Locals walked by wishing her a 'good evening'. She hardly said anything but gave each person a smile and a wave. The fireworks helped liven up her mind and helped her contemplate one advantage she might have. She knew her boss. Calling him at his home in the evening might work more in her favor. He was mellower. She could slant the truth enough to substantiate a few more days in Glenwood.

Smiling in deceit, she recalled how Friday night was card night at his club. Lundquist might even be less combative, even relatively calm, once he got home after a few drinks. She knew his timetable because her own father was also a club member. The two men had been playing cards with each other whenever possible most every Friday night for years...and she'd seen her father waver a bit upon arriving home on many a Friday night. Most importantly, she knew Lundquist drank more than her father did.

MacPherson was about to march over to Sheriff Petracek's office to use his private phone when she was suddenly interrupted by John Bailey. He was leaving the festivities before the dance got underway. Next to him was a younger man about the same height, build, and gait. It was not hard to guess he was John's son Adam. John showed great pride in introducing his son.

Adam was not shy. He shot his hand out toward her. "Miss MacPherson, a pleasure to meet you. My Dad told me about your work on an article. You couldn't have picked a better time to be in Glenwood than during this festival. I hope we can get a copy of what you wrote before you leave town."

Then his eyes lit up like his father's eyes did when he was about to make a kidding remark. "Ma'am, it might be helpful if I saw a draft of your article before you send it in. I could point out the various lies and exaggerations people in this town told you. I figure everyone in Glenwood is giving you the rosiest picture possible."

Adam's eyes were teasing. Most eighteen-year old young men would not be as confident, but only mumble and speak sparingly as they looked down at the ground. But this was far from the behavior of John Bailey's son. He had a self-assuredness coupled with a mischievous but charming manner far beyond his years. There was no doubt he was used to dealing with adults on a regular basis.

She responded, "I might just take you up on that offer. It would be nice if at least some of my magazine descriptions about the resorts and the town were factual."

It took only that small interchange to make both Adam and Lindy discover they could kid with one another. Brought out of her glumness, their conversation brought back her energy. "Adam, your Dad tells me you've been making a nice sum of money these past few summers during festival week. You must really be enjoying yourself out at the resort."

Adam's eyes sparkled. "It's probably the most fun I've ever had. I've been caddying out at the Lodge golf course since I was fourteen. This might be my last summer doing this sort of thing since I'll be going down to the University this fall. Who knows where I'll be next summer."

The three of them sat talking under a tree for the next half hour. She took note how close the father and son were. Never once did they mention anyone else in the family. There was obviously no mother or any lady of the house. That was the first time MacPherson felt real sadness for John, especially come autumn when he was going to lose his son to college.

But, that night the Baileys didn't allow her to be mellow. For two males living on a farm during difficult economic times, their mood was quite happy, almost festive. John related a story about a previous year's festival when a rainstorm drowned out the mayor's welcoming speech. "Many said it was the best speech ever by the Mayor."

As they talked, MacPherson looked beyond the Baileys toward two men sitting at the Presbyterian betting booth just twenty yards away.

It was on the edge of City Park as if the intention was not to make the booth too noticeable. The booth's purpose...a betting booth...seemed very much out of place given that locals didn't have the means to participate in the wagering anyway.

She then took more notice to the larger tent behind the Presbyterian booth. It had been raised just that afternoon.

Two rather surly looking men stood in front of the tent entry as if they were guarding the President. Then a well-dressed couple showed one of the guards a pass. They were provided entrance. Two other men in suits showed up, presented a pass, and were also allowed entry. If ever there seemed like some gaming was going on, that tent fit the image. More folks entered that tent...all showing passes. All of them were generally dressed in better garb than most of the farm folk showing up for the dance. MacPherson doubted these people were entering that tent to play Bingo.

Her attention was broken when Adam let out a howling laugh directed at his father. The two of them had been playfully bickering about who had to get up early the next morning to feed the livestock. Adam was pleading for more sleep since he had to arrive at Chippewa Lodge extra early. John just maintained a wry grin. "Sorry, a deal is a deal. You'll just have to get up a half hour earlier."

Somehow Lindy knew the father would acquiesce given the sunrise to sunset work schedule Adam was doing at the Lodge. Bailey had a very noticeable soft spot in his heart for his son.

Finally the father and son stopped their horseplay. Adam had to return to the Lodge to do some club cleaning and shoe shining for some of the golfers before they teed off the next morning.

She looked at Bailey and said, "And how about you, John. Will I see you at breakfast tomorrow morning at the café?

He nodded. "Certainly...I'll see you about 8:30... after I finish feeding the livestock." She noted he'd already given in to his son.

MacPherson watched the two Baileys get into their respective vehicles. Both the old Plymouth truck and the rusty similar model sedan looked to be older than their actual years...like so many material items in the rural areas. It occurred to her how she hadn't really thought about the economic downturn since arriving in Glenwood. In Minneapolis she saw the abject poverty in the streets every day. In Glenwood, the world looked fresher, more consistent with the attitude of the community that shined so positively. The addition of the late model cars driving back and forth from the Lodge also contributed to an upbeat atmosphere. It was as if the entire town had chosen not to accept the national economic misery.

A broken down 1924 Dodge Victoria Coupe drove by with six young people shouting into the night. Even they seemed happier being in Glenwood. There were four males and two females. One of the males shouted for her to come join them as they drove by. She felt complimented they thought she was in their age group. That night she actually another generation older.

The dance was about to begin and she realized if she was going to call Ernest Lundquist, it had to be soon before he went to bed. It was just past 9:30, he likely would have returned home from the club.

Without further delay, she marched over to the County Sheriff's office where she asked once again to utilize Clarence Petracek's private line. Only one of the deputies was in the Sheriff's office when she arrived. He recognized her immediately though neither had ever met. He was one of the deputies that secretly provided nightly drive-by security for MacPherson by orders of the Sheriff without her knowing it. They didn't ask why. They just followed orders.

Deputy 'Boonie' Radel gave her what had become a normal but tiring greeting. "Good evening, Miss MacPherson. How's the article coming?"

She wondered what people might say to her once the article was completed. Was there not any other topic with which people could start a conversation with her? Of course the article would never be finished. There might be a multi-page warrant for numerous arrests, but not a travel magazine article.

She played along. "Articles going fine, Deputy...thanks for asking. The Sheriff said I could use his office phone if I needed to check in with my...ah....publisher. Would that be all right if I used the telephone right now?"

The Deputy seemed pleased he could be of some help. He nodded and pointed toward Petracek's office. "You're welcome to it. We won't see the Sheriff until late Sunday anyway."

Again to Lindy it made no sense that the County's top law enforcement officer would be out of town on such a busy weekend in Glenwood. He obviously had a lot of confidence in his staff.

Closing the door, she called Ernest Lundquist at his home in the Twin Cities. She envisioned him balancing a bourbon and soda on his stomach while he read some law journal in his study. He would be at his most mellow of behaviors...at least that was her hope.

He answered in his normal gruff tone, but his voice was a bit thick. So far, she'd guessed right. He was half in the bag. She immediately apologized for not calling citing the difficulty of having access to a private line. That whim had just come to her. Surprisingly, Lundquist seemed to accept her excuse...at least to a point.

"Well, Lindy, your explanation is sound even though I know damn well you're lying to me."

She decided to ignore his sarcastic comment and take a more straight-forward and subdued tenor. It would put him off his guard. "Well, Mr. Lundquist, I guess you're right. I don't see anything that needs immediate attention. I'm convinced this gambling accusation is only part of a huge town celebration. It's not on-going as far as I've been able to tell. It's just part of a temporary money making effort by some church. The local police don't seem particularly bothered by what they see. I don't think a minister or some of his church members are going to jail over this issue."

Lundquist chuckled at the other end of the line now assuming his young attorney would be traveling back to Minneapolis that weekend.

There was a pause on the line before she casually began to stir the pot. "Of course, Mr. Lundquist, there is something going on around here that is a lot bigger than some gaming activities managed by a church. I can't put my finger on it, but it'll take too much time to continue the investigation. I don't see anything that's really serious......yet."

Through her few sentences, Lundquist was chortling to himself. He had been right all along. It was now worth the week of having his young protégé out of the office. She had to come down a bit off her perch and had to admit she overreacted to the potential importance of her assignment. Her work had been nothing more than a 'training' exercise making her more valuable in future investigative work.

He leaned back in his comfortable leather chair covering the telephone with his hand while he burped away some remnants of dinner and that last bourbon and seven. He and his friend, her father, Judge MacPherson, had left the club less than an hour before. He was relieved she hadn't stumbled onto something very big. As friends for years, the Judge would have been upset if Lundquist had placed Lindy in some perilous duty.

Trying to be magnanimous and showing respect for the minor assignment she had apparently completed, Lundquist took an extra satisfying drag from his cigar and generously offered, "Well Lindy, if there's no more new evidence, then the anonymous note I got about illegal gambling was probably exaggerated. So....can you wrap it up, get your report done this weekend and be in the office on Monday?"

He was happy with himself for sounding so avuncular. She always tested his patience...and got a kick out of doing so. Truthfully, she'd teased him for years, just not in a supervisor/employee relationship. Her words rarely bothered him. And, she seemed not in the mood that evening to debate any particular issue with him. Of course, he never minded arguing with her. It was part of the relationship they'd built. Besides he knew she was a highly capable attorney with good instincts.

MacPherson remained quiet still hoping the boss would pick up on her subtleties. She was setting Lundquist up. Her silence was a way of making him edgy.

Lundquist broke through her purposeful hush and tried to show his steel. "So, I repeat, my dear, I'll be seeing you in the office Monday morning with your assignment report…and your expense report…isn't that right?"

He heard only silence on the other end of the phone. Exasperatingly he repeated, "Lindy, are you still on the line. I'll see you Monday… correct? You're not going to try any tricks on me. I know you too well… and I'm too old to put up with your shenanigans. You've been on break long enough."

Now the two of them were moving along towards one of their typical wrestling matches. His last comment had given her another idea she hadn't considered. She pinched herself not believing she hadn't thought of this alternative. She stifled a snicker and declared, "Well, Mr. Lundquist, I guess you were right all along about me needing a vacation. I've found a location where I could relax after a hard day and just read and rest. You've been badgering me for so long to take a few days off. I should have guessed that you knew best."

Suddenly Lundquist felt uneasy. It wasn't like her to serve up any compliments toward him. It made him uneasy. He was about to badger her about already having taken a week's vacation, but caught himself. He realized he was in a pickle. He didn't want to demean completely the work he'd authorized her to do. He'd given her the assignment knowing she'd have a couple days to relax. Now she was about to throw a curve at him and ask for more vacation time. He wondered what game she was now playing with him. He sat back sizing up her strategy before responding. There had to be something else going on. The fact that she wasn't disclosing anything as yet meant that she actually might have run into some real evidence. The inference of more vacation time was all a ruse. He knew she wouldn't take a vacation out in the hinterlands of Minnesota by choice. There had to be something of more importance. He didn't want to take her away from an assignment that might have some teeth. Yet he wasn't ready to admit he had misread the situation out at Lake Minnewaska.

Lundquist stayed cagey. He had to make her fight for the extra 'vacation' time she was about to request so he wouldn't let on that he knew she was on a case more important than he realized. Lundquist loved that his mind worked faster when he and she were matching wits.

Then he got an idea, something he'd been teasing her about at various times in her life, even when he knew her as a young girl. In a mock serious tone he exclaimed, "So, a handsome rural chap has caught your eye…and you need more time to get to know him. Am I reading the true meaning of your vacation request?"

They were like two family members testing each other's guile. MacPherson knew he was trying to get her goat whenever he used the 'boyfriend' scheme. But, this time it seemed he was giving her an opening to win her argument…something he rarely did. She was irritated at herself for not having thought about this notion…especially with her unusual interest and success with male companionship since arriving in Glenwood. In the past week she'd met a host of very considerate men who didn't seem to have alternative motives. They were ages from ten to sixty!

She had to give her favorite boss some credit. Teasing her about a possible male friend meant that he still had a twinkle in his eye. For an overweight man sitting in his favorite chair at home with his vest stained in liquor and his breath smelling of cigar, she figured that was a good thing.

Lundquist had just accepted her request for more time invested in Glenwood on the unstated premise that there might be a more significant case to be investigated. Lundquist would save face by basing her stay on letting her get to know some interesting guy out in the sticks. She would have the time to hopefully secure her case… probably through the end of the town festival ten days from that Friday evening.

She chuckled thinking how the two of them had verbally sparred over the years…and where she considered she'd walked away the winner. It would be nice to make him feel like he'd finally subdued her…if her ego would just allow her to accept his next moments of superiority. Getting off the phone had become her next primary aim.

She sweetly replied, "Mr. Lundquist, by gosh, I think you at times can see through granite. Let's just say I have met a couple nice gentlemen and leave it at that. If you see my father at the golf course, don't tell him. He'll be on the telephone nightly to warn me about anyone who might want to tamper with my innocence."

Lundquist laughed openly into the telephone enjoying his victory. She'd won some more vacation time from him…but he definitely knew better. Whatever case she was building, it would be worthwhile for her to remain in Glenwood. By her tone, nothing indicated she was in any danger. That was all he cared about for the present. He yelled into the phone. "O.K., my dear, you've earned it. Have a nice break. We'll see you at the end of next week."

Lundquist hung up the telephone very content. Lindy MacPherson was a lot to handle in the office, but had proven worth his time. He hoped she might be a bit tamer and tanner when she returned. Then he sat there puffing on his cigar analyzing what got said in their conversation. He wondered what was really causing her so much attention.

After hanging up the telephone, she practically skipped back to City Park. The angst had ended. She was going to be in Glenwood for the entire festival. That evening she danced with any male that asked her...old or young....scruffy or dolled up for the evening. The locals... male or female...were delighted how this out-of-town gal had jumped in so willingly to their community celebration. Amazingly no one saw her take a drink of anything alcoholic...and there was plenty flowing through City Park that night.

Lindy MacPherson got back to her cabin after midnight. If that was her first experience with a rural town festival, she had to admit she'd better pace herself. She was exhausted from the non-stop dancing. Her playful nature was totally out of character...as if she was under some kind of spell since arriving in the unexplainably vigorous community. That Friday night she fell asleep not really believing but certainly hoping there would be more discoveries in the coming week. Her anticipation was that she'd certainly have the opportunity to identify more gangsters, especially those currently wanted by the law. It might be as easy as seeing them walking freely around the town or at City Park during the festival. She also figured she'd sojourn a few times out to the Lodge during the coming week as long as she felt reasonably safe. There had to be more evidence of wrongdoing out there. She just wasn't certain what she should be looking for.

As the festival week progressed, Lindy would keep close tabs on the 'gambling' booth at City Park as well as the individuals who went into the large tent behind the booth. She found that the identical set-up was constructed across the road from the Chippewa Lodge entrance. It had taken only some loss of sleep to explore and find out that the large tents contained roulette and black jack tables. It took a special password to get into either tent...in fact a different code each day.

It was Saturday night of the first weekend of the celebration that she'd taken advantage of two lax guards patrolling the City Park tent entrance. They'd had one too many brews from Big Bud Bunson's General Store and she'd been able to slip through the entrance with a group from the resort. Once inside, she witnessed as many as forty to fifty patrons pounding tables and rejoicing or screaming with the money won or lost in roulette and black jack. It was blatant illegal gambling.

As for the Presbyterian Men's Club booths taking bets for the upcoming charity golf tournament, they seemed to care little about the large tents positioned behind their booths. It was also not until Monday night she first noticed the booths were taking wagers on other sporting events besides the coming tournament. These bets were mostly made by the ever increasing number of 'guests' coming into town and staying at the Lodge.

Through those first days of the week MacPherson truly felt she was taking a break from her job. She allowed herself to get lost in the festival activity at City Park. She worked at some of the church booths and generally behaved and felt as if she was a local citizen. She did venture out daily to Chippewa Lodge just to observe the large tent behind the Presbyterian booth and the raucous activities at the resort. She was largely unnoticed given the shear numbers of people...but, not completely. She still got invitations for drinks at the patio bar... and at least three blatant invitations for more late-night activity. It got so she hardly paid attention. The propositions were thrown out like worms on a hook.

It was by the middle of the week when out at the Lodge she saw firsthand the true dimension of the betting going on. She witnessed money being placed on events having nothing to do with the upcoming charity golf event. Wagers were being made on upcoming horse races, baseball games, and even some boxing competitions elsewhere in the country. While standing close to the betting booth across the road from the Lodge, she observed a 'guest' making several bets on horse races at Arlington Park outside Chicago. The money was taken in, a call was made, and the volunteer for the Men's Club was ready to help the next 'guest'. The gambler then went over to the Lutheran food tent after which he returned to the large gambling tent behind the Presbyterian booth.

The mix of church booths and gambling was genius. She looked at the volunteers in the Lutheran food booth oblivious to the wagers being made in their neighboring booth and especially the private tent casino not twenty yards away. 'If they only knew,' thought Lindy, 'that the dollars bet on the golf tournament were like raindrops on a river. Then again, maybe they did...and they could care less!'

What she also found interesting was how the two betting booths were being managed. The mastermind making this business work was using festival week to dull the sensitivities as to any local or otherwise rumors or hearsay about any other gambling activities. Besides, with church and civic organizations making money in conjunction with whatever was bringing more people to the town and to Chippewa Lodge, what would be the reason to want this gift house to end? Watching this entire system work like a ship crew on calm seas made her pleased she'd stayed the extra week.

It also became clear to MacPherson that any locals skittish about the prospect of gambling going on in their town could find solace in that a church group was handling the operation...and secondly, the booth in City Park was not that busy. It was as if that booth was set up in the park for that very reason.

To the contrary, the booth and accompanying 'casino' tent across the road from Chippewa Lodge was exactly the opposite. Since the Glenwood citizenry didn't get out to the Lodge that much, they had no idea the activity. In the evenings during festival week the casino tent by the resort was teeming with patrons.

As MacPherson continued her daily ventures to the resort, she noticed new things with each trip. A temporary telephone line ran from the booth to the largest cabin on the resort property. This cabin looked like a train depot with men constantly running in and out of the building. Curiously the windows were boarded up. Nothing could be observed from the outside looking in. She further noticed several telephone lines running from that same large cabin out to the main telephone cables outside the resort.

Not to grasp how a major betting business was being conducted in conjunction with the town festival had to mean it was being purposely ignored. Furthermore, the set up was so established, she had no doubts the gambling operation was not restricted only to the ten-days of the town festival. It was too big. Private phone lines could keep the business rolling year round within the confines of the resort.

It was very evident that the authorities could roll into Chippewa Lodge at anytime and make some notable arrests on wanted criminals as well as close down a very active and successful illegal gambling operation. Yet, it bothered her that this action would be too easy... too incomplete. Whoever was in charge of this operation could escape prosecution. There was even the chance the responsibility for this gambling operation might center on local townsfolk...whether deserved or not. Henry Hanson would be one of the key arrests being he was chairman of the entire festival and managing the betting booths. But, there were others... Mayor Charlie B. Good...members of the town council...even the minister of the First Presbyterian Church....all these men had a part in the illegalities that were so apparent. Sadly, any raid would arrest too many of the wrong people.

Her real consternation was how deep key leaders in the community were involved in this entire mess. The town was so proud of this Hanson, and he seemed to richly deserve the aplomb. Most importantly, as far as she could see, he gave absolutely no appearance of taking any particular advantages of skimming money off the top from profits from the gambling booths he managed. He lived almost ascetically in a house he didn't own. He drove a 1928 Velie Model 60 Coupe, certainly not a deluxe automobile. If anything from her observations, he was extremely conscientious in training the Men's Club members to handle the wagering with no errors. Yet, how could this genuine local hero be involved with a bunch of thugs at the Lodge who treated law as if it was their prerogative?

As the festival week progressed, she gained a much deeper understanding. Hanson had to be in a serious dilemma. No wonder he looked so exhausted. If anyone understood, he did about the symbiotic relationship between the town and the 'guests' at the resort. The whole thing was just too positive...too profitable...for him to blow any whistles. And, if he did, given the clientele at the Lodge, he could face reprisal in its most final form.

Now she faced potentially the same challenge. She knew if her cover was ever found out, she could face the same kind of reprisal from the 'guests' at Chippewa Lodge.

What held her back was the pure joy that sparkled every day in Glenwood. The emotion amongst the townsfolk was almost fanciful, but it was so invigorating. She didn't want to see the atmosphere end. What was the difference if she waited until the ten-day event was completed the coming Sunday, June 7 when prizes were awarded at City Park and the golf tournament would be completed that afternoon?

The gambling ring would be stopped. Prison escapees hiding out at the Lodge would be returned to jail. Wanted criminals given safe harbor at the Lodge would be arraigned. Deals might be made with some of those arrested that would lead to the leader or leaders of the gambling ring. It was her obligation with the job she had.

With as brilliant as this entire enterprise was, MacPherson feared the true ringleaders at the Lodge would have a well-planned escape or alibi to countervail the arresting officers. Without the arraignment of the key figures at Chippewa Lodge, she would deem her undercover work as inadequate and unsuccessful.

Finally, she knew the arrests would be a very embarrassing legacy the town would have to face for years to come. Glenwood would be known for its ignorance in not recognizing how the mob operated right under their noses...and for so long.

She would end each evening sitting on that same rocker out on her cabin porch no longer bothered by the hum of noise still prevalent from City Park. And, each evening a patrol car would pass by her cabin. If an officer saw her, invariably he'd call out to her. "Evening, Miss MacPherson. Everything all right?"

She'd wave and her soft voice would echo in the humid night. "Yes, deputy, I'm just fine. Thank you. I'm just enjoying the quiet time."

The deputy's voice lowered to respect her solitude. "O.K. then...you have a good night. Hope the article's coming along."

Then he would drive slowly on. He would return hourly even when she was safely in her cabin until he went off-duty. Then his replacement would include her cabin in his patrol.

While she appreciated the attention, MacPherson was very aware other visitors certainly weren't getting this kind of personal attention. She sensed it went beyond the townsfolk wanting a positive article in the magazine. Someone was watching out for her...literally insisting the guarantee for her comfort and safety. Whoever that person was, she'd never feel safer. Then she looked across the lake towards Chippewa Lodge and realized the exact opposite was true if she was sitting on a rocker outside one of that resort's cabins.

Those evenings as she sat on her porch, she would also see young couples meander by her cabin. Some would be barefoot and wading in the lake irregardless of the soft rain that fell two of the nights. They would giggle in their own innocent way involved in their own private longings for each other. A few of the couples would see her sitting alone on the porch. Some would greet her; others would say something to each other, giggle again, and move on.

That repeated scene would cause her an odd sense of downheartedness. How long had it been since she'd had some frivolous fun with a male? Truthfully, even with her former fiancé she couldn't actually remember giggling or sharing some intimate whispers while walking. She and he had been very busy people who tended to accept every social invitation that came their way. They were looked upon as a perfect couple. What she'd come to realize since his unfortunate death was that while they did have a strong bond, the emotion wasn't there. Except for those social engagements, they didn't have a lot in common. They were engaged but never grew serious about a wedding date. She came to understand she'd never loved him and since his death she also accepted the same was probably true of his feelings for her.

Seeing couples lost in their own little world holding hands and walking in the shallow waters of Lake Minnewaska made her wonder if she'd ever enjoy that kind of relationship. As much fun and relaxation as she was having in Glenwood after a week-and-a-half made it very clear she was definitely missing something in her life.

By Wednesday MacPherson had continued her schedule of having breakfast with John Bailey. Various people would eventually join them as the morning progressed including Mayor Good, Sheriff Petracek, Chief Brey, and Nate Morrison. Even Henry Hanson had sat with them that morning of festival week. In his case, he seemed preoccupied and stayed for only a short time. Bailey noticed the same thing and excused his friend's behavior as the stress of running such a large town event.

When their breakfast ended, all went their separate ways knowing they'd all see each other during the course of the day. MacPherson kept up her daily schedule of keeping her eyes and ears open. She only wished she had some hint as to who could be actually in charge of the entire affair going on at the resort.

By Wednesday afternoon, she relaxed in a different way. She played golf...not at the Chippewa Lodge golf course...but at the municipal golf course on the bluff above town just for a break from the crowds in town. She would do so the next afternoon as well. That evening she stopped by a new venue she'd tested the night before...the main watering hole for locals in the back room of Big Bud Bunsen's General Store. That Tuesday night with her investigation completely stalled, she was out just to have some fun. She expected to be the only woman present, but enough locals knew her where she might be accepted. Walking through the alley, she heard a scuffle ahead...something not exactly surprising outside a speak easy. Before the war of words got into fisticuffs, a late model car drove up and two long coated men promptly got out of their vehicle and broke up the fight. They seemed to know what they were doing. She doubted the local deputies could have handled the situation so decisively. She thought it odd how the two men were dressed in plainclothes. She had a strong inclination they were from the Lodge. Her question was why they were performing normal police duties?

When the altercation ended, she continued her march right up to the camouflaged door to the back entrance of the General Store. A local man thirty feet in front of her gave a slow three knock signal and the door was opened to him. Seeing no reason to delay, she walked up to the same backdoor and gave the same slow three knocks. The door was opened and she was in before the guard at the door realized he'd let in a lady. The door guard turned out to be one of Big Bud's sons who she'd already come to know. Bennie Bunsen didn't know what to say.

She beat him to the punch. "Hey Bennie, how are you doing tonight? Can a lady get a drink in this place?"

Bennie again didn't know how to respond. He just motioned her to go into the large room if she wanted. And she did.

At first she wasn't noticed. Then each table of card players began hiding their illegal brews and grabbing their chips as she walked toward the bar. For some reason MacPherson found herself much more comfortable in this environment than a similar one at the resort. She'd become known to enough people in the town that she knew she was considered more a trusted local.

Ordering a drink, she talked with Nate Morrison who didn't feel particularly surprised that she was standing there by the bar. The others in the large room, though, weren't certain of her motives. She might talk to their wives or girl friends. It took Bennie Bunsen to settle the discomfort. He yelled out, "For Christ's sake, fellas, what do you think Lindy's going to do, call the cops?"

The backroom exploded in laughter. Everyone calmed down, especially when MacPherson laughed as hard as the rest of them. From her response, they knew no wives, and especially no girl friends, were going to be told of their presence at Big Bud's. By her being at the busy speak-easy, she was showing that she expected the same courtesy.

As the place relaxed and cards were dealt, she knew she had a new opportunity to listen to some tongues made loose with booze. She even decided to press the situation and sit down at one of the poker tables where she knew a couple of the men. She asked unassumingly, "Is my money good here?"

A startlingly loud sound of laughter burst forth around that table as one of the card players quipped, "Lindy, if you want to lose some of that money you're makin' for writin' your article, we'd be pleased to accept your donation."

Her response was pure Lindy MacPherson...like back at the office. "Boys," she said, "I plan on eating all three meals at the café for the rest of my time here in Glenwood. Looks like you fellows will be picking up the tab. Let's not waste time. Someone deal the cards."

The men around the table guffawed and enjoyed her moxie. She had become one of the 'boys' that evening. As she anteed her first bet, she wasn't certain she liked the designation. She played cards for the next hour and a half buying a round of drinks for the table and having one too many drinks herself. She didn't know how much money she won or lost, but she'd made a lot more friends in that bar that night.

It was Bennie Bunsen who accompanied her over to the city police station when she decided to leave. She wasn't drunk, but he just wanted her to be safe. One of the deputies, Wendell Blake was sitting in his patrol car. No questions were asked; he gave her a ride back to her cabin.

Bunsen whispered to her before leaving, "Lindy, come over any time. You made the place fun tonight." It was as nice a compliment as she'd heard in a long time.

She planned on making Big Bud's a regular stop from then on. On Wednesday night, she gave the three slow knocks around 10:00 and went immediately to an empty seat at a five-person poker table. She knew only one of the other four people, but they had heard of her. When she threw a wad of bills in front of her, she was as welcomed at the table as anyone. That Wednesday night, she only had two drinks. She didn't want to get the reputation that she couldn't hold her liquor. There was plenty of that type of example in the backroom, but no one threatened Lindy MacPherson. She had too many of the boys who would protect her. She felt as safe as she did on her cabin porch.

Again, Bennie Bunsen accompanied her over to the police station down the block just before midnight. Deputy Blake was on duty and was pleased to transport her back to her cabin. He didn't leave until she was safely through her cabin door.

That night she wasn't as tired and read on her porch by gas light until sleep interested her. She felt as comfortable as a bird in a nest. She waved a couple times to a deputy's car as it drove near her cabin every hour. She heard it again driving by as she was falling asleep inside her cabin.

Nothing changed on Thursday. It was just another great day by the lake and another busy festival day...something she now realized she was enjoying too much. Her routine brought her to the Lodge in the late morning after breakfast with Bailey and some more locals.

At the resort, the golf course was already filled; the patio was packed with sunbathing women. She walked around the property hardly noticed, a far cry from her first visit to the resort. That afternoon she again played golf at the public golf course, conversed with booth workers at the park, and stopped by Big Bud's for more poker in the evening. She could tell she was accepted. One of the fellows howled out when she got up to leave with a twenty dollar profit that she was leaving too early.

She laughed openly at their complaints and quipped, "Boys, I have an excuse. I've got my article to finish."

That only brought more jeers. Before she left she left that twenty dollars with Bennie Bunsen to pay for more beers for the guys at her table and the two adjoining tables. It was a small gesture, but it would resonate strongly with the males in that backroom. She was pleased her presence had not caused any friction among the males. She had tried to behave and act towards them like they were 'brothers'. That was her attitude and it seemed to work. The evenings at the speak easy had been quite fun, but futile in terms of picking up more hearsay or worthwhile information.

That Thursday night she accepted a ride back to her cabin this time from Police Chief Rich Brey. They talked for a bit before she went into her cabin.

Brey was especially generous with his comments. "You know, Lindy, I've been in town for a long time. I haven't seen as many visitors get so accepted by the local folks as you. They really appreciate the way you've gotten involved in the festival and seem to enjoy meeting everyone. It's been a real pleasure having you in town. We'll be sad to see you go."

It was a compliment received more in pain than appreciation. She knew that come the weekend that might not be the general feeling about her. Her stomach was already churning in anticipation.

Friday, June 5 began slowly...at least for MacPherson. She'd been at Big Bud's too long the previous night. There were but three days left in the festival, but Friday, Saturday, and most likely Sunday nights were going to be rousing nights to be in Glenwood. When she arrived later than usual at the Glenwood Café, John Bailey, Sheriff Petracek, and Chief Rich Brey kidded her about her late nights without being specific. Whether they knew she was frequenting Big Bud's at night, it didn't matter to her. The way they spoke, though, none of them had any idea. She had a feeling the boys at the speak easy kept her presence as quiet as she kept their secret.

The conversation quickly returned to what the three men had been talking about...how haggard Henry Hanson had been looking that week. They all looked toward the door every time someone walked in, but Henry Hanson never showed that morning.

Their talk soon moved to the festival events for that evening. The new Pope County Lake Queen would be crowned. Some lucky young female was going to win $25 in gift coupons at local stores, ten pounds of meat from Big Bud Bunsen's General Store, and a round trip train trip to St. Paul to tour the capital. MacPherson wondered whether second place would be more preferred.

Extra staging and seating for the beauty contest were being constructed close to the gazebo to handle the expected large pageant crowd. Record numbers of people were also expected that weekend at the lake excursions, the food judging, and the finals in the sailing, water skiing, and boat race competitions. The cow chip throwing contest and the pie eating contests the previous night had drawn big crowds, but nothing like the expectations for crowds both Friday and Saturday nights. A kitten ball tournament was to commence that afternoon with the championship games to be played Saturday before sundown. Of course the biggest event...the charity golf tournament... would bring in the largest hoard of spectators for the weekend.

While MacPherson made certain she continued her public role as a magazine writer, she was now doing so half-heartedly. She went through the motion of again interviewing Mayor Good after she saw him coming out of the back room of Big Bud's General Store just before lunch. He was wiping some beer suds off his mouth when she caught up with him. She knew the Canadian beer would likely make him particularly verbal.

Claiming she wanted an update on the progress of the festival, it was like asking a minister to preach. If Charlie B. Good had an audience even if it was just a magazine article, he was ready to perform.

He expounded, "I tell you, young lady, wait until you see our charity golf tournament starting tomorrow morning. That event brings in proceeds that have helped refurbish so many buildings in town including the school, the fire house, and of course a lot of the churches. We got the best danged churches in the state as far as I'm concerned. Yes, indeedy, Miss MacPherson, we are one lucky Gol danged community. To think it all started just five years ago when some gentlemen from out of state chose our fine community as a vacation haven for their friends and business associates."

As soon as he said what he'd said, he looked like he'd swallowed a pickle whole. He'd said too much.

When Lindy boldly but innocently asked him who those gentlemen were, the mayor's brain suddenly went hay wire. He appeared shaken, looked at his watch, and responded, 'Miss MacPherson, damned if I can remember, but I recall they were just real nice people...and then they spread the word about our fine community. Yes sirree, our town has been just damned lucky....damned lucky."

He raised his chest thrilled that he'd talked his way out of another tight spot. But, he'd sobered up very quickly. He was ready to move on. Waving to an invisible voter across the street, he began to head in that direction. His voice didn't allow Lindy to get a word in edge wise. "Hell's bells, young lady, my public is callin'. Gotta go, gotta be, gotta do...I'm a busy man. Hope you're having fun this week...and make certain you spell my last name in your article with two 'o's. I don't want to be competing with the Almighty."

He exploded in laughter over his own witticism and waddled down the street.

As Lindy watched the Mayor greet everyone in sight, she felt she had just finished interviewing a circus announcer. The man gave a lot of his time to the town, but she'd never met a more intolerable but still lovable self-promoter. She also had a strong feeling he was well aware of the man or the group behind the activities at the Lodge. He would be one man who could never forgive whoever ended the gravy train for the town of Glenwood. He would be particularly disappointed as would most other people when it would be found she was working under cover. She pondered how the kind, thoughtful, friendly eyes from most every citizen she'd met would transform to flashes of disgust and dislike. Even John and Adam Bailey might not think as highly of her when they found out how she duped the town and had not been straight with them.

With these thoughts poisoning her mind, she found her very spirit changing. The contentment she felt since she'd arrived almost two weeks before had dissipated in just a few hours that morning. Come Sunday evening after the obligatory raid, the locals would have to deal with their five year money making festival was coming to an end. They'd been looking the other way for so long...and they rationalized their actions as necessary for the betterment of their community. She would be taking something very important away from the community.

MacPherson absent-mindedly spent her time that afternoon between the booths at City Park and watching the primary betting booth take in more wagers outside the gates of the Lodge. She also heard there was a storm brewing to the west that might curtail that Friday evening's events. But, the crowds in City Park seemed not to care. Their enjoyment superseded any concerns.

It was in the middle of the afternoon she headed for the Glenwood Café just to get away from the crowd of people milling around City Park and to get a late lunch. That decision to walk over to the café would turn out to be very fortunate. On the way she would finally gain a significant lead for an investigation that was going nowhere...and it was entirely coincidental.

It all started with her seeing Adam Bailey parking his Plymouth truck by the back storage shed behind Big Bud's General Store. She was ready to yell a greeting to the busy young man, but his actions made her stop. He began routinely loading the truck with everything from cases of Canadian Beer to frozen containers of meat and fish. He also handled some unmarked boxes with extreme care indicating the contents were probably hard liquor. That scene was no surprise to her. She was well aware booze was being transported into Glenwood a couple times a week from Winnipeg, Manitoba.

She decided to go greet the young man knowing he was just doing a job for some people at the Lodge. If he didn't do it, someone else would be standing in line to carry out the same work.

She sighed. It didn't matter. All this would come to a halt on Sunday. Shrugging, she hustled across the street greeting Adam with a genuine smile. Truly she was happy for him. From what John had alluded, his son was profiting more this week than he or his father would profit from their fall harvest.

He was thoroughly ingenuous and pleased to see her. He kept right on loading boxes of booze as he uttered, "Hey Lindy, I haven't seen you much this week. My dad says you've become so popular in our town that you could be elected mayor if Charlie Good ever stepped down. Of course, we both know Charlie would have to die before that happens. Even then he'd probably somehow get his name on the ballot."

They both laughed knowingly.

Adam finally leaned against the truck to rest. The high humidity was making him sweat profusely. Still he was full of conversation. "Lindy, I hope you're planning on coming out to the charity golf tournament tomorrow? It's a competition unlike any you'll ever see."

She nodded, "Yes, you'll probably see me there eventually."

Then she paused as she watched him throw the last of the unmarked boxes onto his truck. She felt compelled to make a statement. "Adam, you're going to get some kind of award for helping the Canadian economy with all this food and drink shipped in from Winnipeg. You're a growing guy, but I doubt you'll be able to finish all that food by yourself."

He chuckled, "All these boxes? Oh, this is nothing. I make a couple trips a day for Loni. I take care of a lot of errands for him during the festival week. He's got a constant party going on at either his cabin or out on the patio by the golf course. It's a big week for him with all his friends either playing in the tournament or just being here for the social times. The fact is I've been here two other times earlier today just to pick up more food and booze. Usually I just caddy or run errands for him. But this food delivery had become my chief job yesterday and today with the hoard of people at the Lodge. I know Loni really appreciates my help given he has a tournament to run.

Then Adam let go with a small giggle. "You know, I think I've got Mr. D'Annelli figured out in these days before the tournament. I'll bet he's spending all this money on food and drink because he wants all his friends playing in the event to get toasted tonight. He'll have the advantage if they're sluggish and hung over for tomorrow's tee-time. That's Loni...he's always looking to better the odds."

There was a momentary silence in that late afternoon air between the two of them. Adam thought she was just looking out toward the western skies at what had become a huge weather system bearing down on the Lake Minnewaska area. In fact, Lindy hardly noticed the distant cloud cover. She stood there just dazed over what just got said. Just like that, she had learned the name of the organizer and manager of this entire affair. It had to be. She'd heard the name and the reputation, but not for quite a spell. It was as if he'd dropped off the face of the earth.

It made her want to confirm again what Adam had just revealed. Hoping he wouldn't notice her suddenly nervous smile, she asked carefully, "So...who's this guy again? Maybe I can call him for an interview...you know, for my magazine article. Maybe I can get some free tickets to his tournament as well."

Adam continued to show absolute virtue as he openly repeated the name. He seemed surprised she hadn't heard the name already. He repeated, "Sure...his name is Loni D'Annelli. He's from Chicago. I don't really know what he does...something about running a union. We never talk about it. He just seems to have a lot of friends."

Then he quietly admitted, "You know, I think some of his friends are a bit reckless, but they sure are a funny lot. Off the golf course, though, they're not the kind of people I'd want for acquaintances much less friends. But, when you get these guys out on the golf course, I find them all hilarious. I've never laughed harder."

Lindy played ignorant and chanced another question. "So Adam, this Loni fellow, have you known him for a long time. Would I have a chance to talk with him?"

She knew Adam's answer already but wanted to keep him talking. "Oh God no, Lindy. He's especially busy these last couple days through the weekend. I've known him for the past four years. He doesn't want to direct the attention on himself. He's just busy with the charity tournament and keeping all his friends happy while they're at the Lodge. Not a lot of people know what effort he puts in."

Adam showed a satisfaction that he'd just complimented a person who he felt deserved to get more credit than he'd heretofore had ever been given. As for MacPherson, she only nodded with a blank look on her face. She couldn't believe the answer to the ringleader question at Chippewa Lodge was as simple as asking John Bailey's own son.

The name Loni D'Annelli was becoming clearer in her mind. From discussions only occasionally at her Minneapolis U.S. Attorney's office, she knew D'Annelli was a Chicago union kingpin although his true vocation had more to do with being an underworld hustler. Coincidentally, she knew he had close ties to a friend and fellow mob hustler in the Twin Cities named Willie LaCurso. She kicked herself recalling that LaCurso had been one man she'd seen the first time she'd visited the resort almost two weeks before. She'd just never seen or heard of D'Annelli being part of the crowd at the Lodge...albeit the times she visited the resort were limited. He'd obviously done a great job keeping his name under wraps.

Adam didn't notice her glazed facial expression as he jumped back into his truck to return to the Lodge. Leaning out the window he repeated, "So Lindy, I'll see you tomorrow morning at the golf course. Just a warning...if you leave early enough you'll get parking. The traffic gets pretty heavy by mid-morning since there are other lake contests going on close to the Lodge entrance.

She vacantly nodded. "Yeh...ah...thanks for the forewarning, Adam. I'll probably get out to the Lodge kind of early like you suggest."

As Adam drove away, Lindy had to catch her breath. Loni D'Annelli was her man. Whatever time remained before Sunday, she had to re-energize her investigation and concentrate her efforts on the Chicago hood. If she could gain crucial evidence proving his guilt as leader of the gambling ring as well as the man behind the safehouse for various criminals at the Lodge, she could make the police raid on Sunday a real coup.

Suddenly Lindy MacPherson was no longer taking a break. Her mind was pumping as she thought of the additional pieces of evidence she needed. With so many closed mouths, she wasn't going to learn that much more than what she'd just heard from Adam Bailey.

One huge thought then emerged. For D'Annelli to run a gambling operation in such a secluded location, he would need cash...and that cash had to be stored some place very secure. If she could find that location and tie the cash to him, it would be the proof needed too convict this gangster.

Her mind then returned to the person who seemed to be in the middle of everything happening in town. The supervisor of the two Presbyterian Men's Club Calcutta booths...she had to find Henry Hanson. He had to know the story behind D'Annelli. Maybe she could coerce him to talk. But, she knew the problem. Hanson was always on the move. No one would know...or admit...to his whereabouts. She figured to march over to the Mill and wait there until Hell froze just to intercept the town leader.

As she walked there became an obvious problem to her plans. As she looked past the Feed & Grain Mill a couple blocks down the street, she could see the immense proportions of the approaching storm coming from the west side of Lake Minnewaska. It was about 5:00 and it looked like the evening events were going to have to be postponed. Local folks were securing ropes to tents, packing boxes, and covering the tables within the booths with plastic and canvas. Her inclination was to help out, but her mind was on a more critical matter...to find Hanson and convince him to help her. She was mindful that she'd likely have to blow her cover to get him to talk.

Arriving at the Mill, she suspected only Nate Morrison would be in the office. She wasn't disappointed. Morrison was securing windows and doors at the Mill office in preparation for the storm. He was of no help. "Lindy, I haven't seen Henry since this morning and that was for about five minutes. I have to think he's out at the Lodge or probably packing for his upcoming vacation. You know he always takes off immediately after the festival...sometimes even before it ends from what some people say."

She had a funny feeling if she didn't find Hanson very soon, she wasn't going to find him. Jumping in her old Ford, she pressed on the accelerator peeling the tires as she drove out of the Mill parking lot to the shoreline road. The vehicle reacted stiffly having not been driven that aggressively.

Driving along the east side of the lake, she now saw the powerful storm darkening the skies like night on the opposite side of the lake. The wind was picking up noticeably as she drove right up to the Presbyterian booth across from Chippewa Lodge. A few of the volunteers at the booth had already secured the tent and boxed all other papers and paraphernalia. All others were working in the eerie calm before the storm to secure the larger casino tent and its contents.

It was then she saw Henry sitting in a chair in the open air trying to make some final entries in a large book as the wind whipped around him. There was no question what was on that ledger; she would have liked to see the amount...and most of all, where the money was being stored.

She was about to approach Hanson when from her periphery she caught another man advance toward him from a closer angle. She stayed in her vehicle and just watched. The other man was huge...very broad across the shoulders with a barrel chest. The man's hair was jet black. He wore golf clothing and smoked a stogie. Henry was taller, but the other man, though shorter, looked like he could swallow the Mill manager whole.

The two of them got into a cordial but serious discussion. At that moment she knew she was looking at Loni D'Annelli. What was interesting to her was how Hanson showed no intimidation. He was obviously very comfortable conversing with the Chicago racketeer. Henry still looked haggard, but seemed to take great effort not to show any weakness towards D'Annelli.

In less than a minute the two men's conversation was over as the wind increased in velocity. The large man turned and strolled back towards the Lodge watching the impending storm with every step. Henry didn't seem pleased. As he turned toward the vision of the oncoming storm, his shoulders stooped noticeably. MacPherson hesitated. It was not the time to approach the man. What she intended to say to him would require his undivided attention. She figured to catch up with him after the storm blew through.

Her eyes focused back toward the bigger man trotting back onto the resort property. Everyone still outside appeared to be greeting him...even the maintenance workers. He moved and talked with people with confidence. From what she could see, the man was....popular. She thought, 'No wonder people weren't talking about this man. He had the charisma of a successful politician and the presence of a movie star.' She couldn't believe she hadn't seen this man in previous visits to the Lodge. He was hard to miss.

As she watched him disappear into the Lodge restaurant, she couldn't help but hold a certain amount of respect for the man. No matter what he'd done in his past or what he might be involved in at the Lodge, he was enterprising and probably worth more than she cared to imagine. By his very air, she knew she had her man. Now she had to find the proof.

A deep rumble of thunder made the ground quake and brought her out of her trance. The mountainous cloud cover made the grandiose lake seem small. The massive system spread north and south as far as the eye could see. The lightning was non-stop in those bulbous clouds. It was time to seek the safest place to wait out a storm, but she was not going to be stranded with a bunch of hoodlums at Chippewa Lodge.

MacPherson shoved her old Ford in gear. It was then about 5:30 as she drove speedily in front of the storm along the lake front. When she arrived in town, a few people in City Park were still scurrying around securing anything they felt wasn't tied down. It didn't surprise her that two of the men were John Bailey and Nate Morrison. She got out of her car to help but John ran past her shouting in the growing wind, "I've got to get out to the farm to make certain all the doors to the farm buildings and windows in the house are shut." He took off in his old Plymouth without saying another word.

A couple ministers leaving their booths wondered aloud if God was finally paying attention to what was going on at the Presbyterian betting booth. She had to chuckle at that quip. She felt the first drops of rain as Nate yelled for her to head for his truck parked on the edge of the park. They both dove in the front cab as the storm hit with an indescribable vengeance. The truck literally shook as the rain came down in buckets. Some tree limbs snapped falling on one of the booths. They looked at the lake being pounded by the wind and rain. It looked like an angry ocean with small waves repeatedly lapping violently up on shore.

The two of them sat in that truck knowing there was probably a better place to hide out during the storm, but certainly none with a better view of Mother Nature's hostility. A half hour later during a slight hiatus in the wind and rain, the two of them drove the few blocks to the Glenwood Café. Hurrying into the eating establishment, they were greeted by numerous other very soaked citizens who had sought safety in the same place. Immediately she felt safe, almost as if she'd made it home.

About sixteen fellow Glenwood townspeople plus Lindy MacPherson had dinner that night at the café. As much as she enjoyed the laughter and storytelling, she felt a cloud over her knowing that she was within days of disappointing these people. She kept telling herself she had a job to do, but that didn't make her feel better.

As the pelting rain began to lighten, Gertrude Shultz, who worked at the county courthouse, waddled down the street to the café with an umbrella turned inside out. She was soaked once in the café. One of the waitresses got her towels and a shawl. As she drank some warm coffee, she mentioned the call-in from Chief Brey a few minutes before she left the office. He'd reported the sighting of a biplane parked...of all places...beside the barn up at John Bailey's farm. Brey had estimated some crazy pilot had made an emergency landing on the bluffs just east of town on Hwy. #28. He surmised that if the pilot made it to the Bailey farmhouse, he was in good care.

MacPherson paid little heed to the story other than appreciating the good fortune for the pilot. She didn't have much regard for the flyer figuring he had to be some kind of lunatic for flying too close to a major storm. Then she smiled knowing that whether the fellow had a brain in his head or not, John would put the man up for the night and feed him.

When the worst of the storm finally subsided, Nate Morrison drove her back to her car parked by City Park. The young man just a few years younger now seemed years older as he expressed his concern about his Aunt's farm north of Glenwood and whether the buildings made it through the storm. Looking at the young man, she wondered how he would take the aftermath of the police raid...and the possible arrest of

Henry Hanson. Would this new friend even want to associate with her once her true identity was unfurled?

That evening there was a cool breeze coming off the lake as the storm moved eastward away from the Glenwood area. She sat out on the cabin porch with a blanket wrapped around her shoulders and legs. The night was eerily quiet without the festival activities now cancelled or postponed. There would be plenty of need for clean up the next morning at City Park and around the town. For once she would not be helping out. Her plan was to be at the Lodge bright and early for the charity golf tournament. She had one more day before she would be calling in the state troopers. Her hope was that she would have the time to reason with Henry Hanson. But, she was not going to depend on her efforts to persuade him to help her. Instead, she figured to follow the movements of Loni D'Annelli throughout the day. No telling what evidence he might provide just by his actions. Also, staff members at the resort would be at their posts with little to do once the players and the gallery went out onto the golf course. They'd be prime bait for questioning, especially if she used her cover effectively. She would imply that she'd be interviewing D'Annelli later in the day. If she could get just one person to open up, her case against this mobster just might be made more secure.

She eventually moved inside her cabin. The absolute stillness of the night made other sounds more pronounced. The wind was rushing through the trees. The toads and crickets croaked without restraint. Before she nodded off that night, she gave one more whimsical thought about the biplane pilot staying at the Bailey farm that night. Whoever he was, he'd put himself into some unnecessary danger flying into a storm. She wondered if she wasn't doing the same thing to herself by delaying the raid at Chippewa Lodge.

Lindy MacPherson pulled the blankets close to her body that night. She couldn't have known how that Friday night would be her last good night's sleep she'd have for the next couple days. Little could she fathom that the same wild and foolish biplane pilot sleeping out at the Bailey farm had flown into her life that evening. He would begin influencing her life beginning the very next morning. Sitting alone on a cabin porch would no longer be part of her evenings.

CHAPTER

11

MacPherson was up very early on Saturday looking forward to attending the so-called 'charity golf tournament' with excited anticipation, yet mixed feelings. So many things were going to come to an end by the next day. The impact on the town and the Lodge would be an immediate loss of revenue. But, it had to be done.

From a law enforcement standpoint, there was no telling what the state patrol would find when they entered the resort property. She would supply them a list she'd accumulated in the previous week of the crooks, escapees, and bail jumpers along with certain underworld mob figures that she could identity.

She had decided to schedule the raid on Sunday afternoon to give her every last hour to discover evidence against Loni D'Annelli. She planned on making two private phone calls that day...one to Ernest Lundquist and one to her contacts in the state patrol. Lundquist would summon the Bureau of Investigation. From experience she knew an all out raid on Chippewa Lodge could be organized within hours. There would be enough law enforcement people to surround the resort property. Her only real concern was either the state patrol or the impatient boys from the Bureau jumping the gun before she was ready.

Driving out to the Lodge that Saturday morning in her creaking, government-owned Ford, her mind was now mostly fixated on the whereabouts of the exorbitant amount of capital required to run any large gambling business. The cash had to be hidden. It certainly wouldn't be part of an account in some local bank. Further she doubted the operating capital would be concealed at the resort, not with the band of hooligans staying at the Lodge. But, it had to be close, possibly secured someplace within the town.

MacPherson was so engrossed on the possible location of the money, she wasn't ready to face her first challenge when she approached the front entrance of the resort. No longer could she just drive onto the Lodge property. A number of fierce looking men were making certain no one entered without a ticket or proper pass. Slowing her vehicle two daunting, stern looking goons meandered up to her car. She showed them her magazine identification. They were not only unimpressed, they were indignant. A press person would be the last type of individual allowed entry.

One of the men growled, "No ticket, lady, no entrance. Go park your car down the road and buy a ticket like the rest of these people."

Just the way the man spoke raised her dander. She wasn't about to be intimidated by some half-wit gangster. She leaned out the window and directed the man to come closer. He kind of smiled and looked at his friends like he was going to possibly get some action later. When he got close enough, she smiled and whispered to him, "Gee, Mister, Loni will certainly be disappointed if I don't stop by his cabin before the tournament gets started."

The man blanched and suddenly became real polite. He stepped back, his truculent look melting like ice on a hot pavement. He jokingly rebuked her, "Lady, why didn't you tell me about Loni in the first place?"

Looking straight forward and gunning her engine, she responded with no warmth, "That's what I thought."

He motioned for one of his mates to open the gate. The gruff man then pointed over towards the practice area where she could park her car.

As she drove toward the golf shop and practice area, she was quite surprised by the number of people already prancing around the resort area. No doubt there would be quite a crowd by the opening tee time scheduled later that morning. The spectators would add to her difficulty both that day and the next day during the raid. Deciphering innocent ticket holders from the deadbeats living or hiding out at the resort would be a real problem. The pressure of making the right decision was making her head swim.

Seeing two golfers already hitting practice balls, she took note of the condition of the golf course. It was wet but no worse for wear considering the previous night's heavy storm. A maintenance crew was already cleaning debris from the fairways and greens.

Walking by the first tee box, she grabbed some scorecard pencils. She wanted to be well prepared to detail whatever names she might hear or come across during the day, especially those who hung close to D'Annelli.

MacPherson was about to enter the Lodge restaurant in search of D'Annelli when she heard some loud laughter and clapping over by the practice range. It seemed out of place so early in the morning being that it was almost two hours before the tournament was to begin. There was a small gallery forming a horseshoe around one of the players warming up. The golfer was hitting balls with some intensity and then stopping to talk with the folks in the growing gallery. She was impressed that one of the 'sleaze bags' involved in the tournament was being so friendly with the crowd.

Striding over toward the growing horde, she listened to the man whack away at the practice balls while simultaneously keeping the conversation going. She didn't understand why he was being so social. If this man had some kind of criminal background, he certainly would not want the attention he seemed to be seeking.

Nosing her way through a three person layer of people, she came face to face with a very dashing, sharply dressed man. She couldn't get over how crisply he was hitting shots while conversing with the small crowd. His manner and smile seemed so genuine. With his blondish hair blowing in the slight morning breeze, she was reminded of a man who liked the outdoors. He was not at all like the slick back ruffians she hoped would be locked up by the next day.

As he continued to play to the crowd, she noticed how his eyes darted around the crowd and occasionally looking back toward the Lodge restaurant. It was as if he was expecting someone. Then he'd return his attention to the audience asking someone his or her name and where they lived. If he was familiar, he was very open that he'd been in the community. As he cleaned his golf club and replaced it in his bag, he related a story about the time he was in the town. "Yes ma'am," he said, "I was at your county fair a couple times a few years back. I met some great people. I was a barnstorming pilot offering rides in my bi-plane for a couple bucks per person...less if the girl was pretty."

The little joke made the crowd laugh as he pulled out another club and began hitting majestic niblick shots into the sky. She found herself attracted to the man as much as she didn't want to be. The guy had to be a loser if he hung around with the likes of the 'guests' at Chippewa Lodge. Still, she was attracted to his friendliness and style. He was sharply dressed with a purplish shirt and tie combination that made him look more like he was going to a formal occasion than a golf match.

More spectators entering the front gate crowded around the impromptu entertainment. With her curiosity growing, she moved over directly in front of the golfer so she could hear his every word. She whispered to a few people standing close by, "Who is he?"

She got only shrugs. She made a note in her booklet to catch up with him later. She identified him as 'fancy dude', as if a reminder would be needed.

She was about to move away from the group when he began to hit some more sporty shots. She knew golf, so his trick shots caught her attention. She decided to remain as did the ever increasing gallery. Even some of the other golfers arriving at the practice area stood in amazement over some of the shots he was hitting.

He mentioned again to one of the spectators about the time a few years before during his barnstorming days how he'd landed his biplane in their town prior to a storm. That comment finally resonated as she realized this fellow was likely the foolish pilot forced down near John Bailey's farm by the previous night's storm. Her initial positive impression of the man suddenly cascaded. She figured he had to be a complete idiot for having been so reckless with his life.

Nonetheless, she didn't stop staring at him. The talkative younger man seemed more the image of Bobby Jones, the classy national renowned Georgia amateur she'd read about in the newspapers. However, she knew Bobby Jones was a lawyer. A lawyer wouldn't be caught dead playing with a bunch of deadbeats and criminals like the one's playing in this tournament. She could only justify that he was some type of slick operator out for a quick buck...a hustler of the first order with his fancy clothes and confident air.

Her thought about the pilot being a slick dandy was confirmed seconds later when he made a rather outlandish wager about hitting a golf ball out of the practice range in order to scare an innocent lady off her patio and back into her house. The crowd was taken with his roguish self-confidence. To MacPherson he seemed brash and a bit too arrogant for her liking.

It was the first time Lindy MacPherson had ever laid eyes on James Lawton...and her first inkling about him was anything but positive. Still she stayed...as if trying to solve the mystery. Why was he playing in a tournament with a bunch of gangsters? And, why was he so disarmingly friendly to the patrons. The other golfers certainly were not. And, why would he be making such a brazen $50 bet with someone he'd never met in the audience? His chances of winning the bet were low...at least that was the appearance.

She knew enough about golf from her father being a member of the Minneapolis Country Club that the normal practice range ball was soft and couldn't fly as far as a regular golf ball. To hit it out of the Chippewa Lodge practice range meant that the golf ball would have to fly at least two hundred and fifty yards. It was a loser bet. Everyone else in the crowd thought so as well. He didn't hit her as the type who would make that kind of hopeless wager.

Then she started to notice a few things. That morning's practice balls were brand new golf balls...not cheap range balls. The man in charge of the tournament...Loni D'Annelli...was at least trying to make the event as first class as possible. With new golf balls, two hundred and fifty yards became quite possible. The golfer also had a favorable wind. She grinned slightly now knowing the pilot was taking advantage of the circumstances...but that didn't change her mind about him. It only proved again that he was a bit of a swindler...and that maybe he was with his type of people after all.

What followed was his asking her for the flat-headed scoring pencil she was using for notations in her booklet. The flat-headed pencil provided him another advantage. This way he could better hit the golf ball on the upswing and carry the shot longer than normal.

No one in that group of spectators including MacPherson could imagine balancing the golf ball on top of the flat-headed pencil and that it would make a difference in the length of his shot. When he hit the ball with the extra swing speed and the ball elevated three inches above the normal tee height, there was a collective gasp by the assembled crowd as the ball was launched into the early morning sky.

Still, the bet was that his shot had to scare the unaware woman off the patio into her house. That meant he had to hit the ball somewhere in the neighborhood of her house. MacPherson just shook her head in disgust with the incredible adolescence of the wager.

Still she stayed at the practice range watching him. He was definitely entertaining and more skilled than she would have guessed. When that first ball hit the house and hardly got a response from the woman in her back patio, the man's eyes twinkled as he asked MacPherson for another flat-headed pencil. He didn't seem bothered by the lack of success of his first shot. In fact, he seemed more pleased with the reaction from the crowd.

This time Shot #2 rolled by the poor lady sitting in her patio. The ball had careened off the garage and bounced across the patio before settling in some shrubbery. From that distance even the spectators could see the shot had gotten the young lady's attention. She got up from her chair even glanced back toward the golf course not believing a ball from the practice range could make it to her property. Nevertheless, by the resounding crowd noise, she had to realize something strange was going on, though she had no idea she was such a key factor in a bet.

All eyes were back on MacPherson as the golfer looked over toward her to plead for another flat-headed pencil. Her only thoughts were,

'I'll be damned if I'm going to give this lout my last scorecard pencil and be an accomplice to a murder.'

She tried to retreat back into the crowd, but it was impossible. He moved next to her noticing that she didn't like being part of the attention. He leaned toward her ear pleading softly, "Please miss, just one last pencil and I'll not bother you again."

If she denied him the pencil, she knew she'd bring more notice upon herself. She didn't want the crowd booing her. With a skeptical glance, she tossed him another pencil. He gave her a wink as if trying to convince her he was really a decent fellow.

MacPherson had no interest in watching that third shot as she filtered back through the crowd. As that last attempt bulleted high into the Lake Minnewaska sky and eventually came down on that house...and crash through an upper bedroom window...she was already observing some other golfers warming up on the practice range. Thirty yards away she recognized two other hoodlums whose pictures were in her Minneapolis office files. She shuddered when she recognized the evil looking Danny A'Matto. She pondered if that man had ever smiled in his life...least of all having a mother who could love him. Next to A'Matto was the man she loathed beyond description. Willie LaCurso with his ever present small cigar protruding from in his mouth as he swung his golf club had the look of a true competitor that morning.

The thunderous roar from the crowd caught the momentary attention of A'Matto and LaCurso. Their faces showed disapproval about the showboating golfer they'd never seen before but assumed he was a new player in the field.

MacPherson understood immediately that the cunning rogue had somehow won his bet. She looked to the far end of the practice area and saw that the lady was no longer sitting on the patio...and the upstairs window had been shattered. Again, Lindy just shook her head in a 'boys will be boys' response.

Being drawn back to that scene, she then saw something quite unexplainable. As the bystanders were clapping, laughing, and patting him on his back, the fresh-faced golfer raised his arms to quiet the crowd. He declared to the assembly, "Folks, the loss of $50 was bad enough. It was just an innocent wager. But, the cost and hassle of repairing the damaged window...I feel bad about that extra punishment. So, my friend, here's your $50 back to pay for the damage."

The playful golfer could have been elected governor on the spot with the heartfelt cheers from every person surrounding that little scene. The excitement seemed out of place for so early in the morning.

Even the fellow with the broken window took back his $50 with a smile on his face and seemed no longer annoyed.

That little scene caused MacPherson to stop dead in her tracks and stare at the slick but handsome golfer. He acted as if he didn't need or care about the money. That piece of empathy would not have been done by a carnival act type of guy and especially not by one of the leeches staying at the Lodge that week. Now she was even more intrigued by this horse of a different breed.

Just then her concentration was abruptly broken. She noticed Adam Bailey springing from the Lodge restaurant accompanying a huge broad-shouldered man with a stogie sticking out of his mouth. With a hat, bright golf shirt and white pants, she had no problem recognizing the big man as the same one she'd seen the day before talking with Henry Hanson. That morning Loni D'Annelli seemed even bigger as he walked next to his caddy.

She watched as the large man strolled over toward golf performer who was still getting congratulations from members of the gallery. That was her first indication the golfer was not part of D'Annelli's entourage seeing the Chicago hood offer his mammoth mitt in a handshake to the suddenly reticent golfer. It appeared to be the first time they'd met.

What ensued was interesting. They chatted but were closely examining each other's words and movements as they spoke. They then leisurely hit some range balls while continuing to talk. It was apparent they wanted to get to know one another. If their conversation lagged, Adam Bailey seemed to pick up on the small talk to keep the two men conversing. There was another surprise. Adam and the golfer seemed to be quite familiar with one another...as if working together.

Then D'Annelli quit hitting balls and appeared to be talking rather purposefully with the trick shot artist. A moment later they shook hands as if some kind of deal had been struck. None of this made sense to her, but she enjoyed Adam's antics as he walked behind D'Annelli back toward the resort restaurant. Adam turned back toward the golfer and made a comical face while gesturing with a thumbs-up sign. That confirmed her thought. The golfer and young Mr. Bailey had to be in cahoots.

MacPherson couldn't help but smile. If she wanted to know more about this mischievous character on the practice tee, she had Adam to question. For her, the morning had become a bit more fascinating.

The coincidence didn't stop there. Staying comfortably behind him, MacPherson followed the golfer five minutes later over to the restaurant entrance where none other than John Bailey was relaxing on a porch chair smoking a pipe. The two men didn't say much, but the way Bailey's jaw dropped he'd been told something totally unexpected. The golfer laid his clubs down at Bailey's feet and proceeded into the Lodge without another word.

She now was certain something was happening between the Baileys and this interesting, even intriguing young trick shot golfer. She got the feeling that the golfer was as much a fake in this tournament of scoundrels as she was working as a travel magazine writer. So, what could be his purpose? If he were an agent for the Bureau of Investigation, it would be a classic case of two Federal offices tripping over one another on the same case.

Her desire to find Henry Hanson now no longer took priority. Until she found out the golfer's true purpose in being involved in this charity event, her eyes were going to be following both him and Loni D'Annelli.

With a sun hat and sun glasses to conceal her identity from any of the reprobates who may have seen her prior at the Lodge, MacPherson felt safer in numbers. The flow of spectators entering the resort grounds was impressive. For what she had to do that day, she also preferred to stay distant from the two Baileys. There was no reason to get them into any trouble by being friends with her. Besides, she needed to get used to being estranged from the folks she'd gotten to know in Glenwood given what she was obligated to do the next day. That alienation would no doubt include John and Adam Bailey.

Hearing that the players were meeting in the restaurant at 9:30, attending that get-together became her next objective. She didn't look forward to the depraved comments and wicked looks. As she strode toward the Lodge hearing the loud, raucous shouting and laughing, her mood turned dark. How she'd like to cut one of the ruffians off at the knees...figuratively or actually.

When she climbed the stairs to the restaurant, one of the outdoor guards stepped in front of her. He had a lascivious look as he grinned, "Where you goin', babe?"

The words sounded like fingernails on a blackboard. There were a number of responses she wanted to voice, but her goal of getting into the Lodge restaurant prevailed. Through gritted teeth she replied, "I'm going into the Lodge to see my boyfriend. If you boys get in my way again, I'll tell Loni how you physically abused me. What do you think you're chances are that you'll see tomorrow?"

Her threat was effective. Both guards stepped back as if she just admitted to having Tuberculosis. They both showed a renewed respect. With stone-faced reverence, the same man said, "Enjoy the day, ma'am."

Lindy entered the foyer of the Lodge with more confidence. Her next step was to get into the even more heavily guarded restaurant. That was when she saw the trick shot artist standing by the lobby phone. She turned away so he wouldn't recognize her. It helped that his mind was obviously on something else. Suddenly he began to talk animatedly. Grabbing a magazine, she sat in a chair across the lobby from him but within ear shot of some of his conversation. He was talking with someone named 'Charlie' and pleading with the man to hurry. The call was very peculiar lasting but a minute. When the golfer hung up a smile spread across his face as if he'd won a raffle.

This baffling man then sauntered over to the entrance of the smoke-filled restaurant saying some words to the guards who then let him pass into the player's meeting. Seeing that interchange, she knew it was going to be difficult to talk her way by that cluster of guards.

She tried another angle. Speaking to the desk clerk she told him she was hungry and needed access to the restaurant. She hoped he might have some kind of password to give her or suggest another door to enter. Immediately she could see this pipsqueak of a man was not going to help her. He'd seen enough females being passed off as another of the many 'nieces' staying at the resort. He hardly hid his disdain. "Miss, as you should know, you're not allowed in the breakfast area until Mr. D'Annelli finishes going over the rules of today's competition. The patio is open if you'd like to get an early start on your tan." Then he turned away rolling his eyes.

MacPherson wanted to reach over and grab the snooty desk clerk by his nose, but again she remained cool. She didn't have time to waste. She smiled to herself thinking that the clerk's impression of her would likely change after the next day's police raid.

Ignoring the desk clerk's warning, Lindy decided to approach the restaurant entrance anyway. She walked confidently to the door. One of the large guards stepped in her way. "Hey, good looking, who do you belong to?"

That was too much. Both her femininity and her self-worth were being slandered. Her response was quick...way too quick as she stared into the restaurant trying to memorize all the faces seated at the tables. Icily she retorted, "I belong to no one, you big turd. I'm a guest. Don't I have the right to eat breakfast?"

Immediately she knew she'd made a mistake. She should have made reference to Loni D'Annelli. The guard stood even taller now blocking her view. He luckily maintained his calm. "Well, Miss, you can eat in the restaurant in about a half hour. Right now there's a private meeting going on. When you come back, maybe we can have a little bite together...what do you say, sweetie?"

Ignoring the guard's suggestive tone, she backed away mad at herself for letting her pride get in the way of doing her job. However, she wasn't about to give up. She retreated back to the lobby her teeth grinding knowing that she was missing an important opportunity to observe all these mugs together.

It turned out she was delayed only ten minutes. All she needed was some further inspiration...and a $20 bill given to a lucky waitress in the ladies room. She told the waitress the uniform would be returned in a half hour as long as the waitress kept her mouth shut and guarded Lindy's regular clothes. That appeared to be no problem. The waitress grabbed the $20, stripped off her outer uniform, and disappeared into a stall with a magazine saying, "See you in a half hour, honey."

In that same, but ill-fitting uniform, and pulling her hair up in a bun, MacPherson not only walked unimpeded into the restaurant, but she was able to prance freely to and from the restaurant's kitchen into the eating area. The big guard she'd just called a 'turd' didn't even recognize her as she hurried by him. Even then, she didn't escape the suggestive comments. The other guard patted her on her behind as she walked by. "Hey doll, where you been all my life?" This time she only gritted her teeth at the leech. Adjusting her undergarments she turned and put a forced coquettish look on her face and winked.

The two guards grinned at each other lasciviously as they watched her walk toward the kitchen appreciating that more leg than normal was showing.

In the next minute, MacPherson made mental notes of a few more notorious mob figures in that restaurant. She strode by the tables pouring coffee and listening for names. When she got pinched a few too many times, she retreated to the kitchen door as Loni D'Annelli shouted for order and commenced with the rules of the day.

As he spoke she positioned herself at the side of the kitchen. A bigger fellow with the loudest chartreuse shirt inadvertently blocked her from being seen by the restaurant manager. She leaned against the wall and watched the proceedings. The guy next to her with the eye-popping shirt seemed to be studying the men in that restaurant as intently as she was. In fact, he was concentrating so hard he didn't give her a look. In some ways she found that bothersome. Then again with her borrowed, ill-fitting uniform and plain Jane hair-do, she knew she was not the most fetching female in that room.

When D'Annelli finished explaining the rules, all the players began filing out of the restaurant to prepare for their tee times. To MacPherson it was like a line-up leaving the viewing stage. She was writing down names on her order slip as fast as they tromped by her.

Then a strange thing happened interrupting her concentration. That same big fellow with the funny shirt suddenly began behaving like a drunken, boisterous jackass. His talk was slurred and he was challenging anyone within earshot to a golf match. The guy had just been standing...well mannered...in back of the restaurant. For some reason he was making a complete fool of himself. Like everyone else she moved away from him so as not to be accused of being associated with him. What made the whole thing so odd was that she apparently was the only one who knew he was playacting. His purpose for the strange behavior was completely unclear.

The restaurant vacated especially fast with the antics of the supposedly drunken man. The waitresses began cleaning off the tables and MacPherson felt obligated to join in. She did so without taking her eyes off the unexplained action. One of the last people leaving the restaurant was the slimy Willie LaCurso from St. Paul. The big inebriated fellow in the colorful shirt confronted the Twin Cities gangster. Lindy wanted to grab the actor. She knew LaCurso could cut this loud-mouth down to size with a blink of an eye.

The man pretending to be drunk boisterously declared he could beat the small man with three golf clubs while playing barefoot. LaCurso glanced up at the big man and then at his chartreuse shirt. The look in the smaller man's eyes sent a shiver up Lindy's spine. Two of LaCurso's guards moved toward the irritating drunk, but their boss waved them off. It was as if he didn't want his concentration bothered by having to deal with a raging alcoholic. She didn't know then, but all the players were aware of the many tricks that might be played on each other in order to break a competitor's concentration. That was playing in LaCurso's mind. To MacPherson's amazement, he shook his head, laughed, and walked away without another thought toward the inebriated man.

It was when everyone except the staff had gone that she noticed the man now referred to as 'Trick Shot' had remained in the restaurant. He was standing off to the side with the faintest of smiles observing the incident between the drunk and the St. Paul mobster. When LaCurso had finally left, the grin changed to a fabricated concern for the intoxicated man who had just passed out on the floor. The waitress and staff members moved away with disgust from the drunk. 'Trick Shot' moved in closer. As he hung his head next to the intoxicated man, she watched as they immediately began conversing in great speed. Now her puzzlement over this golfer really increased. These two men apparently knew each other...and didn't want any others to know it. It was a very peculiar way of stealing a couple minutes with each other.

MacPherson was alert to their entire game. She couldn't believe other people couldn't see it....or maybe they just didn't care. Guessing that the two were no more crooks than she was, she moved over closer to them. She found them actually trying to muffle their laughter.

Sarcastically she asked, "Are you two boys all right? Shall I call for a doctor?"

Both men waved her away without looking at her. They continued whispering intensely at one another with the fake drunken man still lying on the floor. MacPherson had not seen such weird behavior from two purported adults...ever. She sensed they were up to something... and they were way over their heads. She wondered if they had any idea they were fooling around in the wrong kind of venue. She couldn't imagine what they were up to, but whatever their aims, the final result wasn't worth the chances they were taking.

Then with the brashness he showed out on the practice range, 'Trick Shot' helped his 'friend' up onto the nearest chair and yelled toward the restaurant manager to bring the sorry drunkard some breakfast and "put it on Loni D'Annelli's tab."

MacPherson groaned over the bravado. 'Talk about more guts than brains!' she thought.

As the two men parted, MacPherson had no question something was happening outside the current scope of her investigation. Dumbfounded, she watched the disgusting drunk transform to the calm observer in the loud shirt she'd first seen standing by the kitchen. When he was done with his breakfast...in total solitude...he quietly exited the restaurant showing no signs of dipsomania or craziness. He had done his bit to get the attention of his friend. They were plotting something. Now she had another person to follow.

The restaurant manager ordered her to clean off the table where the big man had been sitting. He looked at her twice not recognizing her as one of his staff, but shrugged and walked away. He had other things on his mind as well. MacPherson ignored him and rushed out the door to the ladies room to change back to her regular garb.

In minutes she had transformed herself back to her normal look with her strawberry blonde hair flowing over her shoulders. With her sundress, sunglasses, and sunhat, her temporary cover as a Lodge waitress had been retired. As she walked out of the ladies room, the restaurant manager was standing by the entrance. He nodded politely,

"Have a good day, Miss." He had no idea she had minutes before been under his employ.

She now had an additional challenge that day. Not only was she going to follow the D'Annelli group but she had to find out what these two friends were planning besides one of them participating in the golf tournament. They were up to something and all indications were that they had no idea they'd just jumped into a swamp filled with snakes.... and some were very big snakes.

She felt obligated to warn them. If they were sharp enough, they would look around and heed her words. Most importantly, whatever their mischief, she couldn't have them interrupting her plans for the next day.

She left the Lodge restaurant chewing on the inside of her mouth. It would be the first of many times the rest of that day where her stomach would grind and she was the one who felt like she'd fallen in the swamp.

CHAPTER

13

As John Bailey stood waiting for Jamie Lawton at the first tee box looking awkward with Lawton's golf bag slung over his shoulder, he was engrossed in watching the unique display of players warming up. The golfers were kibitzing with one another, making more side bets, and generally trying to stay loose until it was their turn to play. To Bailey, it was like a free matinee to be inside the ropes with the players.

Lawton stood off to the side continuing to stretch and swing still not quite believing what he stumbled into. He didn't engage in any conversation...nor was that a desire. He peeked from golfer to golfer realizing this assemblage of men were like a Who's Who in the world of crime. Going by first names on the large scoreboard, he recognized four more players from newspaper and magazine photos. He had a sickening feeling the entire Mafioso was participating in this strange event.

Bailey finally ambled over to him carrying the golf bag like he was hauling a bag of groceries into his house. Lawton rolled his eyes, "For Christ's sake, John, at least look like a caddy." He showed the bewildered farmer and new friend how to throw the carry strap over his shoulder for easier transporting of the bag. Bailey gave him a silent nod feeling more comfortable. Lawton could only shake his head knowing that John Bailey was going to be of limited assistance as a caddy.

Nonetheless, he was heartened that this man would at least be on his side and rooting for his success. Anyway, that was Lawton's hope. He didn't want Bailey to be high-tailing it for the woods the first time trouble brewed.

To make him feel more comfortable, Lawton went over and stood beside Bailey remarking in a very hushed tone, "John, I hope these guys don't start shooting at one another. I wouldn't want to get hit in the cross fire."

John gave him a wry grin, not understanding how possible the statement was. Bailey then moved away from Lawton as if he didn't want to stand too close. Lawton again rolled his eyes. Motioning for Bailey to come back, he seemed hesitant. Lawton finally had to march over and whisper, "John, for the love of God, will you at least walk with me. I'm going to need my clubs!"

Bailey finally saw the humor and gave him a weak chuckle apparently still not convinced caddying for Lawton was a healthy endeavor. Again Lawton tried to relax him with another kidding remark. "John, I'd appreciate if you'd warn me to duck if my life depends on it." Bailey lit a cigarette as if it was his last one and grimly nodded.

Lawton glanced at the discomfitted farmer wondering why this man had held back telling the entire story of this so-called tournament. Had Lawton been aware of even half of what he'd already seen that morning, he'd have flown up to Alexandria and not given Chippewa Lodge a second thought. Playing for $10 with his own friends seemed like a faraway dream. Still, Lawton knew he was in for an experience of a lifetime. He just hoped he still had a lifetime to reminisce about the experience.

Being in the final foursome to tee off, Lawton had the chance to observe each of his opponents as they addressed their first shot. He recognized Big Julie Tagliossa from Milwaukee and his group of law-breakers as the first team of four to tee off on Hole #1. Julie's tummy was so large he had difficulty teeing up his own golf ball. Lawton had never seen a man of his girth swing a golf club...much less move. But, hit it he did, about a 150 yards right down the middle. Then Tagliossa farted and walked off the tee box oblivious to the hundreds of gallery members.

Lawton asked John for his 'spoon'...another name for the three-wood...so he could continue taking warm up swings prior to teeing off. Knowing little about golf, John gave him the most confused look.

Lawton finally pointed to his golf bag and whispered to his inexperienced caddy, "John, it's the wooden club with the 's' on the bottom of the club head."

When John finally pulled it from the golf bag, he pensively presented it to Lawton as if the golfer was about to walk ten paces, turn, and fire. Bailey's action served notice again that John's help on the golf course would be negligible. He knew nothing about the game or the golf course. Lawton would be on his own.

And then his concern evaporated as fast as it developed. Edging up close to him was Adam Bailey. The two of them were partners. Adam was looking at this round of golf as a business venture considering he had a 10% stake in any money Lawton won.

He whispered, "Jamie, put the spoon back in your bag and hit your driver off the pencil, like you did at the practice range. You need a high shot that'll carry over the trees on the left. I take the same shot myself every time I play this hole."

That kind of counsel was like a boost of fuel to Lawton. With the young Bailey having a good golf game of his own, he was heartened to realize as D'Annelli's caddy, Adam would be on the same team. Adam could help any way possible...all with D'Annelli's approval.

Hole number #1 was a Par 4, 310 yard severe dogleg left down a hill. Driving the green was doable with a high majestically hit shot over the trees on the left with a 250 yard carry. The green, though small, was a reachable target. Most importantly, it was a length of hole within range of Lawton's driver.

As Lawton watched each group tee-off, he was able to observe some of the antics and trickery perpetrated by these 'sportsmen'. It appeared there was no limit to any chicanery for the purpose of breaking the concentration of a fellow competitor. He was made aware on that very first hole. With the first green within range from the tee box, the group on the tee lusted after the opportunity to hit into the group still putting on that green. An average drive could roll down close to the green. The hope was that one of the longer hooking drives might not only bother but maim someone standing on the green. Players loved that possibility. If they could lame, injure, or at least agitate a competitor on any of the opposing teams that team felt they had created an edge. With the best two scores of four players on each team, reducing the effectiveness of any one of the competitors could be a great advantage. Lawton just stood there shaking his head thinking, 'My God, this is the first time I've ever witnessed golf being played as a contact sport."

Willie LaCurso, the thin, feisty friend of Loni's, and his band of pirates were the second group to tee-off. Two golfers in Willie's group hit big slices off to the right into the adjoining fairway leaving them almost further from the green to hit their second shots. Lawton made note to make sizeable bets with these two players for the afternoon nine holes.

Willie's third player, though, hit his drive straight and very long right at the group teeing off on the #2 tee box, just thirty yards from the first green. It just missed one of big Julie's teammates, bounced and hit big Julie on the right cheek of his rear end. Whether it was machissimo or he really didn't feel it, big Julie just took a big puff of his cigar and ignored the interruption. He wanted to give no one any satisfaction that he might have been disturbed. He simply addressed his golf ball and hit his drive off the #2 tee box right down the middle.

Willie LaCurso, who looked like he could bend steel with his gaze, was the fourth and last man in his group to hit. Willie was 5 ft. 5 inches, 130 pounds of high intensity. Just by his practice swing, Lawton could tell this gangster knew how to play the game. Willie launched a perfect drive that hooked just slightly and with one bounce landed on the recently vacated green. If he had teed off first, he would likely have laid out one of big Julie's men putting on that green. In fact Willie commented as such and reacted enraged that he hadn't hit first.

This small man with a powerful, athletic swing proved again that size of a golfer didn't necessarily dictate how far one can hit the golf ball. Willie appeared to be about one tenth the size of big Julie, but could hit the ball almost twice as far as the big man. He'd just hit a perfect shot that ended up only twelve feet from the cup with a good chance for an eagle...two-under par. It would be a splendid way for his team to begin the competition.

For Lawton, he couldn't believe how these guys' minds worked. He speculated whether these characters carried their 'hardware' in their golf bag. He sensed all twenty players might not live through this two-day golf tournament. Gazing over at Adam after hearing LaCurso's angry remarks, Lawton just shook his head in mock amazement. Adam simply looked back with a comical look in his eye. It was nothing he hadn't heard before.

The truculent Danny A'Motta and his Leavenworth graduates were next. They all swung the club as if digging a grave was their primary aim. Each of these guys was either nervous or totally inept. If they continued digging into the ground as they swung, Lawton guessed there was not going to be a blade of grass left on the golf course by late afternoon.

None of these guys got their ball even near the first green. While people talked on the backswings of the previous two groups, there was dead silence when Danny and his gravediggers were teeing off. No one wanted to be accused of interrupting their game faces. The only sound heard was Willie LaCurso swearing three hundred yards away after missing his putt for an eagle on the first hole. In two sentences he used the "F-word" as a noun, verb, adjective, and adverb. Lawton had to admit to being impressed with LaCurso's creative obscenities.

The fourth foursome off was the group headed by Vinnie Spagatini, the notorious hitman from Chicago. Lawton figured if introduced to this evil-eyed human being, it would be 'Mr. Spagatini' until this gangster changed the formality. Vinnie and his good friend and Capone associate, Bert Bertinelli, had so many injuries and deaths attributed to them, the newspapers referred to them as a disease. People said that Vinnie and Bert built the Miller's union in Chicago. It was based on whether the individual mill worker wanted to live or not. A vote for Vinnie was a vote for the union worker continuing his life. Some of the workers who voiced loud dissent against joining the union entered another union shortly thereafter. It was either in heaven or hell, but it was definitely no longer on earth. Membership of all the mill workers in the Spagatini led union became predictably quite popular after a couple of non-members ended up as ingredients in several Wonder Bread shipments to the local grocery markets. Lawton found it extraordinary how these two gangsters continuously escaped prison.

But, Lawton had to ignore their backgrounds for the next two days. His only real concern had to be how well Vinnie and Bert could play the game. He was disappointed to see that both men had competitive swings. He was relieved to see both men didn't have the golfing skills to hook the ball onto the first green. Lacking that shot turned out not to be a bother for both hoodlums. They instead aimed their drives directly at the #2 tee box to play havoc with the group in front of them as they were teeing off. Danny A'Motta and his group scowled at Vinnie's group when two incoming golf balls landed on their tee box. Danny and his assassins simply opened their umbrellas for protection, and ignored Vinnie and his team the rest of the round.

Finally it was Loni D'Annelli's team on the #1 tee box. Lawton was biting at the bit to begin play. Loni introduced Lawton to his two other teammates. Their names were Billie McCoy and Whitey Malooley. Lawton felt relieved he'd never heard of either man. They looked at him with neither satisfaction nor disappointment. They had no idea of his golfing prowess. They grunted an almost inaudible greeting and walked away. Lawton didn't care. In no way were these fellows going to be bosom buddies anyway. The important thing was that these two teammates were invited to be on D'Annelli's team for a reason. It was likely both players could play the game reasonably well.

Billie McCoy took a short backswing and directed his first shot on a low arc right down the middle just over 200 yards off the tee thanks to a generous down hill roll off the slope of the fairway. That was his game...short but accurate. Whitey Malooley was a taller guy with a powerful swing and apparently a sweet short game. Whitey hit his shot on a much higher trajectory. It was a major league home run type of hit, but his golf reputation was that he hit it all over the county. Unfortunately the landing area on most golf courses was a bit narrower than the county boundaries. If there was no wind, Whitey had a better chance of scoring well. In the wind, Whitey required most of the immediate real estate to keep his golf ball in play. That morning the wind off the lake pushed his drive far right of the fairway.

D'Annelli decided to hit third. For a large, stockier fellow he had a decent hip turn and hit a nice low hook that rolled down twenty yards short of the first green. Lawton was pleasantly surprised with his teammates. They could play! But, now it was his turn to live up to his showboat persona displayed earlier that morning on the practice range.

Following Adam's suggestion, he teed the golf ball on a scorecard flat-ended pencil once again. Whitey and Billie looked unconvinced. Loni just stood there looking down the fairway. If he was dubious, he didn't show it.

Taking a full cut at the ball, Lawton launched a rocket shot high in the air but unfortunately curving to the right of the 1st green by a good thirty yards. His ball unintentionally was heading directly at the second tee box where the two highwaymen, Vinnie Spagatini and Bert Bertinelli were teeing off.

Lawton's first thoughts were naturally fear that he was going to kill someone on that #2 tee box. As it turned out, it was close. On Spagatini's backswing, Lawton's golf ball hit the ground about five yards away from the gangster. It not only destroyed Spagatini's concentration, but actually made him whiff.

From the first tee box, the last foursome plus numerous gallery members could see Vinnie shaking his fist and yelling enough invectives to make a steelworker blush. D'Annelli, McCoy, and Malooley howled in absolute glee. Malooley commented that Spagatini hadn't been that mad since the last time his gun jammed. Even Lawton broke up laughing on that remark.

The four of them on the tee box then saw Vinnie's partner, Bert Bertinelli move speedily toward his golf bag. He was looking for something...Lawton guessed a 38-magnum. Instead it was something typical of the mentality of the players in this tournament. Both gangsters teed up and simultaneously hit golf balls back at the first tee box in retaliation.

Lawton couldn't believe what he was seeing. There had to be a two hundred gallery members in harm's way around the #1 tee box. John Bailey, standing next to Lawton, dove to the ground with his hands over his head. Lawton ducked behind a tree. Malooley and McCoy held their golf bags up for protection. The large gallery ducked down hoping not to get hit by the in coming golf shots. As for D'Annelli, he just stood there as if daring the two golf balls to hit him.

Lawton's eyes met Adam's who was laughing uncontrollably as he stood behind the large girth of D'Annelli thereby guaranteeing he wouldn't get hit. As for those two balls being launched by Spagatini and Bertinelli, Lawton had never seen something so utterly irresponsible and dangerous done on a golf course. Those two mugs hit those golf balls with no concern for the safety of the spectators. The shots fell mercifully short and only rolled into the crowd, but the sheer brashness of the attack was astonishing. The two hucksters hadn't cared if they maimed anyone. When the small incident was done, the crowd suddenly erupted into a chorus of laughter. They'd heard about the pranks played on the golf course in this particular tournament. They no longer had to wait to have witnessed one of the more hazardous paybacks.

When Adam Bailey came forward from behind D'Annelli, he gave Lawton an innocent shrug...as if to say "you ain't seen nothin' yet!"

The foursome left the tee box in good spirits. D'Annelli inched up to him and said, "Nice shot, kid. That'll keep them on their toes. You're getting the hang of the competition early. Now, get your birdie."

His statement came across more as an order than a request. To Lawton's relief and the team's satisfaction, he did knock in an 8-foot birdie putt after chipping onto the green from the #2 tee box. 'Nice putt, kid' was all he heard...as if the birdie was expected. 'Kid' was apparently going to be his nickname with the group, not so much because of his age but more because of Lawton's perceived innocence. 'Trick shot' was still going to be his moniker on the big scoreboard.

That birdie on the first hole was important in a number of ways. D'Annelli's team was tied for the lead, but more significantly, Lawton proved to his teammates his ability to play the game. Both Billie and Whitey got a bit more talkative on the second hole. Loni just puffed on his stogie with a big grin on his face. John Bailey, the reluctant caddy, even began walking beside Lawton instead of pretending like he didn't know him.

The team did well that first hole. D'Annelli as well made a birdie after chipping his ball from twenty yards away to within four feet of the flag. When the big man made the putt, Lawton found himself already being caught up in the excitement of the event. Whether he was going to gain money for charity or not, he had Charlie's and his $5000 to protect. His team had to at least make second place for him to retain his exorbitant entry fee. Otherwise it would have to be individual side bets on the second nine holes of play that afternoon where Lawton would have to play well enough to recover the five grand. He was pleased to see the determined looks on the faces of his teammates. They didn't want to relinquish their $5000 apiece either. He no longer cared what side of the law they were all on. The four of them were out to win.

Leaving the #2 tee box, Lawton was into the spirit of this blood and guts golf tournament. He had seen all the players tee off on the first hole and had an idea the level of competition. He was surprised to see that a few of the players were better than he expected. Willie LaCurso, Vinnie and Bert...and even Loni were players with some talent. The others had games good enough to still contribute to their team's success. But, it was the ability to drown out extraneous noises and hoaxes that would be a real key to winning that day's event. He would witness golfers aiming shots at opposing players, yelling on backswings, stepping on opposition's golf balls in the rough, laughing at missed shots, and screaming disappointedly at opposition's good shots. These hoodlums were the most unsportsmanlike miscreants Lawton had ever witnessed at any sporting event. It would also turn out to be the funniest day he'd ever spent on any golf course.

What he came to realize was that these players were mostly playing their normal games with their customary behaviors. Decorum was not a word or action in their vocabulary. The thing he found difficult to believe was how they were such sticklers to the rules of golf. He saw no cheating. They must have agreed a long time ago that if everyone cheated, it was just a case of who could cheat the best. In other words, what was the point of playing the game? So, instead they actually followed the rules of golf impeccably. It made the competition more fun. Unsportsmanlike mayhem was perfectly acceptable; cheating was not.

What was also interesting...and somewhat gratifying for Lawton... was that the guys on his team became his closest buddies during those hours on the links. They watched out for each other as one member of the team made a shot. If a club came flying over a tree, a player would yell for his teammate to stop swinging. If a golf ball came flying at the foursome, everyone was warned.

By the third hole Lawton's teammates were slapping him on the back after he'd hit a drive too far left and almost hit big Julie who has plodding down the 6th fairway. The ball rolled between the rotund man's legs. He didn't even notice the ball given his girth, but his teammates saw it. They shouted some profanity back at D'Annelli's foursome causing nothing but laughter from the four of them. D'Annelli, Malooley, and McCoy thought Lawton had done the shot on purpose. He hadn't. With Big Julie being such a large target, Lawton figured he could have done better had he actually aimed at the man.

Meanwhile, Charlie Davis had decided to satisfy some of his curiosity about Chippewa Lodge. After finishing his hearty breakfast with the billing added to Loni D'Annelli's tab, he scurried out of the restaurant ready to find out what was really going on at this resort. With as many known gangsters in one place along with a bunch of evil looking characters he'd never seen before, Davis could only believe there were some rowdy and unlawful things going on at that resort. He didn't expect it would take much effort to get some of the staff personnel to open up and relate to him some stories regarding the Lodge and the questionable 'guests'.

Surprisingly, in that next hour he experienced only frustration. People were highly reserved...as is their job or life depended on their silence. Whenever he inquired about the 'guests' or anything related to the activities at the Lodge, workers suddenly had to get back to their jobs.

Recalling the betting booth outside the front entrance to the resort, he resolved to try a different approach. He asked a resort maintenance worker where he might be able to make a wager on the tournament. While the worker remained reticent, he did put his rake down and in a lowered voice murmured, "You'll have to go out to the Presbyterian gamblin' booth across the road by the lake. You can't miss it. It's by the big tent. Ask for Henry Hanson. He's a deacon for the church. You can trust him to take your wager."

Davis didn't doubt that was true, whoever Henry Hanson was. Wasting no more time, he went in search of this fellow named Hanson. Strolling past the two guards at the front gate, he told them he'd be back. They nodded without changing their facial expression. They wouldn't be forgetting a person with the temerity to wear such a God awful looking shirt.

Striding towards the lake, he could see there was more going on than just the golf tournament. The boat races were in progress. Kids were swimming in the lake with their mothers keeping close tabs. A half-block down the shoreline he saw a sizeable booth in front of a large tent. Many people were entering and exiting the tent. The whole atmosphere along the lake was one of excitement and celebration, much like a 4th of July weekend anywhere else in the country. There was as much entertainment going on outside the gates of the Lodge as there was on the golf links.

Near the booth was another scoreboard like the one he'd seen down at City Park. This one was keeping a hole by hole account of the scoring by each player as well as the foursome best two scores on each hole. It appeared one could make a wager in almost any way on the twenty individual golfers or on the four-man teams.

Davis moseyed nonchalantly toward the booth and watched various people placing bets. That was when he observed not all the wagers were on the golf event. Bets were being placed on professional baseball games to be played that afternoon…and horse races in as far away places as Chicago, Baltimore and New York. Davis' interest was piqued. He sensed this booth and the tent behind it were not for church services.

Davis' attention was then focused on two somber looking men standing guard outside the huge tent. The entrance suddenly opened and two patrons exited the tent. He could see momentarily an assortment of tables inside set up for various games of chance. He also caught a glimpse of a busy bar with well-stocked shelves of booze in the back of the tent. It was apparent the 'guests' at the Lodge had other attractions besides the golf tournament. They had access to tables of blackjack, poker, and craps at their leisure.

What astounded Davis most of all was the pretense that the large tent and booth were run by a religious organization. A sign indicating the tent was the property of the First Presbyterian Church Men's Club was visible and that was a far as the church had anything to do with the activities beyond the signage. Two men and the booth looking like locals the way they were dressed were busy taking wagers. However, the two men standing guard at the tent's entrance didn't seem like members of any church. They were very intent on not letting anyone into that large tent without some kind of identification or secret password.

When another patron, having just walked over from the Lodge, wanted to place a wager on some professional baseball games, he was directed to talk with a tall slender man in the back of the booth. This man was preoccupied with recording bets. He was haggard looking and extremely thin. The way he was rubbing his eyes and moving his head back and forth, Charlie wondered if the man wasn't intoxicated. Talk about the wrong man handling the books.

When the private baseball bets were completed with this tired looking man, a note was suddenly delivered to him by courier. The haggard man pushed himself off his chair and dragged himself over to the large scoreboard to record the latest scores.

Davis had to laugh over this spectacle. The tall, gangly man reminded him of Icabod Crane. The fellow just went about his responsibilities haplessly and methodically while looking as if he hadn't slept in days. Davis wondered why that was. No one worked that hard as a volunteer.

Then two more couples presented their identification to one of the guards at the tent and were allowed entry. Three more people made some kind of bet on the afternoon golf matches. Davis found it hard to believe how indiscreet the public betting was. He'd gambled at many places around Minnesota, but always privately and the location was inconspicuous. After all, public betting was supposed to be against the law in Minnesota.

Davis went up to one of the men taking bets in the booth and asked where he could find the church deacon name Hanson. This man also looked tired, but not as frail as the tall, thin man now back re-tallying the betting receipts. The man hardly looked at Davis. He just pointed at that same unstable gaunt man at the rear of the booth.

Realizing there was not going to be any particular friendly introduction, Davis stepped around the betting table and proceeded to the back of the booth. The man named Hanson didn't even look up. He just continued tabulating the bets. Davis pulled up a chair and sat by the desk where Hanson was working…as if either waiting to make a bet or just taking a load off his feet.

There still was no response from the tall, thin fellow.

Hanson finally looked up and realized someone was waiting to talk with him. The bony man stared for a moment and seemed slightly surprised. Davis wondered if Hanson knew who he was. As far as Davis knew, he'd never laid eyes on this church deacon.

The betting action slowed and the two men's club volunteers told Hanson they were going to get something to eat at the Lutheran food tent. They left and the skinny man sat there with the strangest half-smile on his face continuing to update his books. He seemed very content to have Davis sit there as long as he desired.

For the next couple minutes, Davis and Hanson remained quiet… not even introducing themselves…the church man adding the columns of number in his books and Davis watching the boats on the lake or periodically nodding at ladies as they walked by the booth. Except for some joyful shouting from within the tent, the occasional distant cheer from across the roadway at the golf course, or the motor boats speeding by on the lake, there seemed to be no interest, especially on Hanson's part, to speak.

Davis finally broke the ice. "You the church guy in charge of this whole deal?"

Hanson only shrugged.

Davis perused around the booth and then over at the tent before commenting, "Well sir, you folks from the First Presbyterian Church seem to be doing quite well. Seems to be a lot of activity going on around here."

The tall fellow only sighed as if he knew Davis wasn't there to hand out compliments. "Yeh, I'm in charge of the finances for the church men's club. My name is Hanson...Henry Hanson. I'm the local Feed & Grain Mill General Manager, but I also keep the books as deacon for the First Presbyterian Church. So, I've got to keep track of the wagers on this little golf tournament. I guess that's why they give me the name 'Honest Henry'. I'd better be honest or I'd get run out of town."

Davis gave a nod of approval and openly chuckled over the mild joke. "Well, Mr. Hanson, I hear this little gambling event is anything but little...and it's done with the O.K. of the local citizens and law enforcement. That's a real credit to your men's club in arranging such a lucrative operation for your church."

The thin man stared at him for a moment. Davis thought Hanson was sizing him up...maybe as some kind of lawman. Somewhat surprisingly to Davis, Hanson seemed to make the decision the friendly man sitting by his desk was non-threatening.

Where the deacon had showed obvious signs of not feeling well and not being in the mood to say 'hello', the very manner of the tall, gaunt man suddenly changed. "Yeh, this event is important to our church, but we're not alone. Most every church and civic organization makes a lot of money during our week long town festival. As for this gambling booth, it's simple. As long as we're under the auspices of being a church activity, we're all right with the law. You know, kind of like "Bingo"!

Davis was impressed. This manager of the town's feed and grain mill and diligent auditor of the church finances was sharper than he'd been letting on...and actually very articulate.

Davis decided to push the man for more information. He expected that to be momentary. To his surprise, the church deacon continued to give very direct responses. Davis mixed non-descript questions about the town celebration with more pointed questions about the gambling booth and the assortment of 'guests' staying at the Lodge.

Hanson seemed especially pleased about his church's good fortune in gaining the contract for handling both gambling booths. His eyes caught Davis' as he revealed another startling detail. "Yep...we've really benefited. We get 10% of all bets. The Calcutta pool last year grossed over $383,000. Our Presbyterian group netted $38,000 less the $10,000 fee for the rights to manage the Calcutta. But, a $28,000 net profit for a church...well, it was more than we could have imagined. That kind of money can fix a lot of steeples and upgrade our town."

Davis was floored. Why was this character telling him all this private information? Hanson was all but admitting the betting booths took in many more bets than the wagers on the charity golf event. It made no sense why this town leader was speaking so freely. This gambling booth was performing an activity that was directly against the law. Davis wondered if 'Honest Henry' had lost his faculties... maybe suffering not only from exhaustion, but from too much sun, too little food, and maybe a few too many Canadian beers.

The church man wasn't done. He remarked, "You know, the most difficult part of the job has been the storing of all this cash...especially with the kind of 'guests' staying over there at the resort."

Then he smirked as if Davis would understand his next comment, "...you know what I mean?"

Davis hardly knew what to ask next, but was not given a chance. A white-shirted young man with a bow tie had come running across the road. He approached Hanson politely not wanting to interrupt the conversation. Hanson's attention went promptly to that young man.

As he did so, Davis focused on this strange, unstable man. He was suddenly the picture of stability as he grabbed a parcel obviously containing the money that had been wagered. Hanson gave the slightly nervous young man the parcel as well as a small ledger.

Davis could recognize a runner when he saw one. When the runner took off back across the road toward a group of cabins, another man not as young strode up to the booth with a piece of paper. This fellow was far more social. He had the up-to-date results of the hole by hole scores at the golf event. Hanson took the paper and immediately dragged himself over to the scoreboard to make the scores public. Hanson was obviously a very busy and trusted person in this entire mix.

That made Hanson's admission about the activities at the booth even more puzzling. This apparently very reliable town leader had more or less divulged some very incriminating factors...actual evidence that could be used against the man's church group and anyone else connected to the that immediate booth and adjoining tent. As far as that tent was concerned, Davis figured it was nothing more than a temporary casino.

He couldn't grasp the reason for Hanson's openness. It was as if he didn't care if this little private enterprise would carry on or not. Maybe knowing he was running an illegal gambling enterprise was getting to the small town grain mill manager. The stress had robbed him of all rational thinking. After all, there had been a few stockbrokers who had jumped off ledges after the Stock Market Crash in 1929 when the tension had been too much. This tired looking Hanson was behaving as if he was looking for a ledge.

Just in the short time Davis had talked with Hanson, he had enough evidence to call in the state patrol or the Bureau of Investigation to shut down the gambling booths, the large casino tent, and likely the entire golf event. As an attorney at law, Davis had that responsibility.

But, something wasn't right. Hanson was talking too willingly. Davis had to consider how authentic were Hanson's comments. It didn't get by him that this gambling booth and the adjoining tent were somehow connected to the group of gangsters involved in the charity golf tournament across the road. Davis had a sense that Hanson was baiting the hook for Davis to get involved. It was as if Hanson knew Davis had some legal obligations.

Davis scratched his chin. He didn't know Hanson, but maybe Hanson knew him…and especially that Charlie Davis was an attorney at law. He had a dilemma on his hands. He didn't quite know how he wanted to proceed.

Davis looked at his watch. The first round of play was about to finish. He needed time to sort out all that he'd just heard. Without saying farewell, Davis slipped away from the First Presbyterian Church booth expecting Hanson wouldn't even notice him leaving.

Actually, Hanson's eyes never left Davis even as he continued printing the scores on the huge scoreboard next to the booth. He watched the troubled man in the chartreuse shirt cross the road scratching his head. A slight grin appeared on Henry Hanson's face. He hadn't expected it, but he'd just been handed a gift. He not only knew the man he'd just slyly tipped off about the details of the gambling booth, but he was well aware this man wearing the odd shirt was Charlie Davis, a respected attorney from Alexandria. Davis would have a sense of duty to either report the unlawful actions or at least investigate the matter further before he decided what to do.

Henry Hanson had wished for this day ever since he sent his anonymous missive to the Minneapolis branch of the U.S. Attorney's office. Finally this lawlessness at Chippewa Lodge might be coming to an end. He was the only one in the entire town who knew the depth of this quagmire. Having this knowledge made him the one key person who would be blamed for bringing down the entire enterprise. His life would be in jeopardy. Knowing that fact, Hanson had already planned his escape.

Davis returned to the Lodge property through the main gate. The guards recognized his shirt and allowed him passage. He was in a daze and barely waved at the serious looking sentries. His personality was such that he might kid with the two men, but socializing was the last thing on his mind. He couldn't get over how smoothly those church men, especially Henry Hanson, handled the various wagers and then turned the betting information and money over to the 'runner'. The whole operation ran so smoothly. He was no expert in the gaming industry, but all indications were that this was a longer term business endeavor and not done whimsically during a ten-day town festival.

The crowd noise out on the golf course jolted Davis back to the golf event. The eccentricities going on around him at Chippewa Lodge made the tournament action seem secondary.

Making his way toward the #9 green, he spotted a slightly tipsy maintenance worker taking a break behind the restaurant. Davis wanted more information. He strolled over pretending to be exhausted and sat down on a bench near the Lodge employee. Talking about how stifling hot it was getting, he eventually offered his personal flask to the worker. When the worker grabbed it, Davis had his connection.

He started slowly. "Hell of an event being played out here, especially at a resort so far from town."

"Yes sir," the partially drunken man said, "This resort is making money hand over fist...but it can't last too much longer."

Davis acted surprised. "Really! Why I got the impression this place has all its cabins occupied most of the time."

The slobbering worker scoffed. "I don't know the guests personally, but I know they could leave this place as fast as they arrived and never come back...if things don't stay in their favor. Some of these guys have stayed here for extended periods of time...many as long as three months...even six months...some even longer. When these 'guests' leave, they never check out. The next day they're just gone. Sometimes they return weeks or months later...sometimes we never see them again. But I tell you, none of them are the type of people the folks in town would ever consider having over for dinner...except for Mr. D'Annelli of course."

Once that name was said, it was like the inebriated worker sobered up in seconds. He realized he'd said too much. The man suddenly stood up when a waitress came outside for a cigarette break. He quickly wished Davis a good day and silently retreated back to his job.

Davis picked up where the conversation had died with the first employee. He took a drink from his flask and nodded in a friendly way to the waitress. She looked at his shirt, smiled back, and then turned away. Davis had been rebuffed before. At least at that moment he could blame the shirt.

He pulled out a cigarette and asked the lady for a light. Stone-faced she threw him her match book. When he returned the matches he casually asked her, "I just arrived. Do you know where I could find

Mr. D'Annelli? Charlie didn't know D'Annelli from Santa Claus other than he saw the big man conduct the pre-tournament meeting that morning at breakfast.

The reaction he got from the waitress was unsettling. Just the mention of his name intimidated her. Her eyes got big. She snuffed out her cigarette and began retreating.

Davis stayed calm and called after her. "Sorry ma'am. I just wanted to know where he was."

She put her hands up as if resisting any further talk. Her voice was scared and very low. "I don't know him…I mean I know him but we're not supposed to say anything about him. I could lose my job. I have to leave."

With that she opened the back door of the restaurant and went back to work. Davis now was more intrigued than ever. He got up and made his way out toward the golf course when another older, gray-haired gent with a badge saying 'Golf Course Security' caught his eye. The fellow was supposedly guarding the pro shop while the staff was out on the golf course. He too had a flask. It was resting on his ample belly as he sat on a reclining chair. He looked like he was enjoying his assignment.

Charlie pretended again to be tired and sat down on the steps as he greeted the old man. "Mind if I sit here a spell?"

Then he pulled out his own flask once again and tipped it toward the guard in a mock toast. The old gentleman seemed to appreciate the gesture and tipped his flask in response.

Charlie was more forward with this unprepared security guard. "Well sir, Mr. D'Annelli certainly has done a great job with this tournament…and with this resort, hasn't he?"

The guard fell for the spurious familiarity. "Yes sir, he knows what he'd doing. It was him who introduced the idea of the town festival to run at the same time as this here charity tournament. He got the church and civic groups to help out with food booths, transportation, parking and even ticket sales. You talk about a town being lucky a man like Mr. D'Annelli chose to come to this area. You may not know it, but he keeps these cabins filled with his friends. By golly the town really benefits. And you know what?

Charlie didn't say a word, but held up his hands indicating he didn't know. He just hoped the old guy would continue.

The guy was happy to keep talking. "Well, Mr. D'Annelli insists on not taking any credit. He never wants his name brought up with anything happening here at the Lodge. In fact he gets angry if anyone brings the subject up. He wants all the credit of the town festival and this golf event to go to the townsfolk. Have you ever met a man with less of an ego? I tell you he's a real prince."

The old codger obviously didn't know a gangster from a minister. He just kept talking. "He takes some heat now and again when some of his friends act up. But, how could anyone be against him? His ideas and support have helped the churches make more money supporting this tournament than they could make in a century. Sure beats the God damned hell out of a bunch of bake sales."

The old man broke up laughing over what he considered some pretty sophisticated humor. For Davis, he'd just got his first direct verification that Loni D'Annelli was truly in charge.

Suddenly an ominous looking man wearing a long coat walked by and slowed as he eyed Davis and the slobbering security guard. He gave the two lounging men a sharp look and then moved on. The guard no longer wanted any conversation. He laid his head back on his recliner and began snoring.

Davis got up with his empty flask and moved on toward the noise by the ninth green. He was both astonished and impressed. It was difficult to believe how one man could mastermind such a grand spectacle, yet keep his name out of the limelight. The man had to be an amazing head for business. He had the intelligence, experience, money, and charisma to pull the wool over quite a few people's eyes in the community as well as many of the staff members at the Lodge. And, even if he was carrying out some illegal undertakings at the resort, no one was complaining very loudly.

With the time edging toward 12:30, the foursomes were finishing their first nine holes. After a short lunch break, the same five groups would complete another nine holes of play. Tallying the total scores for eighteen holes, bets would be paid off at the end of the afternoon. Knowing Lawton was in the final foursome, Davis quickened his pace and marched toward the last hole. Seeing Lawton's purple shirt out in the middle of the fairway, Davis eased his way over to the patio alongside the ninth green to gain a better view.

Two big lugs gave Davis a peculiar look. Then gazing at his ridiculously colored shirt, they rolled their eyes and let him into the buffet area. Dressed like that they had to figure he was part of the high rollers.

Davis stood off in the corner after grabbing a beer. The hilarity echoing around the patio area was typical of any country club tournament atmosphere. Wisecracks flowed. Players who'd just completed their first nine holes were bewailing about their lost shots. It was not a particularly unique collection of golfers...other than they were mostly high powered crooks. What was slightly intimidating to Davis was his sense that there was a complete disregard for the law in this group. More frightening was how any one of them could eliminate almost anyone they chose with a blink of an eye.

With his chartreuse shirt, Davis did fit reasonably well into the group of slightly tipsy folk cavorting on that patio. People he'd never seen before including some scantily clad women kept greeting him as if they should know him. He nodded and smiled saying, "Good to see you again" or "Hey, honey, that's a great outfit."

While waiting for Lawton's group to play their second shots into the ninth green, Davis grabbed a plate and headed for the buffet table. Acting like he owned the place, he helped himself to all the food. He smiled thinking that the mob was about to pick up his meal tab for the second time that day. Though hungry, Davis didn't find the food particularly tasty. It had something to do with how much blood was spilled to gain the money to pay for this extravaganza.

Davis watched as two members of Lawton's team hit solid shots on or near the green. The third member caught the pond on the side of the green. Then it was Lawton's turn to play. Davis had seen his friend hit many shots under pressure. With a perfect lie in the middle of the fairway, the expectation was a stylish shot. He could imagine it hugging the flagstick throughout the ball's flight with "ahhhs" from the crowd echoing in the wind once the ball landed.

What he was about to see was anything but a sterling shot. As Lawton swung Davis noticed his friend making a strange pass at the ball. Further, he was using a wood when only a mid-iron was needed. With way too much club being hit, there was no question the ball was going to end up beyond the green. To his horror the ball then began hooking wildly left of the green directly at the patio...a truly horrible shot. The shout of "FORE' was heard echoing from down the fairway at the folks in the patio area.

When the strident scream pierced the unassuming patrons on that patio, people began diving for anything that might give them cover. Davis followed the ball and knew he'd be safe. He just stood there watching the entire group of pleasure-seekers scurrying in panic. He found it kind of hilarious.

When the golf ball hit the patio area, it was like a gunshot when it hit some chairs. For a few of the guests on that patio the sound was really not that frightening. Davis observed a few guys reaching for something in the breast pocket of their jackets until they realized it was just a golf ball.

Lawton looked back up the fairway at his friend. He'd never seen Lawton hit such a poor shot...ever! It was almost as if Lawton had hit the shot on purpose. The very thought was preposterous.

The final outcome of the golf ball bouncing around the patio as if in a pin ball machine ended with some discomfort and more laughter. The golf ball's resting place had finally stopped in the clothing of one Tess Tagliossa, the 26-year-old fourth wife of Big Julie Tagliossa, one of the competitors. That resting place of the golf ball did cause quite a stir. Tess, a former stripper at a Chicago club, was used to wearing a rather limited wardrobe. In the heat of the day, Tess had been innocently lounging in the patio area. She hated golf and just wanted to worship the sun in her latest Lake Michigan beachwear. She cut quite a figure for the males on the patio, though they'd seen her half-naked many times. If local men from Glenwood had seen what she had on, there easily could have been multiple heart attacks.

The golf ball actually completed its journey between her breasts. The golf ball looked quite small indicating the size of her assets. Tess screamed loudly but calmed down when she realized she had not been hurt or bruised. She was looking at the golf ball as if it was something poisonous. She wouldn't touch it...nor was anyone else...given the circumstances.

As for most of the players on the patio, her cries were ignored. They were more enraged because they knew the shot coming in from D'Annelli's group was intentional. Eventually, however, they relaxed and began laughing, especially when Vinnie Spagatini yelled out that the ball had to be played where it rested. Tess didn't like the sound of what she was hearing.

Davis just shook his head and re-positioned himself for a better view of Tess. He, like the others standing around that patio, were interested in how Lawton was going to play his next shot.

CHAPTER

14

As that first round of play continued, Lawton hated to admit that he was actually enjoying the charity golf format far more than he should have. The 'offensive' manner of play and the profanity shared back and forth between groups seemed quite natural in this venue...and truly entertaining. By the 8th hole he had launched a couple of drives that had come perilously close to hitting members of two other foursomes. It was on purpose and the most unsportsmanlike thing he'd ever done on a golf course. His teammates absolutely loved it. Loni would say to Whitey and Billie, "Let the kid hit first off the tee box before Spagatini and Bertinelli get too far down the fairway and out of range. He's got a better chance of beaning someone in that group if he swings first.'

Whitey and Billie totally understood and waited with their adolescent, mischievous smiles for Lawton to launch another missile at the group playing ahead. Beyond the horseplay, Lawton and his group were actually scoring quite well. Lawton had three birdies on the first eight holes. He lost some shots failing to hit over water on two of the holes. He only gambled when his teammates were in good position to make no worse than pars with their own shots. Combining their best two scores on each hole, the D'Annelli team was 5-under par through that 8th hole. Lawton couldn't imagine any other team doing as well given the many strange golf swings he saw on the practice range and the first tee box. What he wasn't taking into account was how much these fellows liked to compete. They had no quit in them.

Adam Bailey was keeping close tabs on the scoring of the other teams. He had a friend report to him after each hole. Adam clued the D'Annelli foursome in before they teed off on the 9th hole. He stated,

"Gentlemen, two teams including the Spagatini and Bertinelli team in front of us are also 5-under par after eight holes of play."

Lawton couldn't believe it. He began wondering whether there really was honor among thieves. Yet, there were too many gallery members and friends of other players for anyone to get away with any cheating on the links. These players were better scorers than Lawton had given them credit. This was turning out to be no cake walk. He would have to play some spectacular golf and get some good support from his teammates if they were to win the event during the afternoon round.

Hole #9 was an uncharacteristically long 420-yard par 4. It played slightly shorter because the fairway careened down a long hill. If a player didn't hit his drive long enough, he would be playing his second shot from a downhill lie. To add to the challenge, on the right side of the green there was a beautiful but noisy and treacherous pond. A ball hit to the right into that water would be met with numerous frogs and toads croaking their discontent over the trespassing golf ball. As a consequence of the pond, most golfers chickened out and pulled their shots left toward the patio area. Golfers usually didn't hit their shots long enough to cause any danger to anyone lounging on the patio. In fact, to actually hit one's ball into the patio area, it would have to be on purpose. The patio was that far off line and beyond the green.

The D'Annelli group waited for Spagatini's group to complete their putts on the ninth green amidst yelling and cat-calling by players and patrons eating and drinking on the patio. The loud noises from anywhere by this time had little impact on any of the golfers. Loni, Whitey, and Billie were used to the boisterous interruptions. Lawton even found he could remain numb and not be bothered too much by these constant interruptions.

He stood there waiting to hit his second shot into the green as Bertinelli sunk a four-foot putt to preserve his team's score of 5-under par. Lawton figured he needed a par for his team, but he was facing a difficult shot. His so-called caddy, John Bailey, stood there holding the bag of clubs smoking his pipe as if not having a care in the world. He seemed content just to be enjoying a nice day walking amongst some beautiful greenery. Lawton figured Bailey couldn't care less about the competition. He really had no idea how much Lawton had riding on this little match.

Whitey Malooley had been all over the course the previous eight holes. From behind a tree, he sliced a big brassie under a tree branch and rolled his ball onto the green some 30 feet from the hole. It was a great shot and a probable par. Lawton felt a bit more relaxed.

From a downhill lie to the middle of the fairway, Billie dumped his ball after a bad bounce into the pond on the right. The croaking frogs could be heard. Lawton was no longer relaxed. With Billie out of the hole it was Loni's turn to hit next. Before he hit his shot he looked over at Lawton with a glint in his eye. "Kid, after I knock my ball onto the green, hold up before hitting. I want to talk to you."

Lawton couldn't help but like D'Annelli's confidence. He also liked the large man's shot into the green from 200 yards out. D'Annelli's ball rolled to the front edge of the green and just barely made the putting surface some forty feet from the flag. Loni was a good putter. A par 4 for him was probable. Lawton relaxed once again. His shot wouldn't be as crucial.

With two fairly certain pars from his teammates on that last hole, Lawton was planning to gamble and play a shot dangerously close to the pond to give his team a possible birdie. But, that thought disappeared the moment Loni sauntered over to him. The big man at first didn't say a word. He looked at the green. Then he looked at the patio to the far left of the green. Lawton's ball was resting on a perfect lie in the exact middle of the fairway. Lawton frankly didn't need a pep talk. He was ready to hit his shot.

Taking the big omnipresent stogie out of his mouth, Loni gazed at Lawton and remarked, "Kid, Whitey and I got some cinch pars. We want you to hit your ball into the middle of the patio...maybe jolt a few of our competitors. You're ball shouldn't matter that much on this hole. I think we got a great chance to really piss off some of our competitors if you launch your ball right into the middle of that crowd."

He snickered, "And, it should be kinda funny to see." His chuckle sounded like a bear growling deep in a cave.

Lawton looked at him like he was crazy. "Loni, you want me to deliberately hit my ball into that patio full of people. I'll kill someone... probably someone not even playing in the tournament!"

"Kid, let me give you some advice. You have a lot to gain if you look like you just choked by hitting a shot thirty yards off line over the green into that patio. Our opponents will be on you like flies to make personal wagers when you sit down to eat lunch. You'll have as many side bets as you want with every guy thinking you'll swallow the potato when it comes to the real pressure of the second nine. Kid, you could murder most of these guys with your golf game. I'm telling you it's to your financial advantage to hit the worst appearing shot you can muster."

He winked and added, "Mark my words."

Then he smirked, "Besides, we'll yell 'Fore'...nobodies gonna get killed. But, by God, it should be the most hilarious thing you've ever seen when a couple hundred people dive for cover."

Lawton couldn't help smiling visualizing the probable scene. Adam began doubling over with laughter. Loni broke into the loudest chortle. Whitey and Billie joined in.

Then Loni added another factor. "Don't get me wrong. With luck you'll mutilate one of our opponents. Their team will be decidedly disadvantaged for the second nine playing with three guys. Hell, even if you miss them, they might injure themselves diving under the tables. It'll be beautiful."

He then went into another deep bellow that had everyone laughing hysterically. Even John Bailey was chuckling loudly.

Lawton put his mashie back in his bag and glanced once again at Loni. Here's a man who had committed any number of horrible crimes over his clandestine career, yet he was like a playful boy choking with laughter over the mayhem he was about to cause. The gaiety in his eyes was positively contagious.

Lawton had about 180 yards to the green and took out a brassie wood.....way too much club for the required shot. He said to Loni, "I believe I could strike more fear if I hit a low pulled hook shot. What do you think?"

With that hoarse, smoke-filled voice, Loni coughed, "Put a sweet swing on it, kid. Let's see you clear out the patio."

Lawton almost lost his composure on his backswing as he held back his laugh. But, he didn't. He put the required swing on the ball to make it curve viciously to the left. The shot came off the clubhead just the way he wanted it. It started out 'left' of the green on a low trajectory. Half way to the green it began veering severely more to the left like a magnet was pulling it toward the middle of the patio. The gallery on the left side of the green started ducking and yelling for people to be alert. Everyone seeing the shot yelled "FORE" loudly to the entire assemblage of people.

The D'Annelli group including the Baileys roared as every golfer and patron on the patio began diving for safety. Only one man did not. Danny A'Motta just sat there in the middle of the patio eating his sandwich and drinking his beer. He didn't even look up as people ducked down and under his table for protection.

As Lawton 'innocently' strutted up to the patio, he was frankly expecting to get mugged for the shot he'd just hit. But, he was shocked. His opponents showed no offense, but were sizing him up as a choker.

Various other guests dining on that patio greeted him with laughter and patted him on the back.

He was led to his golf ball as Danny A'Motta snorted, "Hey, Trick-Shot, you gotta play the ball where it lies!"

That was when Lawton saw where the ball had come to rest...on Big Julie's wife's....cleavage. No one wanted him to get a free drop...except Mrs. Tagliossa and her more than irritated husband. Big Julie didn't like everyone looking at his young curvaceous spouse. He figured they might get some ideas. Of course he was right. Any red-blooded male would have those thoughts anytime they saw Big Julie's wife whether a golf ball had come to rest where it did or not.

Lawton politely asked Mrs. Tagliossa which of the two of them should recover the ball. Tess wasn't certain what he meant. Then she caught on as she coyly considered her alternatives. It was finally big Julie who dug the ball out of his wife's cleavage and threw it out on the grass. He wasn't smiling.

With the 'free drop' to the side of the patio, Lawton actually was given a clear forty yard shot to the ninth green. There wasn't much chance he could land his ball very close to the flag. He also wondered if the "breast" landing of his golf ball had destroyed the impact Loni suggested the shot might have. He wanted his opponents to feel he'd choked badly on that last swing. If it were so, as Loni had said, he would have side bets with anyone he wanted. Players would be standing in line to wager a bet on the last nine holes.

From his free drop position, everyone on the patio was yelling at him on his backswing as he tried to pitch his ball onto the green. He'd never taken a swing under those circumstances. There was no sportsmanship......nor was any expected. It was their form of gamesmanship. In that instance, Lawton decided to purposefully blade his shot over the green and into the pond. It was his only chance to assure his opponents that he would fold under pressure. As his shot hit the middle of the pond, the derisive cheers and laughter from that large mass of people on the patio made him feel slightly embarrassed. He hated to hit a second bad shot in a row, but Loni had convinced him it was the best strategy.

As Lawton approached the green to watch his teammates complete the ninth hole, D'Annelli looked over at him with even more respect. He knew the shot into the pond was done for added effect. He grinned, "Good decision, kid, that last shot will pay you dividends. I'll guarantee it."

Loni and Whitey each two-putted for pars and the D'Annelli team was tied with two other teams for the lead after nine holes with a combined 5-under par score. The other two teams, Big Julie's team and Willie LaCurso's team were only two strokes back.

When the D'Annelli team walked onto the patio for lunch, opponents moved toward Lawton like a hoard of barracuda. They wanted some sizeable individual bets on the next nine holes….just as Loni predicted. Head on head play was still done though they were all involved in a team competition. Each player just had to complete the hole with his own ball even if his teammates had two better scores.

Typical offers for a wager with Lawton were for $500 a hole or a $1000 for the second nine-hole score. And, he wasn't the only one making bets. The betting was frenzied amongst all the players. He couldn't believe the money that was floating around that patio.

Admittedly, Lawton got caught up in the gamesmanship. He was absolutely confident he could beat any one of these guys head-on-head. Certainly he was aware of the $3.59 in his pocket. Even if he lost some matches, he figured to win more than half of them. He could also then repay Charlie his portion of the $5000 if Lawton's team lost the over-all match. As any decent gambler, he had himself leveraged. But, most importantly, he didn't intend to lose to this group of burglars. He wanted to walk away from the golf course that afternoon with as much of their money as possible.

Lawton accepted every bet for the second nine, but insisted that the wagers get documented. He didn't want any huckster to bow out of paying. What surprised him was the reaction. To a man his opponents said, "Don't worry…we won't let you forget."

Of course they figured Lawton was easy money.

With an hour before the afternoon tee time, Davis had motioned for him to meet inside the Lodge. Grabbing a hamburger and cole slaw from the buffet, Lawton made his way to the Lodge restaurant amidst kidding remarks on the patio from players and non-players alike. They considered him now one of them. The camaraderie was nice, but nothing was further from the truth. He would never be one of them.

Looking into the busy restaurant, he finally found Davis. It didn't surprise him that his friend was sitting at the counter making time with one of the waitresses. He wondered how many countless times he'd witnessed that sight.

Since Lawton still didn't think it wise for Davis and him to be seen as associated, he sat down at the counter two seats away and pretended not to know him. Davis gave the waitress some money and she left. He took Lawton's cue and lit a cigarette looking the opposite way of where Lawton was sitting. Then he turned slightly giving his friend a quick glance. Lawton could tell Davis was still not thrilled with the collection of 'gentlemen' he'd chosen to play golf with that day.

They ate in silence until there were no people near them. Finally Davis turned toward Lawton but looked past him. He smiled and waved to no one in particular on the other side of the restaurant. Without glancing at Lawton and maintaining his factitious grin, he chided, "If those shots on Hole #9 were the way you played the entire round, your teammates may hope you stay right here at the counter. That was a hell of a shot into the patio followed by another bladed one into the pond. Since I know you, I had to wonder if you didn't perform those shots on purpose!"

Lawton glanced at him for a millisecond without changing his facial expression and whispered, "Chas, hitting into that eating area... that's closer to the truth than you might believe. I don't know where you've been for the last two hours, but you'll have to see this format to believe it. Guys are yelling at each other during their swings. Balls are being hit at one another. You've got to be ready for anything to break your concentration. It's like a circus out on the course. That's the way these mugs play the game."

A waitress walked by and they turned away from each other. When she passed, they rapidly returned to their conversation.

Lawton continued, "And, as far as that second shot I hit into the patio...that was all planned. Sportsmanship, as we know it, has no place in this tournament. It was my teammate Loni D'Annelli who strongly suggested I make that shot. He felt it would do more good than harm by showing our competitors that I might be choking. And you know what...he was right! I'm now looked upon as an easy mark. Every one of these half-baked bums now wants to make a private wager with me on the next nine holes. It's amazing. Most of these fellows couldn't beat me if I played with one club and a putter. This is like a golfer's dream as far as wagering. I'm not gambling. I'm picking up free money off the table. Charlie, I have the chance to make an incredible amount of money on side bets this afternoon."

Lawton stopped his animated talk long enough to glance over at Davis to see his reaction. Davis just sat there not giving any retort one way or the other. Lawton gave him a kick to his left leg to wake him from his daze. Davis just nodded still lost in his thoughts.

Lawton was bemused. Lowering his voice even more, he said, "I'll tell you more later, when you're listening. In the meantime, where the hell have you been? I figured you'd be out on the course trying to rankle a few of my competitors."

Without looking at Lawton, Davis began talking like a repeat rifle as he kept a hand over his mouth. He whispered, "Jamie, for Christ's sake, you won't believe what I've learned in the past couple hours while you were on the course. There are some strange things going on at this resort. This is no more a charity event than I'm a priest. There is some kind of gambling ring operating at Chippewa Lodge. There are literally booths set up to take wagers on this golf tournament, but it doesn't stop there. I witnessed people making wagers on other sports events around the country. The whole thing is run so smoothly I just can't believe it's just a weekend affair. And, to top it off, the whole operation is being given the appearance that it's run by a local church from town...which is a load of horse...."

A waitress walked by and Davis stopped himself from completing his sentence. After she passed, his tone was even more intense. "....Anyway, I've been talking to a few people...you know, some employees here at the Lodge and even one guy who basically manages the Calcutta. He's a local guy...an apparent pillar of the community. You wouldn't think it to see him. His name is Henry Hanson. He looks like he hasn't eaten or slept in about a month and it appears he's making a wad of money for his church group.

I can't quite figure him out. I swear to Christ he's up to his eyebrows in this whole affair and seems to be going through a guilt trip over what's going on. I couldn't believe what he shared with me. He was either drunk or about to have a nervous breakdown, but his mouth was running full blast. He left no doubt that this charity golf tournament and the weekend Calcutta was just a tip of the iceberg. Yet, I won't believe for a minute he's the brains around this business endeavor. The money they're taking in...I tell you it's just too big for some local small businessman and church deacon to be running. However, he knows more. I plan on going back to talk with this man while you're playing this afternoon. I'll catch up with you later on the golf course."

Another customer strode by silencing the two of them. Davis had a lot more to say. His words kept flowing. "Jamie, I also sense more than a few townspeople have an idea there are some peculiar things going on out here at Chippewa Lodge. But, they won't say a damn word. Maybe you wouldn't either if your community was gaining so much. The local businesses are buzzing. Civic and church organizations are enjoying some high times. Logically the townsfolk don't want this gift horse to go away.

A waitress stepped up and offered to fill their water glasses; they looked away from each other. It gave the two of them a quiet moment to assimilate what just got said.

When the waitress was out of ear shot, Davis looked straight ahead and mumbled, "Jamie, I don't know about you, but God strike me dead if I didn't recognize some of these lowlifes eating out on that patio. I've seen their pictures in the newspapers...and not for anything good. I think many of these good-timers are hoodlums parading around like they're respectable citizens. Some of them should be in jail this very minute. If I was a betting man...and I am...I would wager some significant cash is being hidden someplace."

Then Davis paused and turned toward Lawton and looked his law school buddy straight in the eye. "Jamie, while this Henry Hanson may be in charge of the gambling booths, I'm finding one name that keeps popping up in various conversations. It's your new pal and teammate, Loni D'Annelli."

He was surprised when Lawton just shrugged and responded, "Yeh, it's a shame how a guy and even my other two teammates can be so much fun on the golf course and be so opposite of someone you want to be seen with off the golf course."

They both shook their heads. They both were now on the same page. They sat there at the bar not saying anything...just thinking of what they'd stumbled upon.

Lawton glanced at his watch. It was time for him to return to the patio and get ready for the afternoon match. He leaned closer to Davis. "Charlie, I'll be ready to escape this resort and town as soon as this tournament is over. Right now I'm looking forward to skinning these guys out of a lot of money this afternoon. I've got some healthy wagers already; other guys are waiting for me to establish our individual bets. Whether I even show up tomorrow for the second day of this event will have to be decided later. I may be obligated. As for later this afternoon, you'd better have your old jalopy ready for a quick exit. I don't want to stay around here any longer than necessary."

Davis stared forward knowing Lawton had no choice but to finish that day's competition. Muffling his words through his hands, he said, "O.K., you make some of that tainted money and protect what money we do have in this fiasco. I've got some unfinished business with that church man over at his booth. I get the feeling he's sick of the whole affair and has me pegged as someone who might be able to help him out. Shaking his head, he showed disgust. "I can't believe this charity event has slipped by my consciousness for the past few years. I had heard about Glenwood having a town celebration...of which you would know I wouldn't give a God damned hoot. But, I had no idea a Calcutta and charity golf tournament were connected to this little town festival."

He glanced at Lawton and winked, "Of course, charity events don't hold a lot of interest for me, since I believe myself to be a perpetual charity case. I would have more interest cleaning my boathouse."

Lawton skewed his face while pretending to look across the restaurant. "Well, my friend, I deserve some credit this morning. By getting you down here you've been able to discover a covert mob operation maneuvering right under your own nose twenty-nine miles south of where you live. Your observance these last couple years has been brilliant."

Davis rolled his eyes at the sarcasm, but he couldn't disagree with Lawton's appraisal. As he got up to leave, Davis shot back semi-seriously with his back to Lawton, "Before you go wild on your bets with these crooks, I might remind you that we have $637 remaining after we pay out the $5000 entry fee. On the chance you played poorly this afternoon, you might want to have enough to pay off your losses. I say that just to remind you that it'll be too bad if our friendship is ruined because of your untimely death later today."

With no one around but a couple waitresses, Lawton stood up tall facing his friend. "Charlie, I'm going to beat these guys for two reasons. One...these guys have more confidence in their golf games than their games deserve. If I play only average, I should win more than half my bets. Secondly, and more importantly, I'm out to squeeze as much money from these lunatics as possible...and then give it away. We'll become benefactors for some appreciative charities. Furthermore, I figure my team has at least a two out of five chance of retaining the entry fee. I like those odds given the abilities of my teammates besides myself."

Davis gave him a smile. He'd seen that fire in Lawton's eyes often on the golf course. He liked what the results generally were when his friend was in that frame of mind. Still he couldn't help applying the needle. "Jamie boy, if it looks like you're losing on the back nine holes, you might not see me. I'll be on my way back home. When you get thrown into the middle of Lake Minnewaska in cement shoes by your buddy Loni D'Annelli, I want to be alive so I can attend your funeral."

The two men then walked opposite ways out of the restaurant laughing as they exited. Davis was satisfied with Lawton's chances. Under his breath he couldn't help saying to himself, 'And, this is supposed to be 'amateur' golf!"

Approaching the patio area Lawton noticed Tess had gained some additional celebrity, as if any more was needed. Guests of the Lodge, golfers, and gallery members were joking with her and getting their photos taken with her. She had a golf ball stuck between her breasts reliving the experience with anyone within earshot. She was obviously enjoying her ephemeral glory while Big Julie looked on a bit perturbed.

Seeing Lawton again, his competitors were on him like hungry wolves on fresh kill wanting to finalize a wager. Lawton was ready with pencil and paper to accept and record all bets. His confidence was swelling as he made bet after bet. No competitor was going to conveniently forget the wager. He recorded every bet in detail. It turned out that he had money riding on the last nine holes with every player except of course his teammates. Thirteen of the sixteen competitors wanted to play a $1000 match for the nine holes. Three other golfers wanted to go $500 a hole. The potential for making money in the afternoon was staggering.

As the second nine holes of golf got underway, each four-man team teed off in the same order they had in the morning. Big Julie's team, behind the leaders by two strokes, was the first team off. However, they made up that deficit immediately. When two of his teammates promptly birdied the first hole, their team was back in the fray. They then showed great control and common sense by pulling out umbrellas on the second tee box to shield themselves from drives purposely hit at them from the #1 tee box by Willie LaCurso's team.

As for LaCurso's team, they made only one birdie out of four players on the first hole. LaCurso didn't display any coolness in the least. When the group behind his group hit into them on the Hole #2 tee-off, Willie stomped the ball into the ground, then proceeded to pull his knickers down and moon Danny A'Motta's team standing back the first tee box. The flaw in his action was that three hundred gallery members saw Willie flash his skinny butt at the first tee box. Willie could have cared less.

A'Motta happened to be one of the three fellows who wagered $500 a hole with Lawton. The evil-looking gangster was reading Lawton as a flash in the pan. Lawton in turn had A'Motta figured for a slow pay at best, but took the bet anyway. He figured to let A'Motta pay if he wished. Collecting a winning bet would not be worth his life.

Vinnie Spagatini and Bert Bertinelli were the other two guys who made the $500 per hole bet with Lawton. They were particularly wrathful; their furor emboldened from the first nine holes as D'Annelli's foursome repeatedly hit into them. Both hoodlums went nose to nose with Lawton telling him they wanted the money they would win immediately...or as Bertinelli said, "golf is difficult to play with two broken arms." Lawton didn't blink, but when they left to go warm up for the second nine holes, he had no saliva.

The Spagatini group all hit drives close to the first green but managed only one birdie. When Bert Bertinelli missed his putt from four-feet, the vulgarities from Bert's mouth could be heard over the wind back to the first tee box.

In the D'Annelli group, Whitey Malooley and Billie McCoy and then Loni all hit playable drives within twenty-five yards of the green. Lawton was last to tee off deciding whether to lay up with a 'spoon' shot that would probably land near the green...or take the risk again with his "pencil as a tee" maneuver he'd done that morning. He was inclined to be conservative until Adam saddled up to him. He whispered, "Jamie, go for it. Aim toward the lake across the road on the left. Don't worry! I've played this wind often. It'll blow your ball back toward the green. It's calm here at the tee box, but the lake breeze is really forceful down by the green."

Lawton had to smile. The kid had money riding on Lawton's success.

He put away the three-wood and asked for a flat-headed scoring pencil from the crowd. The crowd started buzzing. Many had either seen or heard of what Lawton had done that morning on the practice range. Following the direction of Adam, Lawton aimed uncomfortably left...literally off the golf course towards the lake. The galley including Malooley and McCoy thought he was crazy. D'Annelli was the only one who showed no emotion. He just said, "Hit it stiff, kid."

With the ball balancing on the top of the pencil about 3-4 inches above the ground, Lawton proceeded to launch a towering drive over the trees about forty yards left of the green straight at Lake Minnewaska. Spagatini's group on the #2 tee box was watching his drive for reasons of self-protection. They needn't have worried. The ball would not come close to them.

As the ball headed toward the lake, suddenly it seemed to be entirely controlled by Mother Nature. It drifted to the right toward the green. If it was long enough, it looked like the ball was hit well enough to make the green.

The ball ended up descending from such a height that when it did hit the softened green, it didn't bounce. The golf ball simply buried itself into the turf...only fifteen feet left of the hole. The crowd went crazy. Even Malooley and McCoy were slapping Lawton on the back. Here was a chance for a two-under par eagle if he could drain that putt.

Dejectedly, Vinnie and Bert turned around and concentrated on their own shots as they strode off the #2 tee box.

Back at the first hole, Whitey almost drained his approach shot and had a gimme birdie. That was one birdie for the team. Loni and Billie hit adequate shots within twelve feet of the hole. The two of them putted first hoping to make their birdies so Lawton could have a free run at his eagle putt. Unfortunately, both players missed their putts. It made Lawton have to be careful not to be too aggressive on his eagle putt. If he three-putted for a par, it would be a major blow to his team.

Lawton's putt was not easy. It was downhill on a very bumpy green given the cleat marks from players in front of them dragging their feet. When Lawton hit the putt, it was so quiet it was as if the three hundred gallery members were not there. The ball seemed to explode off his putter face and was immediately traveling too fast for such a short fifteen-foot lag putt. Lawton's heart was in his throat as his speeding ball began breaking toward the cup. When the ball hit the back of the cup, it bounced straight up in the air...and then disappeared convincingly into the cup.

The eagle had landed. The crowd erupted around the green. Lawton's teammates were slapping his back once again. Their team had managed to go 3-under par on their best two scores on that first hole giving them a one shot lead right out of the gate. He glanced ahead and saw Vinnie and Bert as they trudged down the second fairway. They had seen the heroics. Their shoulders had hunched just a bit more forward.

As Lawton approached the 2nd tee box, Charlie Davis was standing there. The two of them still hadn't acknowledged they knew each other. However, Davis just stood there shaking his head. He knew how lucky Lawton had been. If the ball had not hit the cup it could have rolled fifteen feet by the cup. He just mumbled sardonically "Nice putt", as Lawton ignored him but smiled at the comment.

As the second nine hole competition progressed, there was less tomfoolery going on than the first nine holes. A lot of money was at stake. Lawton made that observation to D'Annelli and he only nodded in his sinister way. Grinning, he said, "Kid, just be ready for anything. You ain't seen nothin yet." Lawton couldn't imagine what malicious things could be awaiting them.

Holes #2 thru #6 saw the D'Annelli team gained three more birdies bringing them to 6-under for the second nine and 11-under when combining their morning score. Lawton had not contributed any more birdies, just that eagle on #1. His three partners had made one birdie apiece. As they stood waiting on the seventh tee, the four of them felt they were in pretty good shape.

Throughout those holes, Lawton had not seen Davis in the gallery. He figured Charlie was back talking to this character named Hanson about the peculiarities happening around the resort.

Finally on that seventh hole he saw Davis standing high on a hill where the #8 tee box was located. What caught his eye was that his friend was accompanying what looked like a very attractive female.

It made Lawton look twice. Davis normally wasn't that lucky. From his vantage point, the female had long strawberry blonde hair that danced in the wind. She was too far away for him to study her face, but if judging by her shape was fair, Davis had stumbled upon a real find.

It was then that the young friend of Adam Bailey's came forward and breathlessly gave Adam an update loud enough for all to hear:

"Big Julie's team is burning up the resort course. His team went 3-under the first nine holes. They are now 8-under for the second nine and tied with you guys at 11-under par. They are playing the last hole. If they get a birdie on that hole, they would be leading at 12-under.

Willie LaCurso's team is right behind at 10-under and were putting for birdies on the second to the last hole.

The other two teams are sucking eggs. They're going to have to do something stupendous to have a chance to win."

The D'Annelli team now had an idea what they had to do on the last three holes. Despite the importance, Lawton found himself staring up at the female with Davis. He had a strange thought that he'd seen her before. He'd had that problem a number of times in his past with other females.

He knew he was missing an opportunity as he watched Charlie giving his top effort to entertain the young lady. She was smiling, even laughing. Lawton gritted his teeth.

With some time to wait, D'Annelli saw his quiet teammate losing some of his focus. Vinnie Spagatini and Bert Bertinelli were ahead on the seventh green ready to attempt their very short birdie putts. The timing could not have been more perfect. D'Annelli drew up to Lawton and retorted, "You might watch our two friends up on the green. Vinnie and Bert have a little surprise coming up."

With those words, all hell broke loose around that seventh green. Some drunken gallery members set off some firecrackers. There were celebratory rockets and missiles flying all over the place. Vinnie was into his backstroke for his makeable fifteen-foot birdie putt when the mayhem started. So startled, he hit his putt ten feet by the cup. He was livid. Throwing his putter aside, he charged toward the gallery to find the culprits. There was no doubt on anyone's mind his aim was to cause some premature deaths or at least impart great bodily harm to someone. Bert caught Vinnie in full stride and held him from committing any felonious attacks. The whole scene finally calmed after the guilty parties disappeared back into the woods.

But, the damage had been done. The chaos had completely wrecked the concentration of those two players. Bert missed his short birdie putt as well. Then Vinnie missed his second putt for par. Both golfers looked ready to machine gun the entire gallery confident they'd bring down those responsible for the clamorous interruption. Residual deaths would not be important. The steam coming out of their ears was almost visible as they marched up toward the #8 tee box.

D'Annelli had been standing next to Lawton watching the entire affair with a satisfied look on his face. Leaning casually towards him, he lamented in mock seriousness, "Gee, it's unfortunate the crowd gets so out of control at times." Then he exploded into his inimitable laughter and strolled over to his next shot.

Lawton would never forget that spectacle. His focus returned and he hit his next shot onto the green as did D'Annelli. Ten minutes later after his team had completed their putts, Lawton noticed D'Annelli amble into the crowd. D'Annelli furtively stuffed some green backs into the pockets of a couple gallery members. There were now no doubts who those rowdy culprits were who fired off the firecrackers when Spagatini and Bertinelli were putting. Lawton heard the two local citizens who accepted the money simply say, "Thanks, Mr. D'Annelli".

The whole thing had been planned for the right moment. Loni had these locals ready to create chaos whenever he gave the word. That word had come at a crucial time for Spagatini and Bertinelli in the match. The results of the shenanigan were about as effective as they could possibly have been.

Lawton again appreciated that Loni D'Annelli had not reached his particular stage in life without brains, good planning, and having people willing to carry out his wants…for the right price.

On the seventh green the D'Annelli team didn't lose any strokes, but they didn't gain anything either. They all missed their birdie attempts from long range. Still, they were tied for the lead with two holes to play.

As they marched up the to the #8 tee box, they heard a big roar explode on the ninth and last hole. They would learn Big Julie's team had birdied at least one ball thereby moving ahead of the D'Annelli team by one stroke at 12-under par. Two birdies on the last two holes would be required to win the Saturday portion of the tournament for D'Annelli's team. But, one birdie would be essential for a tie and a playoff. Unfortunately the final two holes were two of the tougher holes.

Standing on the #8 tee box, the panoramic and spectacular view of Lake Minnewaska made any golfer almost forget about golf. The elevation created a scene allowing one to see the other side of the lake. The hole was a rather unique Par 3 with a dramatic vertical drop from tee to green. There were no traps or ponds just a green that looked like an after-thought far down the hill. The length of the hole was 170 yards but it looked like it was 500 yards with the steep slope to the green. Moreover, choosing the right club to hit was a challenge against the constant lake breeze. Making par on this hole was a good score. Making a birdie two for any golfer was improbable.

Malooley was first to hit and his effort did anything to instill confidence. His shot was so high and so wild to the right; he came back and disgustedly sat down on a bench before his shot hit the ground in the woods thirty yards right of the green. McCoy did better but his shot was ten yards short of the green. Loni keeping his stogie in his mouth then hit a lower shot that looked good until a breeze caught the ball and pushed it pin high ten yards left of the green.

D'Annelli's team had hit three shots and no one had landed his ball very close to the green. At that point the team would be lucky to make two pars. It looked inevitable the team would be lucky if they went into the last hole only one shot down.

With Lawton last to hit, his caddie, John Bailey, actually seemed to understand how competitive the match had become. He was constantly fidgeting with his pipe. Adam, normally a carefree kid, exhibited the same temperament. He couldn't stand still. Malooley sucked on his cigarette like it was his last one before facing the firing squad. McCoy looked like he needed a bathroom. D'Annelli stood on the tee box looking straight ahead chewing on his stogie. There were no hijinks he could perform on the opponents. It was up to the players on his team to hit the required shots or lose. His only comment to Lawton was a rather dimly camouflaged imperious repeat. "Hit it stiff, kid."

Davis was now standing with the attractive female next to John Bailey nervously holding Lawton's bag of clubs. Lawton noticed the female said something to Bailey almost as if they knew each other. Bailey looked at her, smiled, nodded, and went back to fidgeting with pipe.

Davis left the female's side and worked his way closer. Davis had never met John Bailey nor did he have any idea the farmer knew very little about golf. Directing a rather loud whisper at Bailey so Lawton could hear, he whispered, "I saw the previous group hit their approach shots way too high. The wind took control of the ball. You gotta hit your ball below the tree line all the way down to the green to take the wind out of the shot."

It was good advice, even though John Bailey looked strangely at Davis wondering why this man with the loud shirt was even talking to him. Lawton took the vicarious advice and chose a long iron. He didn't even place his ball on a tee. He dropped the ball on the grass. Hitting it flush with the long iron, the ball took off on a very low trajectory towards the right edge of the green. The breeze would have only a marginal impact on the shot. The ball then began hooking toward the middle of the green. Lawton sensed he'd just hit one of his best shots of the day.

The ball lit in front of the green, bounced forward, and started rolling toward the pin. It was moving quickly...way too quickly...and needed to slow down or it would roll over the green. In the next second providence provided some unbelievable luck. The golf ball smacked against the flag with enough force to hear the ball make a clanking sound to everyone back at the tee box. The contact caused the ball to career about four feet away from the hole. Everyone broke out in cheers up at the tee box and in the gallery down by the green.

Lawton's only thought was one of relief. At least his group had one certain par...and possibly that birdie they needed to tie Big Julie's team. Still, his team needed a par from one of his other teammates. That was not a sure thing.

At the green that elusive par happened quickly. D'Annelli made another heroic shot with a chip to within two feet for a tap in par three. If Lawton could somehow roll in that birdie putt, his team would have a chance to win the whole match with another birdie on the last hole.

Lawton studied the break on his four-foot putt and hesitantly approached it. He honestly couldn't tell if it was straight or whether it broke one way or the other. Adding to that discomfort, the players in front of their group had really scuffed up the grass around the cup with their cleats. The short grass between his ball and the cup looked like a war zone. His ball could easily be knocked off line by the spike marks. His only hope was to forget about the cleat marks, stroke the putt with confidence, hit it hard enough to go in, and....hope.

He was about to address the important putt when the D'Annelli group received some reciprocity...some folly by their opponents. Out of the woods next to the adjoining #9 tee box came Big Julie's wife, Tess Tagliossa. She was dressed...mostly... in her innocent two piece outfit as if modeling for a 1931 Lake Michigan beach fashion magazine. She started talking loudly asking people in the gallery where that young man was who hit her with the golf ball earlier that afternoon. People were laughing but trying to tell her to shush. But, not Tess. She just kept on talking loudly about being bruised and how she wanted to sue for damages. She didn't have to make sense. Her assignment was to say anything and say it loudly. She was carrying out her distraction with perfection.

She created enough of a bother that Lawton had to step away from his important putt until someone shackled her high-pitched voice. D'Annelli knew what was happening and came over to offer some support. Patting Lawton on the shoulder, he was like a warm uncle. "Relax kid, you know that's just a ploy by Big Julie to interrupt your concentration. I've seen it too many times. Just forget about the interruption, concentrate, and nail that putt.

Seeing that she had interrupted Lawton's train of thought, Tess just as suddenly quieted down and seductively walked back through the woods toward the clubhouse. She had done her act and done it well. Time would tell if she had been successful.

"Loni," confessed Lawton somewhat unnerved, "I believe Big Julie might have accomplished his goal. I can't decide whether this putt breaks to the right or to the left."

D'Annelli looked at his one-day discovery and could tell Lawton was a bit rattled. The putt was certainly not an easy one.

That was when this man who gambled with most everything in his life showed how he was ready for times like this one. He told Lawton to wait. Then as if he dealt in such matters every day he trotted over to the gallery and approached an attractive lady asking to borrow her scarf. He politely said, "Ma'am, I need it for just a moment."

He came back to Lawton and announced to the now burgeoning crowd, "You all know the importance of this putt. I'll tell you what...I'll bet a thousand dollars with any of my opponents that the "kid" will make that putt....blindfolded with this scarf."

It was pure showmanship showing a nature for risk that was far beyond anyone else's capability.

Lawton almost yelled out, 'Loni, you're nuts!', but he held his tongue. Lying before him was a putt worth more money than he had seen at any one time in his lifetime. D'Annelli had just offered the other players a chance to make what looked like a sure bet to make $1000. The putt was tough enough, and now he wouldn't even be able to see the ball as he stroked it. Additionally, Lawton had an ungodly amount of personal money bet with the other players. His life started flashing before his eyes. He didn't even look in the direction of Charlie Davis. He was certain there was a brand new stain somewhere on his friend's washed but soiled golf and sailing pants.

Up to that point Lawton had been very confident, even at times showing some arrogance just to irritate his opponents. Right then, however, he felt like the first time he had to fly solo in his biplane. Then he hadn't known whether to wet his pants or plead cowardice and stay on the ground. He had chosen to fly the plane.

As D'Annelli's team and the gallery surrounding the 8th green waited for the challenge of the bet to be communicated to all of that day's players having completed their eighteen holes, word came back very fast from the patio. It was unanimous. All sixteen opponents wanted to take Loni's personal $1000 bet...plus there were a couple non-players who wanted in on the action as well. All bets were accepted by D'Annelli.

Loni laughed out loud as he was tying the scarf around Lawton's eyes. He yelled to the crowd, "This will be the easiest money I've picked up in quite some time."

As he positioned Lawton over the putt, he couldn't help but begin to laugh. For certain, this entire day would always be unforgettable. Now, this 'small' additional wager would only add to the memory.

With the scarf over his eyes, Lawton found his nervousness had noticeably declined. If he missed, it would be understandable. Somehow he felt he might just have more of a chance to make it as D'Annelli aimed his putter. All he had to do was hit the ball hard enough so the ball had the chance to drop in the cup. With the ten minute delay, it seemed like two days since he'd initially approached the four-foot putt.

Loni leaned over and calmly said to Lawton, "Kid, you won't miss this, but even if you do, we'll get one birdie to tie on the last hole. Then, we'll beat them in a playoff. Your putter is aimed right at the cup, just stroke it in." His assurance was confidence inspiring.

Without any sense of pressure and the blindfold in place, Lawton just stroked the ball as his muscle memory dictated from his junior days at Midland Hills Country Club in St. Paul. The only thing going through his mind was to hit the ball hard enough.

When the ball glanced off his putter face it seemed like it took a full minute to hear any reaction from the crowd. That reaction would be the only signal whether the putt dropped into the cup....or not.

The crowd let out the beginnings of a moan as they yelled for the ball to get to the cup. 'My God,' Lawton thought, 'I've hit it too soft!'

What seemed like another minute went by and the crowd went from a low "oh" to a second later into the most ear-shattering scream ever heard at that resort. As Lawton pulled off his blindfold, Loni was already picking the ball out of the cup and carrying it triumphantly over his head to the #9 tee box. The birdie putt had dropped. That birdie meant that the D'Annelli team was tied for the lead with Big Julie's team with one hole to play. Lawton couldn't help but appreciate how that birdie would also contribute to some important individual wagers as well.

An added effect was that Charlie Davis no longer distanced himself from Lawton. He had calculated that the two of them had a good chance to come out ahead. Depending on what happened on the last hole, this day could turn into a bonanza. Davis walked next to Lawton to the next tee box holding his friend's arm in the air.

Lawton asked him, "Charlie, why the delayed response from the crowd?"

Davis happily choked a response. "Your putt hit the edge of the hole and rolled around and seemed to stop momentarily on the edge of the cup. It then disappeared. Once it fell into the cup, the place went crazy. You missed seeing a hell of a shot and you're the one who hit it!" Davis looked at the attractive lady next to him. Both exploded into laughter.

D'Annelli made his way through the crowd around the ninth tee box and returned Lawton's ball he had victoriously retrieved from the #8 cup. His smile made his stogie look small. Placing an affectionate hand on Lawton's shoulder he shouted, "Kid, I wish we'd met years ago. We'd have been successful in whatever we did!"

It was said wistfully and within seconds made his smile decrease in radiance ever so slightly. He knew Lawton wasn't one of his kind.

With that he blinked, shook his head, and got back into his normal character. "Boys," he said to his three teammates, "Let's get'em on this last hole."

Loni, having just won at least $16,000 more money on the blindfolded four-foot putt, was greeted with cheers as he stood on the ninth tee box. He looked as if he was Washington crossing the Delaware River. The crowd had grown to over a thousand people gathered around the tee box and stretching down both sides of the fairway. Lawton had not played in front of so many people since the state amateur in Minneapolis at Interlaken Country Club a few years before. Now here he was out in the middle of nowhere with a crowd gathered to watch the richest unknown "amateur" tournament ever played in Minnesota. Loni doffed his cap, replaced it firmly on his balding head, and promptly laced a drive right down the middle of the fairway with cheers following every second of the ball's 240-yard trip. He did a tap dance and bowed to the spectators. Whitey was next and wasn't near the showman. He nervously teed up his ball and hit a high towering drive directly right into the adjoining 5th fairway. Billie, "Mister Consistent", McCoy managed to hit his drive on the fairway but it was weak, leaving him over 215 yards from the green. He'd be lucky to get his second shot to within chipping range of the green.

Lawton was last to hit. He still had the scarf and raised it overhead saying to everyone with earshot, "I'm keeping this scarf in my pocket so Loni doesn't get the same impulse for me to hit a blindfolded drive."

A wave of laughter ensued. D'Annelli's reaction was one of disappointment...as if he'd wished he would have thought of the idea.

As the noise from the crowd subdued, Lawton quickly teed up his ball up before Loni gave it more thought. Lawton knew better. The team needed a good drive just for the foursome to have one more chance at making a sure par and a possible birdie on the last hole. That was all that was needed...one par and one birdie. Even to D'Annelli having his team win $80,000 from his friends and cohorts meant a lot...maybe more in bragging rights than his share of the money. Whatever the case, they wanted to win.

As Lawton teed up his ball, the atmosphere had become suddenly more intense. People were standing too close to the tee box. Both Charlie Davis and Adam Bailey motioned for people to step back so Lawton could swing freely. He took a practice swing to relax his mind and body. 'Oh, the days of an innocent, barnstorming pilot/attorney,' he thought to himself, 'and those days had added up to this amazing spectacle.' He figured he likely had already won most of the individual matches, but how satisfying it would be to win the over all team prize even if he wasn't going to keep the money. The satisfaction was soaking these hucksters out of their ill begotten money.

Lawton was feeling very audacious and somewhat cavalier on that final tee box. He could already envision his ball traveling down the right center of the fairway of this downhill 420-yard finishing hole leaving him in perfect shape for his approach shot to the green.

His backswing felt comfortable. He was doing everything he'd practiced to place a good swing on the ball. His only miscalculation was that he hadn't played in a tournament like this one. Though he'd just witnessed some hijinks during the day by fellow players as well as by D'Annelli himself, Lawton assumed he was done being the target for any other pranks. How wrong he was.

On his downswing with even the breath of a bird not being heard, one of the gallery members broke wind...and he did it in glorious fashion. The sound was so surprising and so raucous that the entire gallery couldn't help but wither into a muffled laughter. Even Lawton felt his body shudder from holding back his own laugh. The circumstances made the foul sound stand out as a classic in poor timing...or great timing depending on whose side you were on.

With the blatant interruption, he was lucky to have made contact with the golf ball. What resulted was the ball being hit off the heel of the golf club and flying on a low trajectory almost beheading some of the gallery who were too close to the fairway on the left side. The ball mercifully missed these people and fortunately began slicing back ever so slightly toward the fairway. Lawton silently begged for the ball to make it out to the middle of the fairway, but that turned out to be too much to ask. An over-hanging branch took care of any further progress as the feeble drive nestled close to a tree on the edge of the woods some 220 yards from the green. The ball was not lost, but it stopped in a horrible position. Lawton mused how he may have done better with the scarf over his eyes!

D'Annelli came over and immediately apologized. "Sorry kid, I should have been on the look out. The crowd was just too big. I should have warned you about the probability that Fanny Rubenstein, one of Big Julie's best friends, was in the gallery. Fanny has a special skill. He can fart on command with three different variations of noise level and length. The man is a maestro. Even if you know it's coming, the noise can still make you jump. He showed you a lot of respect by exhibiting one of his longer, louder ones. Not everyone earns his Grade A effort. Don't worry. I'll stick a couple of my boys on him. Fanny's cheeks will stay silent the rest of the way in."

Lawton smiled ruefully accepting that antics like this one were just part of the psychological play of the tournament. The infamous act by Fanny had served its purpose. Lawton figured he'd be lucky to make a par given the poor position of his golf ball.

Now it was the D'Annelli team whose shoulders were slumped. After tying the leader with 12-under par, gaining two pars to maintain the tie on the last hole seemed remote. Malooley was so far away from the green his teammates didn't even see him until they heard him hit his ball from the adjoining fairway. What followed was a sickening plunk. The ball had submerged in the pond on the right side of the green. Malooley was no longer able to help the team.

McCoy was next to hit. If he could get on or near the green for a good chance at par, Lawton could better consider how much of a gamble he might take on his second shot. McCoy had a difficult downhill. His shot finished twenty yards short of the green. There was a chance he could make a good chip and putt for par, but given the money riding on it, the odds weren't great. It was up to D'Annelli and Lawton to either win or lose that day's competition.

To take some pressure off, D'Annelli elected to hit his second shot before Lawton decided how to play his shot. The big man was 190 yards away and hit his low long iron like he played golf for a living. The ball hit in front of the green and just barely rolled onto the putting surface stopping thirty feet short of the hole. D'Annelli had come through. While the birdie chance would not be easy, the par looked very probable. The team needed one more par to tie Big Julie's team.

Facing his shot, Lawton had a choice between a spoon or brassie shot. What made the 220-yard shot especially difficult was that he would have to aim right at the middle of the pond and hook the ball rather dramatically from a downhill lie. His other choice was to simply lay his ball up short of the green and face a pitch shot into the green from roughly fifty yards out. It would be a lucky par at best. He gazed at D'Annelli who was calmly smoking his stogie but was well aware of the challenging shot. D'Annelli helped make the decision. He confidently rasped, "Go for it, kid". That was his way of saying 'take the gamble'. It was just his way of life.

As Lawton pulled out the brassie and approached his shot, he was relieved to see not nearly the number of people surrounding him like there were on the tee box. Startling noises would likely not happen. To be certain John Bailey and Charlie chimed in and said that if anyone in the gallery moved or spoke while Lawton was swinging, that person would not live to see the setting sun. His two comrades made the threat with such conviction people either retreated away from Lawton's ball further or they silently nodded their heads in understanding.

As he analyzed the required flight of the ball, Lawton realized it was actually a very similar type of shot he'd hit on the same hole that morning. Only this time he'd be trying to hit the ball on the green and not onto the patio.

The swing was solid. The contact had a rich sound. The ball took off at the pond a little further right than he desired. The ball began to hook almost immediately. The question was whether the shot would be long enough. Everyone was yelling, "Hook!!! Hook!!" The shot was on its downward arc and heading for the right embankment of the green adjacent to the pond. It was either going to hit that embankment and bounce into the pond or if it had enough forward power, it might bounce onto the green.

It had the flight time and enough hooking spin to make the essential bounce. When the ball landed against the embankment, it barely skipped onto the putting surface as if scoffing at the pond as it went by. With the pin on the upper right corner of the green, it was plain to see the ball moving determinedly at the flag. For a moment Lawton thought the impossible...that he might hit two flags in two holes. That turned out to be too optimistic. The ball rolled by the pin and settled about twenty feet above the cup on the back edge of the green. The noise from the crowd was deafening. Lawton had just pulled off the scrambling shot of the year out of his bag.

The cheers continued as the D'Annelli team marched down to the green. They now had two legitimate attempts at birdie to win the first day competition…Loni's thirty-footer and Lawton's twenty-footer. As he passed the patio toward the final green, Lawton's opponents just stared at him and were uncommonly subdued. They weren't happy knowing that the 'trick-shot' artist was likely going to win most if not all his individual bets. He was not the choker they had perceived him to be. To add salt to their wounds, he now had a chance to help D'Annelli's team win the big $80,000 first place prize.

McCoy chipped heroically up to within six feet of the cup. Putting first to try and guarantee one par, he missed. It was then up to D'Annelli and Lawton to make no worse than par.

D'Annelli putted first. His thirty-foot birdie putt was up hill and on line but just never had the speed to get to the cup. He was two-feet short. He putted in for the par. Now it was up to Lawton. If he could two-putt from his difficult position above the cup, Big Julie's team and the D'Annelli team would have a playoff for the top prize. To Lawton, just two-putting was something he'd be more than satisfied to take. The birdie putt represented more money than he cared to think about…but one factor kept him calm. He'd never considered any of the money he might win as his. Except for recovering the initial $5000 entry fee, any winning amounts would be donated. His only satisfaction was stripping this money from the pockets of a bunch of professional crooks. That thought helped him maintain his focus.

He knew there would be subtle and unsubtle noises coming from everywhere as he addressed the ball. He put that out of his mind since it was part of the acceptable demeanor of this tournament. Figuring the putt to break about a foot to the left toward the pond, he knew he couldn't hit it too hard or the golf ball would not take the break and likely leave him with a long second putt. If he three-putted to lose the team match, all his previous heroics would probably be minimized.

As he stroked the ball, he was concentrating so hard he was hearing or seeing nothing else. He had effectively closed his mind to all extraneous noises. Later, people said the unbelievable noise from the patio as he hit that putt sounded like a Notre Dame home football game

The line on the putt looked good. Lawton's only concern was that the ball had enough steam to make it to the cup. He could only hope the downhill slant would give him some needed roll.

CHAPTER 15

With the last nine holes in progress that Saturday afternoon, Charlie Davis hadn't become part of the gallery until he met up with Lawton and his teammates on the seventeenth hole of play that day. Besides being too nervous to watch the first few holes of the afternoon round, he felt compelled to witness the action at the First Presbyterian Church's gambling booth and hopefully coerce more information out of Henry Hanson. The obligation to contact someone in law enforcement was strong, but Davis had some other considerations...the least of which was to authenticate what Hanson was saying. Unfortunately there were some personal considerations to be considered. Lawton and he were in a lion's den. To be recognized with a resort full of gangsters was not the best thing for either one's reputation. Even when to contact the authorities was important...the call would be best done anonymously when they were far away from Glenwood.

Now there was another reason for seeking out Henry Hanson, the mogul church man in charge of the betting booth. Lawton could be in trouble at the conclusion of the golf event. On the off chance that Lawton's golfing skills disappeared during the afternoon round or he simply experienced some bad luck, there was not enough money in their money parcel to cover the losses. Davis planned to go to the closest source of money and arrange a 'loan'. If he had to threaten or even blackmail the church deacon into a degree of larceny, he would do so. He had no sense of scruples or morality in the entire matter. The money in the gambling till was illegal. With no respect for anyone or anything there, it opened the door for Davis to be in his most creative mode.

Before making his way across the roadway to the gambling booth, Davis did witness his friend's opening tee shot of the afternoon round.

He was half way down the fairway when he looked back to see Lawton bent over teeing his golf ball on a flat-headed pencil. He'd seen his friend perform this trick often. It meant that Lawton was going to try for the green from the tee box. He followed the flight of the ball as it passed high over the tall pines beside him. The height of the shot was such that when it miraculously actually landed on the green, it stuck like a dart on a dartboard. When Lawton dropped that eagle putt on Hole #1, the D'Annelli team forged into the lead. Davis relaxed considerably. He sensed his friend was not going to lose on this day. Just in case, though, he still intended on having that conversation with Henry Hanson about a possible loan.

Minutes later, Davis was walking across the roadway. It was easy to spot Hanson. He was slumped over his ledger while taking another wager. The dour man looked no better than he had that morning. The activity at the booth had slowed considerably with the final nine holes underway. Bets had been made and the patrons were now directing their attention to the golf tournament. When Davis moved in closer toward the booth, there were two men completing their bets on some horseracing action at Arlington Park racetrack outside of Chicago. Being the only man at the booth, Hanson took the money and recorded the bet. Davis just shook his head in wonderment.

When the two betters left, Hanson was able to sit back and relax a moment. From just outside the booth, Davis saw a truly dog-tired man. He appeared defenseless to any aggressive move Davis wanted to employ whether it was to gain more information or discuss that loan for Lawton.

Entering the booth, Davis tried to be amiable and up-beat. "So, Mr. Hanson, are you pleased with today's receipts? Is your Presbyterian group taking in a few dollars, are they?

Hanson hardly nodded his head. He looked twice at Davis as if trying to recollect all that he'd said that morning. Davis still could not figure out this unusual individual. One minute he was sharp; the next he seemed dazed and confused. Davis found himself feeling sorry for the emaciated fellow. No doubt the guy had scruples to be trusted in handling so much money. However, with the stress the man was exhibiting, it suggested to Davis that Hanson had to be some kind of go-between. On one side he was being entrusted by his church. On the other side.....Davis didn't know. He just gazed across the roadway and stared logically at Chippewa Lodge resort. It didn't take a lot of imagination to guess that a number of hoodlums could be involved. D'Annelli likely was one, if not the leader. Davis just had no proof to that probability.

As Davis eased himself silently into a chair, Hanson tried to come off befuddled, but it didn't work. "Oh yeh, you're that fella I talked to this morning. I probably said more than I should have.

He chuckled while slanting his eyes momentarily at Davis and added, "But, you'll keep what I said under your hat, won't you? Everyone else does."

Davis just smiled and shook his head patiently. He'd become convinced Hanson might have recognized him and knew he was an attorney ...and would likely feel obligated to take some action against the obvious examples of lawlessness at the resort.

He nodded and said, "Yeh, I'm that same fella, Henry...and you should know I'm aware of a lot of things going on out here at the Lodge. I'm not ignorant. I know a lot of laws are being ignored. And frankly, you're in the middle of this mess. You probably can understand it wouldn't look good for you if any law enforcement officer suddenly stopped into your booth."

Hanson showed little reaction. His head simply looked down at his ledger on the table. Davis swore he saw the corners of the man's mouth crease upward. He decided right then to lay some cards on the table in the hope Hanson might do the same.

He leaned toward the bedraggled church man and asked curiously, "Henry, do you know me? I get the feeling we've talked before. There has to be some reason you so blatantly told me this morning about this resort golf event and the town's involvement. You had to realize you and probably a lot of your friends in the community could be in a lot of trouble if law enforcement gets involved...like fines, probable embarrassment, and possibly even some jail time."

That was the first time Hanson truly displayed some nervousness. He shook his head vigorously. "No.....no...we haven't met. Like I said, sometimes I say more than I should. I must have been either tired or irritated this morning to blow off so much steam to you. I hope I wasn't too much of a nuisance to you. And, whatever I said, I hope you'll not be inclined to share it with anyone. I don't want you to get yourself into a barrel of molasses."

He just stared at Hanson. He had the feeling the man was lying despite doing it so credibly. There was no exasperation in his tone... no noticeable degree of anxiety. It was as if he actually preferred the opposite of what he'd just said. Hanson cared little if Davis got himself in hot water...not necessarily with the law, but with the group of gangsters across the roadway.

It took a lot to get Charlie Davis riled, but this was one of those times. His voiced had a decided edge. He wanted to put the fear of

God into this two-bit Feed & Grain manager. "Mr. Hanson, whether you've met me or not, let me be very clear. I'm an attorney. I live up in Alexandria. My name is Charles Davis. Whether I'm a lawyer or not, a person would have to be deaf, dumb, and blind not to recognize the types of people at this breakfast I attended this morning at the Lodge restaurant. It was the closest thing to a mob convention I could imagine. What I saw in that restaurant made it easier for me to notice things like racketeering, aiding and abetting criminal activity, illegal booze, as well as someone's going to be arraigned for providing a safehouse for known convicts. And, now I see a very professionally run gambling house sponsored by a local church. I have a feeling your Presbyterian booth is just a small part of a much larger gambling operation. I wouldn't be surprised if your church booth is nothing more than a temporary façade during your town's festival set up specifically to reduce rumors of gambling impropriety at this resort."

Davis paused before adding, "God knows what else is going on out here."

Henry Hanson just stared at his ledger revealing no emotional response. Most people in Hanson's situation would have asked Davis how they could escape their predicament...and be relieved they were talking with an attorney. Hanson was not 'most people'. He didn't seem to care.

Davis was at a loss trying to further communicate with this stone-faced man. He was apparently too far gone to feel anything. Davis even wondered if the man was drunk. There certainly was the smell of beer at the booth...likely brought in by some of the church volunteers at the booth.

Then Hanson lifted his head. His eyes were lucid indicating he was sharper than he was letting on. His statement was said in a bland almost casual tone as if he hadn't listened to anything that Davis had just said. "So Mr. Davis, you think the situation looks pretty grim, do you? So, when do you plan on contacting the authorities?"

Davis stared at the deacon. The comment was so matter-of-fact. For the first time Davis had the odd revelation that Henry Hanson was more in control of this conversation than Davis cared to admit. The thought occurred to him that he was being played as a pawn by this small town church treasurer.

Immediately Davis backed off. He figured to let Hanson indicate how he wanted to proceed.

Hanson's voice became very measured. It was not the words Davis expected to hear. "Mr. Davis, your interest in our little gambling booth along with your observations about some of the people over at the

Lodge tells me you have a hint there might be a problem our town and the 'guests' staying at the resort. I'll just say this whole ordeal has been going on for too long. As an attorney, you might be able to help. As for me, I can't tell you much more. But, I can say you have the opportunity to take action in whatever way you want. I don't have that option without facing some serious reprisals."

Then he paused before saying, "And that's all I can say."

Any chance for further discussion suddenly evaporated. Another runner wearing a white shirt and bow tie from across the road stopped and stood near the booth. Apparently he'd been trained to stay clear of the booth until Henry Hanson summoned him to approach. It was another example of a very well run operation.

Davis could feel Hanson's further help slipping away. Before Hanson got up from his chair, Davis made one more stab. He hurriedly said, "Henry, I need more substance. Would it help if I told you I'm aware of the name 'Loni D'Annelli'? I know he's involved."

It was the first out and out lie Davis had said to Hanson. He only assumed D'Annelli had to be involved. "Henry, can you share anything else about this guy? I promise something will be done, but can you confirm that he's the kingpin."

Hanson stood up saying nothing. Then, hesitantly he responded, "I can't say. It would be a death warrant for any person who names anyone who might be involved in this enterprise. As you've apparently learned, Mr. D'Annelli is a much respected man both at the Lodge and in town. That's all I'll say about him."

The runner was standing on one foot and then the other waiting for Hanson. Davis knew he had seconds to pry anything else out of this perplexing town leader. "Henry, can you tell me this. If there's an on-going gambling operation centered here at Chippewa Lodge, a lot of cash is needed to run that kind of business. The wagers you bring in at this booth have to be part of that reservoir. Where is the money stored? Whoever handles that cash reserve is the man the authorities would be seeking."

Hanson almost wavered, but kept his mouth closed tightly.

Davis prodded trying to put words in Hanson's mouth. "The cash wouldn't be kept out here at the resort with the background of so many light-fingered individuals staying at the Lodge. Neither would the cash be deposited in a bank. That's too public...and in these times not safe. Henry, can you give me any more help?

But, Hanson only shook his head. There was frustration in his eyes, but also fear. Cutting off the conversation and waving the runner to approach, Hanson looked back and whispered, "If you can find that cash reserve, you'll be on the right track. It's not hard to figure out. It would be a shame if the wrong people were arrested...and worse if the guilty parties got away."

And that was it! With not even a farewell, he strolled over to the back of the booth and got his updated ledger for the runner. It was getting busy for Hanson once again, but he was about to take a break. As frail as he looked, he handled his responsibilities without hesitation. The runner took off with the up-dated ledger and money parcel. Two replacements greeted Hanson and got ready for their shift at the booth.

Davis contemplated taking one more whack at Hanson but ruled it out when the haggard man almost fell off the three-step ladder as he entered the scores on the huge scoreboard.

Both volunteers were right there to catch him, almost as if they expected him to drop any moment. Davis could hear both volunteers showing some concern for Hanson's condition. One of them said, "Henry, you look pretty tired, my friend. Why not stop down at some of the food booths at City Park and get something to eat."

'If they only knew what pressure Hanson was really under,' thought Davis.

Hanson gave them an appreciative nod as they got his sport coat and sent him on his way. Hanson gave them both a very appreciative handshake before leaving. However, Davis noticed something peculiar. It was the length of the handshake almost as if he was saying 'farewell', not just 'see you later'. Even the two volunteers seemed surprised with the warmth of his exit as he placed his left hand over the ritual handshake before releasing the grip.

As Davis crossed the roadway to return to the golf tournament, he caught a glimpse of Henry Hanson pulling away from the booth in his dirty coupe. There was a look on Hanson's face that would bother Davis for a long time. As tired as the man looked, as much tension as he must be feeling, Henry Hanson had a smile on his face...and he was whistling.

The same two guys in long coats guarding the front gates were still there when Davis returned. By now they recognized his chartreuse shirt more than his face. Anyone wearing clothing that outlandish did not represent a threat. They gave him a bored look and let him pass.

As he marched toward the golf links, he felt very much the pawn. He'd stumbled into a uniquely sensitive and shrouded crime scene...

and it was pervasive. Seemingly everyone connected to the Lodge was at least indirectly involved. Worse yet, there was untold numbers of townspeople who were willingly or unwittingly drawn into this mess. The town leaders including Henry Hanson and the organizers at the Lodge were strange bedfellows, but the relationship had been working to the benefit of the town for a long time.

There was a lot on his mind, but he and Lawton would figure out together how to proceed later. As Davis made his way out onto the golf course, he realized he been so engrossed with Henry Hanson, the outcome of the golf matches had fallen in priority. He'd even forgotten to discuss the possible need for cash if Lawton was choking to death out on the golf course. Now he became intensely interested in whether his friend was persevering. That would dictate whether Davis would drive right into Glenwood and flag down Henry Hanson. This time the conversation would not be as cordial. Davis would insist on a loan from the gambling profits or he'd threaten hell on earth for Hanson. He didn't look forward to using such an unprofessional approach, but being in the middle of a huge sham anyway, it didn't much matter what tactic he chose to use to get Lawton and himself out of this predicament.

Davis gazed at the scoreboard by the patio. People not interested in perspiring out on the golf course as spectators lounged in the shade of the tall trees or under a tent partially covering the patio. With their interest in the golf match only marginal, it gave the men more time to drink and win the attention of some intoxicated ladies lying with them.

The scoreboard showed the D'Annelli team was no longer in the lead after just completing Hole #6. The one group labeled 'Big Julie's team' was burning up the last nine holes and was leading by one shot after completing their last nine hole round.

With $5000 on the line, Davis headed in the direction of the #8 tee box. There were three holes remaining; plenty of time to tie up the match. Even if their entry fee was lost, he knew Lawton had a bunch of individual matches. If Lawton could win a bulk of those, they could recover their $5000 and even come out ahead.

As absorbed as he suddenly was in his computations, he'd hardly noticed a good-looking female suddenly appearing at his side. She just kind of materialized out of nowhere heading in the same direction. Davis looked to his side twice swearing he'd seen her before. He racked his mind trying to remember where. She was wearing a sun dress, large hat and sunglasses...and was stunningly attractive. On his last look, she'd even smiled at him. He wasn't used to someone of the opposite sex having such a good first impression towards him.

Given where he was, Davis knew he'd better be careful. While her attire showed class, she could be a girl friend of one of the racketeers staying at the Lodge. He and Lawton were in enough trouble; there was no reason to add any fuel to the fire. His concern only heightened when she asked him if he knew which fairway the Loni D'Annelli group might be located.

Cautiously Davis responded, "Oh, so you're here with the man in charge of this whole tournament." It was a shot in the dark. Maybe the lady could divulge something important.

He gulped when she abruptly lost her smile and glared at him. Her coldness was palpable as she tersely responded, "Hardly. I have nothing in common with that....person."

Then she seemed to catch herself and relaxed her taut manner. "Actually, I briefly met one of the players on his team this morning at the practice range. He was performing trick-shots of all things. I thought he was kind of.....well.....interesting, so I thought I'd watch him play the last couple holes."

Her voice softened even more. "He sure seemed different than the rest of the smart-mouthed wolves playing in this event. He was more innocent, even more conservative despite the show he put on this morning on the practice range. I had a feeling he was not displaying his normal behavior. And, he's certainly friendlier compared to the other players. Why he's playing in this charity tournament....I can't figure it out."

Davis knew immediately she was describing his friend. He wryly skewed his face for a second. He'd never ever heard Jamie Lawton described as 'conservative'...not with the number of times he'd seen his friend stand on his head on the wing of a moving biplane. Additionally, he'd seen Lawton land too many times on roads, golf courses, and once even on a lake. And 'innocent'...Davis couldn't help but guffaw. He'd seen Lawton bet he could hit a golf ball to a practice green next to a parking lot full of automobiles on one side of the green and the clubhouse and patio on the other side of the green...from 150 yards away. On that occasion, the two of them had not stuck around to find the gentleman whose windshield Lawton had demolished after his shot went wayward. They'd left some money on the front seat of the car, but it wasn't enough after paying off the bet. Davis was still reminding Lawton of that bit of immaturity whenever the situation warranted.

Davis figured if this young lady ever got to know Lawton, her impression of the 'conservative' Lawton would evaporate rather quickly. Hearing her devout misgivings towards the guest list at the Lodge that weekend, though, helped Davis relax his caution. While he wasn't comfortable enough to admit that he knew Lawton, he decided there was always time to be friendly with an attractive female. He gave her his best smile and said, "Well, I'm going the same way. Let's go find this foursome."

He and the young lady made it to the highest vantage point on the eighth tee box when they finally saw Lawton and D'Annelli conversing out in the middle of the seventh fairway. By then Davis learned that his new acquaintance was Miss Lindy MacPherson, a free-lance travel magazine columnist. She commented that her task in writing some articles about the resorts around Lake Minnewaska was almost completed.

Any last distrust of her eroded when she commented about the wild 'guests' at the Lodge and the 'perverted' players involved in that day's competition. He noted her disdain was quite serious. It was obvious she'd had some poor experiences while touring Chippewa Lodge. He was tempted to ask her about some other things she might have seen at the Lodge, but thought better of it. It was neither the time nor the place.

It was then that the rockets and firecrackers went off down by the seventh green while one of the players was putting. When the gangster missed his first putt…and then his second putt, Davis and Miss MacPherson watched as that player was held back from charging into the galley. Davis of course had no idea the disturbance was a planned bit of bedlam instigated by Lawton's own golfing partner, Loni D'Annelli. While Davis couldn't help but chuckle over the incident, he noticed the young lady next to him was not humored. In fact, she looked disgusted.

The two golfers were still seething when they arrived at the eighth tee box. Davis noticed the young woman's face suddenly go pale as she watched each member of that foursome. It was then that Davis thought he recognized one of the golfers from a picture in a recent *Minneapolis Star*. He recalled the man's name was Vincent Spagatini. He'd been charged in a Chicago murder case and was currently out on bail. The article mentioned that it hadn't been this gangster's first time with such a charge.

Davis figured being on parole for Spagatini was apparently as normal as some people attending church. He bit his lip and stayed quiet as he watched the hoodlum and his teammates cool down before addressing their difficult shots to the eighth green far down the hill.

The Spagatini foursome actually played some skillfully launched golf shots. Two of the four players made the green with lower trajectory shots hit below the wind with a long iron. The two guys who played a fairway wood hit their golf balls too high. The lake breeze took control of their shots and pushed their golf balls out into the woods forty yards from the green. There was determined silence as that foursome marched off the tee box. They looked like they wanted to kill someone.

When the D'Annelli team arrived at the 8th tee box, Lawton gave Davis the big eyed look as if saying, "Where have you been?" Davis rolled his own eyes in silent response. The two men stayed clear of each other, both thinking it was still safer not to be recognized as friends. Lindy MacPherson looked at one of them, then the other, wondering why they were being so coy. It wasn't the place to tell them she was onto their ruse, though she still had no idea what their purpose was in playing in this mob golf event.

It was then that Charlie Davis edged over to Lawton's caddy, John Bailey, and commented how important it was to keep shots below the treetops because of the strong wind off the lake. He said it loud enough for all the players to take note.

Bailey, not knowing Davis, turned and looked at him like he was nuts. Bailey couldn't care less if there was a raging blizzard; he was just enjoying the humor and the pleasant walk on the golf course. More importantly, though, Lawton heard the intended advice and promptly pulled out a long iron for the required shape to his upcoming shot.

As Davis moved back next to the female he felt all eyes on him from Lawton's teammates for sharing the helpful tip. At first he thought their stares were for his stylish shirt. It took him a couple seconds to realize their focus was on the eye-catching female standing next to him.

From her perspective, the only person Lindy MacPherson was focused on through her sunglasses was Jamie Lawton.

Later that Saturday afternoon, the noise and excitement from the golf event had finally calmed down. It was the end of the afternoon, a couple hours after Lawton's putt 'heard round the Lake' had slipped into the left side of the cup for the win on the last hole. Lawton and Davis no longer felt they had to pretend they didn't know one another. Lawton had made some big money on the golf course thanks to his two birdies on the last two holes. The $5000 entry fee never had to leave the confines of the money satchel under the driver's seat of Charlie Davis' roadster.

There was one additional person with Lawton and Davis as they sat on the patio waiting for some of the bets to be paid off. It was the attractive female with the sun dress, large hat, and sunglasses that Charlie had met…and finally, if hesitantly, had introduced to Lawton. He still couldn't place where he'd seen her before. As for Lawton, he couldn't take his eyes off her. He too felt he'd met her before.

As for that last putt for the margin of victory, Lawton had stroked the ball on #18 green never believing the ball would make it down the green's incline. But, the ball just kept rolling…and rolling. When it barely arrived at the cup…and just dropped in, an overwhelming cheer erupted from the gallery. Lawton was surprised by the reaction he got from the players as he entered the patio area. It was as if he'd proven himself to them…performing and winning under some obvious and ridiculous interruptions. Everyone on that patio began shaking his hand or patting him on the shoulder…that is, everyone except Vinnie Spagatini, Bert Bertinelli, and especially not Danny A'Motta.

Two guests who he'd never seen before placed a mug of beer in each of his sweaty palms. Lawton thanked them and found a place to sit ready to begin the collection of his winning bets.

It was a typical post-tournament aftermath on that patio. Lawton found himself actually enjoying the social gathering despite most of the group being a bunch of scoundrels and criminals. That afternoon he hadn't thought of them in that way. He found himself considering his competitors quite normal the way they complained about their bad luck, bragging about some of their good fortune, or describing a great shot during what had been a truly spirited contest. Lawton even found himself drawn to D'Annelli and his two other hoodlum teammates. Whether he would have felt warmly toward them if his team had finished second or third place was wasted thought.

Thanks to the last two holes, he won every individual bet... even against the players who were white hot playing on big Julie's team. He'd beaten big Julie by two holes and Tagliossa's three teammates by one hole thanks to the birdie on the last hole. That was $4000 of additional winnings to be collected from that team alone.

It was within five minutes after sitting down that Big Julie gruffly walked over, stopped and just stared at Lawton. It was as if he couldn't decide whether to strangle Lawton right then or later. Then he broke into the most respectful smile while laying out $4000 in cash in front of Lawton, Davis, and MacPherson. His voice sounded like he was gargling. He said, "A couple nice putts on the last two holes, Trick-shot. Nice playing." Then the furl returned to his forehead as he retorted, "Now keep your balls away from my wife!" As he returned to his table, his unique laugh sounded more like a wheezing horse after a mile run.

Lawton appreciated the man's play on words, and gave him a nod and a smile. Yet, he was pleasantly surprised for another reason. Big Julie had lost with class.

MacPherson didn't know how to take the 'balls' comment, but decided not to ask. Lawton looked at her and shut down any depraved thoughts by her or Davis. He leaned over to her patting her arm and whispered, "Give me credit for having more brains than what your active mind is thinking. I'll explain later."

As for Davis, he'd seen Lawton's golf ball lodged between the breasts of Tagliossa's wife knowing it would be a story for years and years. He had tipped his glass toward Big Julie as the grossly large man returned to his table. The comment had definitely not gotten by the chuckling Davis.

More golfers followed to gamely shake Lawton's hand and individually pay the money they owed him. Much to Lawton's surprise... as well as to Davis and MacPherson...there were no death threats while money was being paid.

The last three guys to approach him were the three fellows who bet him $500 a hole. Vinnie Spagatini lost three holes and owed Lawton $1500. Spagatini didn't have an inch of class as he simply dead-panned, "Don't spend it too quickly, hot shot. Consider it only a loan. I'll get you tomorrow." Lawton hoped that statement referred only to the upcoming Sunday golf match and not his life. That wager was particularly pleasing for Lawton to accept.

Bert Bertinelli followed with the $2000 he'd lost to Lawton...four holes at $500 a hole. He threw the money on the table and gave Lawton a stare that could have frozen the doors of hell. Lawton decided not to say anything to the gangster...thinking it might be the last words he'd ever speak.

The last guy, "Mr. Smiles" himself, Danny A'Motta had scored a 42 on the last nine holes and was understood to be looking for the greenskeeper to kill or maim. A'Motta sent a messenger over to Lawton with $2500 in cash covering the five holes he'd lost on those final nine holes. He had been convinced Lawton was the biggest choker to ever hold a golf club. His conviction turned out to be dead wrong.

Last but not least, a large envelope was brought out from the Lodge's vault. The vault contained 19 of 20 players' $5000 entry fees. Loni stood up and almost sheepishly said he had forgotten to pick up the entry fee from the 'Trick-shot' that morning. Everyone around the table got suddenly quiet. Good naturedly, Loni continued, "but I guess it doesn't matter now. We got first place."

He looked at Lawton and grinned, "Here "Kid", keep your $5000 in your pocket...and take $15,000 to stuff in that same pocket. Loni then handed $20,000 to Billie McCoy and another $20,000 to Whitey Malooley and kept the remaining $20,000 in the envelope for himself. The four men cherished that moment together knowing that they would never experience that feeling again with the man they only knew as 'Trick-shot'.

It had been a very profitable day on the links for D'Annelli as well. Counting side bets, the big $20,000 team prize, $22,000 he won from Lawton's blindfolded four-foot putt on the 8th green, plus his own side bets, Loni pulled in over $50,000. Not bad for a barrel-chested 'businessman' who smoked too many stogies.

That Saturday Lawton made a total of $19,000 in side bets along with the net of $15,000 from the team competition. The $5000 Davis had brought from his Alexandria home never had to see the light of day....nor did the $3.59 Lawton still had in his pants pocket. All in all, $34,000 was a reasonable day's bounty for a successful day on the links. Lawton had the satisfaction of skinning a bunch of crooks. Already he was thinking what causes he might contribute his winnings. He...and Charlie Davis...wanted none of that profit for themselves. They would keep referring to it as 'tainted' money until they were rid of it.

D'Annelli was still not done. He announced the next day's competition would commence with tee-off slated for 9:30. Lawton listened while looking around the patio. By the baleful looks from some of his competitors, he had the strong feeling Sunday would be anything but a cakewalk. D'Annelli would no longer be his partner since the event the next day would be ten 'two-man' teams competing against each other. The teams would be arranged based on how the players scored on Saturday. $20,000 per team would be the entry fee. With Lawton's winnings of $34,000, his portion of the entry fee...or $10,000...would be no problem. Still he gulped. $200,000 would be on the table on Sunday with the winning two-man team pocketing $100,000. Second and third place teams would get $60,000 and $40,000 respectively. The shear sound of that amount of money for one day of golf took the wind out of his lungs. Lawton also faced the reality that the team assignments would no doubt be rigged. He'd be paired with one of the worst golfers amongst the twenty players assuring himself of an even lesser chance of winning any bets. D'Annelli certainly owed more loyalty to his 'guests' than to someone who just 'happened' to show up to play golf that morning.

When D'Annelli finished his comments, he inched over towards Lawton and stated very seriously. "By the way, kid, the money we all won or lost today stays only within this group. I don't want the locals or even the spectators to hear the amounts of money we've been wagering. There could be a negative reaction amongst the townspeople. So, take your money, enjoy the fact that you won it, and keep the amount under your hat. Got that?"

Lawton nodded not having any problem complying with the demand. D'Annelli didn't want any pettiness or envy that might cause the authorities to be contacted. As for Lawton, he didn't want anyone to know he was even present at Chippewa Lodge that weekend.

As D'Annelli waltzed away, Lawton found himself looking at the skies and praying that rain might wash out the next day's play. One day of golf with these hoodlums was more than enough. He'd accomplished his aim of skinning them for a lot of money. Now he had to face his next quandary. How visible had he become? And, with his heroics that afternoon on the links, players and patrons alike might be more curious about his true identity. It was one thing to be deceptive about his background, but it could be especially prickly if they found out he was a Minneapolis attorney.

Davis looked at Lawton and grimaced, "That's more money than either of us have seen in one place." Then in a lower voice he added, "Too bad we're not going to see if for long."

Lawton nodded back and murmured, "A couple of charities are going to be very happy."

Then they snapped back into the present changing the subject remembering that Lindy was within ear shot. She pretended not to hear as she aimed a steely-eyed look at the abhorrent figure of Willie LaCurso across the patio. Yet, she had heard every aside whispered between the two men she only knew as Jamie and Charlie. It made her highly curious about their behavior. Here they were receiving individual winning bets and $15,000 poured onto the table and her two hosts seemed to care less.

She finally had to react. "Why are you guys so determined to rid yourselves of this money? My God, Jamie, you didn't steal the money. You won it fair and square."

Lawton and Davis didn't really respond as they looked at each other with a slight embarrassed grin.

Lawton tried to appease her. Looking nervously at Davis for support, he quipped, "Hey...this is supposedly a charity tournament. Of course we're obliged to give away a good portion of this money. I'm sure the other players are doing the same thing.

Up to that last statement, Davis was nodding his head. When Lawton said 'other players are doing the same thing', Davis stopped swallowing his drink in mid-stream and started choking.

That comment didn't resonate with MacPherson either. She knew giving away some of the money was the last thought on the minds of the 'other players'.

For the first time she truly gazed at the two men she'd been joking with and taking in the pleasure of their company since the middle of the afternoon. She had an admission she was being forced to make. Why was she even with them? She didn't consider them gangsters, but why would these two men be taking chances playing with such a corrupt and certainly dangerous group of conmen? They must have some idea of the types of characters involved in the tournament. It could only mean they had some other reason for being at Chippewa Lodge.

She suddenly felt naïve. It had been so long since she'd allowed herself to join in some fun. These two high-spirited guys had brought out that reaction in her. Now she'd reached the point where she wondered why she trusted them. They were obviously educated. They were witty and knew what was going on in the world. Just as important, they talked with general disdain at the people who surrounded them on that patio. Most of all, they made her laugh…at times, uncontrollably. She hadn't had such an unbridled good time since…before her fiancé was murdered.

But, she now had become discomfited. Had she misread them? Their names were 'Jamie' and 'Charlie'. That was all she knew. In fact, they were very careful not to include their last names whenever some drunken degenerate came around to introduce himself. People wanted to know the real name of the person everyone called 'trick-shot'. Invariably she'd noticed how both Jamie and Charlie ignored the question about their names…and then changed the subject. She even appreciated when forced to introduce her to someone, they'd both only give her first name as if to preserve her own privacy from the hoard of mobsters.

As the two men collected the winnings and began stuffing the money into the envelope supplied to them by D'Annelli, they were completely unaware of MacPherson's increasing unease. They continued to make uncomplimentary remarks about the players and socialites around them. Once Charlie leaned toward Jamie and whispered something about the soiled background of one of the crooks getting drunk at the next table. When they joked about 'taking care of some of these guys the next day', it didn't necessarily sound like they were talking about golf. It occurred to her for the first time that they might be at Chippewa Lodge for another reason. It made sense since they were being so careful not to let her completely into their closed little sphere.

She kept her focus on them and only smiled as Jamie was constantly interrupted by one drunk after another. As the inebriated man stumbled away, Jamie would look at Charlie and they both would roll their eyes in a way that showed extreme disrespect.

She couldn't see anything they had in common with the element present on that patio…other than golf. She became more and more convinced they had to be planning something. She could just feel it. And, nothing pointed to them being officers of law. If they were undercover, why was Jamie making himself so visible? Both men were too unstructured and spontaneous.

MacPherson tried not to believe what she was thinking, but too many things were supporting her bizarre notion. It could be serious… even to the point of carrying out a plan to eliminate one or more of the mobsters. As outlandish as it sounded, they could be part of a plot. Chippewa Lodge certainly was a perfect venue. It was a den of iniquity, but certainly a relaxed atmosphere. These gangsters used to looking over their shoulders with bodyguards protecting their other shoulder were not as attentive at this resort. This resort property on this particular weekend was a hit man's delight.

She'd been trained in various areas of criminal law...including traits attributed to unemotional and ruthless hit man. Besides disguising himself, a cold-hearted killer could play act and display whatever persona that might be effective in carrying out his deathly purpose.

She considered the joking but watchful man named Charlie. As humorous as he was, there was an observant and serious and even distraught side to this fellow. After she'd accepted Jamie's invitation to join them at the post-tournament party on the patio, Charlie had become more distant. His mind was elsewhere. His level of apprehension had greatly increased about the environment around the patio. His eyes were intense and his icy comments about the people around them showed an aloofness and frostiness toward the entire crowd. He was there only because his friend was there.

As for Jamie, where she'd had an interest in him as the day progressed, she now had to assess his behavior pattern. She'd been impressed the way he'd acquired an invitation into the charity golf tournament. While it appeared Adam Bailey had cleared the path, somehow Loni D'Annelli was willing to take a chance on someone he'd never met. Or, had those two men met before? Could D'Annelli and Lawton be conspiring against someone at the Lodge that weekend? It was conceivable. There were enough hoodlums in the vicinity for their to be targets and pursuers toward any number of these cons. Even his reactions toward all the players were remote...except to Loni D'Annelli.

They seemed to get along like old friends.

MacPherson's mind was running hot and confused. She didn't know what to believe. Somehow she had to collect herself. She knew her frustration about the next day was bothering her. It was up to her to call in the state troopers and the Bureau of Investigation. She just wanted more assurance who the real culprits were who were running the illegal gaming operation. It would certainly be a triumph if arrests were made on the various thugs hiding out at the Lodge whose names she'd documented. But, she wanted the leaders of this whole enterprise and the proof to make their arrests stick.

Now she was facing possible interference from the two men sitting at her own table. As gentlemanly and amusing as they were, these fellows she only knew as Jamie and Charlie might get in the way when she called in the raid. She could not let that happen.

MacPherson need to clear her head and decide what to do. Excusing herself for the ladies room, she was half-tempted just to leave the resort and let what would happen the next day happen. She just wanted to know if these two gentlemen were truly friend or foe.

—m—

When MacPherson left the table for the ladies room Davis and Lawton had no idea their attractive and fun-loving female friend was so upset. Lawton was about to offer to accompany her in order to stave off various male advances, but she seemed very capable of defending herself.

With her temporarily gone, Davis finally had the chance to update Lawton about the second conversation he'd had with the odd church deacon at the Presbyterian gambling booth ...the fellow named Henry Hanson. He claimed to have doubts about Hanson's guilt, that the man was caught in the crosshair between doing good for the town and trying to ignore the goings on at Chippewa Lodge.

Lawton cut him short. "Charlie, it's our professional duty to get the authorities involved. You and I both know there are enough criminals lolling around this resort to fill an average sized prison. If there's some illegal gambling going on, the law could pick up the local perpetrators on the same trip. I don't see the problem. Let's call in the state patrol. I frankly don't want to play the second day of this golf tournament with a bunch of hooligans."

Davis reacted quickly, "Jamie, there's more going on than you can imagine. I've found out things about this place that you'll not believe. First, you're right. This place is a haven for known and unknown criminals. But, this gambling activity is something much bigger than a game of chance at a church booth. There's a tent behind the church booth that could rival Atlantic City with all the black jack, craps, and roulette being played. I believe it's too easy to place the blame on some townsfolk. This thing is too professional to be managed by some local hacks. If the authorities came in right now, some relatively innocent local people could be caught and be falsely accused. This oddball, Hanson, I told you about over lunch, hinted that the true hucksters would escape unscathed if this operation was closed down. And, if the locals start talking, they could face reprisals from mob members. I have the strong feeling Hanson himself could be especially vulnerable to retribution. He was really sticking his neck out talking to me."

The two of them cut short their conversation as John Bailey slipped up to them. "Adam and I are getting out of here. It's not the kind of place for him...or me for that matter. You gents can stay the night at our place to save you having to look for a place to stay tonight and since you'll be right back here tomorrow morning."

Bailey then offered his services as a caddy for Lawton the next day. Lawton looked underwhelmed with that offer, but accepted Bailey's bigheartedness with the overnight invitation with a thankful nod. He realized John Bailey didn't have much to give, but what he had he was being most generous.

Bailey added, "Jamie, since I've got your golf clubs, I'll bring them out to the farm."

It struck both Davis and Lawton the stark contrast between the kindhearted Bailey and most everyone else on that patio.

Bailey then motioned for his son it was time to leave the party. The two of them retreated to the exit as the excited Adam was telling his father some of his earnings that day from D'Annelli. Davis and Lawton were also getting itchy to leave, but Lawton was still a popular figure amongst the party goers. Neither of them wanted any part of the continuing frolics on that patio, but their escape was going to be difficult.

More drinks continued to arrive at their table. Loni D'Annelli was smiling and waving at Lawton like they were old friends. The trouble was their acquaintance was ephemeral...and they both knew it. The next day they'd be opponents in more ways than one. Lawton had been a convenient gadfly who happened to be in the right place at the right time that morning. Lawton waved back at the big man wondering if D'Annelli had any idea how obvious it was D'Annelli would make 'Mr. Trick Shot' would lose big the next day. D'Annelli's loyalty was to his underworld friends.

Shortly after MacPherson returned to the table, Davis let her know they'd be leaving the party. Lawton knew it was best but seemed hesitant. He asked Lindy if she'd be returning to the resort the next day for the final round of the charity tournament.

Davis silently watched his friend's enthrallment. It was a disapproving look. Never had he seen Lawton so bedazzled by a female...and he didn't even know her last name.

Her response to him was friendly but non-committal. Davis noticed a slight change in her temperament since returning from the ladies room. She wasn't as jovial or responsive. Lawton was completely blind to her change in mood.

With no more delay, MacPherson got up abruptly from the table and said pleasantly, "Well, I've enjoyed the afternoon with you gents, but I've got a deadline on my article and tonight is a work night. I may see you out here tomorrow, but chances are it won't happen. I'm really behind on my piece of writing."

To Lawton and Davis, it seemed rather sudden that she appeared eager to vacate that patio...even negating Lawton's offer to escort her through the throngs of conmen. Shaking her head, she retorted stiffly, "Good luck tomorrow...whatever you hope to accomplish." And then she left without even shaking their hands.

Those words left both men looking at each other as she left the drunken patio party. Neither one spoke, but they both had the same questions. 'What did she mean by that remark...and who really was this lady? What had caused her behavior to be altered so abruptly?' She'd been having what they thought was a good time.

Her exit had been so quick and unexpected, Lawton had failed to ask her where she lived. He was noticeably disappointed with her sudden departure. It caused Davis to help his friend return to reality. "Jamie, for Christ's sake, anyone would have to think twice about a friendship with you considering the company you seem to keep. Hell, I've had my doubts about you all day."

Lawton laughed at Davis' remark, but still couldn't help thinking, 'Damn...another time, another place and I'd have better luck with that girl.'

Lindy's exodus was the impetus Davis and Lawton needed to contrive a way of making their own exit. Drinks were still being delivered to their table. It was an obvious attempt at getting Lawton wasted. The worse shape he left the party, it followed the worse his game would be the next day.

It was easier for Davis to leave. He leaned over and shouted above the noise, "Jamie, I'll have the roadster ready with engine running out in front of the Lodge. See you in five minutes."

Davis walked out of the party with little problem. For Lawton, just standing up caused more well-wishers and competitors to crowd around him. He'd been the most talked about player in the field. Everyone wanted a piece of him.

Moving toward the bar, two of Big Julie's teammates corralled him and talked about some bad luck on one of the holes they played. They gave the impression of no ill intent, yet they maneuvered him closer to the bar.

As they surrounded Lawton at the bar, two women came up and slipped a piece of paper into his hand. He didn't have to be that experienced to know he'd just been given their name and cabin number for later that evening. He nodded at the women and respectfully shoved the notes into his pants pocket not wanting to hurt their feelings.

Whichever golfer's girl friend they were, Lawton figured he'd be lucky to leave the Lodge alive if he made any attempt at dallying with either of these females.

Five minutes later he was still desperately trying to find a way to end the conversation with Big Julie's two teammates. He felt like Teddy Roosevelt at a Bullmoose convention. Everyone wanted to talk with him. The only difference was that 'T.R.' would have enjoyed every minute of his audience. In Lawton's case he was deploring every additional minute he had to associate with these reprobates.

Then the adulation...phony or legitimate...got worse. More drunken party-goers spilled drinks on him as they congratulated him on his play that day. Tess Tagliossa suddenly appeared in front of him giving him the eye.

Standing close by were Spagatini, Bertinelli, and Danny A'Motta staring at him with an eye of a different magnitude. Those three guys simply didn't like anything about him. The only things they had in common with Lawton were their interest in golf and their need for oxygen. It struck Lawton that they might want to erase that last commonality. He knew it was just a matter of time before one of them would corner him for the purpose of finding out more information about his background.

Another five minutes went by and Lawton was dumping drinks on the patio floor as fast as they were being placed in his hands. It was so crowded around that bar no one saw the way he was disposing of the liquor. The players interested in getting him drunk had to be thinking he had a hollowed out wooden leg the way he was supposedly finishing off those drinks.

Davis had now been waiting out in front of the Lodge in his A-68 St. Clair Roadster ready to roll for over fifteen minutes. Lawton was no closer to escaping the patio. Then the problem got even worse. Spagatini moved in next to Lawton with his dark evil eyes as black as his groomed hair. He gave the appearance of saving Lawton by faking friendliness and dragging him over to the table where A'Motta and Bertinelli were seated. The interrogation would certainly begin after another drink. Lawton felt like he was caught in a strong current and couldn't swim his way out.

And then something happened totally unexpected. Just as Spagatini began pushing some party-goers aside to open a way to his table, a vision of true loveliness suddenly stepped between Spagatini and Lawton as if placed there by a streak of lightning. Lindy MacPherson stood in front of Lawton, talking wildly, and hanging all over him.

Spagatini showed surprise and stepped back a few feet loving the way this striking female was throwing herself at Lawton.

To Lawton, he realized immediately she was there to save him. She was totally play-acting. He'd thought she'd left the party long before, but now she was back to rescue him from the pack of wolves. He couldn't imagine why she was making the effort, but he was relieved she was.

With her aggressive move, Spagatini had surrendered to the interruption. He winked at Lawton giving him space to operate with the willing female. It was a normal male reaction seeing another male appear to be getting lucky.

Then in front of all those gazing eyes, Lindy gave Lawton a big, flamboyant hug as she whispered rapidly into my ear. "Charlie told me you might need some help. Just go along with me. I'll get you out of here."

She'd caught Lawton by complete surprise. He hadn't expected to be so close to her so suddenly...and he liked it. Her smell was intoxicating.

He whispered back to her, "You lead...I'll follow!"

Her voice was now louder...and seductive. "O.K., big boy, so I lost the bet. When do I have to make payment?"

The guys within earshot, including Spagatini, got wide-eyed and winked at each other. Lawton was not completely dense. Seeing the door open for escape, he grabbed MacPherson around the waist and they headed for the patio exit. His thumb was in the air as they departed. Behind them, there were drink glasses held high in an uproarious toast to the trick-shot artist's final winning bet. Lawton only wished the inference of this 'non-cash' winning wager with this uniquely gifted and beautiful female was authentic.

They dashed off the patio through the Lodge foyer and out to Davis' waiting roadster. Davis stood there leaning against his roadster as if wondering what took her so long. He'd been the one to ask MacPherson for the assistance before she drove out of the resort. She was in and out of the party within five minutes with Lawton in hand. She grinned at both of them as if wondering why either was surprised at her quick success.

Then as quickly as Lawton was delivered, Davis showed no patience. He wanted to get away from the Lodge. Lawton was dragging...as if he wanted to say something else to MacPherson. While his eyes showed interest, he knew he shouldn't try to make a play for her at that place or time. He blinked...and just repeated his thanks to her. His final words expressed hope. "Maybe I'll see you tomorrow here at the Lodge."

She gave no response. The moment had come and passed. It could have been as simple as him inviting her out to dinner. After all, it was the final night of the festival. There was more fun to be had. But, Davis was begging for him to get in his roadster.

He gunned the engine saying, "Come on, Jamie. Let's get out to Bailey's house. It's time to get out of this place."

She stepped aside and Jamie jumped into the roadster. The sports car pulled away as he turned toward her giving a forlorn look as if he wished he wasn't saying farewell. A reluctant wave followed as Davis shifted gears and careened out the resort exit. She returned the wave in equal measure even though she had a strong feeling these two guys had their own agenda for the next day.

Once out onto the lakeside roadway, dust and gravel was spat out from the back tires. In seconds the two friends were zooming down the road along Lake Minnewaska towards Glenwood and onto the Bailey farm.

The shear relief of escaping the resort party and the group of hoodlums was exhilarating for both men. It was as if they had their lives back. None of the mobsters, including even Loni D'Annelli, had extracted Lawton's full name at the patio party. Of course, D'Annelli was busy enjoying his own elation over his win…and getting drunk. As the old saying goes, 'Every day won't be a circus', but that day there was a three-ring circus at Chippewa Lodge and Lawton felt like he'd been center ring. At the very least, D'Annelli had to be in the adjoining ring.

At their speed they made it into Glenwood as if they'd been flying. Approaching the edge of town by the lakeside beach, they observed huge crowds heading toward City Park. As they reduced their speed, Lawton and Davis saw first-hand the true success of this festival. Young folks were already packed around the gazebo area waiting for the band to begin swinging even though the dance wouldn't start of a couple hours. The more innocent game booths giving away worthless prizes for the winners were all active with trusting participants. The church booths full of food were raking in the money. It looked like a grand time. Davis pointed out the scoreboard near the other Presbyterian betting booth with that day's golf event results. He explained to Lawton the large tent behind the booth contained a casino type gambling house. The two of them were personally witnessing the benefits of the affiliation between the town of Glenwood and the hoard of questionable 'guests' at Chippewa Lodge. For Lawton, he was beginning to understand why Davis was so perplexed about calling in the state patrol or the Bureau of Investigation. Who was actually in charge? Who were the people who should be arrested?

Slowed by the throngs, they were delayed getting to the main intersection. As extraordinary as this example was of a dedicated group of citizens, steadfast town leaders, and underworld financial backing from Chippewa Lodge, they knew the bizarre association could fold up like a cheap watch. The mob group would have no loyalty. When they decided to leave the Lodge for any reason, the town would suffer the consequences immediately.

Rather soberly, Davis turned his St. Clair Roadster onto Hwy #28 and headed east out of town with directions from Lawton how to get to the Bailey farm. Their vehicle drove by the sparkling, renovated First Presbyterian Church. It was another example of Hanson's statement to Charlie about how the town was profiting from the mob-involved charity golf tournament.

The engine purred as they climbed the bluff providing a breathtaking sight of Lake Minnewaska. Less than a mile west on the very highway Lawton had landed only the night before, they turned onto the Bailey farm driveway. Out in the country the contrast from the noise and excitement at the resort and in town was incredible. The countryside was peaceful and still as death.

Davis broke the silence as they drove up the long, uneven driveway. "You know, Jamie, we have a duty to get law enforcement involved. However, we also have a few things to consider ourselves. We have to keep our names anonymous and certainly out of the press. Waiting a couple days until we're hardly a memory to the people we've met this weekend would probably be best. Then we could make a nameless call to the authorities and fill in what we witnessed at the resort. Lawton nodded showing general agreement. They still had to deal with the question whether to show up for the second day of the tournament or just be a no-show. Where they wouldn't have to deal with a second day of playing golf with a bunch of gangsters...and losing most of the money Lawton had just won...that action could raise eyebrows. They did not want to give any of these hoodlums any reason to pursue them.

Arriving at the farm, John's old truck was parked in front of the house. It fit well with the picture of the dilapidated and aged farmstead. As ramshackled as the outside of the house looked, Lawton and Bailey knew within that farm home had to be unadulterated joy after Adam's big pay day. In addition, Lawton knew the young man was undoubtedly holding his breath until he got his negotiated 10% fee he and Lawton had agreed upon. Lawton had considered that accord a wishful joke. Who could have guessed that Lawton could have pulled in anything near the $34,000 he'd won.

Before entering the house, Davis looked around the farm and commented sincerely, "Jamie, you know we talked about a worthy cause for the money you won. From what you've told me about John and Adam Bailey, we might consider them as our cause. You wouldn't have even played in this tournament without them. Besides, they seem like really good people who, as you said, had something very sad thing happen to them a few years back. I say if a small but deserved gift just happened to land in their laps, it would certainly give me...and likely you...a good feeling that the money would be put to good use. This kind of money could boost their fortunes and really change their lives. You said Adam was leaving the farm for college this fall; it might give John a chance to alter his life. Staying around this farm doesn't look too positive to me."

Lawton nodded. "It's a grand idea. But, knowing John Bailey and being around him for the last twenty-four hours, I doubt he'd keep the money for himself. He'd give it to other people he considered more in need. He's just that type of man.

Davis shrugged. "Well then, don't make the money a gift. We could buy this damned farm with the money we've got in our parcel. That would force him to take a new look at his future."

They headed for the farmhouse door silently with Lawton nodding his head in thought. "Charlie, so what would we do with this farm, let it rot?"

Neither one could take Davis' brainstorm further. It already looked in that condition. Then they stopped at the porch and relished the spectacular evening view of Lake Minnewaska below the bluff. The last glow of twilight left a deep hue to the lake's color.

Davis added, "It'd be worth the price just for the view."

Then over by the barn sat Lawton's beloved biplane still in as good as shape as when Lawton bought the air machine...which of course wasn't saying much.

Davis' face changed to disapproval. He shared no love for the old spy plane describing it often as a box with wings held together by tape with an engine he wouldn't put in a motor scooter. His standard line to friends was that he wouldn't fly in Lawton's plane unless he was sedated or he had a one-way ticket to heaven.

Davis crinkled his nose as he often did in the presence of the biplane. "Jamie, if you let that flying contraption sit there and decay for a few days, it'll probably just break up into pieces by Thursday. With luck you might make a little money selling some of the parts."

Lawton was used to the playful bantering. He badgered Davis back. "My friend, where is your zeal for adventure...your desire to be part of history. You're showing premature signs of aging. That's a damn shame for someone thirty-one years old."

Davis countered a bit wistfully, "Jamie, that old machine is likely going to make you history before your time."

The verbal sparring continued as they walked through the screen door of the Bailey home. Both men immediately were amused. Adam was counting the loot he'd pulled in that day and his much satisfied father was shaking his head in amazement as he smoked his pipe. Adam looked like Silas Marner counting his coins with John guarding the proceedings like a sentry at Ft. Knox. They were so involved, they were actually startled by Lawton's and Davis' entry. Bailey jumped up as if looking for a weapon with the arrival of their guests.

Davis quipped, "John, I'm glad you look first before you shoot!" Then seeing the startling amount of greenbacks on the table, he gagged, "Holy Christ....what kind of gold mine did you guys wind up with today?"

Indeed there was more money on that table than the two Baileys had ever dreamed of seeing much less having. John's tone became hushed almost in reverence as Adam continued to count. As for Adam, he didn't even greet Lawton and Davis. He just kept tallying.

John whispered, "We're still adding, but so far Adam's pulled in more today than what this farm is probably worth." He got 10% of what D'Annelli made today on the links!"

Suddenly Adam's voice pierced the air like a cannon ball streaking through the room. "By God...I believe I have somewhere close to $5000 lying on this table!" His eyes were as big as saucers.

Lawton looked at Davis and then strolled over to where Adam was sitting and pulled out a wad of bills. "Adam, you may as well add this to your total. Let's see, I made almost $35,000 out on that golf course today. It kind of looks like I owe you 10%. Here's another $3500." He threw a bunch of hundreds and twenties on the table that would more than support that amount.

Then Lawton added big-heartedly, "And might as well count out another $1500 for your father for his part in our little game. He deserves a percentage."

Bailey appeared to resist the money until he heard Lawton's determined tone. "John, that's the least I should give both of you. The plain fact is that I wouldn't have played in the tournament without the two of you. Consider it your part of the cut."

Bailey was utterly speechless seeing the additional money on the table. Both Lawton and Davis saw a tear well up in the eye of the father.

Adam counted the additional money Lawton had thrown on the table until he reached $5000 and then returned the extra...as if he'd handled that kind of currency every day. There was now a stack of

$10,000 in cash piled up in front of the two Baileys. John could have been blown off his chair with a minor sneeze. It was different for Adam. He was all business. The reactions of the father and son were priceless. Lawton and Davis were enjoying their first sense of satisfaction in giving away at least a part of the accumulated winnings.

It didn't take Charlie Davis long to feel at home with the two Baileys. He'd been in the house for only minutes when he yelled out, "God almighty, John, I'm parched. I hope you have some Canadian beer in your icebox." Davis had never been accused of shyness.

John was still staggered by the amount of cash on the table. He blankly pointed toward the kitchen. Davis grabbed two beers tossing one to Lawton. They then retreated back outside to the farmhouse porch leaving the father and son to discuss their new found wealth.

As they plopped down on a couple rockers with their feet on the railings, the two men began discussing whether they should show up at the next day's golf event or not. It was predictable they'd have to give back most if not all the money still in their satchel with the guarantee that Lawton's partner would be ordered to take a dive. The only way Lawton would make any money would be on individual bets.

They were just getting into their debate when their conversation was interrupted by a harsh noise coming from the roadway a quarter mile from the farmhouse. It was the sound of a fatigued car engine speeding along State Hwy. #28. The blare reverberated across the field. Then suddenly, there was a screeching of wheels as if the vehicle was turning onto the Bailey farm road. They stood up to watch a worn-out looking Model 'A' Ford bumping its way along the thin driveway kicking up gravel and dust. The two of them couldn't imagine what kind of emergency on such a calm, quiet Saturday evening could be so urgent. The vehicle then turned toward the house, the headlights momentarily blinding Lawton and Davis as it raced toward the front of the farmhouse.

Abruptly the car screeched to a halt not five yards from Davis' prize Wills St. Claire Roadster. Davis was about to shout something nasty at the driver when he stopped unexpectedly recognizing the person who jumped out of the clunky Ford. Immediately they both were relieved with the sight of the visitor. Marching toward them was none other than their new acquaintance...the female they only knew as 'Lindy'.

They both jumped forward to greet her as she tautly walked across the lawn before bounding the steps to the porch. Their open palms of greeting were left hanging as she breezed right by them and through the front screen door without so much as a knock or an invitation. Only her left arm was up with a finger indicating for Lawton and Davis to follow her.

The two of them looked at each other shrugging and wondering what they'd said or done wrong. Grabbing their half-empty beers, they followed her into the house.

John and Adam were still busily handling their take for the day. When MacPherson barreled through the front door, they were placing the last of the currency in their own leather satchel. Both Baileys exploded out of their respective chairs when the screen door slammed shut. Like Lawton and Davis, the father and son had no idea what was going on.

Paying no heed to greetings or the high finance activity in that house, she moved toward the fireplace in the living room with her back towards the four males. She stood there as if waiting for the right moment to turn around. She obviously was upset and had something very important on her mind.

When she finally turned, all four males observed a different look on the younger lady's face than the relaxed, smiling one they'd gotten to know. They all froze not having any idea the cause for her strange behavior. Her gaze on each of them was as if she was sizing them up for slaughter.

Then she spoke. Her tone was lower, very intense and measured. "Gentlemen, you may as well sit. I have a little story to tell all of you... and you're going to have to make some decisions after I'm done."

Lawton and Davis glanced apprehensively at one another. They sensed they were about to hear something they didn't want to hear. Nothing indicated what she was about to say was going to be either pleasant or appreciated. They nervously retreated to a chair and sofa respectively not taking their eyes off this now transformed female.

The two Baileys also were watching her carefully, but had a more immediate concern. They shoved the last few greenbacks into the burgeoning leather case where it was then lightly dropped onto the floor. Giving her only partial attention, Adam furtively kicked the satchel behind the sofa.

Then she started. Her voice quavered at the start and then grew stronger as she continued. "My name is Lindy MacPherson and I am not a free lance writer for a travel magazine. I work out of the U.S. Attorney's branch office in Minneapolis. I've been doing some undercover investigative work for the past couple weeks here in Glenwood regarding a rumored gambling operation. Well, I can tell you that in my findings, the rumor is true. I can also tell you that I've found more than illegal gambling. I have enough evidence to put a lot of people behind bars….unfortunately not just the bastards occupying the cabins out at Chippewa Lodge. There could be some local citizens who might be in serious trouble as well."

She paused. There was a collective sigh among all four males as if their respective cars had been repossessed. Lindy MacPherson's eyes were intense, her face stressed, and her voice strained. She had come to the Bailey house for a reason and it was quite apparent not a social call. As the four males sat silently, there were only the sounds of crickets chirping, frogs croaking, the omnipresent flies and beetles bouncing against the screen door and the swish of trees in the night breeze. Each one's mind was racing trying to calculate the impact of what she was about to say next.

CHAPTER

17

For Lindy MacPherson watching that roadster peel away from the Lodge spoke volumes. Only minutes before she'd helped the man she knew as 'Jamie' escape a hoard of gangsters at the post-tournament party on the Lodge back patio. Now she was standing in that Lodge parking lot alone. Given the time the three of them had enjoyed in the last few hours, she had expected the evening might continue over dinner or at least a walk through the festival in town. She could have gotten more of a feel for why these two mystery men were at Chippewa Lodge. Nothing made sense why Jamie had played in the charity event. What were their motives? They weren't truly part of this group of mobsters. She'd felt a spark between Jamie and herself, but his friend, Charlie, only had his focus on leaving the Lodge property. She couldn't disagree with the urgency, but he seemed particularly edgy.

Their exit had been disappointing, but it was also odd how they were in such a hurry to head out to John Bailey's farm. If there were two other males in Glenwood she felt safer with than John and Adam, she couldn't name them. Were they now involved in whatever agenda of the two men speeding away.

With her mind a million miles away in furious thought, she roamed back to where her Model 'A' Ford was parked. Her feet were shuffling and her ears not attuned to the sounds of footsteps on broken twigs following her. However, one too many twigs snapped and in seconds her female instincts returned. She stopped and the noise stopped. She took a few steps and the footsteps could be heard. For a single female, Chippewa Lodge was a dangerous place. It was her own fault. She'd not been paying attention and now she was vulnerable.

Increasing her pace across the parking area, the footsteps among the many parked cards kept pace. While there was still some light left in the evening, the overhanging tree branches made the atmosphere darker. Her heart began to race.

Without seeing anyone, she reached in her purse feeling for her revolver as she arrived at her car. Struggling with her keys, a hand suddenly grabbed her arm. The jolt caused her to lose both her purse and her grip on her weapon. The handbag fell to the ground. She looked at her attacker and got a cold reaction. There were two men, not one. Both inebriated, the one assailant holding her arm flashed a wicked grin at his companion sitting on the side board of a car parked next to hers. He was finishing off a flask. It appeared obvious she'd been stalked since leaving the party. There had been an interruption when Charlie saw her still in the parking lot and yelled over to her to please help retrieve Jamie. When that little episode ended and Charlie and Jamie left her, the goons had their wishes answered when she was alone once again.

The situation got nasty very quickly as one of the men slurred, "Hey beautiful, you wanna drink? Our cabin is real close. We could make your evening extra special."

Livid that she'd been caught off-guard, she tried to recover giving a token response. "No....that's O.K. I've got a date with my boyfriend. I've got to go."

That statement had no effect as the two drunks only snickered. She tried to open the driver's side door but the man with the flask stood up leaning his body against the car door. She was now sandwiched between the two aggressors. All she could smell was booze. The sight of their lustful determined eyes made her stomach turn.

MacPherson had to think faster than her assailants. Spying her purse containing the revolver lying on the ground, she gauged whether she could dive for the purse while simultaneously grabbing the gun and firing it at one of them before they attacked her. That idea was far-fetched.

Her choices slimmed down to basic survival; she changed her tact. Instead she gave them a suggestive smile. She used D'Annelli's name. "You boys better be careful. If I had a drink in your cabin and word got out to Loni, all three of us would be in trouble."

The two attackers momentarily looked at each other...and then discarded her words. She sounded willing. Besides, they were too far gone to care. That ploy was not going to work.

One of them slurred, "We won't tell if you don't tell, baby". With this act her only chance, she continued coquettishly. "O.K., boys, let's have some fun. Where's your cabin?"

The two men sneered at each other realizing they'd found the right female. Both men loosened their grip only slightly. Showing no sign of trying to escape, she grabbed their arms as if seeking an escort to their cabin. The inebriated radiance of their lust drooled from the sides of their mouths.

MacPherson then took her advantage. She stopped abruptly and looked apologetically at them. "Boys, I've got to get my purse. It's over there on the ground. Let me get it. I'll need to powder my nose."

They shrugged as she dropped her hands from their arms. Swaying unevenly they waited for her realizing they might need support to find their cabin.

In seconds the entire situation changed. She was no longer the party girl she'd just faked. As she picked up her purse, her face showed scorn and ferocity the likes of which made their eyes bug out. The first blast from the gun traveled between one of the drunk's legs. The next one whizzed by the other man's ear. Stumbling away from her, they repeatedly fell to the ground as she moved towards them. They were sobering up fast as they crawled toward the first cabin in sight.

Regaining their feet, the two men scrambled into the cabin not bothering with the door knob. Lying on the floor, four more rounds were rattled off directly into that cabin. The aim was high. Lucky for them her intention was not to kill, only to make them wish they'd never met her. If one of the rounds had hit one of them, she knew she'd lose little sleep.

If the situation hadn't been so serious, she might have laughed. Approaching the cabin while re-loading her revolver, she finally got control of her emotions and stopped shooting. She thought of her father and Ernest Lundquist. Those two protectors both lived with the desire to shelter her from unpleasant ordeals like this one. This would be one incident they'd never know.

Moving back toward her vehicle, some 'guests' and staff came running out of the Lodge after hearing the gun shots. One gruff looking man with cigar hanging from his lips shouted at her, "Hey Sweetheart, did you see anything?"

She bristled at the condescending 'sweetheart' comment and shot back, "Yes, I believe two of your high quality friends are trying to kill each other in that first cabin on the left. I believe they were arguing over which one of them was going to be first."

The crusty lout glanced at her not following her meaning. "First for what?" he asked.

Her face was red with fury. "...the first to die if they had spent one more second in my presence."

Bitter words coming from such a nice looking young lady made the sloppy oaf do a double-take. He was not one who normally got intimidated by any female, but the cold tone in this one's voice made him think twice about any further talk. He moved away from her toward the cabin correctly sensing he'd be better off concentrating on ending the supposed altercation between his two cohorts.

She turned quickly away from the man realizing smoke was coming from the spent revolver now back in her purse. The redolence of perfume and lipstick had been completely taken over by the odor of a warm Magnum. Enjoying the chaos she'd created, she started up her vehicle and drove slowly toward the Lodge exit. Ten men were hiding behind trees yelling for their buddies to come out of the cabin. She smiled guessing how her two attackers were likely cowering under the bed or behind a chest of drawers to escape the crazy female firing wild shots at them.

While the melee continued, she calmly drove her Model 'A' Ford away from what had become a very comical scene. Eventually the two attackers would exit the cabin claiming they were just trying to help some young girl with car problems. Then she'd started shooting at them. The tale didn't have to make sense. It only had to be sound valid enough to protect their male egos.

MacPherson exited the Lodge property not even shaking given what could have happened. Her heart beat had been rapid but her respiration remained normal. She was a good shot and every round fired into that cabin went where she'd intended. She was glad she hadn't made a body shot; that likely would have caused an uproar. The police would not have been called necessarily, but the group of gangsters would have been on edge making the next day's raid more precarious.

As she continued driving along the east shoreline she watched the last of the sunlight in the evening sky. The smell of the lake and the refreshing breeze relaxed her mind from the ordeal she'd just handled. Now the last thing she wanted to do was sit quietly on her cabin porch or parade around City Park alone occasionally waving 'hi' to the locals she'd come to know. It would be less than twenty-four hours and they wouldn't want a thing to do with her. It was especially revolting that the feeling would be the same when the two Baileys learned she'd been working under cover.

That thought got her even more depressed. Her mind kept thinking back to Jamie and Charlie as well as the smiling faces of the Baileys earlier that afternoon. How had the four of them gotten so close, especially when Jamie had only landed by accident the previous night near the Bailey farm? She thought ruefully, 'If friendship came that easy, Jamie should be running for public office.'

Now even more didn't make sense. Who really was John Bailey, the man she'd repeatedly met for breakfast at the café since the first week she was in the town. Why had the older Bailey suddenly showed up as Jamie's caddy? He knew as much about caddying as she did about farming.

And Adam...he gave the appearance of innocence and not being very observant. She recalled how that very morning the young man had tried to suppress his happiness with his little fist pump when Jamie had gained the invitation from D'Annelli to play in the golf event. Then on the golf course, the young man showed grit as he counseled both D'Annelli and Jamie on their upcoming shots.

MacPherson went back and forth in her mind. How might John and Adam Bailey be involved in this whole matter?

Her mind was getting so twisted she had difficulty focusing on the road. How could the Baileys be involved with the two outsiders? They were too inexperienced...too decent...too comfortable in their skin to get involved in whatever Jamie and Charlie were secretly planning. 'Then again,' she thought, 'maybe they had been swayed by the charm of the two out-of-towners? Or, maybe somehow they could have been coerced?' It was not very likely as she pictured the relaxed interaction when she saw these males together, they all seemed to legitimately like each other.

MacPherson was so certain something was going on. She knew she'd be sorry if she didn't try to uncover their plans. Her problem was time. Her last night in Glenwood could not be sitting on her rocker on the cabin porch. One thing for certain, though, she had to now bring her boss closer to the entire matter. On Sunday she wanted to have the last chance to possibly discover who were the key people behind the gambling operation before any raid ensued.

While she was going to delay until Sunday morning to call Ernest Lundquist who would immediately send out various levels of law enforcement, she wanted to make the call to him promptly. She aimed her vehicle in the direction of the County Sheriff's office to use Petracek's private line to telephone her boss. She had to solicit more help and discuss the timing for the raid at Chippewa Lodge if it was to succeed.

Arriving at the county courthouse only one deputy was there... the others were obviously out keeping order during the festival. She was shocked to hear the Sheriff and Police Chief Brey had taken the day off to fish. It was hard to believe the patrol of the festival was completely left to their deputies. Then she recalled the two long-coated gentlemen the previous night breaking up a potential alley fight outside Big Bud's speak easy. The deputies were getting help from a few plain-coats whether they knew of the support or not. MacPherson sensed the additional enforcement was being done by a mob security group assigned by someone out at Chippewa Lodge. It was in the best interest of the group of gangsters at the Lodge to make certain nothing untoward happened at the resort or in town that could bring negative visibility to festival week. The additional private force had done their job; she was aware of no reported serious offenses during the entire week of the town celebration, not counting public drunkenness.

She asked to use the telephone saying that the Sheriff had been very accommodating given her deadlines with her publisher. The deputy nodded and MacPherson entered the Petracek's office and closed the door.

Knowing at that hour she could catch Lundquist at home before he went to the Minneapolis Club, she expected Lundquist to be unreasonable, incorrigible, and to order her back to the Twin Cities. When she finally got through to Lundquist's residence, she determined she could not allow him to interrupt her with his normal comedic and sarcastic banter.

Answering the phone she found him unexpectedly quiet. She brought him up to date quickly about her uncovering a large gambling operation camouflaged by a well attended ten-day town festival. She added that the gambling operation was likely a year round business. Her voice remained steady as she offered proof that a safe house was being run out at an isolated resort near Glenwood as well. She also related that a sizable booze running operation was located at the isolated resort.

Lundquist maintained his silence as she then named twelve wanted criminals who were long-term 'guests' at this place called Chippewa Lodge. She added that because of a spurious charity golf event going on that weekend at that same resort's golf course, there were likely other wanted gangsters beyond the list she'd already compiled.

Amazingly, Lundquist never interrupted her through her entire discourse. He had not reacted when she expressed her extreme disappointment in not yet having found the unfailing evidence as to who were the ringleaders of this entire operation. When she outlined her suggestion for a law enforcement raid on the Lodge property sometime the next day, she expected his opposition. His only response was "I understand."

When she mentioned her idea that the timing of the raid should be at the end of the afternoon to let the spectators leave the resort property, she heard a slight clearing of throat.

That's when he calmly said, "Lindy...did I hear you say the afternoon?"

Her response had been an assured 'yes'...even though she didn't feel that confident.

There was a pause. He was obviously writing down everything she was saying. At no time had she felt the sting of his anger, the disagreement in her plan, or insistence that she leave Glenwood and let the Bureau of Investigation and the state patrol take over the case.

When she had completed her report, his reply had been steady and respectful. "Good job, Lindy. I might suggest the raid would be better timed for the morning for the very same reasons you just gave. In the afternoon, we might miss the arrests of some of the criminals on your list. They may be in a hurry to check out and leave for their own reasons."

He'd paused again. "But, it's your case, Lindy. We'll follow your lead."

She had been elated over his response. For the first time she sensed she could be upfront and honest with the man since joining the office. Of course, she'd never been on as important of a case.

Her voice had become more self-assured. "Mr. Lundquist, I want as much time as I can feasibly have to locate any further possible evidence that could convict the leader of this whole scheme. I have a feeling his name is Loni D'Annelli, but I have to have better proof. If I can prove his guilt, I can spare a lot of locals from being arraigned...and most importantly, really cause a stir in the underworld. That's why I chose Sunday afternoon. I need the time. In particular what I'm looking for is the cash reserve for the gambling house I believe he operates. I have to be honest. I'm having no luck as this guy is slick. I plan to follow him tomorrow. With the end of this charity golf tournament that he runs, he may have to venture out to where his operating capital is located. It's a weak idea, but I don't want to give up until the last possible moment."

Lundquist's voice soothed her. "Lindy, if you think you can pin some more charges on him...then we should delay the raid until you give the word. However, my advice is to not wait too long. In the meantime I'll contact Jack Murphy over at the Bureau of Investigation office and inform him to have his guys ready outside Glenwood tomorrow and that you'll make the call as to the timing of the raid. And, by God, I'll tell him if he jumps the gun and doesn't follow your instructions, I'll make certain it'll be the last raid he'll ever lead. As for the state patrol, let's contact your uncle up in Bemidji. As Beltrami County Sheriff, he could be a big help. He'd want to be there anyway just to ensure your safety during the melee. I'll ask him to work with the state patrol and insist on holding their action in check until you give the signal to proceed. For now, just concentrate on that final bit of evidence. You've maintained your cover...how I can't imagine. But, if you have a chance to gain an iron clad case against this fellow D'Annelli, then we've got to give you the time. I'll take the responsibility of organizing the raid; you just continue your undercover work. Keep in touch and work through me. I'll stay by my home phone. Good luck."

With that final word he'd hung up as if not wanting to waste any more of her time. She had been bowled over by Lundquist's unquestioned support...as if she'd just graduated to a new level of competency. He'd held her back for so long not allowing her to take risks. Now proof of her capabilities had happened on what he had originally thought would be a rudimentary investigation.

As she'd left Sheriff Petracek's office, she'd felt buoyed...her energy revitalized. Loni D'Annelli and his cash reserves had to be her last priority before the raid. As for the four men out at John Bailey's farm, that mystery had to end. They were not going to interrupt or foul up the next day's raid. She was going to travel out to the farm and threaten holy hell if any of the four of them had any plans of their own regarding the second and last day of the golf tournament.

As she wormed her Model 'A' Ford through the throngs of people at the festival as she headed out to the farm east of town, she kept ruminating how this strange day had developed. She couldn't help but smile...at times even laugh.

Earlier that afternoon as she made her way out onto the golf course she'd noticed the large, comical fellow in the chartreuse shirt marching in the same direction. After having watched his antics that morning with his friend, she at first sensed both of them were naïve in this world of conmen at the resort. Watching this large fellow, she had begun to have second thoughts as she observed his behavior. He seemed quite serious and even perplexed.

Since the big, loud-shirted guy was headed on a similar path out onto the links, she thought it best she get closer to see what he and his friend were up to. Maybe she could warn them at some point how they were in the middle of an oven. She had figured once she forewarned them, they'd be looking for the resort exit as soon as possible.

It turned out to have been very easy to meet the man in the horrible looking shirt. He'd melted in her presence like a high school kid in the throws of puberty."

While he had warmed to her immediately and had her laughing within seconds, she noted upon introduction, he'd only offered his first name. Though joking with her, she could tell his mind was deeply involved in some other thought. As they'd walked, she also had realized the man named 'Charlie' had no recognizance of having seen her as a waitress earlier that morning. In fact, he'd seemed so preoccupied she'd wondered if he could even recall her name she'd given him less than a minute before.

When the two of them had finally spotted the D'Annelli foursome on Hole #7, they continued to higher ground through the woods to the 8th tee box. Charlie was winded when he'd reached the top and looked down at his friend about to hit his second shot onto the #7 green. Catching his breath might have caused him a moment of carelessness as he commented, "Damn, I hope 'Jamie' has been able to put up with all the hijinks. If he doesn't lose his concentration, he could run circles around these players."

For her that accidental meeting of the man named Charlie had been the start of an afternoon she couldn't have thought up. He'd turned out to be completely casual with a penchant for saying too much...as in mentioning the first name of his friend. Still, the guy was irreverent and funny. He'd made a comment about some of the golfers needed to take up a new sport. His evaluation of some of the unique golf swings had her choking with laughter.

Later when finally introduced to Jamie, she'd found the same kind of witty male, but more reserved. The kidding between the two of them was relentless, especially when Charlie voiced his disapproval of what he called 'Jamie's new friends'. Lawton didn't take offense. He'd found the kidding amusing. She'd found herself strangely attracted to this golfer the more she was with him that afternoon.

With Jamie and Charlie having to attend the mob party on the restaurant patio to collect the winning bets, she'd been invited to be with them. Through all the wisecracks and general laughter on that patio surrounded by mostly reprobates, she'd found herself having fun as long as she stuck close to her two new acquaintances.

It had not been until later in the patio party she'd begun having her doubts. Why were they there? What were there intentions? They were completely different from the other players in the tournament. They seemed neither daunted by the group nor interested in getting to know any of them.

Now she was about to find out.

Lindy MacPherson felt an urgency to get past the crowd once she left the County Sheriff's office. Honking the horn a few people moved aside, but there was no way of forcing her way through the swarm of people. It was then one of the dependable city police deputies came to her rescue. He recognized her plight and began blowing his whistle.

While clearing the way, the Deputy yelled over to her, "Hey, Miss MacPherson, how you doing tonight? You gonna finish that article before the festival ends?"

She'd heard that comment once too often. That cursed article seemed to represent everything good about the town. How disappointed the townsfolk were going to be when they'd learn the article was a hoax.

Through clenched teeth she waved her appreciation to the cop. Once again she thought about how accommodating the local county and city law officers had been to her since the very first day she'd ridden into town. It made her wonder what County Sheriff Petracek and Police Chief Brey really knew about her. And here she was, probably causing the end to their jobs and possible jail confinement. For the first time she doubted if she was really cut out for the type of work she had chosen for a career.

As MacPherson left the busy streets of Glenwood behind, she was momentarily mesmerized by the beauty of Lake Minnewaska as her Model 'A' Ford labored up the bluff toward the Bailey farm. She wasn't certain how she was going to approach the four men, especially with her growing negative assumptions about Jamie and Charlie. She suspected she'd probably have to lay her cards on the table and admit to her real assignment. She didn't expect any problems from the Baileys, just disappointment. As for Jamie and Charlie whether they were willing to talk with her or not, once they heard about the planned raid and the overflow of law officers spreading through the resort and the town the next day, she expected their purposes would be put on hold. MacPherson smiled for a moment realizing she had the upper hand. Then she frowned. Or did she?

As sick as MacPherson felt about the probable outcome of the raid on Chippewa Lodge and the town, she was personally perplexed about her own reputation in Glenwood. She knew it was a selfish thought, but she'd never gained so many friendships in such a short period of time. She'd get plenty of credit by her department; certainly the newspaper reports would be generous. But, those accolades would mean little. She was just doing her job. To her, she would really miss those welcoming greetings when she walked through town. The trust she'd built claiming to write some positive articles would end abruptly.

She just wanted to leave the beautiful little town and remember it for the pleasures she'd experienced. She doubted she'd ever be in a place like it again.

Making it to the top of the bluff overlooking the town and the lake, she realized she didn't exactly know the location of John Bailey's farmhouse. Everyone talked as if the Bailey farm was right at the top of the hill. She wasn't thinking straight. What did she expect, a billboard with a shiny light pointing to her destination. She stayed on State Hwy. #28 as it turned east towards the rolling countryside. She imagined a certain pilot the previous night landing his aircraft on the slender highway moments before a killer storm obliterated both the biplane and the pilot. How her life would have been different if that had been the result. She hated herself for thinking that way. She also thought about the laughs she would have missed.

Less than a mile after reaching the top of the hill, she noticed Charlie's roadster parked at the side of a poorly conditioned Minnesota farmhouse. The house looked so lonely...so non-descript...so empty. She couldn't imagine the two Baileys living there...and maintaining such a generous spirit and pleasant disposition. It was a statement, if nothing else, that it was how one lived his life, not where it was lived.

Almost missing the entry to the farm, she screeched her tires onto the long gravel driveway. She felt herself mellow recalling the bits and pieces she'd heard about a family tragedy that had been forced on John and Adam Bailey. She had consciously steered clear of the subject with John during any of their breakfast conversations. However, now seeing the lonesome house, a sense of sadness hit her like a cold breeze. She'd had some grief of her own. It was pointless to compare stories of misery. Nonetheless, she had a feeling she was driving into a headlong wind of sorrow.

Gunning the engine and spitting up gravel, MacPherson accelerated toward the parking area in front of the farmhouse. Out of the corner of her eye she had seen the weird spectacle of a biplane parked by side of the barn, thereby authenticating the story of the forced landing during the Friday evening storm. It only added to the puzzle and her distrust of Jamie and Charlie. Why would he have chosen such a dangerous and unorthodox method of travel that particular stormy evening, especially if he was part of a scheme directed against some gangsters that weekend at Chippewa Lodge?

She felt her head throb again. Nothing made sense to her about the two men she'd met that afternoon.

It was then she saw those same two men standing on the porch trying to figure out who was speeding up the Bailey driveway. Their calm silhouettes against the barely lit sky now made them seem much less provoking than two characters planning something ominous at Chippewa Lodge.

Arriving at the house she slammed on the creaking brakes and kicked up enough dust to cover Charlie's sports roadster parked next to her. She sat there for a moment in the darkness of her vehicle as the two men descended from the porch with worried looks. She suddenly didn't know whether to be angry or relieved that she was back in their midst. Somehow being with Jamie and Charlie quieted her nerves. She felt safer.

Still, something wasn't right. She couldn't be sway with their frivolous humor and carefree nature. This wasn't the time to back off. She had to find out their motives. It was critical she remained as furious as she'd been at times that evening.

Pushing open the driver's door, she marched purposefully toward them ignoring their look of astonishment. Their faces relaxed as they recognized her, but immediately changed to concern as she sped by them with only her finger motioning them to follow her into the house. She had reconciled that whatever friendship she'd had with them or the two Baileys up to that moment would likely end in the next few minutes. But, she had a job to do.

Entering the house she had glanced at the odd sight of John puffing on his pipe as Adam was pushing a large amount of cash into a worn leather case. No doubt it was Adam's payment from Loni D'Annelli. She expected the gangster would be very generous with the young man.

A second later her focus was back on her purpose. She could care less about the money on the Bailey table.

John had gotten up quickly and made two steps towards her in greeting until he saw Charlie and Jamie walk in behind her with eyes widened and hands out in front of them indicating her entrance and behavior was a puzzle to them.

John stopped in his tracks and retreated back to his chair. She'd no longer carried the friendly manner of an outgoing magazine writer. He'd not seen her look anything like she presently looked in the ten days he'd gotten to know her.

As for Adam, he'd immediately read the situation as more hazardous. By the time she'd turned to face the four men in the living room, there was no more money on the table. With the sleight of hand of a magician, he'd dropped the leather satchel on the floor ...his foot nudging it under the sofa.

There was an uncomfortable silence all around the room as she stared at the four of them. Even the crickets and toads seemed subdued in respect for the moment as well.

CHAPTER

18

Lindy MacPherson's entrance to the Bailey farmhouse that Saturday evening had been like an unexpected tidal wave. When she'd suddenly announced her true identity and that she'd been conducting an undercover investigation for the previous two weeks, the four males in that living room had reacted as if the black plague had accompanied her into that house. Their shoulders hunched as she'd explained how a mysterious private communication received at her boss' desk related a concern about a possible illegal gambling ring operating in the local area. That anonymous letter had instigated her being assigned to the Lake Minnewaska area to check out the depth of the accusation.

With that brief introduction, her mood was serious and agitated when she focused in the direction of Lawton and Davis. It was quite the opposite when she turned to the two Baileys. Feeling guilty for having pulled the wool over their eyes for so long, she lamented, "John and Adam, you've gotten to know me like everyone else in town as a journalist for a travel magazine. I only chose that occupation as my cover. The aim was to make people comfortable with me in town and therefore more willing to converse. I hope you'll forgive my deceitfulness, but it was part of the job. You understand if I would have identified myself as an investigator from the U.S. Attorney's office, I would have discovered nothing."

The older Bailey's nod reflected how logical her statement was. His son seemed oblivious to her clarifications. He was more concerned with the cash filled leather bag down by his foot. As she spoke he just kept nudging the satchel further under the couch while maintaining eye contact with her.

MacPherson looked back at Lawton and Davis again exhibiting no trust or warmth. Her tone was sharp. "Let there be no doubt, gentlemen, if I had found this gambling complaint to be connected to the insignificant booth games of chance typical at any small town event, I would have left town that very day. But, from the first day I drove into Glenwood, I observed more than a few odd things, both in town and at Chippewa Lodge, and even in the behavior of the townspeople. They were consistently very tight-lipped about the uniqueness of their town and especially about the unruly group of guests I discovered staying out at that resort. When I visited the Lodge, it didn't take much observation to realize the place reeked of unlawful hanky panky. I could see immediately the resort was operating as kind of safe house for a bunch of surly looking gangsters and actual wanted criminals. Beyond harboring a large number of hoodlums, it was a center for booze buying and distribution. With these details I would have been shirking by responsibilities if I didn't extend my investigation and my time in Glenwood.

What was really strange, though, was that I really didn't detect anything remotely to illegal gambling until days later when the ten-day town festival opened last weekend. Suddenly two very well managed gambling booths rose within the confines of other church and civic organizational booths. These two booths were handled by the First Presbyterian Church Men's Club...one in City Park and the other outside the gates of Chippewa Lodge. Their purpose was to take bets for the upcoming charity golf tournament. That simple aim was non-threatening and certainly gave the wagering booths an image of innocence and credibility. Almost immediately I witnessed wagers at both booths...and on many other competitions than just the golf tournament. Bets were being accepted on various national sporting events... like horse races, baseball games, boxing matches, and even some auto races. That type of extra gambling activity, gentlemen, is illegal.

While all this betting was going on, what really astounded me was how all these activities were going on right under the noses of the people in Glenwood. They seemed not to be aware or even to care. To be fair, it has no doubt been easy not to notice anything improper since not many locals go out to the Lodge. Only the beginning of festival week caused the locals to be anywhere near the resort with some temporary food and game booths along with the First Presbyterian betting booth to be set up by the lake near the resort. The rest of the year there is just no reason for the locals to travel out that way.

Regarding these betting booths, I know the townspeople believe the temporary Presbyterian gambling booths simply close at the end of the festival. Well, I'm here to tell you that in no way does either booth seem like a temporary church betting booth. The wagering that goes on is just too professionally run to stop after just ten days. And, what a great way to thwart rumors about illegal gambling at the Lodge... just make it look like it's a temporary church money raiser. My guess is that the main gambling house at the Lodge simply folds the booth activity back into the confines of the resort. I would expect a raid at the property will uncover the proof of my suspicion. While I've been trying to discover who at the resort might be in charge of the racket, I just haven't been free to move around out there. I take my life in my hands every time I enter the gates of that place. As a result, I'm concerned too many local people...good people...with take the blame when this whole affair inevitably comes to an end. No doubt the culprits planned it that way. All in all, it's an unbelievably well run operation."

MacPherson slowed hoping her comments might stir some remarks by the two Baileys. Seeing the glum looks of Davis and Lawton, she expected nothing of help from them. But, the silence was disappointing. Her eyes only met returned stares as if they were evaluating his own circumstances.

MacPherson was not ready to give up. Her pace to her allegations increased as if telling them all she knew would somehow make at least the two Baileys come out from the shadow of fear that surrounded so many other citizens in Glenwood.

She continued, "As for harboring convicts and wanted gangsters, I was dumbfounded. From mug shots and 'most wanted' lists I've seen at my office, I recognized too many of these sleazeballs. If there were only a few of them at the resort, that would have been bad enough. However, with the festival underway there are more of these shady characters passing through town and ending up at Chippewa Lodge each day...all having come to prepare for the big charity tournament. Still, there are so many more of these gangsters who've already been living at the Lodge for a long time. Again, providing a safe haven for so many of these underworld figures on a full time basis is illegal. It'll be the owner of the resort who will be charged with harboring wanted criminals."

She paused again. Her frustration in not getting any response from the four males was becoming tiring. She tried to sustain her wrath, but was running out of energy. Disillusioned, she lamented, "I find it amazing the length of time this unbelievable venture had been in operation. The shear determination by the townsfolk to remain ignorant about what's going on out at the Lodge has been nothing short of remarkable. Locals seem not to care who the 'guests' are at the Lodge as long as local businesses stay solvent supporting them. I can understand these feelings even though I can't support them. With the struggles caused by current economic hardships, no townsperson wants this advantage to disappear. Moreover, I can also appreciate how this unique relationship can be rationalized. If the safe house and the gambling house weren't at Chippewa Lodge, then they would be someplace else...and some other community would reap the benefits."

Getting nothing from the Baileys, MacPherson then turned toward Charlie and Jamie and glared at them. They were still ensconced in their own problems. They no longer had a look of cockiness they'd had earlier in the day. Whatever casual, even careless, attitude they'd had with MacPherson at the golf course...it was gone. Truly, both men looked like they'd just swallowed a canary.

For an instance she reconsidered her decision about them. They somehow didn't look as conniving or confident as they had. Had she misread their motivations for being at the Lodge?

She shook her head. She couldn't be wrong. There were just too many questions surrounding their odd actions. She could not let herself trust them. There was too much at stake. She could not let her concentration waver.

A voice now monotone, she sighed. "I came out here tonight to give you all fair warning about what's going to happen tomorrow, so all four of you can decide for yourselves your next moves...or maybe reassess what you already had planned. Here's what's going to happen. Sometime tomorrow at my calling, a raid on Chippewa Lodge will commence. It will be conducted by the state police in conjunction with the Bureau of Investigation and my office, the Minneapolis branch of the U.S. Attorney's office. Everyone on the premises including spectators will be stopped, questioned, asked for proper identification, and arrested if found to have anything to do with the Lodge. I have a list of the hooligans who are wanted or have escaped from jail. They will be arrested immediately when found.

To say that the charity golf tournament will be permanently interrupted by this raid will be an understatement. There will be no completion of the second day of the tournament. It should be obvious the unlawful activities at the Lodge will end tomorrow as well. The suddenness of that end will likely have a negative effect on the continuation of the festival in town as well.

As the distressed MacPherson began to finally slow down, Lawton looked over at Charlie Davis. Davis looked like he might need a paper bag to maintain proper respiration...or for possible self-administered suffocation. Lawton masked his true feelings. He wasn't ready to believe this female was going to leave Davis and him out in the cold fending for themselves....even though they really hadn't shared anything but their first names with her.

He calmly turned his head toward Lindy MacPherson thinking intently for a way out of the jam Davis and he were in. John and Adam only shuffled uncomfortably in their chairs. The four males were now looking at MacPherson as if she was a one-person wrecking crew. Untold numbers of people would be affected by her bringing in law enforcement the next day.

Adam Bailey's glare was feigned. He was experiencing some extra distress now that she represented the law. He had selfishly become even more concerned about the leather case under the sofa. That money as far as he was concerned was earned. He didn't want it confiscated. It represented a better life for his father when college started that fall. The farm mortgage could be paid off. There would be enough left over to cover college costs. That bag of $10,000 in his mind was more important to his father than to himself.

Maintaining her stern presence, she became more direct. "O.K., for what it's worth, I'm going to suggest something to help all of you. While I don't believe any of you have any direct guilt in the goings-on at the Lodge, you could still get caught in this police dragnet tomorrow. I'm going to recommend in your best interests just to remain here at the farm tomorrow morning until after the raid. Otherwise, I can guarantee you'll be caught up in the police dragnet and you'll have to explain your reasons for being there. John and Adam, that might not be a problem for you. I have a feeling that's not the case for Jamie and Charlie. Your alibi might be a bit weak. It wouldn't surprise me that the two of you may just be sitting with a bunch of arrested gangsters and hoods in the Pope County jail at this time tomorrow."

Davis complexion turned pale as road kill. As for Lawton, he was having a difficult time understanding why MacPherson had changed her attitude towards them so drastically since that afternoon. Now her furor could only add to their problems about how to excavate themselves from this whole mess.

Davis leaned over toward Lawton and muttered, "The U.S. Attorney's office....My God!"

Lawton whispered back, "Looks like I'll need to fix up my biplane. I hope the barnstorming and air delivery service business is still viable."

Davis nodded, "Maybe I could mow grass at the golf course. I know some people out there. Of course this all depends on when we get released from Stillwater State Prison. There's a silver lining...striped clothing makes me look thinner."

The two of them would normally have laughed at their commentary, but their words seemed dangerously close to the truth. Both were gazing into the depths of hell from a position too close to the fire. Their very vocations and reputations were at stake.

To MacPherson she was certain she'd finally struck a chord with her acquaintances. She kept up the pressure on them. "Gentlemen, I've been following your every action since this morning. Jamie, you might remember asking a young lady for a flat-headed scorecard pencil when you were performing those trick shots on the practice range. I guess you were so intent on getting Loni D'Annelli's attention you didn't even focus on who was supplying you those pencils."

Lawton scrunched up his face. He remembered. It now seemed so long ago. Referring to himself, he mumbled, "Christ, what a dim-wit."

Davis gave him the oddest look having not yet heard that part of the story. Both Baileys couldn't help but stifle a grin since they'd been part of that morning's successful deception.

MacPherson then turned toward Davis with a voice reflecting both disgust and some mirth. "And you, Mr. 'Drunkard', I lost you for a couple hours after your performance at the restaurant this morning. I had to get rid of my waitress uniform."

Davis rolled his eyes and sighed, "God dammit...that's where I first saw you. But, you looked so different...not like you appear right now....."......and then his voice trailed off.

Then Lawton and Davis went into silent mode once again. She kept on. "Yes...I was standing right by you guys in the restaurant when Charlie was acting as if he'd passed out. I overheard you discussing some kind of plan to take as much loot off these hoods as possible. At the time I gathered you were just a couple high rollers not aware of the group you were trying to sting. I thought you guys were entertaining... but foolish. What got me thinking you have more of an agenda was your reaction to all that money you won. I believe the figure was almost $35,000...and you both looked at the cash with little excitement. Actually you began talking about where you might donate the money, as if it was already burning holes in your pockets. That proved a couple things to me. First, you weren't part of the lowlifes staying at the Lodge. That was good.

But, the second thing kept eating at me. I kept asking myself, if you weren't in the tournament to win all that money...and you only showed up at the Lodge and got an invitation to play Saturday morning. There was no doubt you disliked the people who were competing in that tournament. The whole thing begs the question as to why were the two of you were there? Normally it wouldn't matter, but you'll have to understand I can't have anything interfering with Sunday's raid. So, to be clear, if you have any plans to initiate some kind of plot against someone at the resort that might interrupt the police dragnet, I'll personally see the two of you behind bars.

With the confirmation of her fears, Lawton nodded at Davis who still looked perplexed. He still had no idea what might have caused her to believe the two of them could be conspiring against someone at the Lodge. She'd seen them both behave rather bizarrely most of the day, but that shouldn't have been such a negative cue ...especially as far as Charlie Davis was concerned. He behaved that way since Lawton first met him.

Lawton sat there trying to figure a way to convince her that their actions, while ill-advised, were not as devious as she suspected. What was holding him back was the complete ridiculous impression she'd have of them if he really told the truth. Adding to the dilemma, he found himself strangely attracted to this female, even though she all but held his career and future in the palm of her hand. Davis, on the other hand, had nothing to lose. Lawton could sense his friend was going to try and deny everything in an attempt to regain her trust... and would fail miserably.

Showing a look of innocence, Davis gave his attempt. "Miss MacPherson, my friend and I would like to thank you for thinking we're brave enough...and stupid enough...to take on the mob. Fortunately, we're not. We're only here in Glenwood because my friend, Jamie, would tee it up with Satan if he felt he could take him for a few bucks. So, don't worry about us getting in your way tomorrow. Being no hero, I'll gladly slip out of here right now and enjoy another Sunday back at my lake house. The closest I want to get to your raid tomorrow is reading about it in the newspaper."

Lawton was still pondering the 'Satan' remark, and had no particular disagreement with Davis' statement. But, he watched her turn completely frigid to Davis' quite sincere stab at purity. MacPherson wasn't buying a thing Davis said...especially since she had gotten to know his personality that afternoon. Since the man was rarely serious, she took his comments more in a joking way. If anything her decision about the two of them was more solid than ever.

Seeing her look of slight disgust, Davis sat back in his chair realizing quite clearly he had failed. He looked over at Lawton as if the executioner was waiting outside the door with rope in hand.

Lawton grinned back. Nothing they were going to say was apparently going to persuade MacPherson otherwise than what she was thinking. There was little doubt in his mind she cared any more how they might come out of this ordeal. She had given them an out by simply staying at the farm during the raid, but that might not be their best choice. If they weren't at the Lodge during the raid, that might not be in their best interest. He could see Loni D'Annelli looking for anyone who might have been conspiring against his operation. Who better to suspect than a couple individuals who just happened to drop by Chippewa Lodge a day before the raid and now were peculiarly absent from the grounds that morning?

If there was to be any chance of salvage, Lawton knew he and Davis better change their tactics. Until he could see the way clearer, Lawton remained calm, raised his chin, smiled at her, and paid close attention to her behavior. She was on edge and had no patience for any possible obstruction to her next day plans.

It was then that Lawton realized the two of them had a bargaining chip with the information Davis picked up from Henry Hanson. It was just the case of when and how to play that chip to get this determined U.S. Attorney to trust them again.

As for Davis, he noticed his friend's small grin indicating something was brewing in his head. He'd seen the look before from Lawton and was satisfied to sit back and say no more. If Lawton was content to let things develop, then he was as well.

Once again MacPherson took their silence as one of discomfort. Though disgusted, that was fine with her. The more nervous they became, the more apt they were to delay or withdraw their plans.

It was left that only the two Baileys might be able to volunteer some additional information about the real guilty parties. Her voice showed strain. "I'm willing to wager the two of you know a lot more of what's going on at the Lodge than even Jamie and Charlie do. I can only believe you've both been part of that cooperative inattentiveness that seems to have taken over this town like some illness. While I understand why townspeople might behave this way, it doesn't make it right. John and Adam, you have to understand if you know anything that could lead me to making the proper arrests tomorrow...and I think you know what I mean...then the other probable arrests of such key people in town as Henry Hanson, Darrell O'Donnell, Mayor Good, Big Bud, and even the County Sheriff and the Chief of Police all might become unnecessary."

It was a statement that got to the heart of the matter. It left the father and son looking bewildered. They'd both so long been part of the unique environment between the Lodge 'guests' and the town that evidence given out would be to the detriment to the community. Rumors they'd heard and even things they'd seen while living in the town for the past five years now attacked their memories like a repeating rifle. They both looked at her and shook their heads preferring the safety of silence.

To MacPherson, that deafening quiet in the living room caused her to mentally throw up her hands. Her strong entrance to the farmhouse had daunted all of them. The only thing she'd really gained was likely shortcutting the actions of the two men she only knew as Jamie and Charlie. They'd be jumping into a fire if they ignored the imminent raid and tried to carry out whatever competing conspiracy they had planned.

That was it. Lindy MacPherson just sat down on a chair. She felt defeated. She'd lost what was left of her fierce temperament. Mentally she was whipped. She didn't even make eye contact.

As she sat, each of the four males couldn't help but see the trauma. Her frustration was obvious. She'd apparently placed a lot of hope they might come forward and bring new energy to her investigation. Her aims were understandable. She was trying to save some good people in Glenwood from taking the rap from those who were actually guilty. Certain townsfolk had been set up by an extraordinary mobster. The depth of what was about to happen was also sinking in. The long term affiliation between the town and the Lodge was about to come abruptly to an end. The relationship had been positive, but it was all built on a charade. The conclusion was going to have immense ramifications.

With the gravy train for the community about to pull out of the station, the arrests would be almost overshadowed by the immediate and long-term impact on the town. They could see MacPherson's pain. She would be blamed for a job she was sworn to do. The folks who'd gotten to know and like her so much the previous two weeks were now going to be suffering.

It was probably this empathy that caused John Bailey to move toward her. Where Lawton and Davis were still contemplating their exit strategy, Bailey had no such concerns. He showed a kindness that shocked her and got the attention of the others. He patted her on her shoulder and said softly, "Hey Lindy, you look kind of spent. Why don't you relax and we'll talk this out. Can I get you a coke? We've got some cold ones in the icebox."

Her face showed encouragement. She nodded at him. That was the first time Lawton and Davis realized MacPherson and the two Baileys actually knew one another prior to that very afternoon.

As John went to get her something to drink, Adam remained focused on his own predicament. Without being noticed by MacPherson, he slyly removed the leather pouch from under the sofa and casually walked toward the front door. He murmured something about having to go out to the barn. The screen door slammed shut as he went running through the parking area by the farmhouse with the concealed leather satchel. Whatever she might be warning, he considered it secondary. Protecting the newly acquired family wealth had become his primary aim.

With John and Adam out of the room, she leaned toward Lawton and Davis and gave one last attempt. Her focus was different. She wanted to appeal to the two joking, engaging men she met that afternoon. Her tone was apprehensive, yet straight-forward. "O.K., John and Adam are out of the room. What's going on with the two of you? You guys knew the golfers you played with today were not the bright spots of our society. I know you're not part of that group, so you had to have something else planned. You obviously don't want me or anyone else to know your true motives, but I have to know one thing. What possessed you, Jamie, to even play in this golf tournament? Your reasons aren't clear. Even your behaviors I observed with both of you all day seemed curious. How can I not believe the two of you are running some kind of scam against someone at the Lodge?"

Lawton shook his head toward Davis indicating they should not respond. Davis kept the faith that his friend had some kind of idea percolating. For once in his life he didn't say a word.

Lawton sat forward and showed some of his lawyer instincts by not responding and then changing the subject. He asked MacPherson matter-of-factly, "So Lindy, what are you waiting for. Why not call in your raid tonight? You'll catch most of these fellows three sheets to the wind. It would be an easier encounter."

She showed disdain. She mumbled, "You don't understand the entire picture. I believe I know who's behind this whole operation at the Lodge, but I can't prove it. You guys know it as well. Your 'good friend', Loni D'Annelli has to be the brains and energy behind this gambling ring and every other illegal business centered at the Lodge."

Davis stared at Lawton with a knowing expression, but still remained silent.

MacPherson showed her exasperation. "I'm not ready to call in the troops. I have a chance to put Loni D'Annelli behind bars and make the charges against him stick. But, I don't have the conclusive evidence I need. He's brilliant. He's placed himself under the protective cloth of the First Presbyterian Church Men's Club to avoid charges of orchestrating a gambling ring. He's somehow cajoled the law enforcement in Glenwood to look the other way. And he's one of the primary financial supporters of every civic and church organization in the community. I can't charge him with anything. Even a charge of harboring known criminals wouldn't fly. Darrell O'Donnell owns the resort, not D'Annelli. And, as far as the illegal gambling, fingers would point at a church deacon in town by the name of Henry Hanson. He's the one who manages the gambling booths for the First Presbyterian Church.

Again Davis gave Lawton an 'I told you so' look.

Her voice got even lower. "Look, I've got very little time, but I need to find something...anything...that points the lawlessness at D'Annelli and his immediate associates. I can't remove the unfortunate impact on the town after this free-for-all at Chippewa Lodge ends, but I'd like to keep the wrong people from going to jail. The town doesn't want this bubble to burst. They're enjoying the good times when every other town in America seems to be suffering. If you can help me in any way, I'll do everything I can to keep both of you clear of any accusation of wrong doing. If you do have something planned against anyone at the Lodge, I don't care right now. I suggest another time and another place would be best."

John then returned to the room with a Coke. He calmly handed it to MacPherson and then stood watching the three of them in silent thought. Everything she'd said moments before he'd heard. He hadn't worked out in his mind how he could help her out, but the looks on the faces of Jamie and Charlie, they seemed to be working on the same problem.

He instinctively backed away rasping, "I'll be right back. I've got to see about some chores." It was a weak excuse to leave and find Adam. He had a vested interest in that leather bag of cash as well. Despite their anxiety, Lawton and Davis smirked knowing the two Baileys were about to conceal their cash where God himself couldn't find it.

With the two Baileys out of the house, Lawton and Davis were seeing this predicament from far different angles...even between themselves. Both recognized they'd just been offered a reprieve of sorts. MacPherson needed more evidence and had just offered them what amounted to a free ride out of Glenwood if they could offer her anything that might lead to the arrest of D'Annelli. She still didn't trust them. She was still concerned about their own plans against someone at the Lodge.

Lawton knew of Davis' discussions with Henry Hanson, but he wasn't certain how helpful that conversation might be to MacPherson. He was inclined to let her continue to believe they had ulterior motives at Chippewa Lodge. It would give them far more credibility with her than the farcical true reason they were in Glenwood.

As Lawton sat there just thinking, Davis got more fidgety. He had a need to confirm Lindy MacPherson was who she said she was. He hesitantly asked, "So...Lindy...please repeat again...did you say your last name was...well...the same last name as one of the justices on the State Supreme Court. Did you say 'MacPherson'?

She nodded straight-forwardly, not really paying attention to Davis' strain. "Yes, Judge MacPherson is my father."

He winced as if just receiving a blow to the head. Even more weakly he inquired, "I know a County Sheriff up in Beltrami County in Bemidji. "You wouldn't know a Ralph MacPherson by chance."

Blankly, Lindy nodded again. "Yes, I'd better know him. He's my father's brother...my Uncle Ralph MacPherson. My family has a long line of law enforcement people."

The color had all but dissolved from Davis' face. With the chalky look of an albino, Davis motioned to Lawton to follow him outside. Lawton awkwardly excused the two of them saying to MacPherson, "Give us a couple minutes. We might have a way to help you out. We'll be right back."

Davis was standing by his roadster when Lawton got outside. He was smoking a cigarette like it was his last one. He hissed, "Jamie boy, let's get the hell out of here now. Let's just tell her we appreciate she thinks we have something up our sleeve, but that we thought you were playing in a legitimate charity event. Let's thank her for a nice afternoon, bid her good luck in her damned raid, and enjoy a day of golf and fishing at Lake Ida tomorrow. She's got a brigade of cops ready to pounce on that little resort. The information I got out of this Hanson character won't turn the tide of guilt toward your buddy D'Annelli. It's just Hanson with his side to the story. D'Annelli will have a better story."

Lawton wasn't convinced. "Charlie, I think we're in the thick of this thing whether we want to be or not. Remember, if we don't show up tomorrow for the golf event and there's a raid, those boys would have to consider us a stool pigeons. We may get a visit from D'Annelli or a few of his cronies sometime in the future. I ask you, do you want to be looking over your shoulder in the months ahead?"

Charlie stood there puffing on his cigarette. He couldn't disagree.

Lawton continued, "Charlie, the lady obviously thinks we're conspiring against someone in that group at the Lodge. I say let's maintain that image in her mind. If we admitted to the adolescent reason we were there in the first place, she could drop her concern about us like a bad blind date. I'm also arriving at the decision that we're better off working with the lady while we still have some time to control our own destiny. She needs to find something dirty on D'Annelli...or at least something that would tie him to this whole mess. That would work in our best interest. He'd be busy disproving the accusations and evidence against him rather than being focused on who tipped the cops."

He paused. "Chas, tell me, is there anything else you picked up from that Hanson fellow this afternoon that could help her case. Any potential proof could make our position that much safer...meaning that we won't appear as stool pigeons. The raid would then be the result of MacPherson's investigation. We won't have a bunch of conmen looking for us.

Davis thought hard before a light seemed to turn on. "You know, now that you mention it, Hanson and I talked about the money required to run a gambling business. Cash is of course required...a lot of it. People expect to be paid immediately upon winning. Like I told you, I saw a lot of money being bet on various sports, not just on the golf tournament. The betting the charity event was small potatoes. I commented to him about all that money being taken in...and asked him where it was all stored. That was the one question he refused to answer."

Charlie paused. "I know Hanson was seriously concerned about retribution. He might be one of a very few who know of the location for that cash. He could have been signing his own death warrant if he'd told me."

Lawton muttered softly, "Chas, that might be our ticket out of this ordeal. Hanson will no doubt be picked up in this dragnet. Let's tell her this man is the key. I have a strong feeling he knows whereabouts for the gambling operation cash. Hell, we could tell her the raid itself will probably uncover the funds. Then we'll promise to conduct our business with a few of those gangsters another day. We'll never have to get into specifics. I'll try to pick our time to suggest we'll just leave as a way of guaranteeing we'll not impede the police raid in any way.

Davis agreed. "Hanson shouldn't be that hard to find. She scared hell out of us. Hanson is in worse shape than we are. She should be able to intimidate that man with half the effort.

The two men were satisfied their plan with Lindy MacPherson would work. As they headed for the front screen door, John Bailey walked out of the barn heading toward the house. They didn't have to ask what he and Adam were doing. That $10,000 in the Bailey satchel was likely hidden where only archeologists could find it. As for Bailey, he continued to show uncommon composure despite the wrath he knew was going to come down on the town.

Lawton asked him, "John, Lindy's asking us for support against this rather large group of conmen staying at the Lodge. Aren't you the least bit concerned about the repercussions if your name comes up as one who might have assisted her?"

Bailey only shrugged and continued strolling toward the house. Looking back he responded laconically, "I've been in worse situations. Now, let's go help the lady."

Lawton and Davis looked at each other. There was no doubt of the sincerity of Bailey's comment. It spoke highly of the man's character. It was evident something in his past brought with it a coolness in times of great tension or even danger. Bailey's assurance had an immediate effect on them. They felt slightly self-conscious for thinking just of themselves.

Bailey entered the house ahead of Lawton and Davis. Adam trotted up behind and slung an arm of over Lawton's shoulder. His father had obviously had a talk with him. The young man's comment was simple. "We need to help her."

When the four of them entered the house, Lindy was sipping her coke. John sat in his chair where he'd been with a pipe in his mouth as if not having a concern in the world. While appearing detached, he was anything but removed. He was deep in thought.

Lawton and Davis took seats across from her on the couch. Adam sat on the floor beside her. She examined each of four faces staring at her. Her expression showed that these four males had reached some kind of decision. Whether it was to help her or not would be seen. Since they weren't alienating her, her hope maintained some realism.

It was Lawton who spoke first. In just one minute since seeing John Bailey, he'd quelled his own concerns. If the Baileys were going to take a risk, he and Davis had to consider the same. In the long run, crucial proof against D'Annelli would be in all of their interests.

Very cautiously Lawton spoke, but conscious of lightening his intensity. "Miss MacPherson...Lindy...yes, Charlie and I might have some helpful information. During this afternoon's golf tournament, Charlie had a chance to talk with Henry Hanson. We're willing to divulge that discussion because it might help your aim. First, I want to repeat the importance of absolute anonymity for the two of us...and frankly, the same should be said for John and Adam. Wherever this further conversation goes, nothing can be tied to us. Secondly, we have to be further guaranteed that whatever the reason Charlie and I were present at the Lodge golf course today, that cannot be held against us nor cause any charges or even questioning by the authorities. Finally, we have to have your assurance you'll do everything to keep our names out of any investigation or court depositions in your case against any of those arrested tomorrow at Chippewa Lodge.

290

Davis was satisfied with Lawton's deal-making. As for John and Adam, their eyes had grown large. They were impressed that Lawton might be more than a barnstorming pilot. Even MacPherson gulped. Lawton had more or less just admitted by establishing the guidelines that Charlie and he had to be in Glenwood for more than golf. With her agreement, their commitments were no longer the priority. They would help her in exchange for anonymity. She'd gotten as much in the deal as she could hope. Though not completely trusting them, she didn't hesitate. "O.K., gentlemen, it's a deal. You've got my word."

Then she looked over at the two Baileys and said the same thing, but more emphatically. "John and Adam, whatever you see or hear in this house has to stay here for your own safety. You can't ever say a word to anybody about Charlie and Jamie other than Jamie came into town accidentally, he played golf in what he thought was a charity event, and then he and Charlie left town at whatever time the completion of the tournament happened.."

The four men nodded agreement.

Slumping back in her chair, MacPherson had no more to say. Lawton and Davis felt their cockiness returning. Given the discussion Davis had with Henry Hanson, they both sensed the value of that conversation. Lawton nodded at Davis to proceed.

Davis loved being on stage. From experience Lawton knew his friend was going to milk the attention. He rolled his eyes as Davis began exaggerating his own story. "Well...while Jamie was playing with his newly found friends this afternoon, I got a little curious what was going on at this resort. I met the man you all know. Though a church deacon for the Presbyterian Church and manages the local Feed & Grain Mill, he's the man in charge of the betting booths across the roadway from the Lodge and the one at City Park. When I talked with him, he seemed either inebriated or bordering on severe exhaustion. His condition made him quite talkative...at least the first time of the two times I chatted with him this morning.

MacPherson's forehead creased. The jaws of both Baileys slacked. They looked disbelievingly at one another. John was the first to interrupt. "If you're talking about my friend, Henry Hanson, you must be mistaken. Henry doesn't drink. He's one of the straightest arrows I know...and he's a personal friend. I can only say, Charlie, if you saw him that way, it was only because he wanted you to see him that way."

Then it was Charlie's turn to look bewildered. He countered, "John, I swear I've seen my share of drunks...including myself in the mirror some nights, but if Hanson was faking his behavior he was doing a masterful job. If he wasn't under the influence, then he was certainly in pretty bad shape. I was surprised not only of the illegalities he described, but that he was sharing the information with me. I don't know why he thought he could trust me, but it was as if he wanted to get a load off his mind.

Lawton appeared impatient. "Chas, quit wasting time and just get to the part about the money."

Lindy MacPherson perked up when she heard that comment. Davis nodded and continued, "Well, he told me a few things Lindy already mentioned from her investigation. Importantly, though, he never would admit anything dire about Loni D'Annelli even when I asked him directly. Hanson's nervousness about possible reprisals was very obvious. I pressed him again and again about who financed the gambling ring. He wouldn't say a word.

Then he got interrupted with some booth duties and I had only a minute to push him one more time. He let go with one more aside... something about I'd be on the right track if I could locate the cash reserve. Then Hanson also added, 'It's not hard to figure out.'

Then he basically was done only lamenting that it would be a shame if the wrong people were arrested in this whole affair. I swear to God after leaving him, I felt he'd given me the exact amount of information he wanted to give me. I sensed he knew I'd probably not sit on his admissions and do nothing."

There was a momentary silence in the Bailey farmhouse. MacPherson was pleased to have her beliefs corroborated, but disappointed Charlie didn't have more to offer. It was a needle in a haystack where the cash reserve might be located.

Davis then turned to Bailey. "John, you say this Hanson fellow is a friend of yours. I'd be concerned. He looked sickly. If this raid is going to happen tomorrow and this man is arrested, I swear Hanson might be suicidal. I saw a man over the edge. If we do anything tonight, this man should be located and let him know what's about to happen. He might just come around and decide to talk. If he's concerned about retribution from D'Annelli or other mobsters, this might be a time, Lindy, when you'll have to arrange protection for the man. He'd be vulnerable as any person I've ever known."

As they conversed, it was Lawton who was not paying attention. In fact, it was hard for him to show much concern about Hanson since he didn't even know the man. Lawton stood up and began pacing the floor.

It was finally Davis who noticed his friend's distant behavior. He'd seen this look in Lawton's eyes often but under far less precarious circumstances.

MacPherson was about to get up from her chair when Davis placed his finger over his lips and pointed to a chair for her to sit down so she wouldn't interrupt Lawton's train of thought.

The Baileys and MacPherson began smiling at each other seeing Lawton's stare so remote. Lawton himself had no idea he was being observed.

It was Davis who finally ended the silence. His voice was low and raspy. "O.K., Jamie, spit it out. You're driving us crazy. Just start talking. If you aren't making sense, I'll butt in like I always do. Just say it."

Lawton nodded and sat back down on a chair lifting his head to focus on each of the people in that living room. He kept nodding his head as he mumbled, "Lindy, this is not that big of a community. The cash reserve to support the gambling enterprise wouldn't be out at the Lodge...not near that group of cons. If we all just focus on where a tidy sum of cash might be concealed, we might be able to check out a few locations yet this night. It at least would be worth a try."

Not looking for a response, Lawton's voice maintained its cadence. "John and Adam, you know the buildings in town. Since the money wouldn't be hidden near a herd of crooks, let's move into town. It's got to be someplace for easy access. Chances are someone like D'Annelli or one of his associates might enter the location in the middle of the night to deposit some of his gambling proceeds. You can be damned certain it's not going to be a local bank. They wouldn't want any official documentation of his revenue and profits. Besides, he couldn't trust the banks anyway. Who knows which ones are going to be in business tomorrow...or next week...or next month? There have been just too many closings."

He paused to see if he was talking sense. There was rapt attention. Davis had already been down that road with Hanson about the location but getting no response. Now Lawton was pursuing the same course but with more focus. "You've got to believe if D'Annelli is storing a lot of cash, he might also be stockpiling stolen goods as well. The location therefore would have to have a dry atmosphere and obviously be secluded. No natural elements, especially rain water or melting snow could be allowed to breach the storage place."

He looked at John Bailey. "John, you know the town. Where would anyone hide a bunch of gambling profits and stolen goods?"

This was out of John's area of imagination. He just shook his head blankly. "I can't say. You could be talking about any attic or basement in any building in this town.

There was a hush of disappointment with no ideas being said. Then the dead quiet was interrupted by an almost inaudible rasp. It was from a voice not heard often that evening. It suddenly uttered, "Why not the Mill?"

In unison all heads gradually turned toward Adam. He had moved over to the kitchen table drinking a coke and still looking half-interested in what was being discussed.

He looked at them with wide eyes. Now louder as if defending his whim, he exclaimed, "Hey, I'm sorry. It's stupid. I shouldn't have said anything."

The needless apology was ignored and the other four held their heads up looking at each other. Charlie mused, "You know, if I had a bunch of money I needed to be kept secure and hidden in a safe, dry location I might just discuss my need with a man who had become a kind of friend. I might just talk with the man in town named Honest Henry Hanson. This man would know the community and its buildings inside and out."

Lawton gazed at his friend and then over at Adam saying to no one in particular, "And, where does Mr. Hanson work again?"

Davis looked at him smiling, "He's the manager at the Glenwood Feed and Grain Mill on the west side of town. Do you suppose......after all, it's a business... where you store things".... and then his voice trailed off.

Lawton's voice reacted like a pistol shot. "Bingo! That's got to be it. Hanson said to you, Charlie, that it shouldn't be hard to figure out. The man's business is storing feed and grain. Why couldn't the same facility be used to store a sizeable amount of cash and anything else D'Annelli wanted in safe keeping. Why wouldn't Hanson some time ago have offered this gangster some low cost square footage at the Mill after D'Annelli sought his advice for some storage needs? Hanson wouldn't have had to even know D'Annelli's reasons for the space. I can see Hanson offering D'Annelli some place at the Mill for probably very little money. After all, it was for the good of the town to keep this benevolent outsider appeased."

The momentary silence gave way to four of the five people in that living room simultaneously nodding their heads. Davis added, "That would be why Henry Hanson would not talk about the location. He would be the only one who knew the location...and the only one who would likely take the blame if D'Annelli's storage space was breached. If it's at the Mill, it shouldn't be that hard to find."

That was when the fifth member of the group, John Bailey, began to shake his head. "Folks, not to burst your bubble, but I help Henry out at the Mill. I think I know every nook in the entire place. I don't know where the space would be that Henry could have offered."

MacPherson jumped in. "Look, it has to be checked out. We have five people in this room. A couple of us could search out the Mill while the others try to corral Henry. Two or three of us should be able to find this man someplace in town. Once we do find him, telling him what we know might force him to open up and help us."

Bailey then mentioned another stumbling block. "My friends, if you think you can just go down to the Mill and ransack it, you might think twice. The Feed & Grain Mill is across the street from City Park. The street will be filled with people enjoying the last night of the town festival. How many people do you think might witness you rummaging around the Mill...maybe a hundred...two hundred...or more?

MacPherson wrinkled her nose. John seemed ahead of them in his thinking. She looked at him wondering how and why this man's mind worked so quickly and logically. He was supposed to be just a downtrodden farmer inexperienced in matters of investigation.

He didn't stop. "Folks, here's another consideration. Let's pretend you somehow find this money tonight, whether at the Mill or elsewhere. How do you prove whose money it is?"

While the others silently began shaking their heads in momentary defeat, Lawton's eyes brightened. With an evil smile he chuckled, "You know...if I found out that the very source of my business was suddenly missing, I'd be pretty upset. I believe I'd take some action to recover my lost capital. Then I might raise holy hell until I found those responsible."

Looking bemused, Lindy blurted, "I don't follow you." Davis looked equally confused.

Building in confidence, Lawton seemed more assured. "Hear me out. This gets better by the second. If the money can be located, I suggest it gets stolen. I mean take the whole damned pile of dough. You only need to hide the money temporarily someplace until after the raid. Then, if it's D'Annelli we're after, find a way to make him aware of the robbery."

He then looked directly at MacPherson. "Lindy, if he reacts to the theft of that cash, you've got your proof that it's his money."

MacPherson looked doubtful but interested.

The two Baileys remained quiet and non-committal.

Davis just stared at his friend not ready to say anything just yet.

Lawton was unfazed by the combined lack of enthusiasm. "O.K., I admit I haven't thought through this idea completely, but it has a basis for multiple advantages. If D'Annelli self-incriminates himself, the authorities wouldn't be that interested in arresting some of those local folks you mentioned including Henry Hanson. It would also follow that D'Annelli would become the main suspect for any of the other unlawful deeds at Chippewa Lodge."

Davis' gaze at his friend now became more intense. He finally cracked, "Jamie, I think you're delusional. Can we just shoot you and put you out of your misery?"

Then he shook his head in defeat. "However, if I had a better idea, I'd be suggesting it right now. And, if the money can't be found, Lindy, you've really not lost much but some time and probably some sleep.

Then looking at MacPherson, Davis made an uncharacteristically serious suggestion. "Lindy, if Hanson really can't be found tonight, you may as well schedule your raid to start tomorrow morning before a lot of the spectators arrive and all the misfits at the resort are either slumbering or getting ready for the last day of the tournament. Your dragnet shouldn't miss anyone."

Lawton was about to chime in his support to Davis' proposal when MacPherson threw both of them a curve. She seemed to be thinking ahead as well. Her rejoinder came across agreeable to the timing of the raid...even benevolent...at first. "Gentlemen, I think the Mill has to be the place to look for the money. I want all of you to know whether the money is found tonight or no.... or whether I can trace the money to Loni D'Annelli or not.... there has to be an understanding that all four of you had nothing to do with me this night or throughout tomorrow. For your own good, you shouldn't be seen with me anymore. I won't face retribution. I'll be recognized as someone just doing her job. But, if any of your involvement is made public...well, I've seen and heard too many stories of the long term tentacles of the mob."

Then as quickly as she showed that concern, she bounced over to another fact. "Charlie and Jamie, I know you don't want to show your faces tomorrow morning at the golf course, but you should probably re-evaluate your situation. Once you boys teed it up with your new golfing friends today, you jumped into deep water without a life jacket. I don't believe it's in your best interest to simply walk away from this situation. When the police dragnet descends on the Lodge tomorrow and you're not at the resort, it won't take long for some of those gangsters, especially people like Loni D'Annelli, Willie LaCurso, Vinnie Spagatini, and Bert Bertinelli...just to name a few...to wonder where 'Mr. Trick-Shot' is as well as his friend with the fancy shirt. Charlie, you're only involved by association, but that's enough. Both of you will be suspected immediately of some dilly-dallying with the authorities. They never before had a problem with the law at the resort until you two got involved with the golf event.

With the two of you missing from tomorrow's action and the simultaneous visitation by some thirty state officers and deputies at the resort...well, I don't know how you two see it, but it sure seems mighty coincidental. It shouldn't take D'Annelli's boys long to track you down. I just hope you have a believable story...one that you haven't been able to share with me."

She paused looking skyward. "Let's see, Jamie, how would your explanation go again. Charlie and I just happened to be in town and decided to play the Chippewa Lodge golf course. Of course you weren't aware that a huge charity golf tournament was being played at the resort course. You just showed up at the golf course on a whim, began hitting trick shots, and soon you were invited to play in the event."

MacPherson quieted and then smiled innocently to observe if her point had been made. "I'm sure that tale will satisfy everyone. I'm not certain who you'd prefer to explain that whole story to first, the mob or the cops. I'm sure they'll both be sympathetic. Of course, it might get a bit sticky when the subject comes up of your winning almost $35,000 off these bums."

There was more silence around the room. John Bailey let his head nod slightly. MacPherson's summary was difficult to refute. Adam copied the same look. Lawton leaned back staring at MacPherson with a new look of respect...a small grin forming on his mouth. He knew she had him. They had to show up at the next day's golf tournament.

Davis was nodding. He also could see that showing up for the second day of the charity tournament would be their wisest choice. The gangsters would see them being subjected to inquiries by the police just like the rest of the staff and 'guests' at the Lodge. There was a good chance the two of them would be released and able to high-tail it out of the resort before noon. That way they could also miss the long noses of the press and save their reputations.

Lawton shrugged as he looked at Davis. "Well, Chas, looks like we should accept the invitation by the lady to join forces."

Davis had already accepted the obvious. He stood up and drained his last drop of beer before saying, "Well, this will be a new experience for me on a Saturday night. As far as I know, I've never broken into a Feed & Grain Mill...at least while sober."

That statement seemed to summarize the awareness around that farmhouse living room. Everyone knew they'd just signed up for a night that promised to be late.

The relief on MacPherson's face was palpable. If she had any chance to find true justice before the raid, she'd just been given a transfusion to her investigation. Everything seemed possible.

Puffing on his pipe, John Bailey cleared his throat loud enough to get attention. "Folks, before you get too excited about breaking into one of our local businesses, why don't I just give you a key since I work down there when Henry's gone." He produced the key and threw it to Charlie amongst laughter.

With his eyes still dancing, he then tendered one other question. "So let's say you find the money...and somehow even steal the money...I still have to ask you where are you going to hide the cash? Don't mean to spread lye on your plans, but it might be something you'll want to consider. There are a lot of people in this town...some good and some bad. I'd be careful where you conceal the loot."

Then he leaned back again while lighting his pipe mumbling, "You people obviously don't do many heists."

There was more laughter, but with not as much zeal. The shear lunacy and excitement of sneaking into the Mill and possibly discovering a large amount of cold hard cash was keeping them from properly thinking ahead.

It was Adam who again showed his spunk. "If we find the cash, I have an easy answer. Just bring the dough back to our barn. It'll be safe and won't be here for long anyway with the raid happening tomorrow. The authorities will be out here taking control of that evidence as soon as possible."

He smiled, "Besides, it would be kind of interesting. I'd like to see what it feels like to stand next to a pot of gold."

His father didn't look excited about his barn being used as a temporary vault, but it did make a lot of sense. He nodded indicating the temporary problem had just been solved.

The five of them then got busy agreeing on assignments for the evening.

It was only slightly after 10:00 that Saturday night when the two Baileys left in their Plymouth truck to find Henry Hanson. It was up to them to find him, explain what was coming down the next day, and persuade him to tell where the cash reservoir for Loni D'Annelli's gambling operation was located. Lindy MacPherson had given them permission to mention federal protection was available if Hanson feared retaliation.

A short time later MacPherson, Lawton, and Davis headed straight to the Feed & Grain Mill in the Model 'A' Ford discussing every minute how to remain undetected while rummaging through the Mill. The noisy and active street dance on the north side of City Park unfortunately would be only a block and a half away keeping people close to the Mill until very late that night. The predicament they would face would be the Mill parking lot. The lot would be filled with cars and young folk parading around or smoking and drinking in small groups amongst all the vehicles. The three of them would have to be extra cautious not to be noticed inside the Mill office.

As the three drove down the bluff into town, the quiet of the farm surrendered to the noise coming from City Park. The Feed & Grain Mill on the opposite side of town loomed in an almost haunting way with the four-story grain elevator units backed against the silhouette of the bluffs on the north side of town. MacPherson made three passes by the Mill in her old Ford with Lawton and Davis hunched down in the back seat. They were already worried about being seen with her.

She had been right about the number of young people lounging around their vehicles in the Mill parking lot. "Gentlemen, we're going to have to park down the block and come into the Mill from the back door."

They were lucky to find a parking spot between two smelly horse drawn wagons one block from the parking lot and two blocks from the dance. The three warily made their way across the road to the Mill trying not to be noticed. As Lawton and MacPherson ran behind the Mill to the back entrance, Davis remained out front and directly across the street as a look-out. It was decided that if anyone approached the Mill windows or office door, Davis would vigorously honk the horn of the nearest open topped automobile.

Lawton struggled in the darkness wrestling with John Bailey's key to the back door. Crouched over in the dark trying to find the key hole, the two of them were suffocating with the pungent smell of the stored grain. The breeze blowing over the grassy field between the county fairgrounds and the Mill swirled the air and forced them to hold their noses. The odor would eventually become barely acceptable, but it hovered serving as a constant reminder how they were operating outside the law.

Finally giving up on the key, Lawton simply turned the door knob. It opened. That was the first time the two of them broke up into hysterics. They were like two youngsters trying to muffle their laughter. Lawton whispered to MacPherson, "So much for security...a hell of a place to store a large amount of cash."

They slipped through the door and just stood in the back of the darkened office adjusting their eyes to the interior. Toward the front of the office, the sizable Mill office windows brought in the bright streaks of light from the street dance down the road. They stayed low knowing their figures could be seen if they got near those windows.

Now they faced the real challenge...where to begin their search. At first they did the obvious; they rustled around the office area in the semi-dark looking rather absent-mindedly for a safe. None was found except for a wall safe. That was not big enough to house the amount of cash they expected to find.

Their search got more desperate as they poked the walls for empty spaces and quietly stomped on the wooden floor to locate any possible loose boards. They moved the wood stove aside hoping it hid a staircase under the floor. That proved futile. Across the room, there was a ladder leading up to an open storage area. There was some hay and dusty grain bags up in the loft, but no obvious hiding place.

They also checked the ceiling for a possible attic. Everything proved fruitless. It was looking more and more essential that John and Adam locate Henry Hanson. He would be the last effort. Without his help, any further search seemed a waste of time. They would have to think of other evidence that might prove D'Annelli's guilt. But, at that late hour...time was not on their side.

Just as MacPherson and Lawton were shrugging in defeat, there was a loud car engine and flickering headlights shown on the office's three windows. Lawton moved swiftly to the front office window as a Packard Custom Coupe screeched to a halt right in front of that very window. Ducking even lower, he stared wide-eyed at MacPherson. Someone was about to enter that office. They had seconds to hide.

Two men got out of the vehicle and began walking toward the front door of the Mill office. Finally they heard Charlie Davis breaking into a drunken medley of old western songs while pounding on the horn of the nearest automobile he could find. He'd been taken by complete surprise.

Two men suddenly were standing by the back office door rustling with their own set of keys. Their voices sounded disgusted as if they didn't want to be there. MacPherson and Lawton had no other choice but to hustle up the ladder and dive amongst the grain bags and hay in the loft just as the two men noisily clamored into the office.

From their upper vantage, although dim, they were able to watch every move the two men made, but they couldn't make out the men's faces. Their only fear became their ability to remain quiet. The hay was already making them itch. Controlling a sneeze from the dust would also be a concern.

One of the men cursed as he walked toward Henry Hanson's desk. "God damn it...I hate coming to this place. It stinks. Why didn't Loni grab some extra cash last night when we were here? I was just putting the moves on one of the broads Vinnie brought up here. Let's get this done and get back to the party."

The other guy just grunted. "Let's not be too quick...and don't turn on any lights. I don't want any of those kids in the parking lot taking notice."

Just hearing the voices gave away the two intruders' identities to Lawton. They were none other than his golf partners from earlier that afternoon, Whitey Malooley and Billie McCoy, trusted right-hand men for D'Annelli. Malooley was taller, quieter and definitely the more formidable of the two. McCoy was faster-talking, shorter and more rotund fellow with a gift for verbal intimidation. That afternoon Billie had told one of their opponents that he kept one club in his bag for beating people to death. Lawton didn't know if the opponent believed it, but it made that foe retreat.

Malooley and McCoy were apparently making a run on the Mill to carry out an errand for the boss. It never occurred to either MacPherson or Lawton what that task might be. The combination smell of sweat and booze now permeated the office. Both men were feeling no pain from whatever they had been consuming out at the Lodge. They snuck around the office struggling to get accustomed to the dark and staying out of the light cast through the office windows. Swear words were echoing through the office as they bumped against chairs. Finally one of them turned on a small office gaslight causing MacPherson and Lawton to duck even lower on the loft floor.

Suddenly, McCoy glanced over at the back door of the office. He whispered the nickname he called Malooley. "Hey Long Ball, is that back door open?"

Without bothering for an answer, McCoy marched over to the unlatched back door and mumbled, "Christ, why don't we just put a lighted sign outside telling people there's a pot of gold in here and it's theirs for the taking?"

MacPherson and Lawton huddling close to one another turned their heads toward each other their eyes widening. They realized at that moment they'd probably hit the jackpot. They were about to be led to the end of the rainbow.

Malooley chuckled over his buddy's comment and took a drink from a small flask of booze he was carrying in his coat pocket. McCoy latched the door and returned to the desk.

Despite the unceasing itching, MacPherson and Lawton remained quiet as church mice as they watched the two men slide Henry Hanson's desk to the side. Then McCoy reached down to pull the floor rug away. Under that rug was a trap door. He opened it, grabbed the small gas light on the stair well, and descended into an obscure area below the main floor of the office.

For the next minute nothing was heard from McCoy as Malooley stood over the lighted hole in the floor muttering to his friend to hurry up. Finally, some muffled profanity echoed up into the Mill office about the smell and the conditions in that basement storage area.

MacPherson and Lawton had now become miserable lying on the empty grain sacks and hay. Sweat was building up both from the stuffy heat at the top of the room as well as the pressure cooker they now found themselves. There was a point at which they weren't going to be able to lay motionless. The itching sensation was excruciating.

Finally McCoy ascended the steps. He was carrying of all things a shoebox. From his perch above, Lawton saw with help of the small gas light in Malooley's hand a label saying 'Buster Brown'. That was it.

McCoy again complained irritably, "This is all Loni needs for tomorrow. Let's get out of this rat hole. I feel like I need a bath!"

MacPherson and Lawton felt the same way.

Malooley closed the trap door on the floor and replaced the rug. Both men then moved the heavy desk back to its original position. McCoy flashed the light all around the office area as if to see one last time if anyone was there. Satisfied, he doused the gas lamp and set it aside. In seconds, they were out the door, into their Packard, and on their way.

MacPherson and Lawton jumped up and started scratching themselves with no sense of modesty. MacPherson had her blouse off before Lawton removed his own shirt. They were shaking the clothing and wiping off their skin and face. Lawton half hoped MacPherson's disrobing might go further, but she put her blouse back on in the dark of the loft.

She chuckled, "I don't usually do this type of thing on the first date."

Lawton grinned as he pulled his shirt back on. "I guess that's a positive sign, isn't it?"

They scampered down the ladder just as Charlie Davis gave a faint but urgent knock at the front office door. Lawton opened it and a breathless Davis entered. "Holy Christ Almighty," he said, "I'm not used to this life of crime. They drove up to the Mill and were out of their fancy car before I realized they were actually going into the office."

Then his apologetic look disappeared as he looked at MacPherson still brushing hay off her clothing and hair. A smirk came onto his face as he removed some tell-tale hay from Lawton's hair. "So...while you kids were rolling in the hay, did you have a chance to notice there were two visitors moseying around this office?"

The quip was ignored as the three of them ducked down quickly to avoid being seen by a couple walking right by the front windows of the Mill office. Lawton whispered, "Charlie, those two guys were Whitey and Billie from the golf course. They just saved us a hell of a lot of time. Wait'll you see what's under this very floor. We're sitting over some kind of hidden basement that might just contain a sizeable amount of loot. Lindy and I would have never considered a trap door under Henry's desk."

Recovering his breath, Davis snickered, "We were damned lucky. At times I saw your shadows moving inside the office. I thought some people out here in the parking lot would certainly notice. Then that new Packard drove up. I was talking with some young lady and barely had time to run over to pound on someone's car horn to warn you. By God, she must have thought I was nuts the way I dove into someone's vehicle. When I finally got myself out of that car, she was... not surprisingly...gone."

He looked at MacPherson and deadpanned, "I'm used to that reaction from women."

He actually got a chuckle out of her with that small remark. It was the first time he'd seen her smile since the three of them were on the golf course that afternoon. Wasting no more time, the two men moved Hanson's desk, lifted the carpet, and opened the trapdoor. Carefully, MacPherson and Lawton descended the stairs as Davis maintained his position in the office as lookout. Lawton's weak flashlight beam seemed like a floodlight in that cavernous basement.

Directing the light at the walls, what they immediately saw was a shoe salesman's dream. There were untold numbers of shoeboxes stacked on shelf after shelf. Not for one second did they believe there were shoes in those boxes.

MacPherson grabbed one of the shoeboxes and opened it as if it was some kind of special gift. The contents were what she expected. She carefully removed one of the stacks of currency. It contained all twenty dollar bill denominations and there were five stacks in the shoebox. She grabbed another shoe box disclosing the same contents with one exception. This box had stacks of twenty-dollar bills composed of brand new currency. In fact, the new bills were perfectly wrapped in cellophane. They were almost too crisp! The word "counterfeit" came to both of their mouths as Lawton and MacPherson looked at each other wide-eyed.

More shoeboxes were opened. There appeared to be two particular shelves full of the shoeboxes with the questionable currency. Lawton leaned over toward MacPherson and predicted, "You might have yet another charge against Loni D'Annelli."

Standing in that dank basement, both were awestruck by the amount of cash and the number of shoeboxes. They had no idea they would find that quantity of currency. As Lawton shined the flashlight around the remainder of the basement storage area, there were other valuables gathering dust in the subterranean room. Artwork, sculptures, and even gold bars were randomly placed around the windowless tomb.

A new challenge became evident. There would be no possible way for them to strip the room of its contents. There was just too much stuff. They decided to focus just on the shoe boxes. They needed to pilfer enough of the boxes so it would be noticed. It had to look like a robbery had taken place.

Davis had remained by the office windows nervously watching for any more interruptions. Lawton leaned out through the hole in the floor and softly called out, "Charlie, you need to take a look at this. He placed one of the shoeboxes on the office floor and returned to the depths.

Seeing the Buster Brown shoebox, Davis was unimpressed. He whispered loudly, "Hey Jamie, do you have something in Size 13?" Seconds later Lawton and MacPherson heard the predictable gasp from Davis.

Davis' patience was getting thin. Another automobile drove through the Mill parking lot creating more nervous tension. It turned out to be only some kids. Davis whispered loudly into the basement. "O.K., you found it. Let's swipe what we want and get the hell out of here."

Lawton came up from below once again. "Charlie, stick your head down here and see what we're up against."

Looking slightly perplexed, Davis went half way down the storage room stairs and aimed his own flashlight at the walls. The whistle he emitted said everything. "My God! If there's money in those shoeboxes, we're standing in Ft. Knox."

MacPherson had already been tabulating. Her tally was approximately $5000 in each of the two shoeboxes she examined. Her eyes were as big as saucers, but she'd also become somewhat pensive. "Jamie…Charlie…there's still the question of ownership of all this money. We may know its Loni's cash, but our only proof is two of Loni's boys pulling money out of this storage area. We aren't about to admit that we witnessed the spectacle of them down in the Mill basement. That wouldn't be a wise move."

Lawton stayed focused. "Let's continue with our original plan. Let's take as many of the shoeboxes as can fit into Lindy's old Ford… and then leave the rest of the storage area ransacked. We want there to be an obvious scene proving that this Mill storage area had been breached. We'll figure some way for D'Annelli to get the word about the 'robbery'. If he begins to tip this town upside down until he finds the money or the perpetrators, he'll pretty much self-incriminate himself. That should be the proof you need, Lindy."

Davis slipped out the back door to retrieve Lindy's Ford while the other two continued hunting for some proof of ownership of the valuables in that basement. When that proved futile, they began transporting shoeboxes up the rickety staircase to the floor level. It was while they were in the depths of the storage area that an unexplainable sound suddenly occurred right above them. Lawton hurried over to the stairs. Glancing up he thought he saw a momentary shadow at the top of the storage room stairs. He whispered loudly, "Chas, is that you?"

There was no response. Lawton and MacPherson froze for a second before Lawton flew up the stairs. All he saw was a dark office. Looking back down into the basement he whispered, "Lindy, we must be getting a bit edgy."

Ten minutes later she began counting shoeboxes they hoped to take from the Mill basement. Her voice was incredulous. "We've got darn near a hundred shoeboxes. If there's $5000 in each shoebox, then we've collected close to $500,000 from the basement. That amount of missing money should be noticeable, wouldn't you think?"

Before leaving the creepy basement, they made things look disheveled. They then shifted the shoeboxes toward the back door leaving the trap door opened with the rug thrown in the corner and the desk askew. That was hint enough that something was wrong the next time anyone entered the Mill office.

Minutes went by and still no Charlie Davis. He'd been gone far too long. To add to their angst, the street dance was ending. Cars and horse-drawn rigs were driving by the front of the Mill as if in a parade. Lawton and MacPherson stayed low so as not to be see.

Another ten minutes went by and the traffic lightened. Still another horse-drawn carriage plodded by the Mill full of some very inebriated people screaming and laughing loudly. When they finally moved on, Lawton crawled over to the window in hopes of seeing the old Ford. But, the only thing moving toward the Mill was another wagon pulled by two horses with the driver covered with a very old burlap sack. Lawton actually felt sorry for the person driving the wagon. Things were so tough out on the farms in America. The guy didn't even have a coat to wear on a cool night.

Just then the wagon lurched right and went around the side of the Mill. They froze. The wagon halted by the back door, the driver wearing the burlap sack jumped off the wagon and came right into the Mill office. He leaned over and grabbed six shoeboxes stacked by the back door before they realized who it was. Charlie's chartreuse shirt was covered by the burlap sack.

He looked perturbed. "So, I'm going to do this by myself?"

Lawton sighed, "You don't exactly know how to dress for a robbery."

Davis's shrug said enough. There was no way any of the three of them could have guessed they would be rifling money out of a Mill basement past midnight on a Saturday night.

When MacPherson saw the wagon she remarked, "Charlie, if this is your idea of a getaway car, don't ever give me crap about my Ford again."

He chuckled, "Your car was blocked in. I saw the hayride wagons and decided to borrow one. We can transfer the money into your Ford later. Then I'll return the wagon where I found it."

Their 'heist' continued as the occasional car head light flooded the front of the Mill office. The three-person chain would duck until the light passed and then continue packing shoebox after shoebox into the back of the wagon. When the job was completed, Davis pulled the canvas over the back of the wagon and tied the covering down. It now looked like just another horse drawn wagon.

Again they lay low as two vehicles full of young people stopped in front of the Mill. The animated voices wouldn't go away. It seemed like hours, but it was only minutes until the cars finally peeled out of the parking area. Immediately Davis flung the burlap sack over his shoulders to once again cover his effervescent shirt. He gave his two-horse team a touch of the whip and they were on their way.

The plan was for him to drive the wagon over to the adjoining county fairgrounds where MacPherson and Lawton would eventually meet him with Lindy's Ford. There they would make the transfer of the shoe boxes.

Davis' teeth showed from under the burlap. He winked at Lawton. "If my law business goes all to hell, looks like I've got another option."

MacPherson and Lawton locked the back door and crept back around the Mill and approached her vehicle down the block. Staying in the shadows to avoid any chance of recognition, they were suddenly approached by a young couple. Lawton pulled MacPherson over by a tree simulating a romantic moment so the young couple wouldn't see them face on. The boy and girl giggled and passed by them.

A half-block from where the Ford was parked, a police car approached and MacPherson gasped. She duplicated Lawton's earlier effort pulling him toward a large bush and slinging both her arms around him. He only wished MacPherson's car was parked on the other end of town.

She was only slightly embarrassed as the officer drove on. "Don't get excited. I know the cops in this town only too well. We can't let them recognize either of us."

They finally made it to her 1928 Ford Model 'A', a vehicle that looked as lackluster as it had three years before when it was new. The government had leased a number of these vehicles for various department activities. Lawton found himself pleased he had chosen not to work for the government. His Julian Sports Coupe was almost four years old. It was stylish, fast, and the engine purred better than the engine of his biplane. He considered MacPherson's Ford one step above the horse drawn wagon driven by Davis.

With MacPherson insisting, Lawton hunched down in the passenger seat. She drove the side streets until intersecting westbound Hwy. #28. There they saw Davis and his stolen wagon clip-clopping toward the county fairgrounds. Since leaving the Mill, he'd added a farmer's cap to his burlap sack wardrobe. He was the image of a Minnesota farmer traveling homeward from a big night at the festival.

As he turned the horse team into the county fair ground property, MacPherson turned off her headlights and followed the wagon into one of the unlit open barns. When both vehicles were inside, the barn door was yanked closed. The three of them were operating like they performed clandestine late night robberies as a matter of routine.

It took less than ten minutes to transfer the approximate one hundred Buster Brown shoeboxes from the wagon to the inside of the Model 'A'. The boxes were literally spilling out of the windows looking as if the car was headed to a shoe convention.

Davis then got in the rig and headed back to City Park to return the wagon. They should have left the wagon in that county fair barn. The feeling, however, was not to get sloppy. They'd almost completed what they hoped would be the perfect caper.

Ridding himself of the wagon, Davis was to make his way on foot to the opposite side of City Park where MacPherson and Lawton would be waiting for him. Then they'd take on the last nerve-wracking step of the night...driving a car full of very conspicuous Buster Brown shoes boxes through town as they high-tailed it back up the bluff to the Bailey farm.

It was approaching 1:00 when MacPherson and Lawton stopped her car in a dark shadow across the street from Lake Minnewaska to await Davis' return. As isolated as they were, that location proved not to be as private as hoped. About fifty yards away, the community band was still leisurely putting away their instruments and generally enjoying some of the free beer brought over from Big Bud Bunsen's General Store for their post-dance enjoyment.

Ten minutes went by and no Charlie Davis. The stress was stifling. Lawton was beginning to worry. He groaned, "What's keeping him. All he had to do was drop off the wagon. Something's happened. I can just feel it."

They waited another five minutes with not a glimmer of Davis when Lawton kicked open the stuck passenger door of the Ford and rasped, "Wait here and guard our 'shoes'. I'll go check on him. Take off if someone comes near you."

She wasn't about to argue.

Lawton trotted across the dewy, trampled grass of City Park hoping Davis would suddenly appear. Unfortunately, all he was hearing was some loud ruckus on the other side of the park. He slowed to a walk and headed in that direction desperately trying not to be seen by anyone. One short day of evanescent glory out on the golf course could prove to be his undoing if he was recognized. If spotted, a text book robbery by three 'unpracticed in crime' attorneys could be jeopardized.

Getting closer to the melee, he made out the tall figure of his friend. Davis was obviously in a pickle. With the burlap sack tightly bound around his loud shirt and the cap pulled down over his eyes, he was trying desperately to keep from being identified. As near as Lawton could assess, the owner of the wagon team was trying to hold Davis while yelling for the police. Davis was denying the charge even though he was guilty as hell. Lawton smiled at his friend knowing that was Davis' attitude on any charge...especially traffic citations....just deny guilt.

In this case the owner of the wagon was determined, drunk and miffed. It made for a very dicey situation. Davis was using his more popular method of handling the situation...that is, pretending to be completely soused as well. Through slurred words, he was offering the wagon owner alcohol for medicinal purposes from the apothecary shop down the street he claimed to own. The farmer didn't believe him.

Davis then tried to appease the conflict by offering a couple cases of Canadian beer to be delivered to the farmer's home in return for having used the man's team. At that point Lawton knew Davis was running out of ideas if he was down to relinquishing some of his personal beer supply.

From the shadows, nothing seemed to be working. The unforgiving farmer yelled out that he was a Lutheran and didn't drink beer, even though he was practically paralyzed with his own home brew. Some band members had meandered over to the altercation hoping they might see some late-night fisticuffs.

Lawton saw no choice. He was going to have to somehow intercede without himself being recognized. He was about to yell out that a man was dying over at the gazebo on the other side of City Park when, as if on cue, two dark-coated, sinister looking fellows popped out of the dark from across the street. In no uncertain terms they told the people standing around to go home. One of them went up to the farmer, handed him a couple bucks, and told him to shut the hell up, get in his wagon, and leave. The farmer didn't look pleased, but examined the daunting men and the greenbacks, and wisely chose to retreat to his wagon. Davis needed no such urging. He pulled the burlap sack even closer to make certain his entire chartreuse shirt was covered. He moved away from the two men as if they were carriers of rabies.

Halfway across the park, Lawton intercepted him. Davis was striding at a pace of a galloping horse. He wasn't even startled knowing Lawton had likely come looking for him.

In a very hushed tone, Charlie said hoarsely, "Jamie...let's keep moving.....it's those guys with the long coats. They were patrolling the front entrance to Chippewa Lodge this morning. They work for D'Annelli. I saw too much of them when I was walking back and forth between the resort and talking with Henry Hanson. Christ, when I put this shirt on this morning, I didn't think it was going to matter. I don't think they caught a good look at me."

Seeing those two men in the long coats spoke volumes. Davis and Lawton saw firsthand how Loni D'Annelli had his own patrol overseeing the efforts of the county deputies and city police during festival week. If the police weren't around or were spread too thin, Loni's henchmen would take charge in keeping order, probably without the local authorities even knowing. It was all about control and not allowing any unwanted or negative attention to the week long town event. D'Annelli wanted the festival to operate as cleanly and smoothly as a Baptist picnic.

Lawton and Davis finally jumped out of the dark forest where MacPherson sat impatiently waiting for them. They were impressed she didn't shriek. The three of them then slithered into the front seat given the lack of any other remaining space in the back seat. With the load of Buster Brown shoeboxes, she couldn't see out the back of her vehicle. Adding to the challenge, the gear shift was awkwardly placed between Lawton's legs. He smiled as she gave him a coquettish look while operating the gear shift. The lady certainly wasn't a prude.

They slowly drove back toward Hwy. #28. It was the only roadway that ascended the bluff back to the Bailey farm. With the town now deathly quiet and few cars driving around, they chose to take the most direct route... right through the main intersection of town.

As she turned onto the highway, there was the very farmer who wanted Charlie arrested for stealing his wagon and horses directly in front of them. Davis tried to duck down so as not to be seen by the driver, but there was just no room.

Then they all gasped as the wagon hit a bump in the road. Teetering on the very back of the wagon was one more shoebox. The dark interior of the barn back at the fairgrounds had caused them to miss this last shoebox while transferring them from the wagon to the Model 'A' Ford.

All three uttered their preferred swear words simultaneously. Lawton was impressed with Lindy's choice of profanity. He noted that the lady had been around the block a few times.

They had no choice. That last Buster Brown shoebox had to be retrieved. Lindy slowed her automobile as Lawton crawled over Davis to slide out of the passenger side of the car. He sprinted ahead as quietly as he could, grabbed the last shoebox without raising a stir from the driver of the wagon. Then he dashed back to the car amid both MacPherson and Davis collapsing in laughter in the front seat. Even Lawton broke up laughing as he dove back into the front seat of the Ford. His little act of heroics was quite the come down from the gallantry he showed on the golf course earlier in the day. The man in the wagon turned back hearing the commotion, but was unable to see anything but the blinding headlights in his eyes. He methodically motioned for the vehicle to pass. With Lawton's legs still hanging out of the passenger window, MacPherson accelerated past the wagon.

The next obstacle was making it through town on East Hwy. #28 without being seen. Unfortunately, despite no traffic at that hour of the night, providence was not completely on their side. Just ahead were the two long-coated security men who'd just broken up the altercation in the park. As part of Loni D'Annelli's night security shift, they were apparently back at their post ready to take care of any other problems that might occur that night. To drive by them in an old Ford teeming with Buster Brown shoeboxes, MacPherson, Lawton, and Davis may as well stop and inform the two henchmen how they'd just lifted $500,000 from D'Annelli's secret bank account at the Mill.

Unless they could get by those night guards, their perfect crime, within minutes of succeeding, would fail miserably. Without hesitating, MacPherson took a hard right down a dark street to escape their eyes. Stopping under a cluster of overhanging tree branches, she turned off the car's engine. There they sat, perspiring in the cool, but humid air wondering what their next move should be.

It took Davis less than a minute for his impatience to overflow. Disgustedly he hissed, "This is ridiculous. I'm going to do something. Give me a few minutes. I'm going to do something to get their attention. We've got to get them off that street corner. When you see them move, drive past the main street intersection. I'll catch up with you in the block past Big Bud's General Store. If I'm not there, drive over to the First Presbyterian Church. I'll meet you there when I can get there.

Lawton asked, "Should I inquire what you're going to do?"

Davis shook his head. "It'd be a waste of time. I don't know yet."

MacPherson rolled her eyes and looked straight ahead. Lawton only smirked as Davis got out of the car and disappeared into the night.

MacPherson shook her head. "Is he always this inventive and spontaneous?"

Lawton nodded. "Have faith. He's a bit impulsive, but I want no other person in my corner when the pressure is on. You'd better get ready to get this heap going. I don't know what he's going to do, but you can bet he's going to create some kind of chaos. You can bet those two fellows in the trench coats will be running very soon. We'll just have some very limited time to make it past the intersection without being seen."

Another minute went by and any doubts MacPherson had were quickly erased. Suddenly one of the henchmen pointed perpendicularly down the street toward Lake Minnewaska. The two men didn't even mash out their cigarettes. They just bolted. Lawton winked at Lindy and nudged her to start the engine. "I think it's time to go." She just shook her head and accelerated out of their hiding place onto the main road through town.

A block before the intersection a much winded Charlie Davis intercepted them sooner than planned. He jumped in the still moving vehicle and chortled, "Let's get this piece of junk rolling. There are going to be two really angry night guards looking for someone to blame regarding their vehicle." His eyes were shining and he couldn't stifle his own pleasure as to the bedlam he'd created.

As they drove through the main intersection and looked to their right, they observed the two long-coated men chasing a vehicle heading down a slight incline toward the lake. There was no one in the driver's seat.

Davis sadly shook his head. "Gosh, those fellows have to be irritated. You think you've got your car in gear and the damn thing slips into neutral while parked on a slight downhill. It'd be a shame if they have to fish their car out of the lake. What a rough way to end a long night."

Davis then sat back with a self-satisfied grin. Lawton looked at MacPherson with an 'I told you so' grin. She in turn gazed at Davis and then at Lawton as if they both belied their age. Whatever her thoughts, she couldn't complain about the results. The old Ford sped onward unseen and then groaned up the hill on East Hwy. #28 toward the Bailey farm.

By the time they had made it to the top of the bluff, the stress level was seeping out of their bodies like a leaky balloon. They'd just accomplished something totally out of character...a successful night time robbery...something that didn't exactly mesh with their legal training. The late evening suddenly became quite amusing.

Minutes later they were bumping down the long Bailey driveway. MacPherson drove the automobile directly into John Bailey's open barn. Muffling their mirth like three drunks sneaking home, Charlie squeezed out of the vehicle and closed the barn door to keep their actions from waking the two Baileys.

MacPherson insisted they find something to cover up either the car or the shoeboxes. As she said, "Look, with approximately $500,000 in that vehicle, we can't just casually leave this money here in this barn." Conveniently, a large tarp was found in the barn and draped over the automobile.

As late as it was, there was one more piece to the puzzle that had to be discussed. Otherwise their efforts that night would be for naught. In order to link the money at the Mill with Loni D'Annelli, Lawton and Davis figured MacPherson might need some help in coming up with a way to make the Chicago conman aware the next morning that the Mill secret storage area had been breached.

With exhaustion making them giddy, they were still ready to thrash out a plan. To their surprise, MacPherson began heading for the barn door. She was leaving...without any further discussion. It only reminded them that her trust went only so far. She apparently wanted no more assistance from them. Her mood had changed slightly and she wanted them to know she was thinking ahead.

Her appreciation was sincere, but her next course of action would remain private. She said, "Jamie...Charlie...I couldn't have done it without you. I can't thank you enough. Now, it's late. We have a big day tomorrow. I don't want to endanger you more than I already have. I believe I can handle the next part of this plan. I'll be contacting the state patrol in the morning. There are a few more details, but I think I might be able to bring D'Annelli to the Mill...and do it on my own."

Her confidence was so sure. Lawton and Davis only eyed each other in surprise, but didn't question her judgment. She just seemed no longer to be interested in sharing her intentions.

She turned and finally added, "Since you're now going to be at the Lodge tomorrow morning, I'm thinking you should try and dodge the raid if at all possible. Even if you're picked up, I'll make certain you'd be suspected of nothing. But, to make it easier, I suggest you work out an escape plan once the raid begins. We'll settle on how and where before we leave for the Lodge tomorrow morning. The less you have anything to do with the state patrol the better. I believe it would also be in your best interest to be seen by as many of the hoods at the Lodge as possible before the police move in. Then, they'll not suspect you of any possible conspiring with the authorities."

Her suggestions were amazingly lucid considering the lateness of the hour. She seemed to have things under control...even thinking of the best way for them to deal with the raid. They'd done all they could that night to assist her. Lawton and Davis now had no fears about having to playout the second day of the tournament. That meant they could make as many wild bets as time would allow at the breakfast furthering their image of innocence.

The three of them staggered out of the barn and headed for the farmhouse. Lawton closed the barn door as securely as possible, which meant he latched the wobbly dead bolt. It was so loose a ten mile an hour breeze could nudge the barn door open. But, they were too tired to care. The large amount of money in the Ford only had to be hidden under the tarp for a short period of time. The authorities would take possession of the cash sometime after the raid.

Lawton commented as they approached the Bailey house. "You know, I was thinking. If all this works out and somehow the cash and goods in the Mill basement can be attributed to D'Annelli, the money in Lindy's Ford becomes nothing more than superfluous evidence."

Charlie nodded. "Hell, you're right. We could start a new country with that money in the barn."

The three of them enjoyed the whim, but joking no longer carried much appeal. They were all too fatigued. Sleep had become the primary need. The light of morning would arrive way too soon.

It was after 2:30 when they fell into their respective places to sleep. Lindy earned the third bedroom. Lawton took over the couch. Davis fell fast asleep in an old easy chair with ottoman in the living room. Though he snored, it wasn't heard.

Unbeknownst to MacPherson, Lawton, and Davis, there was something else that materialized during their short walk from the barn to the farmhouse. Adam Bailey had awoken to the sounds of MacPherson's Model 'A' Ford charging up the driveway and then being driven into the barn. Whether the muffled laughter from inside the barn or his natural interest in the travails of his three houseguests that evening, Adam was awake and considered joining the fun. However, after the big day on the golf course and the intrigue going on that evening, he decided to remain in his room for the time being.

Shortly, he observed through his bedroom window the three night-time intruders drunk with their success exiting the barn and swaggering across the farm yard to the house. With his eyes and ears to the window screen, he saw their exhaustion and heard their loose whispers. He couldn't help but take note of Charlie Davis commenting about "enough to start a new country". How could that not pique his curiosity? Also that they had chosen to park Lindy's old Ford in the barn instead of haphazardly outside the house meant there might be something being hidden in that automobile.

It wasn't five minutes after the three worn out houseguests had fallen fast asleep that Adam rolled out of bed and moved stealthily across his creaking bedroom floor and down the stairs. He tiptoed out the farmhouse door across the lawn and the gravel parking area to the barn. Unlatching the barn door with but a flick of a finger, his hands found the gas lamp hung where it always was. Closing the door, he lit the gas lamp and immediately saw MacPherson's Ford covered with a canvas parked in the middle of the barn.

He slowly strolled over to the car in wonderment. Then carefully crawling under the canvas cover, he stood up under the canvas and pulled the light up to the windows of the old Ford. What he saw he didn't expect. There were just shoeboxes, lots of shoeboxes, all stacked in the backseat from floor to ceiling.

He looked closer. The name 'Buster Brown' was on each box. Adam smirked to himself, 'What in blazes is all the secrecy?'

He reached through an opened window and carefully removed one of the shoeboxes. The disappointed frown disappeared on his face in the next instance. From under that canvas, the gasp he expelled when he took the top off that shoebox echoed throughout the barn.

Adam crawled out from under the canvas placing his gas light within a foot of the contents of the shoebox. He wanted to make certain what he was seeing. It took but a second to eliminate any further question. He'd never been more stunned as he fingered each stack of $20 bills inside the shoebox. The Buster Brown shoebox held enough cash to make the offertory plate at the local First Presbyterian Church Christmas service look meager.

He sat down on the dirt floor of the barn and began massaging the stacks of money. It was the second time that evening and the second time in his life he'd been exposed to so much money. Holding one rubber-banded stack in his hand, he dreamed of what that amount could buy. Then he began counting the individual bills in each stack. Not trusting his brain, he repeated the process. Each time he came up with the same number. There were fifty $20 bills in each stack and five stacks each held together by a rubber band. He did some quick arithmetic. With $1000 in each stack....there was $5000 in that one shoebox! $5000! He'd hidden twice that amount in the barn earlier that night, but glancing back at the canvas covered vehicle, there was an untold number of boxes stuffed in that car.

Adam got momentarily light-headed guessing how many shoeboxes were being hidden in that old Ford and then multiplying that figure by $5000. He now understood the behavior displayed by MacPherson, Lawton, and Davis just minutes before. If this was evidence found at the Feed & Grain Mill against Loni D'Annelli, his long time friend was going to be facing some irrefutable charges.

Adam crawled back under the canvas and held up his gas light to the window of the car once again. He wanted to estimate the number of shoeboxes. Yet, they were stacked so randomly it was difficult to make an accurate count. Buster Brown shoeboxes were shoved into every space of air with the exception of the front seat of the Ford. Making a cursory count, he figured there had to be over fifty boxes...maybe sixty...maybe even seventy-five.

He scrambled back out from under the tarp and made certain everything looked just as it did when he entered the barn. He looked over at some loose dirt on back corner of the barn floor. His father and he had not buried their leather packet full of $10,000 in that location. They had just wanted to make it look like they had. No, they had another place they were keeping their money until things calmed down. His father and he already had plans for that $10,000. They were not about to let that money get away.

Now here he was with a box full of another $5000 sitting on the dirt floor of the barn. If there were 50 to 75 more shoeboxes, there was likely somewhere between $250,000 to possibly $375,000 stuffed in that Ford. It was an amount so large he couldn't relate to the figure. But, he did understand the amount didn't matter. It was evidence against D'Annelli and would remain in the barn only temporarily.

He stared back at the canvas covered Model 'A' and then at the Buster Brown shoe box in front of him. At that moment it was like a cloud suddenly enveloping him. He began hallucinating. He couldn't help but contemplate if one...or even two...of the Buster Brown shoeboxes came up missing. Who would know? It didn't look like his three friends had neatly made an inventory of the number of boxes...not the way they were haphazardly shoved into the old Ford. Furthermore, he couldn't imagine the loss of those shoeboxes would have any impact on the level of the charges against Loni.

He sat there on the dirt floor of the barn pondering what he could do with the additional money. His mind was not on himself but more on the many destitute families in and around Glenwood and Pope County. While he and his father were known for pitching in and helping folks in time of need, it was always generosity with their time and labor. He and his father had never been able to think in more extravagantly charitable ways since they'd never had resources to consider such a delusion. But, since earlier that evening as he and his father hid their $10,000, he'd had these images of bigheartedness floating in his head. He'd felt somewhat guilty knowing his father and he were only thinking what the money could do for themselves. Now, only a few hours later, he'd discovered enough cash hidden away to make their personal treasure look paltry. More importantly, with the mind numbing amount of money in those shoeboxes, that dream of what the money could do for others was now foremost in his mind.

Adam's heart raced over the possibilities. What if portions of a shoebox full of money happened to land in some local families' pockets? How much good could that do for each of those families? He could name ten...fifteen...twenty...even more families who could be at least temporarily unburdened with just a portion of one stack of twenty dollar bills held in one shoebox.

Adam thought about the undying respect his father enjoyed around the area. Adam had heard too many times how folks were certain if John Bailey ever had any money, he'd likely give it to people in need as fast as he received it. It was just understood he had that type of character and soul.

Now there was a chance to make that impossibility.....possible. There was enough money in that Ford to imprison Loni D'Annelli...plus do a lot of good for some truly needy folks. Adam had no moral problem with his notion...none in the least. He had a feeling his father would be appalled by his thoughts, but that didn't seem to matter. He had an urge just to discuss the whim...one time...with his father.

He picked up that lone shoebox being careful not to drop any currency on the dirt floor and turned off the gas light. Squeezing through a small opening at the barn door, he latched the door and snuck back across the lawn to the house. He knew how to keep the front screen door from creaking by pulling up on it as he opened it. Not even his father knew that trick. Adam had learned that little maneuver only in the last year...a few late night returns from weekend dances in Willmar and St. Cloud required some ingenuity so as not to wake his father. What Adam didn't know was that his father heard everything until his son came home, but never said anything. Unfortunately for Adam, his Dad had no mercy the following morning. Chores still had to be completed.

Adam tiptoed past Lawton and Davis fast asleep in the living room. He didn't have to be that careful. They were comatose. A marching band would be challenged to wake them.

At the top of the stairs, he paused by his father's room thinking twice whether to bother his Dad or wait until morning. He thought about the agreement they'd had ever since his mother and sister had been taken from them only six years before. His father had said if there was something to talk about between the two of them, no hour was too early or too late.

Adam stepped into his father's room and whispered, "Dad....Dad...I need to talk with you. Wake up! I've got to show you something!"

John groaned and rolled over.

Adam sat on the bed and waited for his father to gain consciousness.

John was not irritated in the least...just tired. That agreement with his son would always be etched permanently in his mind. Irregardless, he was still somewhat surprised by his son's excited voice at such a late night hour.

John finally forced open his eyes and whispered back, "Adam, what in tarnation are you doing up at this hour. What's wrong?"

Adam didn't say a word. He just opened up the top of the Buster Brown shoebox and showed his father the contents. John was still groggy. He rubbed his eyes in the darkness and really couldn't make out what Adam had given to him.

Adam reached into the box and pulled out a stack of bills. "Dad, feel this. It's money...and a lot of it! In this shoebox alone there's $5000."

The son was trying determinedly to control his exhilaration Thinking his father hadn't heard him, he repeated, "Dad, there's $5000 in this shoebox! And, out in the barn in Lindy MacPherson's Ford there are more shoeboxes...more than some shoe stores even have. I think they found Loni's storehouse of cash."

John just lay there balancing on his elbow staring into the shoebox. He gave no reaction. Then in a tone he normally didn't use with Adam, he quietly but firmly rasped, "Adam, it's simply none of our business. Return the shoebox where you found it. It's not ours to touch. You can bet its evidence Lindy MacPherson needs to make her arrests on Loni D'Annelli and his people. You remember we've occasionally talked that this type of thing could happen to those fellows out at the resort. Neither of us imagined or wanted to believe Loni had the kind of operation out at the Lodge that Lindy described, but it appears he's guilty as hell. You've got Lindy's proof right here in this shoebox. Now is not the time to do anything stupid or get greedy. We had an incredible day. Loni was generous to you as always. Our new friend, Jamie, was particularly kind as well. Let's be happy with what we gained."

Then he lay back down and in a voice half asleep he murmured, "Now, son, do what I say and get back to bed. We've got work to do before we go to the Lodge in the morning."

Adam got up slowly. He understood the words, but couldn't help be disappointed over his Dad's reaction. Here was a chance to really help some people ...but his father wasn't giving Adam the opportunity to explain his true thoughts.

Adam put the top back on the shoebox and began shuffling toward the bedroom door. But, he turned around and said something not knowing whether it would be heard by his sleeping father or not.

"Dad, I'll return the shoebox where I found it like you say. But, I want you to know what I was thinking. It might not be what you expect. There's more than enough cash in that old Ford to be evidence against Loni. If he and his guys truly are the hoodlums so many think they are, then likely a lot of decent people had money taken by Loni and his men. These folks will never see that money again. I was just thinking that it would be nice if a few people in need could get some of this money instead of just having the government confiscate it for evidence. I wonder how much is needed to convict Loni. And, somehow when the government is done with the money, I think they'll keep it for their own use....you know, bribes to informers to pick up other criminals... stuff like that. I mean, what else would they do with the money?

Dad, I just don't think the government needs all that money in shoeboxes in Lindy's Ford. I'd like to have just half of it. In ten minutes I can list hundreds of people I'd give some of that money."

There was a pause. Then Adam repeated, "But, I'll do what you say. This box will go back to the barn. I just don't have to like doing it."

Then he didn't say any more. Adam tiptoed out of his father's room and retraced his steps back to the barn. He placed the shoebox back in the old Ford in the exact spot he had removed it. Five minutes later he had crawled back in his bed to grab another few hours of sleep before his father would wake him for morning chores.

Throughout that short time Adam had returned to the barn and replaced the shoebox, John Bailey's eyes were wide open. He'd heard every word his son had said.

His son's reasoning about the money and the good that could be done with just a portion of it had stirred him. That buzz would continue through restless sleep and on into the waking hours that Sunday morning.

CHAPTER
20

Sunday morning burst forth way too early for the late night burglars staying at the Bailey house. Sleep for MacPherson, Lawton, and Davis had been a short experience. It was 6:15. Davis had slept soundly on the chair with ottoman not forty feet from a rooster in full volume. His chartreuse shirt didn't seem as resplendent as it had the previous day. The sweat as well as the dirt from the burlap sack had streaked the shirt with ugly stains. Some hay hung from the shirt as well.

It took only the second piercing cackle from the rooster for Lawton to jerk awake and charge toward the window to yell at the bothersome noise. Through that disturbance, Davis never budged.

Lawton went back to the couch and fell back onto it as if it was still nighttime. Sunday mornings were notoriously poor times for the two attorneys. Both had often played golf all day Saturday and stayed out very late the same night. Sunday was recovery day. Golf was usually played, but at a slower pace.

He stretched knowing the day had to start. His consolation was that he didn't have to be in competitive form that morning. The raid was only hours away and all he and Davis had to do was make it out to the Chippewa Lodge golf course and go through the motions of warming up for a golf event that would not be played. Their biggest challenge would be to evade the authorities once they entered the resort property.

He heard a noise in the kitchen and allowed one eye to open as he lay on the couch. Lindy MacPherson survived the night and was rummaging around looking to make coffee. She was wearing an old shirt of one of the Baileys as a kind of pajama. She looked rather fetching as she moved slowly around the kitchen.

In minutes the inviting smell of the brew brought Lawton to consciousness; Davis still hadn't moved. Lawton sat up admiring MacPherson for more than her makeshift night clothing. He couldn't remember meeting any female that compared to her. She'd been uncover for two weeks and had pulled off the scheme without being discovered. How could he not be impressed?

Then, as if trying to keep Lawton's eyes from undressing her, she motioned for him to come to the kitchen window. Her voice was deep reflecting her own lack of sleep. "My God, I don't believe it. People actually get up and do work at this hour. Our hosts are out doing their chores already. Adam is pitching some hay into a fenced-in area containing some cows. John is standing in a hog pen throwing feed onto the ground. Isn't this supposed to be the day of rest?"

Davis jolted awake hearing her voice and staggered with Lawton over to the window. They both groaned and shrugged their shoulders uncertain whether witnessing the outdoor scene was worth their time. Washing up in the kitchen sink, it took Davis no time to choose his attire for the day. It was the only change of clothes he had. The grass-stained pants and slightly streaked casual shirt pulled from the back seat of his roadster the previous evening were a slight improvement to the now soiled chartreuse shirt and slacks he'd been wearing. At least the change of clothes smelled better and had no hay hanging from the armpits of the shirt.

Lawton was more meticulous. He had to dress as sharply as he had on Saturday to continue the ruse that the second day of the golf tournament would be played that day. MacPherson cleaned up as best she could. She didn't have a change of clothing. She'd have to wear the same outfit she'd worn rolling around in the hay at the Mill. Somehow she still smelled all right to the two men.

John and Adam finished their work by 6:30 and strolled back toward the house. Watching the two Baileys, the three wondered whether John and Adam would say anything about the canvas covering Lindy's Model 'A' Ford in the barn. The answer would come shortly. First, however, both males began stripping themselves to their skivvies by the well leaving their dirty outer clothing and manure stained boots in a heap to be cleaned later. It appeared to be a very normal routine of washing themselves before entering the house.

A feminine shout from the kitchen sounded. MacPherson seeing them from the kitchen window yelled, "Gentlemen, "Don't you two dare go any further. This isn't a barracks."

The two of them smiled and waved before toweling off. When they entered the house and looked at their half-conscious guests, Adam was not even subtle. He bellowed, "Good God Almighty! What bank did you guys rob last night? There's enough money in the back of that car to make most bankers jealous!"

John smiled slightly ignoring his son's antics as he continued through the house to his bedroom. He showed no interest in the discovery of the money. As for Adam, he was enjoying the momentary discomfort he'd just caused. MacPherson, Lawton, and Davis could do nothing but shake their heads and laugh. Whether the Baileys knew about the money or not didn't really matter. The barn would only be a temporary repository.

Two minutes later, John freshly dressed, descended the staircase. Pouring a cup of coffee he seemed completely relaxed. Adam was still kidding as he ate some breakfast. "So....are you guys starting a shoe business...or a bank?

Disregarding his son's teasing, John gave the three some well-earned credit. "So, you were successful last night. Where'd you find the loot?"

Davis chimed in. "It was lucky. A couple of Loni's boys showed up at the Mill and virtually led us to where the money was stashed. You apparently don't know about the basement under the floor of the Mill office."

John looking surprised shook his head. Lawton then told the story about stealing the shoeboxes and the challenge of getting the boxes unseen back to the farm. All the while during the entertaining tale, MacPherson was preoccupied. Grabbing the money for evidence wasn't going to be enough unless Loni D'Annelli could be better connected to the cash. She was still processing a plan to lure the Chicago conman to the Mill that morning. Moreover, she was going to need some support once again. She truly hated to solicit assistance from the two Baileys. Being locals, they could be recognized easily. That could not be allowed happen.

As for Lawton and Davis, she was no closer to much about them or their motives for being at the Lodge that weekend. That question really no longer mattered. They'd lived up to their bargain the previous night in helping find the money. They would not be disrupting her imminent raid. It would be understandable that their only interest was to escape from the entire situation as soon as possible.

Adam inquired how much money had been taken from the Mill basement. Lawton made a guess. "I believe we brought back to the farm about a hundred shoeboxes...and that's just a small portion of what remains in that Feed & Grain Mill basement. And, in that basement storage area, we saw more than money. There were other valuables as well. Our problem remains that it has to be proven all that currency and those valuables are possessions of Loni D'Annelli. He didn't exactly leave signage down there declaring it was his property."

MacPherson took over. "Yes…and now I have to somehow get D'Annelli's attention away from his golf event this morning and get his attention toward the Mill. All that has to be seen is that he acknowledges ownership of that money and those stolen goods. Then, I've got my man."

The males watched as MacPherson stood up nervously. She looked at the time and then at the four men. Her decision was made at that moment. She sat back down still staring at them. "Gentlemen, I have a plan, but I can't carry it out by myself. If any of you are willing to help me, I have to repeat the rules for your own safety. For your own good, I will disclaim getting any support from anyone except the state patrol. I don't want you admitting to the state patrol about anything you might agree to do with me this morning. If asked, you'll have to lie about your involvement. I'll back you up and emphatically repeat that I worked alone. That should protect you from any accusations or reprisals…as long as you keep your mouths closed.

There were nods from all four men understanding her explanation and appreciating her concern. Her reference to the word 'involvement' caused each of them to sit straighter and not miss anything she was about to say.

John gazed at her. "Lindy, I've known you for almost two weeks. I know this day is going to be hard on you. You've made a lot of friends in town, and you know this raid is going to end a good run that's benefited the entire community. It's too bad so much good in Glenwood came as a result of the types of people staying out at the Lodge. Frankly, it's time to end this charade. If it's all based on broken laws and criminals hiding out, then it should have ended a long time ago."

Then his wistfulness disappeared and he said earnestly, "You know, I had a feeling this was going to be the last year of the charity golf tournament. What was happening at the Lodge was becoming just too public.

He looked at his son. "Well, Adam, I guess you got your big payday yesterday. It looks like you won't see another day like that one for a long time. But, it's hardly sad. You made more money this week than you dreamed existed."

Adam only nodded.

John leaned in further toward MacPherson and retorted, "So….tell me what else needs to be done. How can Adam and I help?"

Her eyes warmed towards the two of them. Lawton and Davis were again awed by John Bailey. Everyone in that room accepted how he was one of those special souls who could see through the fog and understand the true picture. He was offering to help no matter what the consequences.

Then MacPherson turned toward Lawton and Davis. They hadn't been as spontaneous with any offer to assist...nor did she expect them to be.

Lawton was more terse. "Lindy, let's hear your plan."

Wasting no more thought, MacPherson began to talk fast. "There is a small window of opportunity to bring Loni out of his mole hole at the Lodge and cue his interest toward the Mill...and it has to happen before the raid. If the authorities arrive beforehand, Loni might be able to lay back and disclaim any responsibility for anything going on at the resort other than his civic-minded charity golf tournament. His seeming largess will likely keep him from being arrested... much less convicted... of any charges."

All eyes were on the young lady as she bristled with intent. "Charlie, Jamie and I left the Mill office and opening to the basement last night looking as if there'd been a break-in. I'll make an anonymous call to the Lodge about the break-in at the Mill for the purpose of hoping D'Annelli will hear the news. My plan hinges on D'Annelli being alarmed. That's where you guys at the Lodge could help by starting some quick rumors about a large amount of money having been taken. I figure if he understands how dreadful this apparent robbery could be, there's a chance we could yank him out of his comfy little resort. If we can get him to come to the Mill coupled with his two right hand men being at the Mill last night, possession could then be verified. I'd then make the arrest."

The four of them sat there looking at her waiting for her to continue...but there was no more being said. She'd suddenly gone quiet as if waiting for a general response to her plan...one that she hoped would be positive. Her shoulders drooped slightly when she was met with no apparent enthusiasm.

John cleared his throat about to say something...and then thought better of it and lit his pipe. Lawton and Davis glanced at each other trying not to show approval or disapproval. It was her game. They weren't about to burst her bubble. As for Adam, he continued eating. He was going to follow whatever plan was decided upon.

Then John cleared his throat again...this time while shaking his head. He was showing constraint, but something was deeply bothering him. "So, Lindy, you're hoping Loni will be upset about a Feed & Grain break-in rumor. Is that what I'm hearing?"

She nodded, but not as confidently.

Bailey, in his inimitable calm manner, reacted. "What you don't know is that the Feed & Grain Mill is often times unlocked. It gets broken into routinely. Young people like to scamper up that ladder in Henry's office area and use it to roll around in the hay...if you understand my meaning?

Davis gave him a blank stare. MacPherson and Lawton knew firsthand what he meant. For once young Adam even had a glint in his eye.

John didn't stop. "Breaking into the Mill would carry as much significance as breaking into a church. There's no perceived worth of anything to steal. That you found an amazing amount of money below Henry's office just tells me how secretive that unknown storage area has been. Hell, I've worked part-time for Henry when he's traveling and I didn't know until now that a basement under the Mill office even existed. Loni won't believe anyone could have found that basement when only he and Henry Hanson knew about it.

Distressed, MacPherson replied, "John, then you think something more dramatic has to be done to get D'Annelli's attention?"

Bailey just sat there playing with his pipe, nodding his head up and down...and thinking. MacPherson knew he was right. Even Lawton and Davis allowed their heads to nod. Time was running out if D'Annelli's guilt was going to be proven before the raid.

"Unless....." Everyone again looked at John Bailey. He seemed distant as he spoke. "...there was a time in the Big War that my small battalion had to locate a main enemy supply depot. We located it in a scenic, wooded city called Bielefeld, about a hundred kilometers from Dusseldorf. Rumor was there was enough explosives stored in some buildings to blow up most of France."

MacPherson and Adam knew John had been overseas in the war. Adam was transfixed since his father rarely referred to his war time activities.

Adam coaxed him to say more. "So, Dad, what did you guys do?"

John was almost whispering. "There was a lot of wind....we set a fire...the German townspeople were desperately trying to put out the flames. They were concerned about the potential burning of their town, but many were quite aware of the explosives and ammunition being stored in their town. As the fire spread, the German soldiers were ordered, as we expected, not to let that fire get near certain buildings. From the woods with our binoculars, we could tell which buildings were being protected because the soldiers surrounded those structures and kept soaking the outside walls where the armaments were stored."

Adam was caught up in the story. "So what happened?"

John blinked and finished his coffee. "We came back a few days later and blew up those buildings one by one at night. That was it."

John's face showed embarrassment, like he hadn't meant to share anything about that time in his life.

Charlie reacted with some wit. "So John, what's the point of your story. Do you want us to arrange a bomb run on the Feed & Grain Mill and blow those elevators to kingdom come?"

There were some short spurts of laughter except from John. He was dead serious. Gradually the point of John's war story became clear to MacPherson and Lawton. They'd seen a dry grassy area between the fairgrounds and the Mill. It didn't take much to visualize John's idea.

Lawton said to John. "I think your suggesting a small grass fire could be set in that grassy area northwest of the Mill. The smoke from that field will get everyone's attention in town...including, if I understand your point, certain folks looking across the lake from Chippewa Lodge. If the smoke from that fire can get Loni's attention, he's got too much to lose to ignore the possible disaster approaching the Feed & Grain Mill. The hope would be that the volunteer fire department and the townsfolk will rush out to the fire and get the ground blaze under control before it touches the Feed & Grain Mill... but not before D'Annelli rushes into town. Have I got your meaning?"

John nodded. "Damn certain got the attention of some local folks in Bielefeld, Germany."

There was a silence around that farmhouse kitchen for a couple seconds. Then heads started nodding...even Adam's head.

Bailey was not done. His steady voice had a tone that gave confidence to each person in that house...as if his wartime experience was naturally putting him in charge. MacPherson seemed relieved to give him the floor.

He looked at MacPherson as he spoke. "With Adam, Jamie, and Charlie at the Lodge, I'll position myself with you near the Mill. Lindy, you'll be the one to start a small grassfire by the fairgrounds, the wind typically off the lake should blow toward the Mill. The smoke should erupt quickly and make the scene look worse than it actually will be. The real concern will be the velocity of the wind. I'll contact the volunteer fire department in time to put the fire out before it spreads to the Mill. We certainly don't want to burn down the whole damn town! It would help if you three out at the Lodge might keep your eyes peeled across the lake for the smoke cloud. Somehow Loni needs to understand the seriousness of the fire and the consequences if the flames reach the Mill. If he ignores the threat, Lindy doesn't have much of a case against him."

MacPherson was suddenly intense and exhilarated. It was the kind of idea and assistance she needed to have any chance of arresting the right people. Her response showed impatience and a readiness to proceed. "It's the best idea we've got and it keeps you guys from being seen with me. I'll call my contacts and have the state patrol ready to raid the resort yet this morning. I'll time it so they'll not make any moves on the Lodge or in town until D'Annelli is given the chance to see the fire and shows up at the Mill. That'll be my proof. Then I can signal for the raid to begin."

It was agreed that 9:30 would be the time the fire in the field would be ignited. It would coordinate with D'Annelli in the Lodge restaurant going over that day's rules with the players. That room offered a huge picture window view of the lake and the distant sight of the grain elevators at the Mill.

With nothing more to be said, the five of them readied themselves for what seemed like a simple, straight-forward attempt at deceiving D'Annelli. It would be the last chance to scheme against the Chicago gangster. If he took the bait, imprisonment was guaranteed. If not, his lawyers would likely get him absolved of any possible charges. The raid would not be a bust, but the kingpin of the Chippewa Lodge affair would probably escape prosecution.

John Bailey still remained deep in thought...something each of them took notice. Standing out by his old Plymouth truck, he asked his other four compatriots, "What about Henry? We can't forget about his safety. Adam and I looked for him last night. He was no where to be found...not at his house or at the festival. I know it doesn't look good for him with the money in the Mill and all, but Henry's no more a crook than I am. I believe if we could find him, he'd be more in favor of bringing down D'Annelli than you might think. He knows the town has gained a lot, but it's come at a price. I believe that was why he was so open with Charlie yesterday afternoon."

MacPherson couldn't say much at that moment, but made a commitment she hoped she could keep. "John, I'll just do my best to keep Henry's name clean. He's been under a lot of strain and in a tough situation...and he's done it for the good of the town. I'll protect him in any way I can whether we land Loni D'Annelli or not."

It was 7:30 when they left the farm. The sky was clear, but the wind across the glimmering Lake Minnewaska had already reached good sailing conditions. Davis, Adam Bailey, and Lawton charged out of the farm in Charlie's roadster heading in the direction of Chippewa Lodge. That strong breeze made all three slightly edgy regarding the impending fire.

Adam blurted out the obvious. "My God! I hope my Dad and Lindy know what they're doing. That's a hell of a wind to be starting a fire so close to the Mill."

Davis and Lawton didn't have to say anything. Their heads nodded as a gust of wind caught the jalopy as they descended the eastern bluff into Glenwood.

At that early Sunday hour, the town was especially peaceful. The townsfolk were getting a slow start to the day after a raucous final evening festival at City Park. The First Presbyterian Church looked positively palatial with the beautiful pillars in front. The sidewalks as well the curb and gutter looked clean stretching all the way to the main intersection. The money it took to pay for these types of civic improvements had come as a result of the town's involvement with Loni D'Annelli and his group.

Turning left at the main intersection, they headed along the lake shore appreciating the vast beauty of the greenish-blue lake. They trusted that same vista would be as gorgeous the next day.

Less than ten minutes later, they arrived at the front gate of the resort and were greeted by the gruff looking guards in the long coats. Davis and Lawton felt their throats get dry...but not Adam. He called them by name as he wished them 'good morning'. Then he informed them he was bringing in one of the players and his caddy. The guards weren't about to doubt him. They knew the kid was special to D'Annelli.

The two guards actually grinned at him as they waved Davis' roadster through the gates. Adam played his role well as he returned the wave. His smile disappeared immediately once the roadster was through the entrance. Lawton and Davis were well aware the morning would be tough on the young man as well. His experiences at Chippewa Lodge with the funniest, craziest, and most morally wrong fellows he would ever meet again would abruptly be coming to an end. In the coming years he would recall those summers of his high school years and a smile would form on his mouth. Seconds later that smile would fade as he would remember how quickly that memory had concluded just two weeks after graduating from high school.

Davis parked the roadster by the tennis courts at the edge of the resort with hopes of giving them a possible easier exit. He grabbed Lawton's golf clubs as if he was really going to tote the bag. Then they dragged themselves to the practice range while Adam went into the restaurant to locate Loni D'Annelli. There was not much talk among them once they parked the roadster. They all had a role that morning, but were more transfixed on how that morning would work out.

Some of the players were already warming up on the practice range. Lawton had none of that dedication. His energy was quite the opposite from the previous morning. He no longer was seeking attention. Davis was even worse as he plopped down by a nearby tree and pulled his golf hat over his eyes. As for Lawton, he had to give his warm up shots some effort to show his fellow competitors he was ready for the last day of the tournament. It was not easy. His head ached from little sleep and the anticipation of what was about to happen very soon that morning.

He looked over at Davis and muttered, "Chas, my swing feels loose...too loose. I couldn't beat the worst golfer out here today."

A good caddy would normally build up his player. Davis made no attempt. Instead he languidly moaned, "What do you say we put the clubs back in the roadster and have some breakfast. That's about the only thing I'm qualified to do on a couple hours of sleep...and you don't look qualified for much better."

Staggering to the restaurant, they positioned themselves near the picture window overlooking Lake Minnewaska where they could gaze across the lake. From their table they could see the far away elevator silos of the Feed & Grain Mill protruding above the rest of the town. It was less than an hour before the fire would be set.

Lawton now had plenty of time to stroll through the restaurant in order to be seen by most players. Most of them looked in poor condition after what had to be a Saturday night of hot women and cold booze. Still, no player let Lawton walk by without reminding him they wanted a wager on that day's play. He gave them a dutiful wave and spurious smile while swearing at them behind his teeth as he continued his walk through the Lodge. That day's event was fixed against him and the greedy bastards were out to reclaim their lost money from the previous day.

Finally Lawton sat down and watched as more players slowly wandered into the restaurant. Some had girls hanging on them. To a man these fellows looked like they were in the same decrepit condition as Lawton and Davis. It caused Davis to lean over toward Lawton and remark, "Jamie, as tired as you are, you could still clean these guys' wallets if you did have to play today. I swear some of them are going to need transfusions to make it through the day. If a couple of them open their eyes, they'll bleed to death."

About fifteen minutes later Loni D'Annelli strolled into the restaurant with his entourage of friends, associates, and sycophants. His caddy, Adam Bailey, trailed behind looking a bit forlorn, but faking the best smile he could muster.

Breakfast was quieter and more leisurely that morning given the fatigued condition of the golfers. D'Annelli didn't have the same look of affection for Lawton as he did at the end of the previous afternoon. That day was gone. D'Annelli knew Lawton was going to lose on Sunday...and lose big time.

As the time grew closer to 9:30, Lawton, Davis and even Adam turned their heads more and more toward the picture window. Seeing the two tall elevators on the Mill property standing far across the lake on such a clear, windy day, they knew the fire MacPherson and John Bailey were shortly going to create would be eye-catching enough to provoke some legitimate concern from that restaurant.

Adam, sitting next to the joking and bigger than life D'Annelli, picked at an egg and bacon placed in front of him. He continually got up and wandered by the large restaurant picture window as if enjoying the beauty of Lake Minnewaska. Obviously upset and not really realizing how his mood was affecting his behavior, his disposition began to make Lawton and Davis nervous. Finally Davis sauntered over to the young man as he stood by the window and whispered something sharp that got Adam's attention. Acknowledging the comment, he immediately replaced his grimace with a grin and quietly moved away from the window. He'd taken the hint. Still, he glanced momentarily at Lawton shrugging his shoulders ever so lightly as if asking the same silent question all three of them wondered. "When is this fire going to be struck?"

As for D'Annelli, he was sitting at his table like a king on his throne amidst loud joking, playful, and sarcastic comments from his friends and fellow players. With the bonanza he'd received the previous day in winning, he was enjoying the good-natured ribbing. Three waitresses brought his warm breakfast. He went after the eggs, sausage, ham, and toast like he hadn't seen food that month.

From their corner table, Davis leaned over to Lawton and joked, "It's like he's enjoying his last meal. He must know something!"

Of course he didn't. It was just his normal manner of eating.

D'Annelli then looked around until he found his caddy, Adam. His eyes showed concern. "Adam, my boy, eat up. We got a long day. You need to keep up your strength."

Adam gave him that same devoted smile with not quite the enthusiasm. But he sat down in his customary chair next to the big man and dug into his breakfast. D'Annelli patted the young man affectionately on the shoulder. The image didn't get lost by Lawton or Davis. The mobster always seemed to be looking out for the young man, as if they were related by blood. Adam would be the closest thing to a son the Chicago mobster would likely ever have…at least the kind of son he would want. Once D'Annelli saw Adam plowing the food down, he was satisfied the young man was content. Then he turned and began joking again with his cadre of hucksters.

More players streamed in for the player's breakfast with only ten minutes remaining before D'Annelli would stand up and announce the two-man teams, the competitive format for the day, and the tee times for each group.

Still there was no smoke seen on the horizon across Lake Minnewaska.

As for Lawton, he began accepting bets from every player...writing them down just as he had the day before. It was so obvious no one wanted to miss out on a sure thing. The bets were anywhere from $1000 to $2500 for the total two-man team score as well as wagers on his individual score against other individual opponents. If the tournament was actually going to be played, Lawton would not have anywhere near the money required to cover his bets even if he had retained all his winnings from the previous day. He'd already heard his new partner was Jake 'The Knife' Bellini...and that this greasy gangster still had his head in the toilet from his excursions the night before. For this man to even stand up and hold a golf club would be remarkable. It didn't matter. Bellini was being paid to throw his portion of the match. With that as his only responsibility on Sunday, he had no reason not to have gotten completely plastered.

Lawton and Davis kept rolling their eyes with each bet. They just couldn't get over these hoods would actually believe Lawton could not be aware that the team competition was fixed against him.

When Danny Amato strolled by with a look in his eye that could melt steel, he growled, "Yesterday was only a loan, kid, only a loan. Hope you didn't spend your winnings yet. Count me in for $3000 on our team bet."

Vinnie Spagatini and Bert Bertinelli didn't even say 'good morning'. They both just retorted, "$2000 on the eighteen hole two-man team score...another grand on our individual scores." They didn't even give Lawton time to respond. The bet was final as far as they were concerned.

Then Lawton caught the glare from Willie LaCurso sitting across the restaurant floor. He gazed squarely at Lawton holding up two fingers apparently indicating the same $2000 bet that Spagatini and Bertinelli had just unilaterally made. Lawton gave a slight nod in acceptance and the St. Paul gangster gave him a sinister grin in reply. The coolness of the gangster's sneer could be felt even from that distance.

Then Big Julie Tagliossa and his buxomed wife, Tess, entered the restaurant looking like the oddest couple since Lincoln and Mary Todd. He gave Lawton no nod or welcome, but Tess strolled by with her overly made-up face flashing a teasing grin. She was playfully shaking a finger at Lawton formulating the silent words on her lips, "You naughty boy."

Lawton sheepishly waved back hoping Big Julie wouldn't see her subtle little act. Davis just rolled his eyes and whispered, "Jamie, as far as she's concerned, you're on your own."

When the wagering was finally completed, Lawton ended up agreeing to well over $40,000 in wagers. Many of the bets were individual bets that he actually had a reasonable chance of winning. However, even then, if the tournament was to be played and Lawton had to participate, he'd be doomed with the guarantee that all his team bets would be losses. It made him anxious enough that he began peeking over at the huge picture window every ten seconds.

It was 9:25 when Loni stood up after eating enough food to satisfy a small village. The large man lumbered around the restaurant intending on completing some bets of his own before speaking to the group. All the while the eyes of Lawton, Davis, and Adam switched from Loni to the picture window...back and forth...back and forth.

When the clock approached 9:30 there was still no indication of smoke from across the lake. Davis leaned back and said in a voice only Lawton could hear, "Anytime now Lindy....any time!"

Stopping next to Lawton, D'Annelli retorted, "Well, kid, it ain't going to be as easy for you today. I'm afraid we aren't teamed up. You'll have only one guy as your partner today. The drawing has already been done so you've got yourself a mate. I'll announce the teams shortly. Your new partner will either be your buddy by the end of the day....or he'll want to kill you."

D'Annelli let go with a huge guffaw as Davis and Lawton lost their coloring. It was an intended joke, but the truth was more within range of reality than was comfortable. Showing his true colors, D'Annelli declared a $2000 team bet with Lawton and his partner.

Finally just minutes after 9:30 Loni D'Annelli stood before his 'guests' to introduce the two-man teams and clarify the rules of that day's competition. He lit a big stogie, farted, and yelled for everyone to shut up. Adam got up from the table and gradually moved over toward the restaurant picture window. His look was one of anxiety. Lawton and Davis didn't need his slight shake of the head to know he was seeing no smoke as yet.

The room silenced as Loni passed out the listings sheet with the two-man teams and their tee-off times. As he covered the format for that day's event, Lawton gazed down the list and saw the name of his teammate. Though only nicknames were used on the printed partner sheet, seeing 'The Knife' by his name meant that his partner was indeed the notorious Jake Bellini. Jake worked for Vinnie Spagatini and tried to cover the scars on his face with whiskers. His pockmarks were so rough, he had little choice but to use a scissors versus a razor to shave. Lawton was surprised he had someone of Bellini's caliber as his partner. He witnessed the man playing on Saturday. He had a decent game. Interestingly, the only player not in the restaurant that morning was Bellini adding truth to the hearsay that 'The Knife' might need help navigating himself around the golf course.

Lawton's stomach was beginning to knot up as Adam again looked at him and then at Charlie while slowly shaking his head. It was still all clear across the lake.

Davis had become so fidgety he finally had to stand and move toward the back of the restaurant. Whether the fire was going to be lit or not, the state patrol was also waiting down the road for the signal to start the raid. He wanted to be in position to escape the dragnet.

Lawton remained seated trying to look composed while unconsciously looking at his watch every fifteen seconds. He kept going over in his mind what could be going wrong. The fire should have been started ten minutes before. A cloud of smoke should already be covering the Mill. John Bailey should have already alerted the volunteer fire department.

But so far...no fire...no smoke...no nothing.

Now it was Davis who'd become so preoccupied with the vision out the big picture window. Lawton gave his friend the big-eyed look hinting to stay away from the picture window.

There was then a chorus of laughter as D'Annelli made some crass comment about a waitress who passed in front of him. Lawton faked a wide smile. He had no idea what had been said.

Now troubled, all three conspirators looked at each other sensing that something had gone seriously wrong. D'Annelli was finishing his comments. Seconds later the players would be filing out of the restaurant to get ready for their tee-times. If the grassfire west of the Mill didn't materialize in the next five minutes, the advantage of pointing out the fire to D'Annelli and creating some sort of panic would be lost. The restaurant picture window offered a perfect screen to witness the blaze. Everyone would crowd around the window. That scene would add to the sense of disaster and alarm...and maybe enlarge D'Annelli's own concern.

But, that opportunity looked more likely it would be missed. It was more evident that the only thing the three of them would have to deal with was dodging the incipient police raid. In itself, that would be very challenging, but not impossible. They'd worked out a plan to escape. But, for what the result that morning could have been regarding D'Annelli, the disappointment on the faces of Lawton, Davis, and even Adam Bailey was beginning to show.

The breeze was more evident than preferred that Sunday morning as MacPherson readied herself to start what she hoped would be a controllable grass fire by the county fairgrounds. Located just a few hundreds yards west of the Feed & Grain Mill, the inspiration of the fire causing a smoke cloud seemed less dangerous to the grain-filled and highly flammable storage elevators at the Mill.

Before positioning herself at the fairgrounds, she had again phoned Ernest Lundquist to give him the more specific timing for the raid. As he had promised, he was waiting patiently by his telephone in Minneapolis for her call. They wasted little time talking. Immediately he then alerted the state patrol and a small group of agents from the Bureau of Investigation who also were standing unseen a few miles outside of Glenwood.

MacPherson also made direct contact that morning with her Uncle Ralph, the Baltrami County Sheriff in Bemidji, who had driven down to Sauk Centre, just east of Glenwood to await word of her final plans. It was his responsibility to keep the state patrol from jumping the 9:30 gun as they remained hidden a mile down the lake shore road from Chippewa Lodge. Everything was in place well before 9:30.

She scanned across the grass field staying low to the ground from her position at the county fairgrounds until she spotted John Bailey. He was barely discernable across the street from the Mill camouflaging himself amongst some overhanging dogwoods. She gave a slight wave and he returned it. The public telephone to alert the voluntary fire department was but a few feet away next to a gasoline station.

As Bailey stood waiting for MacPherson to strike the match, he was becoming more agitated. It had been his suggestion to arrange the fire and now the wind was blowing at a frightening velocity. He thought back to almost fourteen years before when he and his troops had started that strategic fire on the outskirts of Bielefeld, Germany. Then they hadn't cared if that city burned to the ground. This intentional fire was quite different. It was his town this time.

With each passing minute and the increased wind, the fairgrounds and her location next to the grassy field suddenly didn't look as far from the Mill. If the fire reached the Mill elevators, the entire complex with the dry grain would flame up like a torch. It would do untold damage to the evidence below the Mill office floor. Worse yet, the town buildings loomed just beyond the Mill to say nothing about the danger with the gasoline station where John Bailey was standing.

MacPherson looked at her watch. It was five minutes beyond the time she planned to have the fire in full volume crossing the field. She had to make a decision. If the fire would be too calamitous then she may as well call and let the state patrol commence their raid.

It was John Bailey who helped her make that decision. He suddenly stood away from the bushes where he was concealing himself and raised his hand toward her. He was giving her the 'O.K.' sign with his finger and thumb together. It made her smile. Though understanding her concerns, he was expressing confidence in her and signaling that she should proceed. It was the boost of self-assurance she needed.

She lit the match and threw it on some dry straw she had found to supplement the fire. The straw exploded into a nice flame. As it touched the dry grass, a grayish white smoke began billowing into the crisp clear air. It was now out of her hands and the responsibility of John Bailey. She could only assume he was already contacting the fire department. The smoke had already obliterated her view of him.

With that part of her task completed, MacPherson had to intercept the state patrol as it entered town from the opposite side of town. Racing across the north side of the fairgrounds, she leaped a fence and took a semi-circular route up to the back door of the Feed & Grain Mill office. She was surprised how already thick the smoke had become as it blew past the office window. She gazed through the back door window and saw everything was just as she, Lawton, and Davis had left it hours before...the desk pushed against the wall, the rug thrown over in the corner and the trapdoor opened to the basement. Everything was set up for D'Annelli's possible entrance. She now had to depend on her three comrades out at the Lodge to point out the fire and stir up the emotion in D'Annelli about the potential damage to the Mill.

With the trap set, she retreated a few blocks north of the main intersection and then circled around to the front of the Glenwood Café.

From there she could intercept the state patrol to keep them in check while they waited for Loni D'Annelli to possibly take the bait. It was a ten-minute drive into town from the Lodge. She was hoping D'Annelli might do it faster.

Like clockwork she then heard the town fire alarm. John had made the call. The volunteers would be arriving shortly. She gulped watching the smoke get thicker as it spread across the grass field. It was even beginning to blow past the Mill to her location causing her to cough. She closed her eyes hoping she wouldn't have to witness the two Mill elevators flaming up like two candles. Across the street the gasoline station and a small sewing and gift shop sat vulnerable to a runaway fire. She could visualize the tanks at the gasoline station exploding and causing the flames to spread further into town.

MacPherson started wondering where the town fire department was. She kept wiping her eyes with her sleeve anticipating the vision of one fancy car speeding into town from Chippewa Lodge.

Finally one of the fire trucks raced down the street to the Mill. Then another followed driving past the Mill to the grassy field where the firemen immediately began their work. Her heart began to sink. There was no sign of anyone from the Lodge, not even one of D'Annelli's men rushing toward the Mill. Adding to her disappointment, she now saw three state police vehicles moving slowly down the street from the east side of town toward the main intersection just blocks from the Mill and City Park. They were following instructions but reluctant to hold their ground too long. There was public safety at stake.

She ran back up the street toward the officers to intercept them. There was still time. They needed to wait. She called for the officer in charge and he was in front of her in seconds. She shouted, "I'm Lindy MacPherson with the U.S. Attorney's office. I'm the one who set up this raid. The fire department is on the scene. Stay back. Just give me a couple more minutes before you approach the Mill. It's imperative you stay out of sight until I give you the signal to move in. Once I give you a wave, radio your people assigned outside Chippewa Lodge to begin their raid. Can you do that for me?"

The officer in charge, J.D. Smoltz, a Captain in the state patrol, knew exactly what she was trying to accomplish from the conversation he'd had with MacPherson's Uncle Ralph that morning. Smoltz and Sheriff MacPherson from Bemidji had often hunted together up near Leech Lake. Ralph had described her as an attractive blondish gal who'd been undercover the previous two weeks in Glenwood. Smoltz gave MacPherson the once over noticing the mussed strawberry blond hair and the blackened streaks of perspiration smudged on her face.

He could hardly believe she was the one behind this curious operation. She also looked so young. But, he gave her the benefit of the doubt.

The Captain then returned to his patrol car to contact Sheriff MacPherson who was waiting impatiently and under cover less than a half mile from the resort entrance. Sheriff MacPherson assured Smoltz the raid would not begin until the Captain called with the go-ahead from his niece. Hearing the word 'niece' at first threw Smoltz. Then he figured if the intense, grimy young lady was kin to his friend on the other end of the line, she was of good stock.

Scurrying back down the street toward the Mill, MacPherson felt she was losing her mind. Her ploy to bring D'Annelli into town not only was failing, but was now endangering the Mill and other town buildings. The case against D'Annelli would have to ride on the merits of the proof she had so far. While it would end the lawlessness out at the Lodge, there simply would not be enough evidence to convict D'Annelli. She'd done everything she could, but it had not been enough. While the day would be proclaimed a success by her office and other law enforcement groups, she would always be disappointed that the Chicago mobster would walk free.

She stood at the main intersection by the Glenwood Café as more and more locals trotted past her toward the excitement of the fire. Captain Smoltz was holding his hands out in front of him appealing for her signal. She couldn't bring her hand up just yet. She could sense what was going to happen next and it disgusted her. The authorities would confiscate the cash and the other valuables in that storage area. In a short time a mob lawyer from Chicago would lodge a claim to recover the money. The attorney would claim to be representing a number of organizations and people who were innocently storing their private funds and personal treasures with Henry Hanson within his Feed & Grain Mill storage basement.

The attorney would not mention his clients by name; however he would have a detailed account of what was stored in that Mill basement less any knowledge of the purported counterfeit money. The attorney would suggest Henry Hanson should have to explain that part of the findings. Loni D'Annelli's name would of course not be part of any claim for the money or material items. Henry Hanson would be given the 'credit' for offering the Mill basement as the safest place anywhere in town, including the two local banks, to store all this cash and personal belongings. He would come off looking like a dolt.

All those organizations and people making claims would be under the auspices of Loni D'Annelli. The real money and the valuables would eventually flow from that attorney back into the clutches of Loni D'Annelli. MacPherson felt her teeth grinding in furor.

As the firemen worked feverishly on the grassy field and by the Mill, she had one more emotion...that of guilt. In her blind quest to lock up a big-time Chicago hood, she was risking the burning down of the west side of Glenwood. Besides that, she was playing with the lives of four men who had done nothing but support her in her quest.

She could only hope Lawton, Davis, and Adam Bailey had figured some way to dodge the imminent raid. As for John Bailey, she was relieved to see that he'd already slipped away unnoticed. Her hope was that he was already back at his farm safely doing his daily farm chores.

She leaned against the outside wall of the cafe downcast as she watched the firemen get control of the fire. They were letting it burn its way out. There was only one section that still endangered the grain elevators, but even that looked like the firemen were winning.

That brought to mind what would be the unfortunate situation for Henry Hanson. He'd be arrested and interrogated by both the state patrol and the Bureau of Investigation about his role in hiding money and valuables in the basement of the Mill that he managed. He'd be in the untenable position of facing charges and staying mum...or facing D'Annelli and his boys if he consented to talk to the authorities.

Her frustration level had reached its peak. Life wasn't fair, but this was particularly unjust to a person like Hanson.

As more local citizens were heading in the direction of the fire, she ruefully thought what better to see the spectacle of an inferno from hell only moments after a fire and brimstone sermon that Sunday morning. She looked back at Officer Smoltz up the main street on East Hwy. #28 a few blocks from the main intersection. He was waiting for her signal, but all the while moving his six patrol cars ever closer to the scene of the fire. His impatience was palpable. She could sense he was going to move forward with or without her signal in the next couple minutes.

Finally, the sigh she gave was almost audible above the wind and sirens. There was no more reason to wait out at Chippewa Lodge. Waving to Smoltz, she gave the signal to radio the law enforcement group to commence the raid at the resort.

She watched him make the call. The odds were good that D'Annelli might still be stuffing his face with eggs, sausage and toast at the Lodge restaurant as the police arrived. She hoped he'd gag on the food.

It was hard for MacPherson to admit defeat. Captain Smoltz's small force of patrolmen was still waiting for her second signal so they could move forward towards the Mill. There were people to protect. They had an obligation to perform. She finally stepped out into the middle of the intersection by the Glenwood Café. All she had to do was turn and wave Smoltz forward.

She shook her head. The results could have been so much better.

Loni D'Annelli was having the time of his life that Sunday morning. When he stood before his throng of brothers in crime, the stupendous ovation was like a warm shower of praise. Rarely did his group enjoy such a private affair away from pesky police and nosy reporters. The secluded Chippewa Lodge had proven once again to be the hallmark of confidentiality with only curious and innocent bystanders showing up at the Lodge property to view a very unique charity golf tournament. While the event had become more public, it still enjoyed relative obscurity thanks to the ten-day Glenwood festival that had become the primary attraction...as he'd hoped.

That morning he had a feeling this day would prove to be the last time for the charity golf tournament at Chippewa Lodge...but certainly not the last tournament he organized. Next year he'd just find a different location. Rumors had been floating around Minnesota about the participants. That spelled potential investigations and trouble. He wanted to keep his business operation at the Lodge until the end of the year. Then he'd pull out and move to another similar secluded location, maybe closer to Chicago...like in the Waupaca area in central Wisconsin.

The good-natured shouting and laughter from the players at the Lodge restaurant was like music to D'Annelli's ears. It served as another endorsement for the positive image he'd built with his mob comrades back in Chicago. Many of them were sitting right there in the restaurant having relaxed and enjoying the week completely free from their own challenges back in their home city.

Like a pompous, rampaging Southern Baptist minister, he raised his arms and the restaurant turned to silence waiting for him to speak. Loni D'Annelli at that moment had reached the pinnacle of his career in crime.

As for Jamie Lawton and Charlie Davis, they were sickened by the entire scene. That feeling was only multiplied by the delay of the impending fire near the Mill. The holdup had now been long enough that Davis, Adam Bailey, and Lawton had to admit the fire would not be set and D'Annelli would be remaining right there at the Lodge. He'd be arrested along with others in his group, but with no proof of guilt, he'd be set free yet that afternoon.

The three of them nodded at each other to begin moving for the nearest exit to escape the looming raid. The noisy visit from the state patrol could begin at any moment.

Davis meandered over toward the front entrance as D'Annelli began announcing the two-man teams that day as well as the tee-times. Lawton kept his seat but nodded to Adam to begin shifting toward a back exit. The three of them had agreed they would leave separately but eventually head through the trees to the #4 tee-box far enough from the restaurant that the raid would not locate them. They planned on simply playing golf on those golf holes away from the main buildings of the resort until things had calmed down on the resort property.

As the boisterous and profane D'Annelli continued bantering with his audience while he communicated the rules of that day's competition, Lawton got up and strolled toward a side door exit. He assumed Adam had already moved from the picture window.

Not seeing Adam, he looked back to see the young man unexplainably riveted to the large picture window...as if in a trance. Something was happening. Lawton's heart began to beat more rapidly. It was Adam who was supposed to shout if he saw any smoke across the lake. However, he was not saying anything loud or otherwise; he was just staring, his finger pointing urgently out the picture window.

It was then that all hell broke loose. Adam suddenly began wildly motioning with his arm. Whitey Malooley noticed Adam's bizarre behavior. He'd known the kid for a long time and never had he seen this type of emotion from the well-mannered young man. Malooley quickly moved toward the window. His sun-tanned face seemed to pale. He nodded urgently at Billie McCoy to join him at the picture window. McCoy's face froze when he arrived.

Charlie Davis stopped his exit and moved back along the perimeter of the restaurant toward another window that gave him a vision of Lake Minnewaska. As for D'Annelli, he was yet in his own glory not noticing any peculiarities. He just kept on talking and joking with his room full of mob brethren.

Davis looked through the window and then immediately at Lawton. The two of them had often communicated non-verbally. This was one of those times. Charlie simply gave one nod. Lawton then knew...finally...the fire had been started and the 'sting' was on.

He too moved toward the picture window...and there it was...a huge, dark, ugly cloud of smoke appeared to be engulfing the Feed & Grain Mill. Adam was wide-eyed and silent. He appeared not to be acting in the least. Malooley and McCoy didn't know what to do... whether to assume the fire was being handled...or interrupt the boss.

Lawton and Davis maintained cool heads. The time had come to 'sell' what might be happening in town.

D'Annelli was still laughing at one of his quips when he noticed the waving arm of his caddy. His smile began to fade. He too had never seen Adam Bailey behave in that way. D'Annelli moved quickly across the room to the window as the entire crowd quieted. When D'Annelli was presented with the picture of the huge cloud of smoke, his respiration was interrupted and his eyes seemed to glaze over. An apparent fire in town was the last thing he expected.

It was then Adam yelled, "Holy shit! That fire is right by the Mill. Those two elevators full of grain will blow up like bombs if the fire reaches them."

D'Annelli digested Adam's emotional outburst in seconds. He stared intently across the lake not wanting to accept what he was seeing. At that moment the blowing smoke made the two Mill elevators totally disappear. Though flushed with too much food and drink, his face drained of color.

Adam then added fuel to the fire. He shouted, "Jesus H. Christ! That Mill is made of wood! The whole place will be ashes in a half hour!"

Those were the words that made the mobster's eyes bug out of their sockets. Where the young man was slow to get into his role, he'd made up for the delay with an award winning performance in front of D'Annelli.

D'Annelli didn't wait another second. He and his two associates, Malooley and McCoy, ran from the restaurant. Seconds later they were peeling down the lake side road in Loni's Cadillac...the tires barely making contact with the ground. Some of the players decided to follow in their own late model vehicles just to see the spectacle. The tournament was obviously going to be delayed. What they couldn't understand was why D'Annelli was reacting so panic-stricken to a simple Feed & Grain Mill fire.

While the rest of the players milled around in the restaurant to await D'Annelli's return, Davis left the restaurant and began his own small bit of chicanery. With the looming raid and to discourage potential escapees, his small jack knife provided just the required instrument. Marching by the cabins close to the Lodge, he casually stuck holes in tires of every fancy car he saw. Davis then pocketed his small penknife and nonchalantly walked over to his roadster, grabbed his golf clubs and promptly marched toward the agreed upon meeting place with Lawton and young Adam... the #4 tee-box out on the golf course.

While Davis had been completing his small assistance to the police, Lawton and Adam remained in the restaurant to maintain their own visibility and image of innocence. They re-filled their coffee cups and continued making small talk with the remaining players, girl friends, 'nieces', and a few wives. Like others, they were drawn to the big picture window behaving surprised but blasé like the others.

In reality their stomachs were churning. From their distant perspective, there was reason to believe the plan was working to entice D'Annelli to barrel into town. The new predicament was that the blaze might just take down the town in the process.

Still, Adam and Jamie's now primary aim was to get out of that restaurant before the police raid ensued. They had just moments to high-tail it out onto the golf course toward the #4 tee box before all hell would break loose.

Big Julie Tagliossa and his entourage including wife, Tess, hadn't moved a muscle when D'Annelli had rushed away. It was none of their concern. While moving toward an exit, Lawton decided to establish one more image of himself at the restaurant at that exact time. He stopped by the table to solidify his bet with Big Julie as if they were actually going to play the round of golf that day. Tagliossa had difficulty holding back his enthusiasm about the 'sure-thing' bet he'd made earlier with Lawton. Knowing that Lawton's partner, 'The Knife', was going to take a dive that day, Big Julie was unusually nice. He said to Lawton, "So...Trick-shot...you had quite a take yesterday. How about we triple our little bet today?"

It was easy for Lawton to nod his head and even kid the gangster. "Sure Julie, you just pick the figure you want to lose today."

Tagliossa and his boys looked at each other like they'd just robbed a bank and the bank's alarm didn't work. With Lawton's ignorant jibe, they couldn't even feign seriousness. Seven hoods and Big Julie's wife all broke up in mirth so uncontrolled the large man almost choked and Tess almost lost her top. Lawton knew he had the last laugh as the Tagliossa group would remember Lawton's presence still making bets as the fire burned in Glenwood.

Adam caught Lawton's eye from across the restaurant. He looked desperate. Both knew it was past the time to have exited the restaurant. With a nod from Lawton, Adam inched toward one exit as Lawton headed for the Lodge lobby...but not too speedily.

Strolling by Spagatini and Bertinelli, Lawton couldn't resist making one final image. He said to the two conmen, "Hey...I'm going out to hit some practice balls. Send someone for me when they all get back. I wouldn't want to be late for my tee-time."

Vinnie Spagatini responded with a big smile. "Yeh, Trick-shot, you do that. Go hit some practice balls. I'm sure it'll help."

Spagatini, Bertinelli, and their friends at the table then broke out into unbridled laughter of their own. Lawton walked out the restaurant door pretending not to understand their hilarity. Once free of the lobby, Lawton's gait turned into a trot. He swore he could hear the rumbling of a herd of vehicles approaching the Lodge property.

He immediately saw Adam standing over by a tree with Lawton's golf clubs over his shoulder. They nodded again at each other, but walked in the opposite direction. Two minutes later they both emerged from separate groves of trees and met on the third fairway on their way to the #4 tee box to join Charlie Davis.

They were quiet as they strode along as if enjoying the serenity of the early morning on the golf course. The dew glanced off their shoes as they marched ahead. Besides the chirping birds and the squirrels rustling in the woods, there was only one other very unmistakable but obvious sound they began to hear. It was the low hum of those approaching motors …like an entire army of vehicles…as they pounced on Chippewa Lodge.

Lawton looked at Adam and commented, "You remember reading about Lot's wife in the bible?"

Adam smirked and nodded his head. He said quietly, "Let's not look back." Neither of them did.

Arriving at the fourth tee box, Charlie Davis was whittling a piece of wood while sitting on his golf bag to keep his pants dry.

"Hello, gents," he said, "Care if I play along?"

They all silently but contentedly hit their tee shots with Adam using Lawton's clubs. They'd chosen that particular hole because it headed away from the main buildings of the resort. Playing golf was the last thing on their minds, but the best place for them at that moment. In the distance they could see the dark, billowy clouds of smoke still blowing over the town of Glenwood. Lawton didn't say it, but it reminded him of hell…as if a statement from above was being communicated to the many townsfolk for allowing obvious crooks and mobsters to operate right under their noses for so many years.

'Then again,' he thought, 'who am I to judge when it came to bearing the hard life in a 1930's farming community. Who's to say anyone might ignore certain improprieties for the good of the town.'

As they continued playing the next couple holes, none of them were playing very well. Adam's face showed strain. By day's end he would experience the demise of the four-year annual charity golf tournament he'd caddied in since age fourteen. The ten-day annual Glenwood festival that fed off the charity tournament and was supported by Loni D'Annelli would unceremoniously end that Sunday morning. Most of all, there were fellows he'd grown to like during his summers at that resort. Now he'd likely never see any of them again. Adam had deduced a long time ago that many of these 'guests' were people who lived life on the wrong side of the law. But, he didn't see that side of them when they were living and golfing at Chippewa Lodge.

And the one man who treated him so well...Loni D'Annelli...would assure Adam how he'd always carry a positive memory of his high school summers. He had a hard time allowing himself to accept that Loni was a gangster. He saw D'Annelli only as a Good Samaritan to the town and tremendously generous to him.

The two of them held a special bond. D'Annelli was the one man besides Adam's father who'd ask him about his grades in school, his successes in high school sports, his dreams of attending the University...and above all Adam's future goals and interests. He'd tell Adam about some of the mugs that came to the Lodge. He wasn't very complimentary. And he'd remind Adam again and again that he could enjoy the company of the 'guests' at the Lodge, but never to become one of those types of people. Loni D'Annelli, interestingly, never saw himself as one of those bums. He saw himself as a businessman and a supporter of the union movement in Chicago...and of course the benevolent soul who helped raise the prosperity of the town of Glenwood.

As Adam strolled alone down that 5th fairway he contemplated how he knew that very summer of 1931 would end his time at the resort and the interaction with some of these strange but hilarious men... including Loni D'Annelli. He was going onto college in the Twin Cities. Different paths would be followed and those bonds would disappear. He had banked on the fact that over the summer and into the fall he'd gradually say farewell to his life at Chippewa Lodge. That would now not be the case. The end was happening that day...that very hour. His life at the resort had come to an abrupt finish.

As the three of them stood on the 6th tee box, Charlie gave his ball a whack and watched it sail towards the woods on the right. He swore at the mishit as if the shot was a surprise. In all the years Lawton had known Charlie, he'd never seen him hit the ball left. Despite his mind on everything else but golf, Lawton cracked sardonically, "Gee, Chas, a slice! What a surprise."

Charlie directed a choice piece of profanity back at Lawton and then stepped aside to watch Adam take his turn. No matter what was going on in their lives, when Davis and Lawton competed on the golf course, ribbing each other was customary. That morning was no exception...despite all that was going on at Chippewa Lodge and in town at that moment.

Adam, playing with Lawton's clubs, aimlessly launched an impressive drive down the middle of the 6th fairway. Lawton then followed with a pulled hook that headed for the trees on the left.

Davis dead-panned, "I guess we're seeing an example of a one-day wonder. I think you're easy pickings today, Trick-Shot."

He then lit up a cigar and bounded off the tee box oblivious to anything else happening whether at the Lodge, in town, or anywhere else in the world. He looked at Lawton and jibed, "Buck a hole like normal, counselor, from this hole forward. I'll take a stroke on all holes but the par 3's."

It was Charlie's way of getting himself and his friend back into the fun of playing the game. Lawton's natural competitiveness responded. "The hell with you! You get only three strokes on nine holes like always."

Davis shot back, "Bullshit! I haven't played since last weekend. You played yesterday. You have the advantage. I need more strokes."

Lawton yelped back, "Davis, you crook. I'm so tired I can barely walk. You should be giving me strokes."

Adam Bailey walked behind the two friends not believing their good-natured bantering. It was a typical exchange of two golfers trying to get the edge over the other.

Adam figured that was the way it would always be.

The three of them went off in separate directions to find their tee shots. The quiet returned. All three of them still had a lot on their minds.

Once John Bailey saw that Lindy MacPherson had started the fire, he waited for the flames to pick up with the breeze before alerting the volunteer fire department. It didn't take long to decide. The wind built up the smoke and flames as if ordered to do so. Bailey hurriedly picked up the public telephone by City Park and waited for the operator. When she came on the line, his only words were "Send the fire department! There's a fire on the field west of the Feed & Grain Mill...Hurry!!'

It took just over a minute for the fire alarm in town to sound. The screeching siren was alerting all volunteers whether in bed, sitting in the pew of a church, or about to sneak off to go fishing instead. From his position adjacent to the gasoline station, Bailey watched as men down the block in suits and one man still in his bedclothes were on the run to the fire station.

Bailey was satisfied with the timing, but had become disturbed with the uncontrollable speed of the fire. The gusty wind was propelling the fire across the meadow like there'd been gasoline poured over the grass. The rain on Friday night and even the morning dew was not having no slow down effect. The large land area west of the Mill was like a meadow composed of dry straw.

He would recall the incident was like a tennis match....one way was the growing fire; the opposite way were the firemen congregating to fight it. So far it was no match. The fire was winning. Then the blaze began to spread wide to the back of the meadow. It looked like it was going to overtake a small building on the edge of the county fairgrounds, as the furor of the fire momentarily moved away from the Mill.

He gulped. Again he thought about Bielefeld, Germany. Thanks to the fire he and his men had started, they'd destroyed a major supply depot of German armaments. Allied lives were saved. That's what he wanted to believe. Considering he risked his life and those of his men....and then the medals they received for valor...it verified that others felt the same as he had.

Concentrating on the immediate blaze, this conflagration was altogether different. The inferno was moving too fast making it possible the Feed & Grain Mill elevators could become torches. With the wind, the fire could spread right up the street into downtown. Now he felt what it must have like to be one of those citizens of Bielefeld.

As one of the fire trucks rushed by Bailey heading toward the burning meadow, the vehicle disappeared into a dark cloud of smoke. John looked up and could barely see the two storage elevators. Another fire vehicle drove right up to the Mill and began watering down the outside walls of the office and the elevators. Some clumps of grassy fire flew across the street and landed in some bushes right next to where John was standing. He ran over and jumped on the fire until it was out. Other bystanders began doing the same thing down the street closer to the fire.

John didn't forget as part of the plan he was supposed to leave and not be part of the scene around the Mill. It got him thinking about Henry Hanson. He hadn't seen his friend since Friday and had come to realize Henry might have taken off on his usual post-festival vacation before the actual conclusion of the town celebration. He hoped that was the case. Hanson had left on Sunday the year before as well and had been gone for two weeks.

Rumbling through his mind, Bailey thought of Charlie Davis' description of Hanson...a man unstable and possibly intoxicated. He'd never heard his friend described that way. In the years they'd known each other he'd seen Hanson handle any number of challenges whether it was farmers upset about farm prices...locals concerned about the impact of the general economy...or more specifically the civic and church organizations vying for better advantages regarding the ten-day festival. Henry had been chairman of the event since its 1927 inception. He'd handled any number of disputes. Davis had made it sound like Hanson was cracking up. It didn't make sense.

Bailey decided to stop by Henry's home before returning to the farm. Someone had to inform Henry with what was happening that day. The man had to be ready to answer many questions...some of which could put him in ominous straights with the law. If ever there was a time Hanson might need a friend, the impending circumstances dictated it was now. After all, Hanson had been there when John and Adam were dealing with their own family tragedy a few years back.

Bailey hurried across Hwy. #28 down an alley equidistant between the Glenwood Café and the Mill to keep himself from being seen. He then hoofed another four blocks north until he arrived at Hanson's house.

His concern was immediate. Something was wrong. Henry's car was not parked under the rickety wooden car port in back of the house. It was gone. In fact, it looked like there had been no movement around the house that morning at all. Even the morning paper was still on the porch.

To be certain, Bailey went up to the front door and peered in. There was not a sound. He tried the door knob. It turned. The house was unlocked. He quietly walked in yelling out, "Henry, it's John. Are you home?"

There was no response. He shouted again. The same result. He continued wandering through the house trying to notice anything unusual. The bedroom at the end of the hall showed the bed had apparently not been slept in. Walking back to the kitchen, he noticed an envelope on the kitchen table. It was not sealed. John looked around as if someone might see him, and then pulled the contents out of the envelope. It was a letter of resignation addressed to the shareholders of the cooperative who owned the Feed & Grain Mill. It was dated the day before on Saturday, June 6, 1931 and signed by Hanson.

Bailey reread the first paragraph of the letter. It didn't make sense. Bailey and Hanson were close, but Henry never mentioned even once he was leaving town for good. He'd often left a day before the festival ended, but the letter indicated this time he was not going to return. Bailey felt a sudden deep, guttural emptiness.

He read the remainder of the note. Hanson explained he'd accepted another job offer out of state and that he would be taking on that task one month later after his overseas trip. There was no mention of his new location. His friend ended the note apologizing for being so poor with his 'farewells' and that with the conclusion of that year's festival, it seemed like a good time to leave. No forwarding address was given.

John shook his head. Henry had always said 'good-byes' were tough for him. His farewell letter fit his character and preference. Interestingly, Henry had mentioned nothing about Chippewa Lodge or did he reveal anything about any money stored in the Mill basement. There were no regrets...no statements of sorrow. To Bailey, Hanson showed himself to be ever the innocent man. If he was guilty, why would he have left any message at all? Bailey knew his view was prejudiced. Something quite dramatic would have to be proved for him to be dissuaded about his opinion regarding Henry Hanson. His friend's focus was always on what was good for the community.

He looked around. All the furniture was still in the house. John remembered that Henry had been given the home and the furniture rent free by the Cooperative. They owned the entire property and everything in it. Henry had only his automobile and his clothing. It hadn't taken his friend long to pack.

Bailey read the letter once again and then replaced it in the envelope. He found himself saddened, but also relieved for Henry's sake. Hanson had not been happy working at the Feed & Grain Mill for some time. The important factor now was that Hanson was safe wherever he was going. John placed the envelope back on the kitchen table and left the house exactly as he'd found it.

Hurrying down a side street back toward his truck, the smoke was still thick but not as seriously. He thought about his son out at Chippewa Lodge. If the timing was right, the raid had begun. Certainly Charlie Davis and Jamie Lawton would protect Adam. No violence was expected, but nothing was assured.

Bailey's Plymouth truck was parked right down the side street from the café. There was not a soul on that street. Everyone had migrated to the scene of the fire. There was a shout from down by the main intersection that the fire was now under control except for a small building at the fairgrounds that was still burning. It looked like the Mill had survived.

That was all he needed to see. He got in his truck and drove away from the scene. Strangely, he felt more forlorn than he'd felt in years. Too many things were coming to an end....the town celebration....the popular golf event...and now Henry Hanson was gone. Soon, his own son would be moving down to the Twin Cities for school that autumn. Even the enjoyment he had meeting the two crazy guys from out of town would end. Jamie Lawton and Charlie Davis would be leaving town and pleased to be doing so. There would be no reason for them to pass through town again. Even his two-week acquaintance with the attractive Lindy MacPherson would conclude with her going back to her U.S. Attorney's job in Minneapolis. Even though theirs was only a friendship...nothing else...he come to enjoy their conversations at the Glenwood Café each morning.

He found himself not caring whether Loni D'Annelli was going to be arrested or not. There would be plenty of other arrests. Lindy MacPherson would earn a lot of accolades for her undercover work even if she didn't put D'Annelli in prison. A sense of loneliness began to pervade his very soul. Life was moving on and leaving him behind.

He reached the top of the Hwy. #28 hill toward his farm leaving the thick haze of smoke behind him in the valley below. It dawned on him how symbolic that dark cloud was. He'd lived a responsible, clean life. He was highly regarded in his community. He was a good father. Life was tough, especially as a farmer, but he'd persevered. He'd been dealt some horrible cards a few years back and his son and he had survived thanks to people like Henry Hanson and other kind folks in town. This was the first time he'd felt a vast emptiness about his future. He still wanted the responsibility of bringing up his son; that wonderful task was more or less done. He hated that it was. What was going to follow next in his life? Was he destined to try to eke out a living on dry, infertile farmland? He was not one to complain, but this inescapable sense of loss was overpowering.

He turned onto the dirt road leading to his property. Seeing the farm drew him out of his melancholy for the wrong reasons. There were chores to do everywhere. He drove his Plymouth truck with the squeaky chassis up by the barn and parked it. The day was still early... plenty of time to get some projects done before Adam, Jamie, and Charlie returned from the aftermath of the Chippewa Lodge raid. They had explained their arrival would not be until later in the afternoon. Their plan was to hide out on the golf course until the raid had settled and all the arrests were made. The three of them would only leave the golf course when the resort property was clear of the state patrol.

Lindy MacPherson had mentioned that she'd make it out to the farm much later. It was understandable she'd be busy until evening with the arrest warrants and identifying as many hoodlums on her list as possible.

With time on his hands until they all returned, Bailey decided to vary his normal routine for a Sunday. He hated to miss the hoopla going on down by the Mill, but he knew it was best he stay away. Ever active, he took on some work that needed to be completed. The barn door latch had been broken for almost a year. He was going to fix it. Once that was done, he could clean the inside of the barn. That was overdue.

He wouldn't admit it to himself, but the projects he was planning all centered on the barn...the same barn that housed the canvas-covered Model 'A' Ford owned by Lindy MacPherson...and the same vehicle Adam had disclosed to him contained thousands and thousands of dollars of 'evidence' against Loni D'Annelli.

He opened the barn door and saw the spectacle of the canvas over the Ford. Adam's final question to him vibrated through his head for the twentieth time that morning. He'd asked about how much money was needed to find Loni guilty.

John had only grunted a response. He had no idea.

Then Adam had left the room at that late hour mumbling about how much even part of that money could help so many impoverished folk in the area. It was a notion that was etching itself deeper and deeper into Bailey's conscious. That thought had become inebriating.

Grabbing some tools, he began to fix the barn door latch. His eyes were half on the latch. He kept glancing over at the canvas-covered Ford. His mind kept swaying to that innocent, righteous idea from his son. The beauty of Adam's statement was that it was said with no selfishness in mind.

Bailey moved slowly around the barn circling the tarp. A voice in his head kept repeating what just some of that money under that canvas could do for so many people. Adam said there were so many shoeboxes stuffed in that old Ford that no one could make a correct count. And in each one of those Buster Brown shoeboxes were stacks of twenty dollar bills...some even having stacks of fifty dollar bills. In the box Adam had showed him there was $5000.

John's mind almost went blank with the potential amount of money in those shoeboxes. But his mind remained quite sharp. What if one or two...or even ten of those boxes came up missing from the back of that vehicle? Would it matter? Would anyone notice? Would anyone know enough to care?

Finally John Bailey just sat down in the middle of the dirt-floored barn and just stared at the spectacle of the loosely covered vehicle... and the veritable gold mine it contained.

What he was thinking was like a bad itch in an inaccessible place. It just wouldn't go away.

CHAPTER

22

It was just past 12:00 on that Sunday noon as Davis, Lawton, and Adam sat on a bench at the highest point on the golf course overlooking Lake Minnewaska. From that Number #8 tee box, there was still traces of smoke still hovering over the town. Most of the dark fiery fog had been blown away by the continued wind gusts off the lake. They had played just four holes and were unable to concentrate on any type of quality golf. They were preoccupied with what was going on both at the Lodge and in town.

Nonetheless, they agreed it was important to remain undetected. Where best to be but at the far reaches of the golf course until things settled down. If they could just remain patient until the raid had finished its purpose, they could venture back to the Lodge parking lot, load up the golf clubs in Davis' roadster, and sneak back to the Bailey farm.

The continuing noise echoing across the golf course as the state police raided the Chippewa Lodge property put them on edge. They could hear the screeching wheels and brakes as more and more cops stormed the quiet resort. Because of the announced later tee time, not many spectators had arrived when the raid had begun. Those innocent bystanders that had come through the gates early would no doubt be detained until they could prove their own identity. The state patrol was not going to let anyone just walk off the resort premises. With a resort full of criminals staying as 'guests', no one was going to slip through their hands.

A half hour later they were still sitting on that Number #8 tee box discussing whether MacPherson's sting might have worked on D'Annelli. Catching their second wind, they got back to playing golf... repeatedly playing Holes #4, 5, 6, and 7 out of view from the action at the Lodge. They played every kind of golf betting game imaginable.

They played until 3:00 when hunger and tiredness convinced them to make an effort to leave the Chippewa Lodge facility. If the three of them were stopped in the Lodge parking lot, their excuse would be that they were visitors and had just come out to play the golf course. They would say how pleased they were that the golf course seemed free of other players. It was as creative as they felt they needed to be.

Finally ending their golf on Holes #8 and #9, they paid off their bets to each other. For all the golf they played, Lawton won a dollar from Adam...and made him pay. There was principle involved.

Lawton also took three dollars off Davis despite giving him the higher number of strokes. Davis complained that he would have played better had MacPherson and Lawton not kept him out so late Saturday night.

As they walked away from the green on Hole #9, they began to get a bit nervous. There was still a host of police cars in the Lodge parking lot. 'Guests' were still being led away in handcuffs...people who Adam had never seen before. That only meant there were more cons and criminals staying at the cabins than imagined. Not all the 'guests' played golf.

Charlie's A-68 St. Clair Roadster was parked off to the side of the resort by the tennis court. It was blocked in by patrol cars. They sensed a problem with their quiet escape. Even at the front entrance of the resort they could see law enforcement officers patrolling where the two long-coated D'Annelli guards had been stationed throughout the tournament. There was no question they'd better be ready to be questioned by the police or return to the links for more golf.

The three of them were just turning around to march back onto the golf course when a police vehicle approached them from out on the course. Now the three of them no longer had the choice. They were going to have to talk their way out of a sticky situation.

Lawton and Davis looked rather grave as the car stopped. Out popped an equally grim looking officer. He walked up to the three of them. Davis and Lawton were mentally already fabricating a story to protect their innocence and evade arrest. Even Adam was considering what lie he was going to tell.

Then as if the sun came out from behind the clouds, the officer grinned at them. He inquired, "By chance are you fellas the ones who my niece has been bragging on? Lawton and Davis glanced at each other. They'd both been quite 'friendly' to a lot of women in their lives. They both racked their brains over what niece he might be referring.

Davis, though, didn't miss a beat. "Officer, we certainly are. We missed your name."

The officer gave them a toothy smile and held out his hand. "My name is Sheriff Ralph MacPherson. I'm a bit out of my jurisdiction. I'm the County Sheriff up in Baltrami County. I just came down to help out my niece, Lindy."

The sighs of relief from Lawton and Davis...and young Bailey... were audible.

The Sheriff continued talking not realizing how joyous the three of them were in meeting up with him. "Lindy told me you boys were with her all day yesterday while she was finishing up some of her...ah... interviews for her magazine article. She said there were some pretty shady characters around this here resort...and you guys were just out here watchin' the tournament and keepin' her safe. I want to thank you."

Charlie practically shouted out, "Interviews...article...oh yes, she said she was hoping to finish the article today. Yeh, we came out to watch the action yesterday and met up with your niece...a fine girl I might add. We just came out today to play some golf and got ourselves caught in the middle of some sort of police action. I guess there's some hoodlum you guys are trying to catch."

The Sheriff smiled patiently now knowing who they were. He chuckled at their attempt at playing dumb. They were taking no chances. He appreciated the difficult situation they'd found themselves.

He then made a suggestion. "Lindy said you boys might have a hard time leaving the resort given the number of law enforcement officers questioning the guests here at Chippewa Lodge. She asked that I might find you someplace on the golf course and usher you boys out of here. How does that sound?"

The smiles on the faces of Lawton and Davis were as bright and sincere as the day they luckily graduated from law school. Lawton took over the conversation not allowing Davis to continue his charade of virtue. "Sheriff MacPherson, we'll need to get our car and we'll just follow you back into town."

And that's exactly what they did. Lawton and Davis positioned themselves in the back seat of the Sheriff's car hunkered behind his seat like two guilty car thieves. They wanted there to be no last chance of someone recognizing them. Adam delightfully accepted the job of driving Charlie's roadster back to the farm. The Sheriff was waved through the exit gate by two officers with Adam happily following like a movie star parading down Hollywood Boulevard.

Fifteen minutes later Lawton and Davis were deposited in front of the Bailey farmhouse. Sheriff MacPherson bid them farewell saying, "I'll see Lindy downtown at the courthouse. I'll let her know you guys were safely delivered out of the resort to the front door of this farmhouse.

Lawton's calm appreciation belied the relief and exuberance he and Davis felt. "Thanks for helping us out, Sheriff. Let Lindy know when you see her we'll look forward to meeting up with her later when she can slip away from her duties."

He seemed pleased. "I'll pass along the message." As the Sheriff's patrol car took the Bailey long gravel driveway back to State Hwy. #28, Davis turned to Lawton and asked, "Jamie, how much do you suppose that old Sheriff really knows about our involvement?"

They watched the Baltrami County Sheriff speed up his vehicle on his way back into Glenwood. Lawton answered, "You know, Chas, I'd say it really doesn't matter."

Charlie nodded slowly as they strolled toward the farmhouse to find John Bailey. They didn't expect Adam for a while...not with the chance to drive Charlie's roadster around town. They had bets that it would be at least an hour before Adam showed up back at the farm after showing the vehicle off to a few of his friends. Lawton and Davis knew they would have done the same thing.

Davis won the bet as Adam didn't arrive back home for almost an hour and a half. He claimed he got lost. Charlie asked him how many of his friends got to ride in the roadster.

Adam laughed, his unbridled honesty spilling forth, "Maybe fifteen...maybe twenty."

It was late afternoon when Lawton and Davis arrived at the Bailey farm...Adam Bailey, as mentioned, a bit later. When they walked into the house, there was no John Bailey. Then they heard some noises from the barn and trotted in that direction. They were about to open the barn door when John opened it himself from within. He was perspiring he said after getting caught up on a weekend's worth of chores in just a few hours. What was strange was how strangely exhilarated he looked with dirt and sweat from head to toe.

John welcomed them and suggested they go to the house for something cold to drink. Bailey led the way practically skipping across the gravel parking area to the house.

Davis murmured to Lawton, "No one should be that thrilled after finishing farm chores."

Bailey heard the joke and chuckled. Then his face turned stiff. "Where's Adam?"

Lawton was quick to respond. "No worry. We got a ride out here from someone else. We're betting Adam took Charlie's roadster on a little spin to impress some friends. We're betting he'll be back...but not real soon.

Bailey showed relief and then voiced what seemed like a practiced response about working so hard...and on the Sabbath. "Yeh, there were some extra things I decided to do until you guys returned. They're done now. I'm going to get cleaned up. You boys are welcome to some clean clothes in the house. They might not be the most stylish, but they're clean. I put some beer and sodas in the ice box. We can sit on the porch and enjoy the view until Adam and Lindy return."

Bailey and Lawton smiled at one another over Bailey's generosity. He didn't have much, but what he had he offered it without delay.

Bailey seemed a bit wound up relative to his normal behavior. As if not wanting a pause in the conversation, he pointed at the western sky. "That storm cloud coming over from the Dakotas looks like it'll go north of us, but it'll be a beauty to watch. I'll be out in just a few minutes." Then he went in the house.

Davis looked at Lawton. "Christ, what's with John. Count on a farmer to talk about the weather when there's nothing else to say. Maybe he had a few bottles of his home brew while he was working. He should be exhausted with the work he's put in. Instead he looks like he could harvest the west forty acres this afternoon.

As John washed up, Lawton and Davis checked out the condition of the biplane for Lawton's return trip to the Twin Cities. While working on the air machine their discussion drifted to an important bit of unfinished business...where to distribute the money Lawton had won at the tournament. Both men considered the cash nothing but refuse burning a hole in Davis' leather satchel. They wanted no part of that money. Since giving a portion of Lawton's winnings to the Baileys the night before, they still had in excess of $29,000 remaining. They never did have to touch the parcel of money shared by each of them. It was still hidden under the seat of Davis' roadster.

Lawton suggested dividing up the money and give it confidentially to at least five benevolent organizations. However, it was Davis' more popular recommendation that they find a way to place the money in the hands of John Bailey. They had come to have nothing but respect for the man. While they didn't know the details, it was apparent the Baileys had some tragedy in their backgrounds. Despite that load to carry, Lawton and Davis had come to learn from MacPherson that both father and son were highly regarded in the community.

But, the clincher for them to get the money to John was the fact he was going to be alone on that humble farm come that fall with Adam going on to school. While loneliness and despair were common feelings in the harsh rural life of the 1930's, Lawton and Davis could not let this good-hearted soul waste away on his farm. They had the money; all they had to do was figure out a way to carry out their intentions without John Bailey thinking he was getting a hand out. The man had his pride. The last thing they wanted was for him to feel disrespected.

They finally agreed to a plan. They could hardly wait for Adam to return as they'd need the young man's help to persuade his father.

When Adam finally did return home joining them on the porch, Davis could barely wait to launch into his little scheme. He tried to be calm, but ended up blurting out, "Hey John, Jamie and I were thinking about something. You ever be interested in selling this farm?"

John took a huge swig of his Canadian beer and began chuckling as if Davis was kidding. He was unmoved. "Yeh, maybe some of D'Annelli's friends will stop by the farm after they pay their bail down at the courthouse and offer me a price with the money they have left over." Adam respectfully laughed at his father's comment. Lawton and Davis did not.

Davis didn't miss a beat. From his own experience on real estate value experience in that area, he'd estimated the Bailey farm was probably worth less than $16,000, if there was even a buyer to be found! But, Lawton and he didn't care.

To John he simply repeated the statement in a different way. "No John, you don't understand. "Jamie and I want to buy the farm if you're willing to sell it. We've talked it over and we'll not pay a dime more than $29,000."

John looked both Lawton and Davis straight in the eye waiting for them to finish their gag. But, their looks showed they weren't cracking a joke. John turned serious as well. "Boys, don't be funning with me. This farm will never sell for much of anything with the markets and farm prices the way they are. Besides, this farm ain't worth anywhere near $29,000."

Lawton and Davis just stared at him as if waiting for his true answer. Bailey gazed in a cock-eyed way at both of them before finally blinking. "What are you guys saying? You can't be serious."

Davis pulled open his and Lawton's leather parcel and poured the remaining cash out on the porch table. "The money from this bag is yours if you'll sell the farm for our price. I believe you'll find $29,000 on this table.

There was silence on that porch as John Bailey appeared mystified while the wide-eyed Adam seemed to be holding his breath. The cash on the table was awesome. The previous day the Baileys had gained $10,000 from their take from the golf tournament...an exorbitant amount at any time. Now, they were staring at almost three times that figure. The offer was not only serious, but overwhelming.

Lawton eased into the discussion to quiet the sudden tenseness. "John, Charlie's and my offer is perfectly legitimate. So you know we're not going to be gentlemen farmers. Once you sign the papers for the farm over to us, we plan on donating the farmland and the farm buildings over to the University of Minnesota Agricultural Department. That school has been involved in some interesting crop research. However, before we make the endowment, we'd want you to get your full value from your harvest this fall. Whatever profit you make from your fall yield is yours. We also suggest you sell your hogs and chickens. Those profits are yours as well.

As for the house, we'd plan on keeping the farmhouse. Whenever you move from the house...and that's your choice when... we'll eventually plan on having the farmhouse maintained by a service organization in Glenwood. It can be used for civic or church meetings. As for the upstairs bedrooms and the rocker and swinging chair here on the porch, well, that's our reward. We'll keep access to these parts of the house. You never know when any of us might need a roof over our heads. Besides, we like the view of the sky and of Lake Minnewaska from this porch."

All John could do was stammer. Adam looked at his father as if he wanted to help lift his father's arm to consummate the deal with Lawton and Davis. There was a tear in John's eye as he slowly lifted his hand unaided. He finally responded, "You know, I've been kind of wondering where my life was going with Adam gone from the house. If you boys are sure, I guess I'd be kind of loco if I didn't take you up on your offer. I think I've had enough of my life here on the farm."

His hand was barely extended when Lawton and Davis happily grabbed it so as not to allow John to think further about his impulsive decision. Adam was overjoyed...mostly for his father's sake. He hadn't liked the picture of his father single-handedly managing the farm and dealing with the loneliness that would certainly come to pass. His father now had a chance to alter his own life and leave the rural life if he chose.

If was difficult to decide who amongst the four of them were the happiest. Everyone knew that counting the previous day's $10,000 and the farm sale price of $29,000...plus the profits from the fall harvest and the sale of the chickens and hogs... the two Bailey's had a veritable fortune in their pockets relative to the times.

When MacPherson eventually arrived at the farm, she thought all four men had been drinking. Adam eventually explained the deal that had been struck. MacPherson seemed overjoyed by the agreement. The doubt she was having over Lawton and Davis took a major meltdown.

And that was it. The gambling money earned by Jamie Lawton on the first day of the charity golf tournament was gone…and for a good cause. That mutually advantageous agreement with the Baileys would cement a friendship that would exist for the rest of their lives.

There was one other situation that was discussed by Lawton and Davis before Lindy MacPherson made it out to the Bailey farm that evening. After handing the leather packet of cash over to the Baileys, Davis and Lawton were cleaning up from their day at the Lodge at Bailey's well. Davis was ready to go back home.

He pushed his friend to leave. "Jamie, what do you say we leave and have John give our best to our favorite investigator, Miss MacPherson. So far she doesn't know anything about us, even our last names. I think we're better off if that continues to be the case. You know, she still doesn't really trust us…and, why should she? While we helped her last night and today, she still thinks we had ulterior and evil motives against someone at the Lodge. If we admit we had no dastardly deeds planned, it's not going to help matters. It'll still make no sense why we got involved in a mob run golf tournament. Worse yet, when she finds out we're both attorneys…and lawyers with some respected background…I think she'll be disgusted with us. Hell, I'm disgusted with us. We could have ruined our reputations much less our lives if things hadn't worked out the way they have."

Davis thought he was making a strong argument. Disappointingly, he sensed his friend was dragging his heels. Davis would not let up. "So, Jamie, we dodged another calamity…and this one was a big one. I say we thank the two Baileys for the hospitality…and a most unique weekend… and have a late dinner in Alexandria. We can drive back here tomorrow, so you can fly your contraption back to the Twin Cities."

Lawton's reaction remained slow and his response weak. "Charlie, don't you think we should at least wait for the lady and thank her for keeping us out of a potentially very messy situation."

Davis wasn't used to Lawton being so undecided. He countered, "For Christ's sake…write her a note. Let's get out of here."

When he saw the almost indiscernible shake of Lawton's head, he finally had to submit there was some other factor playing in his friend's brain. It didn't take much to guess that Lawton had acquired an interest in this female. There would be no leaving the Bailey farm until Lawton found out if there might be even a speck of reciprocal interest from MacPherson.

Davis tried one more time. "Lawton, you get interested in a lady and you lose your mind. I don't like what I'm hearing or seeing. What did the two of you talk about when you were rolling around in the hay at the Mill last night? It's a hell of a way to begin a courtship."

Lawton only smiled but didn't say a word. But, Davis sensed he was right on point. He pushed. "Jamie, let's get out of here. You don't have a chance with her. She knows the only reason we helped her was to save our skins. If she knew you played in this golf tournament with a bunch of gangsters on a whim...and you had a choice to have walked away...by God, she'll run away from you so fast we'll hardly see the dust. She'll think both of us are two lunatics oblivious to trouble. Usually we don't make it so easy for a person to figure that fact out so quickly."

Lawton had to chuckle over his friend's assessment. He countered, "Chas, just give me a little time to talk with her after she makes it out to the farm. I'd like to be a bit more straight-forward with her. Maybe she'll discover I'm not as bad as she might think..."

His eyes lit as he added, "....despite my association with you."

Davis shook his head in disgust...not totally in jest.

Lawton continued, "Once I have a chance to talk with her, then we can leave. I promise. I'll wait a while to call her when I get back to Minneapolis...maybe a week...maybe two weeks. With her investigative experience, that'll give her time to do some background on us. That probably won't make her happy when she finds out we're reasonably appreciated members of the legal community. She might concentrate more on how we helped her than why I played golf with a bunch of lowlifes in a golf event.

Davis rolled his eyes and scoffed, "You're optimism overwhelms me at times. So...you want to be more straight-forward. For Christ's sake, have I been talking to the wind? She doesn't trust you and you want to pursue a relationship hinged on frankness and truthfulness. When has that ever worked out for you in the past?"

Lawton tried to be defensive but only laughed. "Well......I can't name one in recent years, but that's always been my goal with any lady I've been inclined to date."

Davis kept up his playful ridicule. "Hell, even if there is some attraction between the two of you, your entire one-day relationship has been based on anything but honesty. You both have been living a life of deceit with each other since you met yesterday. One could argue that might be the basis of your mutual appeal. However, we don't even know if there's a 'mutual' anything right now. And, when she discovers you're a lawyer in the very city she lives in, I hate to see her response. She'll figure you were at the mob charity tournament recruiting clients. She'll be livid that she placed any trust in us at all. Even more, she'll want to distance herself from you just because you'd be a danger to her career."

Lawton hated it when Davis actually made sense, especially about women, a subject Davis was mostly incompetent. Still, Lawton remained determined. He said, "Charlie, I want to at least make a proper introductions. With my full name and her investigative background, she'll check us out. I'd like to think our records would stand up against our periodic miscues.

Davis snickered, "Yeh, miscues…I'd say this weekend was more than a miscue. You do make one good point. By delaying any further contact with her for a week or two before you call her up, we might come up with some other acceptable story about our being at Chippewa Lodge. There's a possibility you might be able to prove to your Miss MacPherson you're not a complete idiot."

Lawton gave him wrinkled face, but smiled. Davis knew he'd lost the debate. Of all the women in Lawton's life Davis had met, he saw no future in Lawton pursuing this one. It was a huge waste of both of their times. In frustration he went into the farmhouse to get another Canadian beer from the ice box. The Bailey porch was going to be his domicile for the next few hours.

Lindy MacPherson finally left the Pope County courthouse after a long day that Sunday evening. She'd finished her paper work and arrest warrants on the forty-five gangsters and wanted criminals detained that day. The state patrol had been impressed with her cover-up efforts. Even the more arrogant agents of the Bureau of Investigation gave in and showed her some respect.

With her vehicle out at the Bailey farm, she gained a ride from a local deputy she'd come to know over the previous two weeks. She hoped but wasn't certain if the two men she only knew as 'Jamie' and 'Charlie' would still be at the Bailey farm. With their level of discomfort in finding out her actual identity, she expected them to be long gone.

Driving up the east bluff overlooking the town and Lake Minnewaska, an enormous hazy cloud in the western skyline represented her feelings about what would be happening to the town she'd come to appreciate. Whether the storm would eventually hit the Glenwood area was put aside. Nothing could tarnish what the raid at the Lodge had accomplished.

MacPherson wanted so much to share the success of the day with the four men she'd gotten to know. They'd provided the support, even the laughs, that helped her make it through the stressful weekend. She pictured the excited and satisfied looks on each of their faces when she told them of all the arrests. It would be a very laugh-filled and pleasant evening, especially when relating how she convinced the state police the town leaders were not part of the gambling operation. That meant Mayor B. Good, Big Bud Bunsen, and even the mystifying Henry Hanson would not be arraigned.

Most importantly, the names of Jamie, Charlie, and the Baileys had never come up in any of her conversations that day with her law enforcement colleagues. Her obligation to all four of them was to protect their names from ever having any affiliation with the sting she'd pulled on Loni D'Annelli. As for the two outsiders, Jamie and Charlie had lived up to their part of the bargain. Now, she had to do the same. Their reason for being in Glenwood was unnecessary for her to know and no longer important. That didn't mean she wasn't curious.

Now, sadly, she'd be returning to the Twin Cities the next day and likely not see them again. It was necessary. She had to keep her relationship with them silent for their own safety.

As MacPherson and the deputy ventured up the long, rut-filled driveway, the farmhouse seemed vacant of anyone. Then she saw the Bailey vehicles, Charlie's roadster, and the biplane parked almost unseen behind the barn. She chuckled. She knew her four conspirators were somewhere, but possibly hiding upon seeing a local police car approaching the house.

She quickly got out of the car thanking the deputy for the ride. He nodded and pulled away looking at her oddly why she wanted to end her day at the Bailey farm. She stood in the dusty parking lot looking around, taking in the large weather system moving toward Lake Minnewaska, waiting for the deputy to get back onto Hwy. #28, and wondering where 'they' were.

Then the front door opened and all four of them came out to meet her. For all her misgivings, her apprehension ended the second she saw the delighted looks on their faces. It would be a moment she'd never forget. While the Baileys had to be uneasy about the impact of her actions on their town, they knew the right thing had been done. The satisfaction on the faces of Jamie and Charlie was also quite rewarding. This day would be one none of them would ever forget.

It wasn't five minutes since her arrival at the farm that she was seated on a rocking chair on the porch with a coke placed in her hands. She felt like royalty.

Holding up the bottle with pride, she motioned for a toast. "Gentlemen, I'd work with all of you again without a second thought."

The laughter was genuine and the comment appreciated. Her follow-up was more serious. "I believe you know last night's discovery or today's results would not have happened without all of you. I have to admit when I saw that dry field of grass this morning I almost didn't light the match. The breeze felt like a monsoon. It was one thing to create a fire to lure D'Annelli into town, but it was quite another to burn down the whole town. But, I knew you guys out at the Lodge were not going to let D'Annelli miss the threat to the Mill."

She looked appreciatively at John Bailey. "And, it was John's little signal to go ahead and start the fire that was the wave of support I needed. The fire on that meadow was frightening; it took off so fast... like straw soaked in gasoline. The smoke build up made it look even more alarming. had to race around the meadow and up the street to intercept a small group of state patrolmen who were moving into town too fast. Convincing them to hold back and allow our little sting to possibly work out was difficult. If D'Annelli had made it into town and saw those cops, he might have turned around and gone back to the Lodge. Our scheme would have been ruined.

But, things were not happening as hooped. Time dragged and there was still no D'Annelli. I finally had to give up. It was more important to control the fire in the field and save the Mill...and the buildings in town. I felt so stupid having started that fire and putting the town in peril just to catch D'Annelli red-handed."

Taking another long swig of her coke, she caught her breath. She was excited. "I gave one of the officers, a Captain Smoltz, the word to call my Uncle Ralph who was holding back the state patrol outside the Lodge property to now go ahead and commence the raid. Then I waved Smoltz and his fellow officers to move forward toward the Mill to help out the fire department. Townsfolk were coming out of their homes and churches to witness the blaze. The police needed to control the growing crowd. At that one point, it was the most depressed I'd felt since coming to Glenwood.

Then, it was like a miracle happened. As if speeding in from the depths of hell was none other than Mr. Loni D'Annelli in his classy Cadillac along with his two right hand men. I couldn't believe what I was seeing. I feared he was still going to turn around to evade the police. Instead he was only focused on the Mill. There were firemen all over the place surrounding the Mill and soaking the building as well as the two grain elevator towers with water. One fireman was even on the roof of the Mill office putting out a small blaze.

D'Annelli stormed out of his Cadillac and ran up the steps to the Mill office with a key in his hand. That was my first realization our plan just might work. I was transfixed...observing his every move...and watching every detail of our idiotic plan materializing as if rehearsed. He was in a panic and swearing at the fireman on the roof as he opened the door and raced inside the Mill office. You could then hear cuss words echoing from that office.

That's when I rushed up to the Mill office door with Captain Smoltz and we both saw Loni half way down the steps leading to the basement. But, as luck would have it, he was momentarily blocked by two firemen climbing back up the steps.

The two firemen were shouting, "Look what we found......there's money all over the floor down there." They had stacks of cash in their hands.

I believe Loni D'Annelli's life crossed before his eyes at that one moment. His mouth was ajar realizing his secret vault had been breached. Frankly, I can't tell you the satisfaction I felt seeing him in that predicament, especially considering the misery he and his people have caused so many people during his many years of crime.

I could barely understand his statements given the profanity pouring from his mouth. His two henchmen, Malooley and McCoy, didn't know what to do. They were standing there in their knickers and golf shoes not knowing if they should get Loni out of there or protect what was left in the Mill basement.

Then two state patrol cars came driving up. Four officers got out of their vehicles. They entered the Mill office witnessing D'Annelli still out of control. Smoltz ordered two officers to go down the ladder to explore the storage area below. The other two officers began questioning Loni about his knowledge of the money...and for that matter what he was doing in the Mill. Loni was still frothing at the mouth in abject rage. He shouted out, "Well, it's my God-damned money down there. For Christ's sake, shut the God-damned floor door so the fire won't get down there."

MacPherson grinned. "I swear I heard a band playing. He'd just self-incriminated himself."

There was excited applause on that porch. She showed no embarrassment...only an empty glass. John went and got her another coke as she continued. "Then one of those two officers came back out of the basement with a shoebox full of brand new bills. I heard one of the officers say to one of his partners, "Sam, these bills are so clean and so neatly stacked...almost too clean...and too neat...if you know what I mean."

It was then that I saw Loni roll his eyes. At that point he knew was in big trouble...and not just with the law. If word leaked to his gambling clients how they might have been paid off with counterfeit money, the underworld was going to come down on Mr. D'Annelli very hard. Adding to his problems, that discovery meant the authorities would be confiscating D'Annelli's entire bounty in that basement to examine.

D'Annelli was immediately arrested and taken down to the county jailhouse. When Malooley and McCoy saw their boss falling to pieces with the state police, they discreetly backed away from the scene. I didn't even see them slip out of view. I also noticed some of the other hoodlums who had followed Loni into town silently departed upon seeing more state patrol arrive...but not before hearing about possible 'funny' money being found in D'Annelli's secret bank vault. While they didn't like seeing what was happening to D'Annelli, I saw some very disturbed faces on some of those 'guests' who had followed him into town.

With D'Annelli in custody and knowing the raid was underway out at the resort, I had a chance to return to my cabin, get cleaned up, change out of my smoke-filled clothing and readied myself to appear as a representative of the U.S. Attorney's office. When I showed up at the county jailhouse with a skirt and blouse, my hair up in a bun, wearing my glasses, and my U.S. Attorney identification, no one really recognized me. None of the local deputies, even that officer, Captain Smoltz, recognized me. When I re-introduced myself, I had to tell them to close their mouths.

Throughout the afternoon I brought the state patrol and a couple agents of the Bureau of Investigation up-to-date with my undercover work. There was literally a parade of gangsters, convicts, and petty robbers being ushered into the courthouse. When I left a little while ago, we had in custody at least four prison escapees, five men wanted in surrounding states for robbery, four attempted murder suspects, and the rest arraigned on bootlegging and racketeering charges. There were some very angered mobsters standing around that county jailhouse in their golf clothes."

She smiled. "It's been a great day for the good guys. Even those Bureau of Investigation fellows walked out of various interrogation rooms at the courthouse with grins on their faces. It was a heck of a round-up. All this time, Loni D'Annelli was fuming in the Sheriff's office under armed guard trying to get a hold of his attorney in Chicago. Sunday afternoon made it difficult to locate the people he needed by telephone. I have to tell you, none of us felt particularly sorry for him.

I chose not to be near him. After all, it was only yesterday I was drinking some of D'Annelli's booze with Charlie and Jamie on the Lodge patio. I wanted to do nothing that might help him recall my being with the two of you. With my change in appearance, he barely looked at me given the troubles he was facing. I just didn't want to take any chances."

Lawton and Davis raised their beverages silently in an appreciative toast to her caution.

She continued, "As it turned out, I needn't have worried. D'Annelli was not at his best; he was spitting mad. He of course denied any wrongdoing. Yet, I kept slipping direct questions to the interrogators showing Loni what was already known. He literally blanched a couple times when told of the various charges that would be filed against him. He eventually got control of himself and told the agents questioning him he was through talking until his lawyer called him back. But, smoke was coming out his ears. He did ask the state patrol a couple of times, "Have you brought Hanson in yet? I'd like to see him for a moment when you do."

In response, I repeated to the state patrol that I'd already checked out Henry and had reasoned he was completely clean. I further stated that if there was any more need to question Henry, I'd handle the responsibility myself implying that he'd been working with me on the case. They understood and never brought up his name again. Facts might prove me wrong, but for the time being we have Henry in the clear...at least from the perspective of the law. How he might fare with D'Annelli and his boys is another story."

Lawton then asked, "So, what happens now?"

MacPherson's satisfied grin grew wider. "D'Annelli will be held in the Pope County jail until orders come to extradite him to the Twin Cities. I'm sure his lawyers will meet with him there and he'll be out from behind bars immediately. But, he's got some major charges to overcome. His standing in the mob community has taken a serious hit once the rumor spreads that 'funny' money might have been financing his gambling operation. He's going to be a marked man until he can convince them otherwise. His associates in the underworld don't like to be crossed. D'Annelli is in big trouble as he sits in jail tonight. He may not admit it, but for now, he might be safer behind bars.

As for some of Loni's friends, Danny A'Motta, Vinnie Spagatini, Bert Bertinelli, and even Big Julie, they were all picked up in the Lodge restaurant. Back at their cabins, their bags were packed to leave the resort after today's golf event. They were highly agitated about being questioned and taken down to the county jail. Chippewa Lodge was supposed to be off limits to the law. There was nothing to hold these men, so they were let go by early afternoon. But, their names will always be associated with Chippewa Lodge and the raid. I would imagine they will continue to distance themselves from this resort and even from D'Annelli as time passes.

Bailey finally returned from the kitchen with another drink for MacPherson in time to hear his son inquire about the cash in the barn and whether it was needed as evidence. John had completely missed the discussion about the possible counterfeit money stored in the Mill basement.

Accepting the soft drink, MacPherson snickered, "You know, what's interesting is the cash stuffed in the back seat of my vehicle in the barn will only be added to the rest of the evidence. Once the money reaches the U.S. Attorney's Office in Minneapolis, it will be decided who should take possession while the case on D'Annelli is being litigated."

John had a strange reaction to her statement. He skewed his lips and just shook his head. Adam just stared at his father and duplicated the reaction.

Davis and Lawton only shrugged realizing their late evening 'heist' of some of D'Annelli's funds from the Mill basement had the net effect of making them lose some sleep. Davis commented wryly, "You know, the man who has been strangely invisible since I saw him yesterday afternoon has been our friend Henry Hanson. John and Adam didn't find him last night. I wonder if he blew town, even though yesterday he didn't seem to be in good enough shape to go anywhere."

Bailey vacantly shook his head. He was not about to give any indication he'd stopped by Henry's home and had seen the letter of resignation. He knew Henry was gone...and the longer head start the man got, the better off he was.

During all that time on the porch, MacPherson and Lawton would cast periodic looks at each other when the other wasn't aware. Davis noticed the awkwardness between the two. He was unsympathetic.

Nothing had changed in his mind. Lawton's interest in the lady had no chance of success. As far as Davis could see, any attempt by Lawton to explain his appearance and reasons for risking his career as well as his neck at a mob run golf tournament would be interpreted as hair-brained and impulsive...to say nothing of ridiculous. He could see MacPherson giving Lawton a blank look while looking for an exit.

Davis had only one reason for not pushing Lawton to leave the festive time on the porch. He enjoyed seeing his friend wiggle around in discomfort like a small boy in at a long church service. This was fodder Davis planned on using to kid his friend unmercifully at various times in the future.

What he didn't pay as close of attention was MacPherson's level of frustration. She was ready to forgive Lawton and Davis for practically anything they had planned to carry out at the Lodge that weekend... almost including murder. She just wanted to know. She wanted to understand if this man named 'Jamie' was worth any more of her thoughts. Her obligation was not to pry.

As the conversation amongst the five finally eased down, there were emphatic and quite serious repeats about their each one's commitment to silence. There could never be a word breathed to any other human being about their little weekend escapade. It was understood their very lives depended on that silence.

MacPherson stood up to leave about 9:00. She looked tired but still intoxicated with the results of that day. With a sideways final glance of disappointment toward Lawton, she claimed the next day would be another busy day down at the Pope County courthouse before she drove back to Minneapolis.

Davis offered a quick farewell as if sensing there would be little reason he would ever see MacPherson again. The Baileys set up a time with her to stop by the farm to pick up her cash-filled vehicle the next day.

As for Lawton, he was the quietest Davis had ever seen. His friend's final words to MacPherson were strangely impersonal for the interest he'd expressed in her. Davis wondered if even Lawton had finally realized it was futile to pursue the lady.

Blandly Lawton wished her well. "Lindy, I hope your case ends exactly the way you want. You made a tremendous effort and it all paid off."

That was it. Picturing the hay falling off of each of their clothing the previous night, Davis was slightly surprised the farewell was so distant.

MacPherson reacted similarly...very remote. She nodded at Lawton and then looked at the four males she thought she might not see that often, if ever, in the future. She looked like she had plenty to say, but not ready to say it at that moment. Adam volunteered to drive her back to her cabin in town. As she got in Bailey Plymouth sedan she repeated, "Gentlemen, I couldn't have done it without you."

She left with but a quick wave. As Adam and she drove back down the bluff, she felt satisfied she'd not pried into the two men's private business at the Lodge. She also felt slightly demoralized about her own private life. She was already sensing her interest in the man she only really knew as 'Trick-shot' was all in vain. But her downheartedness was more an anxiety since it appeared unlikely she'd ever see him again.

She whispered to herself, "Such is life."

By Monday morning Lindy MacPherson arranged a ride back to the Bailey farm with her uncle, Sheriff Ralph MacPherson. He was on the way back to his actual jurisdiction up in Bemidji. He promised silence for anything he saw regarding the three golfers he'd met during the aftermath of the raid at Chippewa Lodge. He even dropped her off at the highway entrance to the Bailey farm claiming not wanting to meet anyone else or hear anything more regarding her case. She knew he had an idea those three individuals had somehow helped her. He further understood why she had to remain silent about their involvement.

As she walked up the long driveway, she noticed Charlie's roadster was gone...as was the biplane. The two men had left at dawn apparently anxious to get Glenwood as far behind them as possible...and to use Hwy. #28 as a runway before too many vehicles were on the road.

John and Adam Bailey were already doing some morning chores. The hog pen had been cleaned. Despite selling the farm, there was essential work that continued. Inside the barn, they helped her remove the tarp covering her government leased Ford. All three were still awed by the number of Buster Brown shoe boxes stuffed into the interior of that car. Being rushed, she quickly kissed the two Baileys and promised to be in touch with them...already admitting she had no intention of ignoring the friendship they'd formed. They all knew there'd be curiosities and information regarding the on-going saga of the Loni D'Annelli case. She'd want to know about the town's reaction and the changes that would be taking place in the community. The Bailey's would have first hand knowledge on that front. John and Adam would more simply want to know if there'd be further investigations in Glenwood...including of themselves.

She departed having asked nothing about Charlie and Jamie other than how the take-off went on the highway. Adam laughed how the two of them had made a bet on who would make it back to Alexandria first... with Charlie getting a ten-minute handicap. That was the first time she'd gained one small snippet regarding either of their backgrounds. One of them apparently lived in Alexandria. But, without their last names, it seemed useless to track either of them down.

She took a deep breath and shook her head. Already she was closing down her thoughts about the two men. She just had to accept both Jamie and Charlie would always be a mystery to her...and it would be better for them if she was.

As she drove back into town looking like a 'Buster Brown' traveling shoe sales person, she should have been happier. Once she turned the cash in the shoeboxes over to the two agents of the Bureau of Investigation awaiting her return at the county courthouse, she would get back to her life in the Twin Cities. She expected a heightened level of respect amongst her U.S. Attorney compatriots.

When all the shoeboxes were out of her Model 'A' Ford, she spotted a small folded note taped to the passenger seat where some shoeboxes had covered the paper. She opened it. There was no communication of any sort other than 'J. Lawton' written clearly on the paper. The note was unsigned.

She broke into a smile. One of them...and she couldn't imagine which one...had decided to share that information with her. Someone was inviting her to make a background check on one 'James Lawton'. She finally had his full name.

There was an extra bounce to her step as she signed some papers in the courthouse office officially transferring the contents of her car over to the agents. She did notice one possible discrepancy. The agents counted only eighty-five boxes in her inventory. She thought the estimate was one hundred boxes, she reconciled that the lateness of the hour Saturday night had caused their count to be inaccurate. Her memory of that night was non-stop tension, chatter and laughter with her two partners followed by shear exhaustion. Keeping a correct audit had been impossible.

When she arrived at her Minneapolis office later that afternoon, she admitted privately to her boss, Ernest Lundquist, "Eighty-five boxes...ninety boxes...or one hundred shoeboxes...it didn't really matter. Evidence was evidence."

She wouldn't find out until a couple days later that the shoeboxes full of money she'd taken from the Mill were of even lesser monetary importance. Many of those eighty-five Buster Brown shoeboxes were not filled with real money. There were stacks of counterfeit bills in some of those boxes. Whatever the case, they were all camouflaged. Many of the stacks of currency only had a twenty or a fifty-dollar bill on the top of each column. Underneath the singular bill was newspaper cut to the same proportions as dollar bills. The result was many of the boxes instead of having $5000 or more in each shoebox now only contained $100. It was thought to be another beautiful job of deceit done by Loni D'Annelli. While artfully done, she couldn't imagine nor could the state patrol and Bureau of Investigation offices understand why D'Annelli would disguise the stacks of money in those shoeboxes. The interest in this little ploy was soon lost, since there was other indisputable currency from the Mill basement, both real and counterfeit, that was hard evidence against Loni D'Annelli.

With MacPherson's return to the Twin Cities, she was caught off guard by the fanfare she immediately began receiving as a result of her 'solo' escapade that weekend. The *Minneapolis Star* had given her front page coverage starting with the Monday afternoon edition. When she left her office that evening, there were reporters hovering. Ernest Lundquist and the U.S. Attorney office staff were pleasantly perplexed. Their office had never gotten as much press coverage on one case.

As for Charlie Davis and Jamie Lawton, that Monday morning they were up at dawn at the Bailey farm. John and Adam had already eaten breakfast and could be seen feeding the hogs until their help was needed. The two Baileys and Davis patrolled State Hwy. #28 so Lawton could make an uninterrupted take-off from the roadway with no vehicles coming up the bluff from town. Their farewells were filled with laughter. Davis mentioned he'd have the papers drawn up to turn the farm over to Lawton and him...and they'd be in contact very soon.

While Lawton and Davis left that day not admitting their true vocations, it didn't matter to John and Adam. They already knew the full names of the two men and the four of them were already depending on one another for confidentiality. Trust was not a question. There was no talk of Lindy MacPherson upon their departure. It was understood for the foreseeable future no communication would be advised.

They made it to Lake Ida with Charlie driving his roadster back to his house and Lawton beating him by twelve minutes while flying a couple circles overhead as Davis raced north on Hwy. #29. Lawton won a five-dollar wager who would arrive first at Davis' lake home.

They fished for a couple hours on Lake Ida before Lawton flew back to Minneapolis later that afternoon...under clear skies. With Monday being a normal workday, they were the only ones on the lake. The solitude was striking compared to the wild weekend they'd just experienced.

He and Davis also resolved to tame down their future weekends and concentrate more on lake sports and golf. Taking on the mob was not something they wanted to make a habit.

CHAPTER
23

By Sunday afternoon, most cabins at Chippewa Lodge had been vacated. Those 'professional businessman' who'd been questioned by the authorities, but not arrested, had packed and left hurriedly...most without checking out. There was no mention of any charity golf tournament any more. People holding tickets for the golf tournament were told that the event had been cancelled. They were directed to get refunds from whatever religious group in town who'd sold them the tickets.

The golf course at Chippewa Lodge was as quiet Sunday afternoon as it had been boisterous and unruly only the day before. That solitude would carry on and unfortunately become the normal atmosphere on those links from then on. Chippewa Lodge had lived its highest level of so-called prominence on Saturday, June 6, 1931. It would never again see that activity or revenue it had enjoyed during those years of the annual Glenwood festival.

Sheriff Petracek and City Police Chief Brey had remained out of town fishing until late Sunday afternoon. One of the biggest cases ever in central Minnesota had happened that day and the two top law enforcement officials in Glenwood were no where to be seen. Nothing about their absence had to be explained to the authorities. The various law enforcement offices knew very well why the County Sheriff and the City Police Chief scheduled themselves out of town on that particular weekend. The same thing was done by other local law authorities in various other communities around the state during town celebrations. Games of chance were common during these types of festivals. As long as the local officers of the law were not on duty, they didn't necessarily observe these illegal games and therefore be obligated to halt them. Petracek and Brey were simply carrying out a normal habit done by others in their same role. What the state patrol and the Bureau's agents didn't know was the more stressful dilemma Petracek and Brey had been mired in for many years. For the good of the community…and a small stipend for themselves…they had been looking the other way from some questionable activities at Chippewa Lodge for a couple years.

On Monday morning, June 8, Loni D'Annelli was still languishing in the Pope County jail waiting to be extradited to Minneapolis. D'Annelli was told his attorneys had finally gotten the proper papers to have him moved to the Hennepin County jail. Bail would be set at that time.

Before leaving the Pope County Courthouse Monday afternoon, he was allowed visitation. Whitey Malooley and Billie McCoy had stayed at a rooming house in Sauk Centre on Sunday night before returning to Glenwood. They didn't feel particularly comfortable at Lake Minnewaska with all the law enforcement and newspaper people in town. When they arrived, they had to listen to the whispering rage of their boss from the confines of a private room at the Pope County courthouse. The jailhouse was so crowded D'Annelli had been held in the sheriff's office. He had Sheriff Petracek's cot to sleep on that Sunday night.

The Chicago mobster was practically spitting blood from chewing on his tongue. His entire enterprise at Chippewa Lodge had been toppled. His secret storage facility at the Mill had been discovered. As bad as that was, he recognized his primary trouble would be with his mob associates. The counterfeit money found mixed in with his actual working capital had quickly cast aspersions on his reputation among the entire underworld community. He knew that quandary had to be handled with absolute priority the moment he was released on bail.

Unfortunately for D'Annelli, he knew the accusation about the counterfeit money was partially true. There were times he used the funny money…as in land deals and payouts to government officials and politicians…and at times, with certain independent contractors, that is, murderers for hire or low-class hoods hired to carry out a petty crime. For certain, though, he never used the counterfeit money in his gambling business…but that perception would now follow him. His only recourse was once back in Chicago he would have to douse that misconception face-to-face with his underworld associates or his future could be endangered.

D'Annelli did have one other obsession that he voiced to his two associates that morning. He wanted to find the person who had set him up.

Malooley leaned closer to the boss when he spoke so no ears from outside the office could be heard. He whispered, "Boss, I can't believe it would be anyone staying at the Lodge. They had no idea about our businesses...or that our cash reserves were being stored at the Mill. I don't think any of the townspeople including Henry Hanson had any notion about the size of our operation. God knows the members of the Presbyterian Men's Club and the City Council were too naive and inexperienced to have any idea."

McCoy drew closer nodding his head. "How about Police Chief Brey and Sheriff Petracek...maybe they got cold feet and planned this entire sting just to get you in trouble."

D'Annelli spat back, "Nah, what would have been their motivation? We were helping the town. We had these two guys bankrolled with the trumped up private security job. They got used to the extra money. They weren't about to let that little gift horse get away."

There was a slight pause from D'Annelli. He'd had all Sunday night lying in that cot to ponder who the guilty party was. Finally, he looked his two right hand men squarely in the eyes. His voice lowered and he rasped, "Whitey...Billie...I need you to find me Hanson. It's got to be him. He knew too much. He might have looked like he couldn't fight his way out of a paper bag, but he's a smart guy. Maybe a little too smart. Nobody's seen him since Saturday. He wasn't brought into the courthouse by the authorities. The damned guy has just disappeared. I think we gotta track him down. I got a feeling he knows who set us up...and I think he's part of it. So, for Christ's sake, find him! I want his head!"

Malooley responded confidently, "Yeh, boss. We'll find him."

"....and Whitey," interrupted the furious D'Annelli, "I'm going to have some people gunning for me. I have to get back to Chicago and repair some of the damage this counterfeit money rumor is causing me. Call up some of the boys in Chicago and let them know I've been set up."

By Monday night Loni was at his new quarters at the Hennepin County Jail in Minneapolis. By Tuesday noon he was having lunch with two of his attorneys at the railway terminal waiting for the train to take them back to Chicago. He could only guess how much danger lurked in front of him. His popularity amongst his Windy City mob brothers wasn't in shambles, but even his attorneys agreed his image had taken a serious hit with the rumors about counterfeit money. He had to depend on Malooley and McCoy finding the only person who could have pulled down his world as he knew it. In his mind, Henry Hanson was a dead man.

Sheriff Clarence Petracek and Police Chief Brey finally returned Sunday evening to a town they hardly recognized for all the state patrol cars parked around the county courthouse. Fishing had been highly successful on Lake Osakis, one of the three lakes they favored during absences from previous Chippewa Lodge charity golf tournaments. Their determined ignorance about anything going on at Chippewa Lodge had kept them in good stead with the local citizens of the county and town. It was a convenient, unstated deal as long as nothing went wrong. By the number of state patrol roaming around the courthouse, there was no doubt something had gone seriously wrong. While they showed astonishment upon their arrival at the courthouse, in truth they were not surprised at all. They had been warned by a person with whom they had the utmost trust how this weekend would likely be the end of the D'Annelli era at the Lodge...one way or another.

Knowing that inevitability, they devised their own plan. It would have to serve two purposes...one to free them from the devilish claws of Loni D'Annelli...and the other, just as important, to dodge the predictable question marks about negligence in their duties.

Immediately upon arriving at their offices they exhibited shock and disappointment. They voiced dismay when informed of the unlawful activities being conducted at the Lodge not just during the ten-day festival, but for years prior.

When the state patrol queried them about any past observations, they expressed indignation that anything like a gambling operation could thrive in their jurisdiction. Their portrayals of innocent, ignorant small town law officers was almost deserving of award status. Also, divulged to them how Chippewa Lodge had been a safe house for convicts and known criminals for years, they acted dumbfounded. They would show further surprise when it was revealed that the gambling business' working capital as well as stolen goods were discovered in the basement of the local Feed & Grain Mill.

In fact, that last finding was the only actual detail that did astonish them. They had no idea there was a basement at the Mill.

As Sheriff Petracek finally proclaimed to a couple state officers, "By God, can you imagine...mob people in our peaceful little town. Who would have guessed?"

Their unawareness was so perfectly portrayed that the Sheriff and Chief of Police were not charged with anything. They did have to face the disparaging looks and disrespectful comments from the higher law enforcement authorities now taking over the case. This alienation from the state patrol was an unexpected byproduct of their plan. It didn't make it any easier to take. They gritted their teeth and displayed no defensiveness, only understandable embarrassment. They knew this discomfort would only last a short time until they took their next step. That would come two days later...another part of the over-all plan they'd outlined with none other than Henry Hanson.

Mayor Charlie B. Good and the town council were not charged with breaking the law that weekend or anything done previously. With the ten-day festival ending so inauspiciously, they called an emergency meeting for Monday night to assess the damage. It was inconceivable how the world had caved in so dramatically. The image of the town would take a strong hit with all the disapproving newspaper reports and articles in the days and weeks ahead. The ten-day festival was all but gone. It unlikely could be revitalized. The most critical loss was of course there would be no more support from the 'guests' out at Chippewa Lodge. They were gone never to return.

On Wednesday evening the Mayor called a town meeting at the local high school gymnasium. It was a packed but very subdued meeting attended by what seemed to be most of the town's population. Much of the meeting seemed to focus on how to answer to all the accusations of outsiders as well as pointed questions by the hoard of reporters assigned to this big story. With the unparalleled damage caused by the raid and ensuing arrests, the townsfolk did understand that life was going to get much rougher in the weeks and months ahead. And those difficulties would not only be economic. They also understood the town would become the butt of some very cruel jokes based on community greed and convenient ignorance. Townsfolk would hear sufficient excuses and trumped up responses by Mayor Good and the town council members to help the citizens respond to even the most uncomfortable questions by the many reporters covering the juicy story.

Reporters would arrive as far away as Duluth, Sioux Falls, Fargo, Grand Forks, Winnipeg, Manitoba and of course the Twin Cities. Other reporters from more neighboring communities were too abundant to count.

Curly Gaston, the town's barber stood up and expressed how the town, being so innocent and inviting, had been preyed upon. He tried to express outrage that those 'guests' at the Lodge had represented themselves as fine, upstanding citizens. This claim of virtue was so shallow that a good many locals sitting in the audience had to muffle their laughter. But, another observation by Big Bud Bunsen that the Chippewa Lodge group certainly behaved like law abiding people when they came into town. As he sadly stated, "Any town wouldn't have suspected any of them of wrong-doing given how supportive they were to our community."

Locals applauded Big Bud for that statement. He wasn't known for his depth of thought. But, that night he was emotional. He was the one local businessman who was going to be heavily impacted by the disappearance of the constant food and beverage needs at the Lodge.

Justifications were also made that the resort was far enough from the town of Glenwood where most citizens rarely ventured. How could they have known of any improprieties? As the tailor, Fred 'Thread' Nelson offered, "Why, most of us in town never traveled out to the Lodge. It was a place for vacationers, not locals."

Everyone seemed to like that excuse as well.

Outwardly the town's leaders developed an indignant posture whenever questioned by journalists. Privately, they were inconsolable about what the town was losing. The channel of money gained from the town festival, the charity golf tournament, and the Calcutta had overnight become a thing of the past. The town's charities and church groups would not enjoy ever again the phenomenal windfall experienced the past few summers. It now would be back to the bake sales and bingo games to squeeze money out of the cheap Scandinavians, the tight Hollanders and the querulous Germans living in and around Pope County.

As for Loni D'Annelli, many townspeople in Glenwood would never accept why their Chicago benefactor had been arrested. They heard about Chippewa Lodge harboring criminals and conducting gambling operations year round, but they wouldn't accept that Mr. D'Annelli had anything to do with those types of crimes. It was their belief that 'word of mouth' brought more and more of the wrong kind of people to the Lodge. Besides, the locals believed D'Annelli wasn't around the resort that often. He had his businesses back in Chicago. The general feeling was that he was framed…that certain 'guests' at the Lodge had taken advantage of his absence. It was felt that D'Annelli was just too generous and decent of a man to be caught up in such a messy affair.

And, Henry Hanson, he enjoyed even more loyalty by the local citizenry. Folks saw the authorities remove many things from the Mill basement storage area that Sunday morning when the grassfire looked like it was going to overtake the Mill. They observed a lot of Buster Brown shoeboxes being very carefully removed from the Mill office by the state police. The shoeboxes were understood to simply contain the records of receipts and bills that the Mill Manager, Honest Henry Hanson, filed and saved year after year.

The locals were proud of their Henry. Those shoe boxes just showed again how conscientious and organized he was. Townsfolk would find out, but not for weeks and even months later, that those same shoeboxes actually contained stacks of money...but also learned the cash was not the property of their dear Henry. By that time, it was understood Hanson just rented that private storage space to Loni D'Annelli.

As for Hanson's abrupt departure from Glenwood, local citizens expressed disappointment, but no surprise. They said it was normal for Henry to take a long vacation after the festival. Their 'Henry' had worked hard and guided the town through another annual successful festival. In previous years he'd taken off later on Sunday or at least by Tuesday after the celebration. The fact that he left apparently on Saturday meant nothing ominous. Townsfolk reconciled that if their 'Henry' left a day before the completion of the celebration, it just meant he was probably tired, yet confident the event would finish as smoothly as it had in previous years.

Even when the letter of resignation was made public after a couple days, many thought it was a hoax. People just wouldn't believe he was leaving the town for good. Folks said, "Henry would never leave our community. He is part of our Glenwood family."

With verification by Sheriff Petracek, though, that letter cast more of a cloud over the community than the raid, the fire, or even the arrest of Loni D'Annelli. Glenwood... without Henry Hanson...it was unimaginable.

Mayor Charlie B. Good was especially disconsolate. He had hoped to lean on Henry at the Wednesday post-festival town meeting with all the church and civic organizations. In the past this meeting was well attended and generally a very clamorous, greedy affair. While everyone should have been more than satisfied with their financial results from the town celebration, civic and religious groups had habitually used past meetings to vie for more favorable advantages and considerations for the next ten-day festival. Mayor Good had always relied on Henry Hanson once he returned from his annual vacation to defuse the emotion and suggest that everyone should smell the roses while the 'smellin is good'! Henry had a way of calming people when they got too excited or upset.

This prevailing attitude amongst the citizenry secured Henry Hanson's legacy. He would always remain beyond reproach. No one would accept any ill word or negative thought that might taint their Henry. Eventually, when it was finally accepted that Hanson was gone permanently from Glenwood, many townsfolk claimed they had foreseen the probability. They reconciled that Henry had outgrown the town and needed a change.

There was a short term interest by various citizens as to where Henry had moved, but mostly they just wanted verification that he was all right. Close friends like John Bailey, Reverend Olson, and even the new comer, Nate Morrison who worked at the Mill, mollified people's concerns by reminding them of Hanson's penchant for travel. John Bailey and Reverend Olson reminded folks how Henry had often talked about a world tour and implied that he'd been saving money for a few years to cover the cost of such a trip. They even let the rumor spread that he might be working on an ocean liner. If that was the case, there was no telling when he'd return to the States. There was no basis of truth to any of that garble other than Henry truly did like to travel. Nonetheless, that tale about his nomadic ways was reiterated enough that the locals just accepted that he now lived on some other continent.

By the end of June, where Henry had gone became less of a topic. With the on-going trail of newspaper reporters blistering the community, many folks no longer wanted to know where Henry had gone or when he might pass through Glenwood again. The general feeling was why put him through the same purgatory they were experiencing.

Visitors and journalists continued venturing to Glenwood for the rest of the summer...and periodically for years after to find what they called the 'real truth' about the Chippewa Lodge gambling operation and mobster safe house. They got less and less information as time went on.

By July, 1931, there was a general attitude within the community to simply ignore the entire D'Annelli affair as if it had never happened. The belief was that the memory would disappear sooner that way. The only remembrance would be 'Honest Henry Hanson' and the oft asked question as to his whereabouts. When questioned, locals eventually echoed the same response. "It was time for Henry to move on." Reporters' inquiries got no deeper than that explanation.

The fact that he never said a personal farewell to the town was also accepted supported the understanding how terrible he was at saying 'good-by'.

Regarding Chippewa Lodge, the changes were dramatic. After struggling through the rest of June and having only ten percent occupancy in July, the Lodge decided to close for the summer and the remainder of the year. The owner and manager, Darrell O'Donnell, who'd been exonerated of any wrong doing in the D'Annelli affair, felt he needed a new advertising and sales campaign to bring in more families and tourists for the spring of 1932.

The problem was that the next spring was still in the height...or depth... of the Depression. Solvency at Minnesota lake resorts, if they had even survived to 1932, was not common. Chippewa Lodge ended up not opening its doors again as a resort. A benevolent organization bought the property inexpensively and made it into a very thriving commune aimed at providing downtrodden folks a place to live until they got back on their feet. In payment the appreciative borders helped with the upkeep of the property and lent help in the fields, i.e. formerly the golf course. The untilled portion of the golf course disappeared under a growth of clover, long grass, prairie flowers and various assortments of weeds for the pleasure of cows, goats, sheep, hogs and deer. It would not be re-built as a golf course for another generation.

Glenwood was forced to return to an ordinary oppressed and demoralized farm community. In the following years the town festival was attempted but reduced to a weekend affair and finally to a one-day event. It had the same boat races, evening dances, and church booths selling food and dry goods, but not the excitement or the draw without the charity golf tournament. It was a lot like other town celebrations. There were plenty of parking spots available. It was only attended by locals.

Of course, Glenwood did have one consolation that would never go away. They still had Lake Minnewaska and the beautiful view from the bluffs above the town.

CHAPTER
24

In the months following the D'Annelli affair, Lindy MacPherson was given much acclaim for her undercover work in Glenwood and for alerting the authorities to the lawlessness going on at Chippewa Lodge. There was still talk both in the community as well as among reporters that she couldn't have done it all alone...that she must have had some accomplices. Even in her own office, her associates found it hard to believe before the police raid she'd performed the entire sting on Loni D'Annelli by herself. Her setting the fire was especially suspicious. How was she able to alert the fire department so quickly? The Mill could have burned down possibly taking with it the evidence under the Mill office. Worse than that, there was the potential destruction to many town buildings. It just didn't seem her gamble was worth panicking D'Annelli into coming into town to protect his personal gambling operation profits.

Yet, the fact remained her plan had worked. There'd been no serious damage to the Feed & Grain Mill or the town. Most importantly, the right man was arraigned. When questioned, she just smiled and admitted that luck had been in her corner. Again and again she'd repeat how her efforts had not been done alone. She gave ample credit to the state patrol, the support she got from Ernest Lundquist as well as her uncle, the Beltrami County Sheriff, and the hard-working volunteer fire department in Glenwood. With these humble accolades, she was able to defer and eventually end the doubtful questions while preserving the confidentiality of the four individuals who actually assisted her.

MacPherson was also given repeated credit for identifying some long term wanted criminals staying as 'guests' at Chippewa Lodge. She became such a popular figure to the Minnesota public that early in 1932, she was named as interim head of the U.S. Attorney's Minneapolis branch office when her boss, Ernest Lundquist, was forced to step down due to illness. The 'interim' title disappeared six months later when she became the over-all Director of that branch office. Some said her fast promotion occurred because she was the daughter of the current Chief Justice of the Supreme Court of Minnesota. Other jealous types suggested her good looks had something to do with the promotion. For those people who really knew her, knew better. There was no doubt she had the qualifications for the job. She was known for her resolve, her ability to plan, her intelligence and her initiative. There was no question the constant praise she got for her performance at Lake Minnewaska only added a glow to her actual abilities.

With her promotions, the newspapers gradually accepted she'd planned the raid and outfoxed a major underworld figure. The stories always justified it the same way. She'd been undercover for a couple weeks and had plenty of time to plan D'Annelli's downfall with the state patrol.

Every time that explanation was reported in future newspaper stories of the raid at Lake Minnewaska, there were four males who smiled.

It was within a week after both Lindy MacPherson and Jamie Lawton returned separately to the Twin Cities that MacPherson indeed made her inquiries about the background of James Lawton. That note saying simply 'J. Lawton' she found in her car that Monday morning when leaving the Pope County courthouse was all she needed to initiate her own personal investigation. Though buried with paper work from the raid, she singularly made the search.

It didn't take her long. When she found out Lawton was not just a gadfly but a capable Minneapolis attorney, her initial reaction was one of anger and disdain. While he wasn't in criminal law as she was, she'd even heard the name of his firm. However, it had meant nothing to her at the time.

Her irritation soon turned to exasperation and slowly to laughter all within an hour of finding his identity. She'd been put through a lot of mental anguish by Lawton and his friend that Saturday at Chippewa Lodge. Now after rehashing all that had gone on that weekend, she wondered how she'd convinced herself the two men had evil intentions towards someone at that golf event. She blamed it on her frustration in not finding until the last moment that Loni D'Annelli was the kingpin in the gambling scheme at the resort. She felt foolish the way her mind had slipped into believing something so outrageous.

She also learned that Lawton's very close friend was named Charlie Davis also was attorney and lived in Alexandria. She could see the rarely serious, never embarrassed, and always funny Davis was an understandable balance in the two men's friendship. They were both intelligent, quick-witted, decisive, but very reckless. She considered Lawton the worse between the two friends. He was too confident and his risk-taking was impulsive. He was likely the one who got Davis into more predicaments...the incident at Chippewa Lodge being the prime example.

While Lawton still intrigued her, it made no sense that he would gamble his life and occupation by involving himself in a golf tournament with a bunch of gangsters. She would never believe he had a client amongst those 'guests' at the Lodge. And, there was another side to him that she witnessed. It was not just his ability to play the game of golf well, but it was his burning competitiveness displayed on the links. She tended to believe in this instance that this trait might have won out over reason. Could he have rationalized that playing in the charity golf tournament was not so much a risk as it was a unique opportunity? Could he have also accepted that his golf skills were at the level where he couldn't lose? It would be the one time he could stick his fist in the face of the mob...and get away with it. That money he won...that was his measuring stick to judge success. And, when he'd won, that very cash became more a bother than a reward.

Hearing that buying the Bailey farm she figured was another crazy impulsive decision until she realized it was a way of transferring his winnings into the hands of the Baileys. When the reason came out that the farm would be donated to the University of Minnesota agricultural research, she was as mystified how Jamie and Charlie thought up the idea as much as impressed they'd talked John Bailey into the sale. It still warmed her heart that the very deserving John Bailey would be leaving that farm.

Having learned the identities of Lawton and Davis, she held back from making any contact with James Lawton. He was one of the more unique men she'd ever met...very respectful to her yet teasing in manner. She liked the way he looked at her, especially after they'd rolled in the hay together at the Mill Saturday night. However, she still considered him crazy and a bit out of control. Yet, he was a respected attorney in the city. It didn't make sense.

In the days that followed she kept reasoning that the two of them should keep from meeting each other. That was the way it had to be. It was too dangerous for him to be seen with her and possibly recognized as being in Glenwood that weekend. She'd lost one former boyfriend to a mob-related murder. She couldn't stand having the same thing happen to Lawton. She had to admit, though, she was attracted to him.

It was less than two weeks since the Chippewa Lodge incident when James Lawton could wait no longer. He had a bet with Charlie Davis about his first telephone contact with Lindy MacPherson. Lawton wagered that his call would be accepted by MacPherson where upon she would abruptly hang up on him… but only after telling him that he was the most despicable, irresponsible, and reckless person she'd ever met. Davis almost didn't take the bet because he thought MacPherson might come up with some additional shameful adjectives describing Lawton's character. Despite that discouraging prediction by Davis, Lawton wanted to hear her voice…and her words…himself. It would then be more definite she didn't want a thing to do with him.

The telephone call to her office turned out to be quite a surprise. She had definitely found out his identity. When she picked up the line at her office, he was momentarily stunned. Her tone was neither sharp or agitated as she responded, "Hello counselor, how can I help you?"

She had the same relaxed lilt in her voice as when he'd first met her. He could even tell she was smiling on the other end of the line.

Their short conversation ranged from his congratulations about the accolades she was receiving on her case to her asking about his flight back to Minneapolis. To his absolute amazement, their telephone call ended with them deciding what restaurant might be more private and away from prying eyes. They decided on a secluded little eating establishment a few miles north of Lake Johanna in St. Paul. They didn't wait long. The date was set for the next evening.

Following that three hour dinner engagement, Lawton offered her an invitation to take a pleasure ride in his beloved biplane the following weekend. They ended up at Lake Ida. It wasn't much of a coincidence that John and Adam Bailey happened to have been invited to Davis' lake home that same weekend…for the purpose of having John sign some papers giving Lawton and Davis the rights to the Bailey farm.

Over that summer, it became known at her office that Lindy MacPherson was dating a local, young Minneapolis corporate attorney. As was her habit, she didn't talk much about her male companion hinting that she didn't want to hex the budding relationship.

Nonetheless, when asked where they met, her practiced response was typically vague. She'd say hazily, "I believe it was at some business meeting or social affair." Then she'd change the subject. It was her standard response from then on.

Those friends also commented how spectacularly her life style had changed after meeting this attorney. It was rumored she went on jaunts in her beau's biplane often to an unknown lake west of the Twin Cities...and it was not Lake Minnewaska.

In the following months and years these five people who came together so coincidentally maintained a very close friendship. They never revealed anything about their combined actions on that June weekend in 1931. They would fondly refer to that time as the end of the 'affair', since it was...between the town and those unique 'guests' out at Chippewa Lodge.

The realization that one verbal slip could jeopardize each other's lives made them steadfast in their loyalty to one another. With a number of close calls in each of their lives in the ensuing years, these incidents served as reminders how vulnerable they could be to reprisals by the underworld.

While Lindy MacPherson, Jamie Lawton, Charlie Davis, and the two Baileys respected what a remarkable, life changing event that weekend had been for them, they also paid close attention to how so many others involved in that incident had been affected. From countless local townsfolk to those 'guests' at Chippewa Lodge, the impact from that June weekend was so pervasive and so impressive in changing other people's lives.

The former Polk County Sheriff, Clarence Petracek, and the former Glenwood City Police Chief, Rich Brey, had displayed such humiliation over the group of gangsters working right under the noses in the days after the arrest of Loni D'Annelli. No one knew it was an act. They both summarily resigned their positions in factitious embarrassment the day after D'Annelli was extradited to Minneapolis from the Polk County jailhouse. They appeared so humbled by the wave of illegal activities at the resort that their resignations seemed appropriate and punishment enough. The subject of their after-hours security job never came up in the post-investigation since D'Annelli never talked directly again to the authorities after leaving the Pope County jail. It was another part of the story that disappeared in the rubble left over from the raid at Chippewa Lodge.

Townspeople of course were shocked by their resignations, but even more surprised how matter-of-factly and quickly the two men left town. It was as if their bags had already been packed. Normally there would have been some sadness and awkwardness over losing their jobs. There was neither emotion. While Petracek and Brey claimed to be discomfited over the appearance of dereliction of duty, there was a bounce to their step when they exited the town. By the next day they had moved their belongings to a shared cabin over by Lake Osakis...a location where they liked to fish.

When some friends tried to look them up later that summer at that lake cabin, they were told the two men rarely spent time at Lake Osakis. Much later, it would be found that the cabin was owned by a development company based out of state called Triple 'H' Development, Inc. The cottage served primarily as a storage unit for the belongings of Petracek and Brey. The two men obviously lived elsewhere...and apparently hadn't taken long to become gainfully employed after leaving Glenwood.

About a year later it was learned the two men worked at two high profile Minnesota lake resorts...one on Lake Mille Lacs near Brainerd and another along White Bear Lake, north of St. Paul...both owned by that same firm, Triple 'H' Development, Inc. Glenwood citizens were satisfied that despite the two law officers' unfortunate exit from town, life had moved on. They were pleased that former Police Chief Brey and former County Sheriff Petracek had landed on their feet and had found jobs during such difficult economic times. It was only too bad, was the thinking, the highly regarded men had to take on employment at such a 'low level', as it was termed, probably performing some kind of maintenance duty.

What folks in Glenwood didn't know was that both former officers were salaried managers of those two lake properties. They'd somehow been trained in all aspects of running a lake resort while still working in Glenwood as law enforcement officers...and then continued with more on-the-job training once they had re-located. Locals had no idea both men had planned to leave their law enforcement jobs later in 1931 whether there'd been a Chippewa Lodge scandal or not.

As for Mayor Charlie B. Good of Glenwood and a couple members of the town council, they also left town before the end of the year after the raid. They had been aware of some irregularities going on at the Lodge, but had played dumb masterfully for the good of the community. Former Mayor Good moved to Alexandria and decided to run for the state legislature in a district that included Pope County. Folks outside Glenwood thought if Mayor Good had been so instrumental in helping bring those wonderful years to Glenwood from 1926-1931, then he'd be a great elected official down at the state legislature.

After winning that state senate seat in 1932, the former Mayor got mixed up in some indiscretions with some Twin City underworld types. Folks said he was ignorant of the big city ways and got set up to fail. He was forced to give up his seat in late 1933. He surprisingly got a job rather quickly just a couple weeks after his state senate resignation. He was hired as a business development manager at a White Bear Lake resort. Folks heard that former Glenwood Police Chief Rich Brey helped him get the job. People in Glenwood were proud that one of their own former citizens had the good heart in helping their former mayor during his difficult personal crisis.

Many of the golfers who played in that final tournament at Chippewa Lodge were in prison or dead by the end of the decade. Some of these hoodlums went to jail for many years as a result of being arrested at Chippewa Lodge. Others served time for criminal activities accomplished after that extraordinary weekend.

Vinnie Spagatini and Bert Bertinelli were hired by their mob compatriots to seek out and eliminate the key associates to Loni D'Annelli when it was determined the D'Annelli gambling operation probably ran on counterfeit money. As well, both these gangsters had themselves won and lost a lot of money within the D'Annelli gambling enterprise. They felt they'd been played for suckers having been paid off with fake money. Whether that perception was true or not, their assignment was personal. They looked forward to finishing off D'Annelli's right-hand men, Whitey Malooley and Billie McCoy, and ended up following the trail of these two gangsters for a couple years before finally facing off with them.

Danny A'Motta was incarcerated in 1933 for passing counterfeit bills and being an accomplice to a couple of gangland style killings. He claimed he was framed having been paid with counterfeit money from his winnings through the D'Annelli gambling house. Curiously he didn't deny anything about the gangland killings. He was let out of prison at the start of the Second World War. After changing his name to 'John Peterson', he enlisted in the military and fought in the Italian theatre...on the Allied side. He was awarded a purple heart and received an honorable discharge. A'Motta stayed in Italy after the war and resurrected his former name and his life of crime. He was killed in 1951 in an execution style murder on the island of Sicily. His killer was never found or brought to justice.

Willie LaCurso, the St. Paul mob figure, went to prison twice in the 1930s for very short periods of time. He continued operating his many business interests from his cell. He maintained his underworld activities effectively until he died in a small plane crash of dubious origin along the French-Italian border at the beginning of World War II. His estate was large. It gave large endowments in the name of his first daughter to a small Catholic girl's college in St. Paul. That oldest daughter was the only one of his three remaining daughters who didn't get a chance to graduate from that respected institution. Her life had been cut short by an act of vengeance against her father. Many who knew him said he just wasn't the same after that tragic loss in 1935. That thought was further accentuated by his highly strange death. It was reported he was actually flying the plane when it crashed. He'd never piloted an airplane in his life before that day.

Big Julie Tagliossa went back to Milwaukee after that June weekend and never returned to Minnesota. He said he didn't like the cold! He died in 1934 after an exhausting weekend wedding anniversary trip with his fourth wife, Tess, up in Door County in Wisconsin. Tess' period of mourning didn't last too long. She married one of Big Julie's bodyguards two weeks later. She said she'd been very lonely since big Julie died.

What happened to Loni D'Annelli was even more unbelievable primarily because of the speed with which his life spiraled downhill after his arrest in Glenwood. He was killed on July 4, 1931, while approaching a cab in Chicago. It was less than a month after his golf tournament and his business fortunes had ended so abruptly on that Sunday, June 7 at the Lake Minnewaska resort. He had been trying to salvage his name and reputation with his Chicago mob brethren when he was gunned down. It was a classic mob hit. His bodyguards had mysteriously disappeared as he was exiting a LaSalle Street office building. He was an easy target for the six gunmen.

At his death, most of Loni's gang expressed relief that he was gone....in order to save their own necks. The word was that D'Annelli had crossed the line on the principle of "honor among thieves". So many of his underlings expressed sincere disappointment in 'the boss' to stoop so low as to use counterfeit money to pay his gambling losses. They of course had no idea if he really had. It was just an essential comment made for purposes of their own pride.

D'Annelli's primary lieutenants, Billie McCoy and Whitey Malooley were playing golf at a suburban Chicago golf club in St. Charles, Illinois, the afternoon D'Annelli was hit with those multiple shells from the six revolvers. While having lunch between 'nines' in the clubhouse restaurant, they'd heard about the boss' death on the radio news. They knew their closeness to D'Annelli would automatically make them the next targets. McCoy and Malooley were not seen in the Chicago area ever again.

Then there was the mysterious Honest Henry Hanson, the Feed & Grain Mill General Manager, Treasurer of the First Presbyterian Church Men's Club, and the man who supervised the Chippewa Lodge Calcutta and Glenwood town festival. His story was wrapped in mystery for the rest of his life. But, it was a life that would blossom after that wild and arrest-filled June weekend. Hanson pulled the wool over everyone's eyes. He escaped that Saturday night from his life in Glenwood and the possible consequences he would have faced following the predictable arrest and downfall of the D'Annelli business racket. He expected the state patrol would want him for questioning. That would be the least of his problems if he'd remained in Glenwood another day. He knew he'd be perceived the obvious stool pigeon by D'Annelli because of their close collaboration over the years. There was no doubt in his mind various members of the Chicago mob loyal to D'Annelli would determinedly hound him until he was found and disposed.

Knowing there was nothing he could say that would change D'Annelli's perception, he planned his disappearance...especially since the Chicago mobster's viewpoint about him was quite true. It was Henry Hanson who sent those confidential letters to Ernest Lundquist at the branch office of the U.S. Attorney's office insisting that an investigation be done to get to the bottom of a gambling ring in the Lake Minnewaska area. Without those letters, Lindy MacPherson would never have been given the assignment that sent her to Glenwood.

Henry Hanson had left the state by the time of D'Annelli's arrest. He remained out of sight except for limited communication to two trusted colleagues back in Minnesota. When he heard from Clarence Petracek and Rich Brey about the gangland shooting death of D'Annelli one month after leaving Glenwood, his entire life changed. Any reasons for the law enforcement people finding him and questioning him about the Chippewa Lodge affair became mute. With D'Annelli deceased, the case was equally dead.

About the same time, the U. S. Attorney's office in Minneapolis issued a statement written by Lindy MacPherson declaring no citizen from Glenwood was thought to be involved in the D'Annelli operation at Chippewa Lodge. That statement completely cleared Henry Hanson from ever being wanted for questioning by the authorities.

However, Hanson's new lease on life didn't completely resolve the vengeance aimed at him from the mob side. By the time of D'Annelli's death, Hanson was already a hunted man by none other than Whitey Malooley and Billie McCoy. In time their own motivation changed from just avenging their boss' death. Malooley and McCoy were convinced Hanson had procured a portion of D'Annelli's fortune and somehow parlayed the money into his own bank account. Fortunately for Hanson, these two gangsters faced a constant predicament of their own. They were being pursued by hired guns, Vinnie Spagatini and Bert Bertinelli as they tried to find the whereabouts of Hanson. This dilemma became a constant interruption in Malooley's and McCoy's quest to find Henry Hanson.

Hanson remained very low profile in the immediate years after leaving Glenwood, but quietly developed his business interests. Though he never changed his name, he often thought he should have. He didn't consider he'd become as successful as he did. He also never expected his last few days in Glenwood, Minnesota would follow him so closely. But, as his story is told in another volume, he would come to realize his past would never completely be out of view.

And then there was John Bailey. By the end of June, the deed to the Bailey farm property had been signed and the farmland and farm buildings transferred over to Charlie Davis and Jamie Lawton. Within thirty days the deed was transferred again, this time to the University of Minnesota as an endowed gift.

With the fall harvest and the sale of the Bailey hogs and chickens minus a bank loan that had to be paid, the Bailey net profit plus the money gained from that extraordinary June weekend amounted to over $45,000. While his son, Adam, made regular weekend jaunts up to Charlie Davis' lake home on Lake Ida to join Davis, Lawton and MacPherson, John was often too busy. He claimed he was traveling around discussing possible opportunities with different business people in central and southern Minnesota.

It wasn't quite the truth. In fact, he was performing a dream he'd formulated ever since that Sunday morning in his barn when he stood transfixed aware of the contents in those shoeboxes in Lindy MacPherson's old Ford under the canvas cover. Indeed when

MacPherson turned that evidence in the Buster Brown shoe boxes over to the authorities that Monday morning, she unknowingly was short much of the money she, Lawton, and Davis had pirated from the Mill. After all, there was no reason to believe any money in those shoeboxes hidden under that tarp could be missing.

At first Bailey only decided to take fifteen shoeboxes. It hardly looked like anything was missing from the backseat of MacPherson's old Ford. He estimated there was at least $75,000 in those shoeboxes now in his control. In fact there was a lot more.

Then his idea got larger...to remove more money from as many other shoeboxes as he had time to complete before Adam, Lawton, Davis, and MacPherson showed up back at this farmhouse. His scheme was to cut and shape newspaper to fit under individual twenty or fifty dollar bills appearing at the top of each stack in the shoebox. He cut newspaper strips feverishly for a couple hours that Sunday afternoon before using them as camouflage in over twenty-five more Buster Brown shoeboxes. He would be astonished by the amount of money he'd siphoned from those shoeboxes

Those twenty-five camouflaged shoeboxes then were placed back in MacPherson's Ford under the canvas. The cash pulled from these boxes was hidden with the money from the original fifteen shoeboxes in a temporary location in the barn. The entire process took just under three hours and well before his son, Lawton, and Davis returned from Chippewa Lodge that afternoon.

Coincidentally, from August through October, many good people around central Minnesota found some helpful cash in an envelope in their mailbox or tucked under their front door. Consistently, these people were leaders or pillars of their communities who'd run into some bad luck or personal health issues. The money appeared like a temporary antidote to help these families get back on their feet. No one could figure out where the money had come from...or who was the benefactor.

The newspapers glommed onto the story as if it was the 'second coming'. The press named the giver 'Robin Hood'...a popular figure from old England days who robbed from the rich and gave to the poor. No one actually knew or cared whether the money had been stolen since the cash was landing in some very deserving people's hands. Unfortunately, when the newspaper coverage became too pervasive, the gifts ceased. The general feeling was that the compassionate giver, whoever the person was, did not want to be identified. That was exactly right.

Later in 1931 John Bailey announced to his friends and neighbors in Glenwood he was sick of the cold and he was going to spend the winter in the south since he no longer had the farm. He'd always dreamed of seeing sunny days and green grass in the harshest months of winter. When he left, he had no destination but told everyone he'd keep driving until he found the days warm and the evenings mild. During his extended trip, he stayed in touch with Charlie Davis and son, Adam. By then Davis had become Bailey's lawyer and investment counselor for the $40,000 windfall...as well as that additional exorbitant amount of money John had acquired with the intention of giving away. How he got that money remained privileged between lawyer and client.

A few years later, John could be seen in the summers working and repairing cabins and buildings at of all places...the former Chippewa Lodge. As mentioned, the property had been sold...to an anonymous benevolent organization. The former resort became a type of commune and collective farm for hard hit homeless folks in the Pope County area. John was only a volunteer, but took an unusual interest in the place. His actual home was a comfortable lakeshore cottage down the road between the former resort and Glenwood.

While Bailey certainly had visitors at his lake home, rarely if ever did anyone venture out to his storage shed where he kept his tools and his hunting and fishing gear. If they'd walked inside, they would have been impressed how well organized was Bailey's shed. And, though it would have meant nothing to them, they might have noticed the containers holding all his fishing and hunting equipment. Stacked across a top shelf were fifteen very old and worn Buster Brown shoes boxes.

In the fall of 1931, Adam Bailey did start his college career at the University of Minnesota. He lived at Lawton's Lake Johanna boathouse while going to school.

As the weather cooled there were fewer flights up to Lake Ida by Lawton and MacPherson. Instead, Davis tended to travel down to the Twin Cities to combine some business with pleasure. Whether attending a University of Minnesota football game or re-scanning his repertoire of speakeasies in Minneapolis or St. Paul, he stayed in the other remaining Lawton boathouse sleeping quarters from where Adam Bailey slept...the same one room Davis used during law school. The group of college and business friends who so often frequented

Charlie's lake home on many summer weekends now switched their venue to Lawton's home on Lake Johanna at least one weekend a month. Except for no golf during the colder months, their winter activities were quite similar to their social activities of the summer.

When he was in town, Davis would go out for dinner at least one of those weekend nights with Lawton and Lindy MacPherson. Adam would often join the three of them when he wasn't burdened by his college studies and part-time job. Somehow when they were all together, their conversation always reverted back to that remarkable June weekend the previous summer. While their voices stayed quiet, their laughter was anything but hushed.

Oh yes…over that winter whether Davis made it down to the Twin Cities or not on the weekends, Lindy MacPherson and Jamie Lawton… just the two of them…still went out to dinner. In fact, they went out to dinner quite often. As time went on, those evenings eventually ended with breakfast.